SHADOW OF DEATH

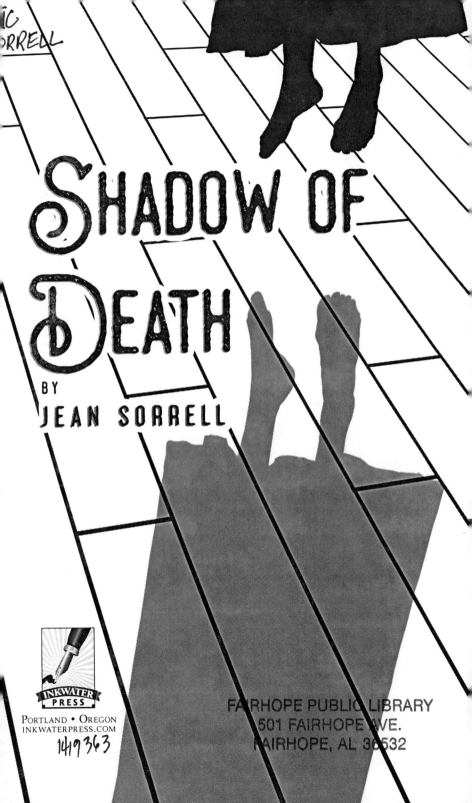

SHADOW OF DEATH

BY
JEAN SORRELL

INKWATER
PRESS

PORTLAND • OREGON
inkwaterpress.com

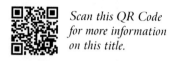
Scan this QR Code
for more information
on this title.

AUTHOR'S NOTE: The Louisiana Leper Home was established on a permanent site in Carville, Louisiana in 1894. In 1920 the Home was turned over to the United States Government and became a national leprosarium. It is now called The United States Public Health Service Hospital.

Publisher: Inkwater Press | www.inkwaterpress.com

Library of Congress Control Number: 2017902267

Paperback   ISBN-13 978-1-62901-424-1 | ISBN-10 1-62901-424-9
Kindle   ISBN-13 978-1-62901-425-8 | ISBN-10 1-62901-425-7

Printed in the U.S.A.

3 5 7 9 10 8 6 4

To Aubrey and Margaret,
two special sisters

Those who have leprosy must tear at their clothing and leave their hair uncombed. They must cover their mouth as they call out, "Unclean! Unclean!" ...
They must live in isolation.

—*Leviticus*

CHAPTER ONE

New Orleans, 1940

I STOPPED ASKING FOR DOLLS AFTER I murdered three of them. Mama said I killed the first one with love, a sad death really, the poor thing dragging behind me everywhere I went until it ended up in shreds. The second one died on the operating table. Examined minutely, part of a child's exploration I suppose, and when I extracted the china head from the rest of the body, then unscrewed its other parts, I decided it was dead. I interred it inside a shoebox in a burial plot in the courtyard under a camellia bush and asked my sister, Gretchen, to pray over it. She was always good at praying, which I was sure came in handy after she became a nun.

My third doll I threw over the banister of our second-story balcony when Gretchen told me Mama had died. I was nine years old and knew that killing a doll was probably not a sin, but the anger I had in my heart for my mother leaving me would surely send me straight to hell. I tried to put it away, all the sadness and hurt. It was just Gretchen, Papa, and me now. Mama and my younger brother, Joseph, both died from the yellow fever that summer. The fact I was still alive made me feel more guilty than ever. When the doll was returned to me, its head cracked but otherwise intact, I told our maid to bury it with Mama and Joseph. I turned away and vowed I would never ask for another doll, and I would not think the thoughts as before because they always got me in trouble.

I thought of my dolls today, although it was more than twenty years ago, and gathered a quilt around my shoulders. I sat in my favorite chair on a crisp December day in the courtyard of my home on Prytania Street in New Orleans. The air was still. Nothing moved, not the debris of leaves, faded pink camellia blossoms, or the single sheet of paper I held in my hand.

The rustling of a brown thrush searching for food under an azalea bush, the distant sound drifting in from a ringing bell on the St. Charles Avenue streetcar, even my own heart beating were superfluous.

Like the dolls.

"You got to go, Miss Catherine."

Grace Maillet, my maid, stood at the door. Well, actually she leaned against it. It would have made a nice portrait. She was already dressed for the day in a starched black uniform and white cotton apron, with her hair pinned back. Yes, she would have made a nice subject for a painting of a handsome black woman, except her expression ruined it. Streaks like drops of rain ran down creases on her face, and her swollen eyes were not black pearls anymore, just dots filled with pain. The door where she stood was more than support. I sensed she would topple over if she moved.

"You read the letter." It wasn't a question. I knew she

had read it, would have done so if for no other reason than to protect me. The letter had been delivered by special messenger at six o'clock in the morning. Of course she would have read it.

I didn't notice when she disappeared back inside the house. The paper left my hand, floated onto the bricks. I stared at it, watched it fall. A man's gloved hand appeared then and picked it up.

"Did Grace call you?" I asked.

"Yes." He read the letter silently.

"They didn't say how she died," I said. "Don't you think that odd?

"I do." Yves sat down across from me, his eyes filled with tears. Why couldn't I cry? Grace's tears ran like a river, and here was my teacher, and loving friend, also weeping.

I stared at lichen growing through cracks in my brick courtyard.

It was sometime later I was persuaded to go into the house, although by then the chill of morning air was dissipating and sunshine promised a blue, cloudless day. Windows and doors would be left open, airing out the house, inviting any tiny, decipherable breeze inside. I was dressed in a long morning gown of beige wool with my artist smock over it, still smeared with a bit of paint from yesterday. Would there be a ceremony for my sister at Carville? I wondered. What should I wear? I'd owned only one black dress in my life, purchased to wear to my father's funeral when I was eleven. Except I didn't wear the dress or attend his funeral. Gretchen saw it one day years later in my closet. She looked at me and frowned, saying, "Haven't you thrown that horrible dress away?"

Our father was murdered, found in the alley behind his club, robbed and beaten to death. Any child who loved her father would have put the dress on and attended his funeral. Yet I refused and Gretchen didn't object. It's quite right to say I hated my father and Gretchen knew it. So the matter was settled.

I didn't escape the funeral completely, though. After his graveside service, many of his business associates and their wives came to our house. I hid in my room. I lay in bed and covered my head, trying to block out their voices. It wasn't a pleasant memory. Almost twenty years ago, now.

Yves and I sat in the drawing room with a cup of coffee. It was a place I enjoyed, attached to my favorite space in the house, a sun room, my studio now, with six French doors permanently adding sunlight and warmth in winter or open to capture any breeze during the long summers in New Orleans. I was content sitting there, breathing in its smell of paint and canvas nearby and several easels with projects in different stages of completion. Heavy, faded fabric sofas faced each other in front of a heavily carved, wooden Victorian mantle, a dying fire in the fireplace below. A huge hand-carved armoire sat rather sadly against the wall, its dominance erased in a flood of faces and bodies. For years I'd covered all the walls and doors in portraits of faces I liked. Or painted faces that paid my bills, like the one I was currently working on: Father Brennan from the Church of the Holy Name. I felt comfortable in this room, in my house; as grotesque as others might think it, it was a safe place for me.

Yves had nothing to say. Grief must slow thinking because my mind was also blank.

When he spoke his voice sounded far away. "We must talk about what to do, Catherine."

"I know." A thought then. "I just don't understand why the Mother Superior doesn't tell me how she died."

He stared at the letter again like one wanting to decipher Chinese. "She asks you to come. To tell you then, I think." He handed it across to me.

I shook my head. "I know. But I don't know if I want to go there. Grace's voice drifted into the room, "You would leave your sister in that place where nobody wants her?"

I rose. "Someone needs to tell Tante."

Yves spoke, rather angrily I thought. "We must call the Mother Superior. Ask her why their own Sister Mary Gretchen isn't to be buried in the cemetery at Carville."

I paused and turned, watching Yves stand then pace in front of the fireplace. He was a slight man, but his small stature, with a lean, sculptured face and salt and pepper graying hair accentuated enormous, penetrating brown eyes. There was kindness behind those eyes and empathy for a child he'd nurtured from ten years old. He was what I'd wished my father would have been to me, I thought. No judgement. Enduring patience. When I turned to leave, he asked suddenly, "Perhaps it was Gretchen's wish to be buried next to her mother and brother and father?"

"Yves, for heaven's sake. Next to Papa? I don't think so!" I started for the stairs. My aunt's room once belonged to my mother and father. She had moved in following his death to take care of Gretchen and me, and her move became a permanent home. Not unusual, except she owned a plantation of a thousand acres on the Bayou Teche near St. Martinville.

"You call her," I threw back to Yves. I felt his eyes following me up the stairs. He was concerned for me. Truthfully, I was concerned for myself. I wondered if in the next minute I would crumble into a thousand pieces.

I knocked then peeked into my aunt's bedroom. She

sat in her dressing gown sipping from a porcelain cup. "I'm glad to find you awake, Tante." But she wasn't. Not really.

"Who is there?" She spoke softly, a voice cultured by generations of Southern women, a voice that sounded so much like music it had the power to soothe like silk against skin.

I reached out for her hand. She denied it. Today was not going to be a good one. Lately, I had noticed bad days outnumbered the good ones.

"May I sit with you, madam?"

"Of course." Manners remained. Even strangers were not denied hospitality. I was offered breakfast tea. We spoke of the weather. "It will be a fine day, I think," she said, smiling.

"It seems so, yes."

Tante stared at me. "My dear, you seem so sad. Forgive me, but I can't help but notice it."

"I've just heard this morning my sister, Gretchen, has died."

"Oh dear."

For a moment I thought I saw something in her eyes. But then it faded, just as quickly. She offered her hand then, as one would do to anyone who was suffering.

"I'm so sorry, my dear."

A quarter of an hour later, I shut the door softly behind me, retraced my steps to the drawing room. "It's a bad day," I said to Yves. Grace left us immediately.

I walked out into the sun porch and began to mix paint. I stared at the unfinished portrait then threw my pallet and brush against the window. "How ridiculous."

Yves reached out to me but stopped short of touching me.

"If there was something I could say, Catherine."

"There's nothing, is there?"

He turned, left me in my studio, sat again next to the fire in the drawing room, his head down, covered by his hands.

I stared out the window at my courtyard.

It was thirty minutes later when Yves called the Mother Superior.

"She says she very much hopes you will bring your sister home for burial, Catherine."

"But how did she die?"

"An accident."

"What?"

"She wouldn't discuss it with me. She said the party line in Carville isn't conducive to private conversations. She'll tell you what happened when you get there."

I uncovered a painting on an easel. Whistler's *Mrs. Vanbrocken.*

"I don't know ... Look, I'm nowhere near finished with the Whistler portrait."

"I'll talk to Harper. They'll wait."

"I doubt it. When does the exhibition open? Friday?"

"They will wait. Or I'll do it myself. You can't worry about repairing a painting right now.

I looked at the man across from me. He must have been close to fifty. We'd known each other twenty years. I looked into his dark brown eyes and still saw Gretchen's and my teacher, a slight young man with amazing fingers, who moved a paintbrush into the most wonderful scenes. Gretchen told me God had sent us an angel and we must not to give him away to Papa. I never did. Monsieur Antoine gave Gretchie her wings, helped her understand how life could carve itself into her dreams. He encouraged me to think for myself, to embrace the world as I wanted to see it, not outside, because I was terrified there, but in my house, where I could create what I wanted. Books. Art.

Faces. My house was filled with people, from Michelangelo's angels to the milkman at the gate.

"You must think me so odd," I'd say to Yves on one of his daily visits for coffee.

"Never, Catherine. It's your house and you've made it sing with art."

And then, five years ago, Yves Antoine proposed a new life for me. "Have you ever considered painting portraits for money?"

"No." I stared at the back of the parlor door and its panels filled with mine and my sister's faces when we were nine and fourteen. "Am I good enough?"

"Yes, you are."

And so our business had begun. Yves sent clients to me and I painted their portraits, or their children's portraits, even recently, two Pekingese dogs. He also brought me paintings he'd restored but that needed touch ups. It was so satisfying to match color and brush stroke to a painting by artists I'd only read about in books. When my work was praised, it was exhilarating. The world that had moved past my door entered it just a bit, and I was content.

Until today. My mentor and business partner sat there now insisting it was necessary I go to Carville. In her letters my sister called it "the saddest place on earth."

"I'll go with you, Catherine, if you need me," he said, "but I really think this is something you should do by yourself."

Grace cleared her throat. A large black man stood beside her, holding his cap with both hands. I noticed she had not allowed him to stand on the rug. "Miss Catherine, this is my brother. He can carry you to the leper colony."

"I is Mister, miss."

I looked at Grace.

"He's a hand on a barge that stops in at the lepers at Carville. Ain't that right, Mister?"

Mister nodded his head. "We stop in every week. We's leavin' tomorrow."

I excused myself and left all three standing there waiting for my answer. I had nothing to tell them. I climbed the stairs, entered Gretchen's bedroom, and stood there. I turned to her dresser, looked at myself in her mirror. I had blue eyes like Mama's and dense black hair from ... Papa's family tree. My olive complexion belonged to a Creole great-grandmother, I thought. My *paternal* great-grandmother, whose faded wedding picture Gretchen and I discovered years ago. My skin was as dark as hers. My facial features, except for the color of my eyes, were the same. It was like being recast from an older mold with Creole genes skipping their way into me.

How ironic. Papa must have cringed every time he looked at me. I studied my face. At the black hair I'd sheared off very short. From Gretchen's dresser I picked up a photograph of my sister and brother and me, the three of us, laughing into the camera. Gretchen, Joseph, and me. What summer was it taken? Maybe the year before Mama and Joseph died. Replacing the frame, I crossed to Gretchen's bed and lay across it. The linen smelled musty, unused, changed perhaps only two or three times in the almost ten years she'd been gone. But staring up into the coverlet above the four posts I could imagine myself here again, sleeping beside my big sister, feeling safe. Someone had needlepointed the top, with flowers and leaves, in pink, yellow, purple, and different shades of green. Gretchen often admired it. She thought it must be very old, from a member of our family we'd never met and would never know. Yet it was presented to her, placed there to be admired forever, if she wanted. Or to pass down to someone else. An odd thing struck me suddenly, that hadn't occurred to me before: Gretchen could see beauty in anything, even in those years after Mama and Joseph died. She often pointed to it when I crawled into bed to sleep beside her and said over and over again, "Isn't it fine? Isn't it marvelous? Look at the colors. The tiny stitches. Every flower is perfect, isn't it?"

How could I go to Carville? My sister wouldn't ask me to leave my house. She knew how afraid I was on the few occasions it was necessary I do so. I could say no. Gretchen would understand. But as I studied the needlepoint hanging above me and thought of how she spoke of passing down the legacy of such a fine piece of needlework, I remembered something. It was the promise Gretchen had made out loud, not to let something so exquisite just rot away, forgotten by all.

"Cathy, let's make a vow to each other, a pinkie vow, that we'll protect her beautiful needlework, whoever it was that made it, shall we?" Our intertwined little fingers promised to honor an artist whose masterpiece was stretched out above her bed, though we'd never know who created it.

Lying across the bed on my back, the tears that wouldn't come before rolled down my face. I sat up. "Oh God! I must go. I must go! My sister needs me!" Because it was the first time, wasn't it? All those years when the madness had lived in this house I had needed my sister to protect me. But now she needed me.

CHAPTER TWO

"**THERE'S NO PLACE FOR A** passenger, Grace."

"Oh, I think Mister has made a place for you, Miss Catherine. You be hidden somewhere on that barge. Some place safe."

I stood on the dock looking at a flat-bedded barge stacked with all manner of crates and two men securing ropes around them. "I don't know. I don't know if I can do this."

Grace stood beside me, motioned to Mister to put my suitcase, shoulder bag, and a food basket on board. She squeezed my hand. "But it's been up and down the Mississippi so many times; you know it's gonna be fine. And Mister going to take care, ain't you, brother?"

He grinned. "This old barge knows the river, Miss Catherine. And you going to enjoy the ride today 'cause the sun is shining and you can just sit back and take a nap it be so smooth!"

Mister Maillet was a lovely fellow. He was someone whose face deserved space on one of my walls. I had guessed before Grace told me that his first name was his mother's invention, to make sure everyone treated her boy with respect. Looking at him, one could hardly do otherwise. He stood head and shoulders above me, and I wasn't a short person. What I liked most about him was his smile. It reminded me of Grace when we first met, when her mother, whom we called Miss Virginia, was our housemaid. How important her laughter was to me when we were children.

I took a few steps cautiously, suddenly regretting my decision to go alone, without Yves.

Mister offered me a hand as I crossed a short gangplank. "You be in Carville before the sun sets, Miss Catherine." He guided me to a spot near the middle of the vessel, where I sat between stacked crates covered by tarpaulins on either side. I was grateful to have something to hold on to and that still afforded a view of the river if I looked straight ahead.

He handed me a folded sheet of paper. "Mr. Antoine asked me to give you this, miss." And he then was gone. The crew began to untie ropes at the side of the vessel. I overheard, "Hammer, pull it over," obviously referring to Mister's last name. Then the order to heave the anchor over the side. The barge was ready to set off. I was suddenly lightheaded, not sure what was happening to me. "I can't!" I said loudly, my voice competing with a grinding engine noise signaling the barge was underway.

"I will pray for you every day, Miss Catherine!" Grace yelled. I offered a tentative wave back, a forced smile on my face, trying to cover my inner terror.

"God wants you to do this, Miss Catherine. You be brave, you hear?" And then again, "Miss Gretchen callin' you, Miss Catherine!"

We slid away from the dock, and I steeled my body

to stop shaking, pulled the provided heavy quilt over me and looked straight ahead. Once I warmed up, my head cleared. I crossed my fingers anyway. The fine weather had held. "It's gonna be a good day to be on the river," Mister said loudly. I nodded and offered another weak smile.

My hands trembled so much I could hardly read Yves's note. "*Call as soon as you can after you arrive.*" He ended with, "*Have perfect faith in Mister. Don't worry. You can do this.*"

An hour later, I decided to stand up, holding on to the ropes. My legs held me and I took a deep breath. I was surprised to see what seemed to be two other passengers, two men in uniform, standing down front.

"They're the guard, Miss Catherine."

I turned to see Mister standing nearby. "You be feeling good, Miss Catherine?"

I smiled. "I'm getting braver, Mister. I just wanted to stretch my legs, to see a bit more of the river."

A broad grin broke out on his face. "That's good!"

I pointed to a large plantation house coming into view. "Isn't that a large house? Very grand looking."

"Sho' is, Miss Catherine. Sho' is."

The river was so wide in places it seemed like we were a mile from land. And, suddenly, a turn brought us close to shore again. Sounds of water rushing against the low-lying barge filled my ears as the passing landscape of trees and impregnable growth of all manner of vegetation passed by. A great blue heron along the bank disappeared, startled by the sound of the barge and the disturbance of the ripples from our vessel.

Around noon I asked Mister if he could join me for lunch, since Grace had packed so much food. He said no but tucked one of her sweet dough pies inside his shirt and laughed. His smile was infectious.

I proposed he invite the passengers up front to join me, and they were happy to oblige. They ate Grace's deviled eggs and ham sandwiches, nodding in satisfaction. I poured strong black coffee laced with cream from a thermos and allowed my curiosity to ask them questions.

"So you're here to guard this barge?" I asked.

The two young men, probably still teenagers, were propped upon the crates beside me. They laughed.

"No, Miss. We're heading for our port in Baton Rouge. We had leave for two days."

"Hitching a ride. That's it," the second boy said.

"United States Coast Guard then?" Nods. "Your boats go up and down the Mississippi?"

"And into the Gulf."

When had this started? I wondered. I knew Hitler was in power in Germany. He'd occupied Austria, Poland, and just recently, France. The ugly little German dictator was at war with England and Russia. Yes indeed, there was good reason to have the United States Coast Guard on the Mississippi River. A whole lot of things must be happening outside my courtyard.

One of the men shyly asked why I was on board.

"My older sister is," I corrected myself, "*was* a nun working in the hospital at Carville."

He caught my meaning and bowed his head for a moment, crossed himself, a gesture I hadn't expected, so spontaneous and kind that tears sprung to my eyes, and it took a moment to pull myself back.

"You're going to her funeral then?"

"Not exactly." Of course they were curious. Weren't we all? The burial rituals of the nuns were as unknown and mysterious to me as the turns of the river. "I'll be bringing her body home in seven days, when this barge returns."

"So sorry, ma'am."

Our comfortable interlude with Grace's food was over. The guards thanked me profusely for lunch, and when they returned to the front of the vessel, I unexpectedly dozed off, letting the motion from the river rock me to sleep, warm under my coat with the sun on my face.

Sometime later, the corpse of an unfortunate cow floating in the river bounced off the side of the barge, jolting me awake. The momentary shutter and roll of the vessel was enough to send me into a slight panic.

Mister was beside me at once. "It be why we all keep back from the sides, Miss Catherine. If we hit a log or something, then you might be in the river."

Not an idea I wanted to entertain. I sat in my chair with a tighter hold on the ropes that secured canvas over our cargo. I tried to put the picture of the huge, swollen carcass out of my mind, to concentrate on the conversation last night between Mother Superior and myself. At Yves's insistence, I had called again to tell her my travel plans.

"When you are here, we will explain all, Miss Lyle."

"Please, Mother, call me Catherine. Forgive me, but was it my sister's wish not to be buried in your cemetery?"

Her voice had been clipped: "I look forward to seeing you, Catherine."

I stared at the river and thought of seeing that swollen body of the cow floating in plain sight. What other obstacles were out there, weighed down by heavy, solid masses of rock or tree branches? The river looked smooth; the vessel created ripples onto the shore, yet how deceptive it was. I shivered and held the rope tight. There was danger. The river could keep its secrets while drowning a person at the same time.

CHAPTER THREE

MISTER WAS CORRECT. WE ARRIVED on time. The barge slowed noticeably and glided close to the eastern side of the river. The sun was about to sink behind the tallest trees. I judged it was near six o'clock, almost twilight on this winter day.

Indian Camp Plantation came into view. Its columns gleamed with blinding whiteness against the setting sun. It stood close to the river, its balcony, absent a railing, reminded me of what my sister had written:

> A deserted mansion, left to decay without a living soul who cares for it anymore. But, dear Cathy, it is beautiful beyond compare. I want you to see it someday and paint it for me. I haven't been able to do it justice.

The captain sounded a shrill horn several times. Half a dozen people came running down the levee toward us. Three young boys the color of coffee jumped for the ropes and tied us off. Then one of them hoisted the gangplank into position.

"Lay along there, boy! Tighter! Get a good loop in it!" the captain yelled. One deck hand tossed a canvas sack of mail onto the ground. It was retrieved by another boy waiting for it.

At the top of the levee, a cloud of white wings approached us. How strange. It was just like an Antoine Gautier painting. The illusion was momentary. What I really saw were the Daughters of Charity of St. Vincent de Paul. They lengthened into a single line, following a path down the earthen levee to the river, bobbing up and down, their white cornettes shining like diamonds against the setting sun.

The nuns moved nearer, so I called out, "Hello," and they waved back in response.

Sundown was fast upon us as the barge was made secure and the group of nuns reached the side of the river dock. Their gray habits, long blue aprons, and white, starched cornettes created a unit, not individuals. Until one spoke to me.

"Hello, Catherine."

"Mother Superior?"

"Be careful!" It was a male voice.

But I lost my balance and stumbled across the ropes on the flimsy gangplank.

The short man with blond, wavy hair who had warned me steadied my near calamity and smiled when I literally fell into his arms. Noticing his collar, I said, "Thank you, Father. I almost arrived soaking wet."

He moved out of the way, I steadied myself and Mother Superior put her arms around me. "Oh, Catherine. You have come. Good for you." Then she took my hand in hers and we looked into each other's faces in the last of the sunlight. Her smooth, flawless face framed by her wimple had deep, searching black eyes, quite inconsistent with the tightness in her lips and mouth. I sensed she hid a natural gentleness she was not willing, perhaps not able, to share with many. But the grip on my hand was uncommon, strong. She would be a complicated subject to paint, and what a challenge she would present to an artist. She was certainly of the Gautier image of women, with the godly presence I had always imagined. Yet she was a real person, not a painting. How awesome was the reality, I thought, and in that single, fleeting moment, looking at the woman who had summoned me, I knew how right it was for me to come.

The gentleman who saved me from falling in the river said, "She must be someone very special for all of you to come and greet her, Sister Emily."

"This is Catherine Lyle, Mr. Bremmer," Mother Superior said. Then turning back to me, "Catherine, you must call me Sister Emily. We don't stand on much formality here."

"Thank you." I smiled at her and reached out to shake Mr. Bremmer's hand. "I'm very much in your debt, sir, and please excuse me for calling you Father. I assumed you were a priest."

Immediately, we had to move out of the way of crates coming down the gangplank, being stacked along the dock. Mr. Bremmer waved my mistake away, laughing, "No harm done. We're in the middle of commerce, aren't we?"

"Are you the Bremmer on this invoice?" the captain asked.

The man directed his attention to the captain. "I am, yes."

"All these crates belong to you then. We can set them on shore, but you'll have to move them up the levee yourself. You can handle that, sir?"

"Oh, yes. Yes." With his hand Bremmer waved at two men standing above us on the side of the levee. "Polanie! Hoanui! Come quickly," he yelled.

Sister Emily frowned, not at me, but at the men she saw coming forward.

"Our pews, Sister," Mr. Bremmer said.

"Why are Hoanui and Polanie here, Mr. Bremmer?"

"How else would I be able to move the pews to the church, Sister?" He smiled, but it was not returned by Sister Emily.

"You know it's not allowed, sir."

The men summoned by Mr. Bremmer stood next to one of the crates.

"The Samoans can't do this work, Mr. Bremmer. You know it."

"Who else then? I can't move the crates by myself." He shrugged his shoulders, a sharp, forced expression of a smile pasted upon his face. Perhaps in an effort to defuse the moment, he turned to me and said, "Our pews will give the Protestant congregation something nice to sit on, Miss Lyle, instead of the falling apart chairs we have now."

I left the two of them to follow the other nuns up the path. Their voices floated away behind us. We crossed a road, a loose description, because it was not much of anything but gravel.

As though a nun had read my mind, she said, "The highway ends about a quarter-mile from here, toward Carville."

So, I thought, the US Marine Hospital Number 66; though, Gretchen wrote it was simply called Carville by everyone here, after the village a short distance away. A hospital for Hansen's disease, stuck away in an isolated place literally at the end of the road. But at least the river didn't end. Perhaps a small consolation to those who must come here.

The woman closest to me reached out to take my arm. "Samuel is taking your luggage to your quarters, Miss Lyle. You'll be over in a house across the street from Dr. Mills's quarters. I'm Sister Clara."

"Nice to meet you. Please call me Catherine."

"Sister Emily will join us as soon as she finishes with Mr. Bremmer."

Another nun looked back at me. "He's a missionary who brought the Samoans here six months ago."

"Why?"

"They have Hansen's disease. Leprosy."

"Oh. Yes."

Another voice said, "And patients are not allowed to work."

"Mr. Bremmer knows that." A nun carrying a lantern smiled. "Hello, Catherine. I'm Sister Paul."

Sister Clara said, "We encourage exercise, of course. But there's also a rule about being at the dock when a boat comes in."

"Mr. Bremmer knows that too."

Sister Clara's arm tensed around mine. "The hospital is over there, behind the hedge. Can you see it?"

"Just barely." I was too busy watching where to put my feet on the path. I glanced over in the direction she pointed. "It looks quite large. I see the outlines of several buildings."

"Yes, the hospital is just one. There are also the patients' living quarters, a library, a chapel, a Protestant church, and the dining hall. Our quarters are also there. You'll be able to see it all in the morning."

"We've just gotten our electricity, but not in all the buildings yet."

"I think it won't be long. Hello, Miss Lyle. I'm Sister Adelaide."

I smiled at her. Not much more than twenty years old, I thought.

Sister Clara said, "We've been told there's confusion about who's going to do the work. The government owns the hospital and all the property, but the state of Louisiana is still negotiating with who will do the rest. It will probably take some time."

Sister Paul spoke again. "It's very dark out here, isn't it? But I like it, don't you? The stars seem to pop right out at you from the sky."

"Here we are," Sister Clara said. "Careful, the stairs are steep."

We stood in the center hallway of the old mansion.

In the dining room, I was given a place of honor, next to the fire. Its warmth revived my spirit some. The table, covered by a linen cloth, and chairs were the only furnishings in the room, in fact the only furniture I'd seen since entering the house. There were no paintings on the walls. It was an empty shell of a place, except in this room, where the fireplace, candles, and kerosene oil lanterns provided us with light.

Sister Clara said, "The house has been empty for many years. It's not used for much of anything now. The government officials wanted us to use it as our quarters, but it didn't suit us. I guess that's why they didn't electrify this place. Nobody wanted it."

Of course the sisters wouldn't accept such a grand place to live. I knew about these women, the Daughters of Charity. Gretchen told me how they lived next to those they helped. No convents. No cloisters. They lived on the streets of New Orleans or wherever they were needed. It seemed like such a hard life, yet it was the order my sister had chosen. She had never looked so happy as the day she told me her plans.

Sister Clara made introductions as I sat down. Sister Paul, Sister Adelaide, Sister Edith.

"There is one more of us. Sister Anne is on duty at the hospital tonight. You'll meet her in the morning.

Dinner was served by the women I guessed were the two youngest nuns, Sister Edith and Sister Adelaide. Truthfully, they might have been any age. All their faces were unlined, except for Sister Clara's. No, I judged Sisters Edith and Adelaide younger because they moved quickly, serving hot, steaming bowls of rabbit stew kept warm by the fire. With bread and wine, it was a very satisfying meal.

Their voices didn't give me an impression of age either, because once the introductions were made, after a prayer thanked God for our food, conversation ceased. It was like a veil had dropped over us. The chatting about stars and electricity and hospital buildings was over. Each woman ate in silence.

Sister Emily joined us before the meal was over. She sipped wine but declined food. She was staring at me when I looked up from my bowl.

"Catherine, we all know how difficult it was for you to come."

The rest of the women nodded.

"We chose to introduce you to this house tonight because this is where your sister was found."

"She had her accident here?"

Sister Emily rose, "Not in this room. We'll take you there."

I followed Sister Emily and the others, each holding a lantern or candle. We entered the central hall of the house, and I realized our first entrance had been a side door. We now stood in a ballroom-sized entry, two large front doors to our right and a curving staircase leading up to a balcony with several doors spaced across the breadth of a second floor. A third floor lay above all, but it was cloaked in darkness. It was cold and the air smelled foul, as though the house itself emitted an empathy to patients living on its grounds: the open wounds and scabs on the bodies of lepers I'd seen before in books. *How must they smell?* How ridiculous the imagination, I thought, and turned my head to focus on the five nuns instead, their solemn faces, some with eyes downcast, surrounding me within a dim circle of yellow light.

Sister Emily said, "I haven't told you the whole story, Catherine. I'm sorry."

I could see her breath in the air as she spoke, her face cast in the yellow glare from the lantern she held. "Your sister didn't die of an accident. She was discovered hanging from the balcony." She pointed, "There."

Silence. It took a minute or two to process those words. A shiver passed through me. I could only stare, seconds passing. I was aware of the undercurrent in the room, of the nuns watching me, holding their breath.

"What did you say?"

They had formed a protective circle like moths drawn to light. Sister Adelaide wept softly, her shoulders sagging as if she carried a heavy, one-hundred-pound weight.

I looked up. In the black space above the balcony, I thought I saw a face. How could I conjure a painting in my mind at this moment? Yet I saw it clearly, my imagination running wild, a woman's face staring back at me. The thought of Pisanello's *Hanging Corpses* hovering high above me. I saw his bodies on canvas transposed, one became my sister, hanging from the balcony. Bile rose in my throat, I turned, losing my dinner on the floor. The nuns ran back to the dining room, returning with the table cloth, the younger ones quickly cleaning away my mess.

"I'm sorry," I whispered.

Sister Emily said, "It's a shock, of course. I wish I could have prepared you. But you understand now why I couldn't tell you over the telephone."

"When did she hang herself?"

"She was discovered here night before last."

I stared up into the blackness, at the space, adjusting my eyes, banishing the painting from my mind, and around me sparks of light illuminated our breath like fog, spiraling up the staircase. I could hear my heart beating inside my ears. I whispered, "Why? Why would she do that? Did she say anything? Did she leave a note?"

"We have no idea why. And she didn't leave us any explanation. Sister Adelaide was the last person to see her."

Sister Adelaide spoke, tears streaming down her face, her voice heavy, words slurred. "We had a cup of tea together at two o'clock ... in the pharmacy. She was in good spirits, she told me about the portrait of the dog you'd finished. We laughed about it. Who would pay money to paint a dog?" Sister Adelaide looked totally distraught. Her voice rose, "Nothing. I saw nothing wrong!"

Sister Clara put her arms around the younger nun. "There, there, Sister. Of course you didn't. None of us did."

"From all accounts, Catherine, not one of us saw your sister as unhappy. On the contrary, she seemed very content."

I stared from one to another. Sister Edith's lips moved

in silent prayer. Sister Paul's candle trembled in her hand. The others nodded their heads in obvious agreement with Mother Superior.

"Sister Mary Gretchen always found a way to cheer up even the saddest of our patients."

"That's true, Sister Paul," Sister Emily said. "She had an inner peace about her that everyone responded to."

"Dr. Mills said she was a wonderful pharmacist. She was very careful with medicine. Everyone trusted her." Sister Paul added. The nuns nodded again in agreement.

Sister Emily said, "We have laid your sister's body in the root cellar, below us. One of the boys is almost finished with a casket. It's not at all necessary for you to see her. It's been a very long day. You're tired. Let Sister Clara and Sister Paul show you back to your quarters now."

"No."

"You want to see her body tonight?"

"Yes."

Sister Emily hesitated. "This way then."

Our shadows created a macabre dance upon the walls as they led me toward the back of the house. We entered a narrow hallway with uneven, creaking floors, moving in single file to a room I thought might be a kitchen, though just a few feet away it was as dark as pitch beyond our arcs of light. I passed the outline of a massive fireplace and hearth. It looked like some black hole into hell.

"It will be very cold in the cellar, Catherine, but it's why we put her there."

Outside, we moved down some steps. Wet grass and weeds brushed against my slacks, then the nuns stopped. Sisters Edith and Clara raised their lanterns to reveal a raised mound of earth with a door on top. Sister Adelaide moved to pull the door open, grunting, and Sister Paul stepped over to help her, exposing several steps down.

My sister's grave. So this was how the nuns chose to honor her, in a hole under a deserted mansion.

"You placed my sister's body in a root cellar?" My face flushed with heat, though the temperature was close to freezing.

"We wanted to preserve her body until you came. This is the best place. It stays cold down there year-round. It's also isolated, never used by anyone. I doubt it is even known to exist by the rest of the staff or the patients."

I was led down some dug-out, uneven steps into a dark pit carved out of the earth, into a tiny room with empty shelves lining the walls, a dirt floor, and a table, on which the body of my sister rested.

In the dim light, she looked only as if she were sleeping, covered in a light muslin gown, her hands resting, folded peacefully across her breast.

"Catherine," Sister Emily said, "You'll be with us a few days. I hope you'll learn how much your sister was loved by all of us, and not just by us; the patients loved her more than anyone else."

I sought to connect my eyes to the body on the table, though my mind recoiled with anger, and I began to shake uncontrollably. The nuns stepped closer, but when I threw out both my arms toward them, they stopped dead-still. No one moved a step closer.

I turned to the body. Touching her folded hands, staring at my sister's face, I trembled at the memory it brought to me. I was a young girl again, no more than nine years old, standing next to my sister's bed, shaking her. "Wake up Gretchie, wake up!"

Lake Pontchartrain, 1919

"Wake up, Gretchie, wake up!"

Joseph put out his hand like Catherine did, to shake his big sister on her back. Gretchen moaned and rolled over in bed, an amused smile appearing on her face. She raised the mosquito netting between her and her younger siblings. Sometimes she thought they treated her more like a mother than Mama.

"Let me sleep! Go away!" she said.

But the little ones were relentless. "No, no, you must get up, Gretchie, so we can go to the lake! Joseph wants you to."

"Oh really? It's Joseph I must get out of bed for, is that it?"

"Yes, yes, let's go! Mama says it's going to be a fine day at the swimming beach. We've only been waiting for you to wake up!"

The entourage included Mary Louise Lyle, her three children, their housemaid, and a hired man, Josiah, carrying a basket of food and water, two large umbrellas, and two blankets tucked under his arm. Mary Louise Lyle possessed the beauty of an English rose, a flawless complexion, at this moment hidden behind a large-brimmed hat. She had blue eyes that sparkled when she laughed, but that today were pinched together in pain. She'd suffered with a migraine since yesterday but had taken Sal Vital around two o'clock in the morning and slept the rest of the night. She felt better this morning.

It was a special day to her children. True, they would remain in their rented cottage for the entire summer. But today was the first day. She didn't want to disappoint her children, and though she felt hot, a bit dizzy even, she had convinced herself a relaxing day under the umbrella, with the breeze on her face and a cool lemonade in her hand, might make the pressure she felt behind her eyes, and the other nagging symptoms of illness, fade. A nap in the fresh air under their umbrella was what she needed.

The small group traced their steps down a heavily used public dirt path between two large houses that faced Lake Pontchartrain directly.

They crossed the road and felt the coarse mixture of pebble and sand between their toes. Catherine stopped, letting the others go ahead. She squinted, raised her hand to shade her eyes against the startling brightness. The lake was so smooth, like glass, its sheen spreading itself as far as she could see.

"Come on, slow poke!" Joseph yelled back at her.

Catherine ran past her little brother then, dropping her towel on the ground, and into the lake, splashing water, its sand and muddy bottom squishing between her toes. Joseph was close behind her, oblivious to his mother's warning, "Be careful, Joseph. Stay close to shore." They splashed water in each other's faces and jumped up and down laughing. Gretchen joined them. At waist deep she carried both of them, one on each arm, out into the lake with an admonition that they must hold on tight lest the little fishes eat off their toes.

"Can we really walk clear across?" Catherine asked. It was mysterious to her that the lake was so very big one couldn't see across but shallow enough a tall person might walk all the way to New Orleans on the other side.

"Oh, there are deep parts in here. But I think we could walk very far and my head would still be above the water."

Catherine loved it. When she got tired of swimming, she sat on the edge of the shore, her legs extended in front of her. Small wavelets of water found their way beneath her bathing costume, and with a stick and pebbles, she made pictures in the sand, of Joseph skipping pebbles, of two boys swimming toward the floating dock about fifty yards out into the lake, and of a woman struggling with a portable folding chair. Several children splashed each other, their laughter floating above her into the trees behind them. Catherine lay down at water's edge, letting its ripples run through her hair without covering her face. She closed her eyes feeling its cold, silky wetness against her skin. She listened to the sounds of the water, of the voices around her. Joseph laughing, "That was a good one. Did you see it?"

Too soon, it seemed to Catherine, she heard her mother's voice from under the umbrella. "Come in, children! It's time to eat!"

The afternoon brought with it clouds, their shadows extending across the lake creating ribbons of light and dark. Catherine felt a soft breeze and a welcome shade beneath their umbrellas. Her mother dozed with Joseph next to her. Sitting beside Catherine, Gretchen was busy at her sketch book.

Catherine's body relaxed. She sighed, closing her eyes. It was so peaceful here. When she grew up, she might live in Mandeville. She would own one of the big houses facing the lake. From her front porch, she would paint the lake every day, no matter what the weather. And in the evenings, she would sip a cool drink and watch the sun set into the water.

It seemed only a minute had passed when she awoke to Gretchen shaking her. "We've got to go."

Catherine caught the panic in her older sister's voice and jolted upright, standing, as Gretchen picked up the blanket. "What's wrong?"

Gretchen turned away to shake sand out of the blanket saying, "It's Joseph. He woke up and said he felt sick. He vomited. Maybe he swallowed some of the lake water."

"Where's Mama? Where's Miss Virginia?"

"They left a while ago. Mama said she was getting her headache back. Miss Virginia went with her 'cause she needs to start supper." Gretchen's eyes were very large, her voice strained.

Catherine looked around. Except for the lady further down from them, the beach was empty. "Where is Joseph now?" she asked.

"Josiah's carrying him back to the house." She began to make a pile of umbrellas, blankets, picnic basket, and water jugs. "He said to leave all this and he'd come back and get it."

They were walking quickly, but suddenly, Gretchen stopped and turned around to face her younger sister. "Oh, Cathy! I was to watch out for him!"

Catherine blurted out, "If he swallowed some water and it made him sick, it's not your fault!" They continued walking again, along the path. Josiah was crossing the road ahead of them, her brother's small, limp body in his arms. She suddenly felt the same panic as her older sister but said nothing.

When the sisters reached the house, they found Joseph in the bedroom shared by Catherine and her younger brother. It was stifling hot inside because Miss Virginia had pulled the curtains to shut out the sun. Gretchen fetched a pan of cool water and sat down beside Joseph, bathing his forehead with compresses in-between holding a bucket for the tiny boy's dry heaves. Mary Louise appeared at the doorway, her own face shining with fever. She had trouble standing so Miss Virginia and Gretchen helped her to lie down next to Joseph.

"What else should I do, Mama?" Gretchen asked.

The housemaid was directed to fetch the medicine chest. Gretchen sifted through its contents of castor oil and Sal Vital, iodine and alcohol, until she found what she wanted. Gretchen was able to convince Joseph to swallow a spoonful of paregoric.

Within the hour, Josiah brought Dr. Nichols from the village. He was a young man, solemn and intense. A new graduate of Tulane's medical school, he hadn't been practicing medicine for even a year yet but knew the yellow fever when he saw it. He'd seen it often enough at Charity Hospital in New Orleans. Both the son and his mother had the yellow eyes, fever, headache, and vomiting that accompanied the virus. And though he knew his first responsibility was to his patients, it was for those not yet infected whom he worried about most.

He motioned silently for Gretchen and Catherine and Miss Virginia to follow him into the next room.

First, he addressed Miss Virginia. "They both have yellow fever. You and I will have to wear gloves and a mask to tend to them." He waited for her nod then turned to the girls. "You must stay in here or in your room. The disease is especially hard on children. You shouldn't be exposed."

Catherine choked out the words, "Are they going to die?"

Gretchen held her little sister, asking, "Are you sure its yellow fever? Mama was suffering with migraine. Joseph has a stomach ache. I think he must have swallowed lake water, that's all!"

"I'm sorry. Lake water would not turn the whites of his eyes yellow."

It was several moments later that Gretchen said quietly, but in a determined voice, "Then I must be with them. I understand about Cathy. But you must let me help. Miss Virginia has children of her own she must attend. She can't stay here night and day. I can."

Dr. Nichols admired the resolve she expressed. She seemed more mature than most girls. And truthfully, she would probably be more help to him than the frightened black woman standing behind them. Yet he hesitated to subject her to the agony of suffering she would see. Perhaps not today or tomorrow. But within the week. He'd watched patients who lingered, who hung on to life for days, even weeks. In agony. He watched as the family members hoped and prayed fervently with each passing day that the victim would recover. A few did. But never the small children.

He said, "I can't approve that."

"You don't have to." Gretchen rose from the sofa and spoke

to their maid. "Papa will come as soon as he hears, so you'll need to prepare for him."

"Yes'm."

"Where are my mask and gloves, doctor?"

"I'll have to tell your father you're acting against my orders."

"Tell him whatever you like."

Catherine grabbed at her sister's skirt. "Don't do it, Gretchie! Don't do it! Papa will take the switch to you. Don't you know he will?"

"No. Papa will approve. He would want me to tend to Mama and Joseph."

"Please, Gretchen! Stay with me! Please, please!"

But her big sister had torn Catherine's fingers from her skirt and left the room, leaving her all alone.

CHAPTER FOUR

I STARED AT THE BODY ON the table. Gretchen wasn't in pain, or sad, or angry. She would never experience any kind of emotion ever again. She'd no longer lift her chin, walk into the room where our mother and brother had languished ... watch over them, speak softly, and bathe their fever-laden brows. My sister was dead, her skin white as chalk. Her face, a death mask, taut, but remarkably subtle in her expression. How truly like a ghost she seemed, lying in repose, marred only by a blue scar left from the rope she'd had around her neck.

I imagined her voice ringing in my ears, "Catherine, please don't cry. It makes me cry too."

I touched her neck. I asked, "Tell me how it happened."

Sister Clara answered. "She made a rope noose. That's how we found her. Hanging from the balcony."

I was stunned. I stared at her for a minute at least, trying to get my mind around her words.

"A noose?" I asked.

"Here it is." Sister Paul picked up a hangman's noose

from the corner of the room. I took it and turned it over in my hands. It was actually perfect, skillfully knotted at the end of a long length of greenish colored rope.

"My goodness. I'd say this would kill anybody very well, wouldn't it?" I felt the blood rushing to my cheeks. I held the noose in front of me, just over the body of my sister, letting it swing. Sister Adelaide gasped and turned away. *Well,* I thought, *why shouldn't I be the crazy sister?*

I exploded, saying angrily, "Did I say something to upset you?" I glanced around, taking all of them into the question.

Sister Emily said, "We should leave now. Tomorrow you can watch as we prepare Sister Mary Gretchen for burial. When Captain Gentry returns a week from now, you can take her home. I'm glad you came, Catherine, but we should leave her now."

"Leave if you like, Sister Emily. All of you can go. Leave me a candle."

"That's not wise."

"Why not, Sister Emily?" I caressed my sister's hair, so remarkably soft in death. "Tell me again how loved my sister was?" My mouth was full of spit. "And then please explain to me why she's not fit to be buried in your cemetery? No answers?" I placed my cheek against Gretchen's, peering up at Sister Emily.

Suddenly, a low whistle, more an expelling of breath brought me back into the moment. I turned to Sister Clara. "It was not our decision to—"

Sister Emily interrupted, "That's enough, Sister Clara. Catherine, I only meant we can't leave you here alone, but if you want privacy, then we'll wait outside until you're ready to retire to your quarters."

They set two lanterns upon the table and their candles

on the shelves, and began to climb the steep steps to the outside.

I spoke out loud, my thoughts spinning. "I know, Gretchie. I'm horribly rude. But your Sister Emily is all about the rules, when sometimes rules must be broken. Would you scold me, Gretchie?" I let my tears drop upon her chest. "Is your Mother Superior always so rigid? At the river, didn't the pews need someone to carry them to the Protestant church? I'm not going to apologize. They should give you a proper burial so that all the people who love you can mourn your death."

I knelt and put my head down on the table, next to her. "Like me."

I really was very tired. Between sobs I said, "Don't go, Gretchie. Please don't leave me alone."

Then I saw something. A bruise on her arm. I pulled at the garment covering Gretchen and began to examine her body. Bruises under both arms. Bruising on her back. The kind of bruises Gretchen had after Papa beat her with his belt.

"I see blue marks. Did Daddy make the marks on you, Gretchie?"

I looked down at my sister's dead body. What awful memories. It was when I began to whisper our father's name as "Monster Papa" after that.

I examined Gretchen's icy hands as they lay beside her lifeless body. For several seconds my breathing was suspended. Answers sometimes jump out at you when you least expect them.

I sought the opening in the cellar and climbed the steps to where the nuns huddled together. "Sisters, please come back inside." When they saw my sister's naked body each woman reacted similarly, with great surprise, whether with a hand across the mouth or eyes filled with fear. They must be thinking I truly was the crazy sister.

"What have you done, Catherine?"

"I'm sorry, Sister Emily. I wasn't planning to undress her, but when I saw the bruise on her arm, I—"

Sister Adelaide stepped forward. "Bruise? What bruise?"

"And on her back." I pointed them out to her. She leaned close, adjusting her glasses. When she looked up, her glance took in all the nuns. "Look at these."

"Why would she be bruised?" I asked.

Sister Adelaide whispered, "It's almost as if she'd been beaten about the arms and on her back."

"Didn't any of you see these as you undressed her?"

Silence. I moved the candle, focusing light on her upper back and under her arms. Sister Emily said, "They were most probably made when her body was retrieved."

Sister Clara spoke. "I don't think so. Not in those spots. I watched the sheriff retrieve her body. When they lowered her to the floor, I cradled her in my arms. When they moved her here she was carried like a baby by one of the deputies." She looked away from the body. "I only saw the scar from the rope around her neck. It was dark blue. And horrible."

Sister Edith said, "I undressed her. It was dark. I only had a candle. I guess I wasn't looking for bruises under her arms or on her back."

I picked up one of Gretchen's hands. "There's also something that looks like blood under her fingernails."

Sister Adelaide said, "What does that mean?"

I don't know. But I wonder why there wasn't an autopsy." No one spoke.

Finally, Sister Emily said, "Sister Gretchen's suicide is the third, possibly fourth one this year. Not here. We've never had death inside this house, but inside the compound, usually in the patients' own quarters. It's hard to understand how anyone could take his or her own life, but for some, the disease becomes quite hopeless."

I didn't know at first if Sister Emily was the one speaking. It seemed like a disembodied voice from the darkest corner of the small cave room. I felt a chill pass through my body.

I said, "So the sheriff saw what he always sees and didn't think to question suicide. He made no examination. Certainly no autopsy since you have her body."

Sister Emily spoke softly. "It was suicide, Catherine."

I held up my sister's hand. "This looks like blood under her nails. Why would she have blood under her fingernails? She might tear at the noose, having second thoughts, but it doesn't explain blood."

Sister Paul leaned into the light staring at Gretchen's fingers, "No it doesn't." She looked back at Sister Emily. "It might be dirt," she paused, "or it might be blood."

I said, "Take a sample. Scrape some from under her nail, look at it, test it for blood." I felt flush, like a fever was falling over me. I picked up the noose. "And explain this, Sisters: a perfect hangman's noose. Where would my sister learn of knots or things like a hangman's noose? Do you just have these things stashed away in a closet in case someone wants to use it?"

Sister Emily said, "What is it you want us to believe, Catherine? That your sister's death was not by her own hand?"

"What else could it be?"

Sister Adelaide whispered, "You think someone forced her to hang herself?"

Sister Clara spoke rapidly, "We have to think about

this." She looked at Emily. "I mean, we must consider. It's what we've been saying, that Sister Gretchen had no reason to take her own life."

Sister Edith said, "No reason we are aware of."

Sister Adelaide spoke. "If it is blood, how did it get there?"

"Enough!" Sister Emily looked at me. What did I see? Challenge? Her composure regained, she said evenly, "Sisters, listen to yourselves. I know what you want to believe, but even if it is true, and I don't think it is, it's obvious why: you loved Sister Gretchen, and her death is intolerable to all of us." She turned. "Most especially to you, Catherine."

"Who knotted the noose for her?" I asked.

"I don't know how she got ahold of it. But she did."

"I see. There can be no other explanation than the one presented to you. Death surrounds you in this place, but not murder. That's it, isn't it, Sister Emily?"

"She wasn't murdered."

I stared into Sister Emily's eyes. "I believe she was," I said. "And—" but I didn't finish the sentence because I was interrupted by a rush of air that entered the hole above us, swept down the steps, extinguished the candles, creating a whirl of dirt circling our feet.

I stared at the body of my sister. Did I shiver against her or did she move? Was it my imagination or the wind against her face that seemed to make her eyelids flutter?

When the candles were lighted once more, we all looked at her body on the table as it was, but I could swear her hand was in a different place than before.

CHAPTER FIVE

WHERE AM I? **RAIN POUNDED** against a small window on the other side of the room. My suitcase lay open on a twin bed next to where I lay. My coat hung on a hook attached to the walL. There was a cross above the doorframe. My shoulder bag had been placed upon a small desk, an old wooden chair next to it.

I felt a soft pillow under my head. As the fog lifted from my brain, I sat up and turned on the bedside lamp. A small alarm clock read ten minutes past seven. In the morning? I got out of bed and walked to the window. Yes, it was daylight, but the storm outside made it seem like night. So much thunder.

Sister Adelaide appeared in the doorway. "Oh good, you're awake."

"Quite a storm."

"Yes. It just started a few minutes ago." She smiled. "Coffee? I brought some fresh ground coffee from the kitchen. Would you like some?"

I nodded.

"I hung your robe in the closet."

I retrieved it and pulled out a chair at the table in the small combined kitchen and living room. Sitting, I asked, "Do you know if Sister Emily has gotten in touch with the sheriff yet?" Sister Adelaide poured hot water over the coffee grounds and pressed them through cheese cloth into the pot.

"I don't know. I didn't speak to her after chapel. Hot milk?"

"Yes, thanks."

She found a jug of milk in the icebox and poured some into a pot, placing it on the wood stove.

"Me too. I like it *au lait*."

When the cup was placed before me, I stirred in two liberal teaspoons of sugar and took a sip. It was delicious.

Sister Adelaide sat across from me. Green eyes behind a pair of small round spectacles accentuated her round, pink cheeks. Her expression left no doubt of a genuine concern over something, perhaps for me. Or another problem. I wasn't sure. She was young, even younger than I assessed last night. If she didn't have her veil, wimple, and spectacles, I could imagine her with flaming red hair, a Titian woman. A face that reminded me of his *Venus*, which no doubt would have embarrassed Sister Adelaide greatly, I thought ruefully. How could my mind conjure up such silly things?

"You make an excellent cup of coffee."

"Thank you."

I was drawn to her dimpled smile, the expressive eyes, but her pensive look returned. I asked, "Sister Emily hasn't changed her mind, has she?"

"No. At least I don't think so. She sent me to my quarters last night after leaving Sister Mary Gretchen. The last thing I heard her say was to Sister Paul, that she wanted to go with her to the laboratory to check the sample. I left the two of them and went to my room. Sister Edith and Sister Clara went with me."

"She'll stand by what she said, won't she? If the sample is blood, we'll call the sheriff?"

"I'm sure she will." Her voice trailed away, as though while speaking the words her mind had wandered on to something else. I watched her hand shake when she grasped her cup and took another sip. She raised her eyes and stared at me. "Catherine, can I tell you something? I need to tell you, if I don't ever tell another living soul."

I was surprised. "Of course."

She drew her eyebrows together. "First, you must know I loved your sister. So much. She never made me feel different. Even if I was. The other sisters have been to school. I only finished fifth grade." Sister Adelaide blushed. "Gretchen fought for me."

"You too?"

"What do you mean?"

"My sister protected me her entire life." I patted Sister Adelaide's hand. "I'm glad she was here for you. But I guess it surprises me that you would need fighting for in this place."

"Oh, there is disagreement. There's a lot more going on here than anyone knows." Her face had changed, the muscles around her mouth tense. "That's not what I want to tell you, though."

I waited. She set her cup down. Whatever it was she wanted to say, it was obviously painful.

"Miss Lyle, do you really believe Sister Mary Gretchen was murdered?"

"I do. What else could it be?"

"I don't know. I want to think so. Isn't that a terrible thing to say?" She sucked in her breath and sighed, "But I do want to think so because I knew her and loved her. She wanted to live, not die! She loved helping others. It was her calling." The spectacles made her eyes huge.

"What is it, Adelaide? What do want to tell me?"

The sobbing came suddenly, as if a pin had been stuck into a baby during diapering. I jumped, in spite of myself. Sister Adelaide spoke in syllables, hard to understand at first, breathless. She said, "I've been keeping something from the others. I don't know why. It wouldn't have mattered if she killed herself, but now, well, I don't know what to do!"

From her pocket she withdrew a crumpled piece of paper and, wiping her eyes, tried to smooth it out on the table, then she stood and walked to a window, her back to me.

I stared at the words:

Don't trust the Samones.

The sound of rain, or hail, like pellets from a gun, hit the roof above us.

"I don't know what it means," she said in a trembling voice. She sat again. "I found it in her desk. I wasn't hiding anything. The sheriff was gone. I decided to clean it out, in case she left something for you." She wiped her eyes. "That's not true. I wanted to find a note to *me*, to explain why she did it. I just couldn't believe Sister Gretchen would leave me, not tell me if something was wrong."

"I don't know what it means either. The letters look like a child's printing; they're not my sister's pretty hand-writing. I think the writer meant 'Samoans' and didn't know how to spell it."

"Yes."

"You say you found it in her desk?" Sister Adelaide nodded. I examined the paper, lined, like a page from a penny notebook used in school. The writing was in pencil, the letters written as if by someone who didn't write very well or, I must admit, maybe someone in great distress. I sighed, folded the paper and put it in my pocket. "Another mystery. I don't know what it means. But I'll turn it over to the sheriff when he comes. It may be important. Or it may not even be Gretchie's but a note given to her by another patient. We just don't know, do we?"

"No. You're right. But I didn't know what to do with it."

I gave her a hug and tried to smile. "I wouldn't either." The minutes ticked on in silence.

Suddenly, as though she'd just remembered, she said, "Catherine, I was supposed to tell you, your friend Mr. Antoine called."

"Oh! I forgot to call him. He'll be worried about me."

"Dr. Mills said you can return your friend's call from his house. He's at the hospital all day." Sister Adelaide pointed out the window. "That's his house."

"I'm eager to get to the hospital."

"Then I'll take you now."

"But I need to talk to Yves. And it won't take that long."

"It will be more private there than at the hospital."

"You're right. Just give me a few minutes to throw on my clothes."

We found ourselves on the porch of the doctor's substantial two-story residence. We knocked and a black woman finally opened the door to motion us inside. We entered, completely drenched in spite of umbrellas and the short distance we'd come across the street.

The woman motioned us inside, "Come in. Hurry

now, you both goin' to be drown like rats if you don't get out of this rain!"

Sister Adelaide introduced me to Rose, Dr. Mills's housekeeper, as she extracted our umbrellas and led us down a center hallway, then quickly took my coat and Sister Adelaide's shawl, saying, "I'm going to put your wet things out in the kitchen."

"The phone is in Dr. Mills's study," Sister Adelaide said, pointing to the small room immediately to my right. "Don't you want to dry off first, though? I'm sure Miss Rose has the kitchen nice and warm."

"I'm fine. I'll join you in a few minutes."

It took longer than I'd anticipated to make the long distance call, from operators switching off from one to another and numbers repeated, and I sensed many people listening along the line, clicking in to hear these new voices. Our conversation would entertain people over their dinner tables tonight, what was said by some woman to a man in New Orleans. I had to repeat that it was "person to person," also an unusual request, I was sure, but one that perked the ears of party liners I imagined, *Well, this must be a really important call for her to pay for person to person. I'd better listen closely.*

Would the storm stop the call from going through? Finally, a ring, and Yves's voice, almost breathless, answered.

First, Yves had to identify himself to the operator. Then I heard, "Catherine, tell me you're all right."

I was shaking but hoped it didn't transfer to my voice. "I'm soaking wet right now. We had to cross the street to get to a phone. It's storming here; are you getting this weather?"

"Yes, it just started. Tell me ..." he paused, realizing we were probably not alone on the line, and changed his tone. "I'm glad you made it safely."

"Yves, we're on a party line."

"I know."

It didn't matter. "Gretchen was murdered, Yves." I steadied myself against the desk. My mouth went dry. "Are you still there, Yves?"

"Yes."

"This is like a living nightmare, Yves."

"Oh my God!"

"Gretchen was found hanging in the old mansion next to the leper hospital."

He didn't answer for several seconds. "Hanging? But you said 'murdered.'"

"She was murdered. Someone wanted it to look like suicide."

His voice was barely audible. "I'm so sorry you had to face this alone, Catherine."

"It was murder. Not suicide. I can't explain it all to you. Not until an autopsy is performed."

"I should be there with you. I'm coming as soon as we hang up."

"I'm surprising myself, Yves."

"What do you mean?"

"Everyone here, including the sheriff, I assume, believes Gretchen hanged herself. But it's not true. I've proved it's not true."

"Tell me."

"I don't think I should go into the details on the phone. Yves?"

"Yes?"

"I don't want you to come right now. I know how much you want to protect me, but I really need to do this alone."

"It's not necessary."

"I think it may be."

"Catherine, listen—"

"Give Grace a big hug for me and tell her Mister was so kind. Tell her all the hands on the barge respect him; they've given him a nickname, 'Hammer.' Tell her that."

"All right. but ..." His words hung out there, a sentence unfinished.

"I can call you, Yves."

"Why didn't Mother Superior tell us right away Gretchen hung herself."

"No, Yves. You're not hearing me. Gretchen was murdered."

"This is a nightmare. You're right. It makes no sense."

"I know."

"And you want to face it by yourself. It's an incredible decision you've made, you know that, don't you?"

"Maybe. But in a way, I'm actually glad I'm alone." Did I mean that? Maybe. "Gretchie needs me now. I always needed her. I leaned on both of you my whole life. I can finally do something for her."

I could see my teacher and partner computing this information. He stared away from the phone, out at the storm perhaps, or at the floor, at the walls of his apartment in the French Quarter. I read his thoughts. This was not the idea, not what he wanted. The experience on the river was to prove that I could walk about in the world and not fear it. Retrieving my sister's body was the opportunity, yet had he known the horror awaiting me ...

His voice pulled me back. "You have the strength to do anything; you've always had it, and I'm so incredibly proud of you right now."

"I'm not afraid, Yves." I thought, *That's not quite true. I'm terrified.*

"Because you're furious."

I smiled through my tears. "You're right. You know me. But I'll try not to throw a tantrum if I can help it."

"You'd be justified. How monstrous."

"Absolutely. I've got to go now."

"Be very careful, Catherine. Will you promise me that?"

"I will. I promise." He had spoken our code set of words. *Be very careful.* And in the ensuing silence between us was an unspoken message, and painful memories from long ago.

✦ ✦

NEW ORLEANS, 1920

In the drawing room of the Lyle's home on Prytania Street, a log fire had been lit, and in front of it sat Mother Beatrice and Sister Eugenie. The tea offered to them on the late Mary Louise Lyle's Limoges china sat on its tray, unpoured, getting cold. The nuns were not there on a social call. Mr. Avery Allen Lyle, Catherine and Gretchen's father, had turned his back to his company, briefly, poking more life into the logs on the fire. But when he sat down again in his chair, they could see clearly his whole demeanor was one of barely repressed agitation.

Avery Lyle was a big man and he wore his sideburns like great puffs of smoke, his thinning hair brushed slick, revealing a widow's peak at his hairline. Today, as every day, he was impeccably, fashionably dressed in a handmade shirt and buttoned collar, and a silk cravat fastened with a gold fleur-de-lis stick pin, under a finely tailored suit. There was nothing untidy about the way Avery dressed. It was only in his flaccid body and drooping jowls, and the redness spreading across his nose and cheeks that one could find fault in and that pointed to excesses in food and drink. Or, perhaps, the color in his cheeks today was a temper ready to explode.

The two nuns saw how angry Mr. Lyle was but chose to ignore it. They taught his daughters every day at the Academy of the Sacred Heart on St. Charles Avenue. For more than six months the faculty had watched and counseled both girls through their grief. But recently there had been undeniable evidence of something else.

Mother Superior Beatrice spoke pointedly to Mr. Lyle. "There are certain excuses that we're concerned about. Gretchen claims she has fallen down stairs, run into doors, and slipped getting out of the tub. Far too many of these accidents have occurred, we think. The most recent was discovered by our nurse on call, a terrible bruise on the girl's arm and, when she was examined, more bruises on her back and buttocks. Nurse is very concerned for your daughter."

Avery's graying eyebrows lifted sharply; his mouth formed a tight smile that didn't reach his eyes. "Well, that is disconcerting, Mother Beatrice. Yet I wonder if your nurse has the medical training to jump to a hasty and perhaps illogical conclusion. I know, for instance, that my eldest daughter has a fickle disposition. I'm afraid she's always been prone to accidents ever since she was a child. She's very much like her mother in that respect."

"Mr. Lyle, doesn't it seem a bit strange Gretchen has suffered so many of these accidents? Is it possible her grief over the loss of her mother and little brother has contributed to, I hesitate to say it ... to hurting herself?"

Avery's lips parted. He let out a huge sigh. He folded his hands together like one in prayer. "It is certainly possible. This has been a very sad house, Sisters. And Gretchen probably feels very guilty over the death of her brother."

"Of course you've explained to Gretchen she's not responsible."

He paused, deciding how far he wanted to extend the conversation, but plunged in anyway. "If Joseph had been watched more closely and his mosquito netting secured over his bed, and had he not been allowed to play during the times of day the mosquitos swarm …" He frowned, his mouth a tight line as he continued, "One must ask if my son would have contracted the disease. The answer is, probably not."

"Your daughter was but fourteen, sir! She wasn't your son's primary caretaker. Surely not."

"Yes, she was."

The Mother Superior's sharp intake of breath divulged her outrage. She dared not open her mouth until she could calm herself. Tonight she would have to confess the anger in her heart for this heartless man.

Avery enjoyed seeing the shock on the Mother Superior's face. He couldn't help the smile crawling about his lips. What was she, after all, he thought, but a sour, bad-tempered old woman used to dictating to others because she wore a veil. He beamed at the nuns, thoroughly enjoying the moment. "And I think you can be certain whatever Gretchen said to you about her accidents was true. My daughters know better than to tell stories. She wouldn't lie."

Mother Beatrice finally composed herself, finding a still place in her mind. She didn't return Avery's smile. "Gretchen is both fragile and vulnerable. And the fact that you didn't know about these accidents tells us she needs closer supervision. It's why we want both girls to move into the boarding school. As soon as possible. Even today."

An unnatural silence took over the living room. When Avery spoke again his voice had a distinct edge to it.

"You have provided my daughters with a superior education

at the academy. Now I see you are also concerned for their health. I thank you for your suggestion, which I will consider most carefully, I assure you."

"Thank you, sir. I know after you've thought it over you'll decide this is best for your daughters. We can watch over them." Her eyes bore into Avery's. "We will protect them from harm."

Avery's cheeks turned blood red. He stood. The interview was over.

Everyone, even the maid, tiptoed around the house after the nuns' visit. The girl's aunt, Tante, stopped coming to the house when she told her brother she agreed with Mother Beatrice, that the girls needed closer supervision than he gave them.

"Papa told her she wasn't welcome here anymore," Gretchen said sadly.

A week later, Avery announced to his daughters they would not be going to the academy anymore.

Gretchen said she had expected it. The nuns shouldn't have come.

"In a way," Gretchen said, "we should thank Mother Beatrice."

It was a statement Catherine thought so wrong. Didn't the Mother Superior make their father so mad that he took them out of school and away from Catherine's best friend?

"No," Gretchen said, "we should thank the nuns because Papa decided we should be taught at home by Monsieur Yves Antoine. I'm so happy for that."

"He is the son of Samule Antoine," their father told them at their dining table, which meant absolutely nothing to the girls until he explained. "Samule Antoine is the leading tenor for the New Orleans Opera."

Catherine said nothing.

Her father chewed a piece of meat in his mouth, explaining, "His son, Yves Antoine, is French by birth and recently graduated from Tulane." He stared directly at Gretchen. "He wants to be an artist. Does that please you?"

Gretchen nodded and looked down at the uneaten food on her plate.

"Then why the devil can't you show it! Lift up you head and say something!"

Catherine couldn't swallow. She thought she might choke on the bread in her mouth. Gretchen slowly raised her head, meeting her father's eyes. "Thank you, Papa."

He slammed his hand on the table, making both girls jump. Miss Virginia appeared briefly at the door before disappearing again. Then Avery Lyle rose and left the room.

A few moments later the front door slammed. Gretchen smiled at her sister. "I am happy, actually. We'll be taught by a real artist, someone who has studied art. And I'm sure he'll teach us French too."

"I'm glad he's not old, like Papa."

Miss Virginia came in to clear the table.

"So am I," Gretchen said. She stood and went to Catherine, hugging her little sister. "I have a good feeling about Monsieur Antoine."

The new tutor learned, in just a few weeks, that things were not right in the Lyles' household. When Monsieur saw a bruise on Gretchen's arm, a look not lost on the ten-year-old Catherine passed between them. Sometimes, when Catherine came into a room, Gretchen and Monsieur would stop talking. Then Monsieur Antoine would hold out his hand to her, say something funny, and they would all laugh.

Days stretched into weeks and months. Nearly two years passed. The teacher and his charges grew to love and respect each other. Most of their days were spent in the sunroom attached to the drawing room of their house. But sometimes Gretchen and Monsieur Antoine took walks alone, outside the courtyard, on the sidewalks that led into nearby neighborhoods. Gretchen explained that Monsieur Antoine and she talked about many things but recently about the future. She had always dreamed of going to Sophie Newcomb women's college. She was old enough now.

Catherine had a feeling their walks were about something else too. She believed her sister told Monsieur Antoine how they dreaded their father coming home drunk. Those times Catherine hid her in the upstairs closet, unfortunately, not far enough away she couldn't hear the sound of Gretchen screaming, "No, no!" heard through the closet door.

Sometimes, just as he was ready to leave, Monsieur Antoine would wrap his scarf around his neck, put on his wide-brimmed hat, kiss them on their cheeks, and say, "Be very careful, girls."

The warning was at first confusing to Catherine but said so seriously she took her older sister's hand and held it tight. She would learn it usually meant either she would hide in the closet or they would sleep together in Catherine's bed. The door would be locked from the inside, and if Papa knocked when he came home from a party or his club, if he slurred Gretchen's name, or hers, saying "Catherine, it's Papa. Open … door!" She wouldn't answer. The two of them would face each other under the covers. Or if he rattled the doorknob, raised his voice, spitting out, "You hear … me, bitch?" Gretchen would put a finger to her lips, a signal to be silent, to fearfully listen until his heavy, thudding footsteps retreated from the door down the hall to his bedroom.

Luckily, the next day, their father never seemed to remember his actions or what he'd said.

CHAPTER SIX

SPOKE INTO THE PHONE, "I will. I promise. I'll call you as soon as I know more." I replaced the receiver on its base, still staring at it. Was this really the right decision? Would anyone listen to a thirty-year-old woman? If Yves were here he would know what to say to the sheriff. He would speak with authority and people would listen.

"We found her body, you know."

I jumped at the voice behind me. When I turned around, there was a girl, not more than twelve or thirteen, standing just inside the door. She stared at me with an intensity more mature than her years, and in a voice so matter of fact, she might have been discussing what she ate for dinner.

"Who are you?"

"Clarice Mills." She stepped into the room and plopped herself on a large easy chair, swinging one leg over the arm. "Dr. Mills is my father. I live here."

"I see."

"Me and Jack found Sister Gretchen. Did they tell you?"

"No."

"I guess she might never have been found otherwise." Clarice was eating what looked like a biscuit. She took another bite. "Nobody much goes in that old house."

"And why is that?"

She finished off the biscuit, licked excess butter from her fingers before saying, "Jack says it's haunted, only he says 'hanted' cause he talks funny. He says the ghosts in the house are Indians, and they're upset 'cause it was built on top of one of their sacred places." She sat up suddenly, as if to make a point. "It used to be my mama's house. She grew up in it and sold everything to the government."

Clarice cocked her head to one side, as if puzzled. "So you think Sister Gretchen was murdered?"

I knew chastising her for eavesdropping would be a waste of time. "And you don't?"

"Well, I guess I never thought about it." The girl paused, pointing to the ceiling. "I saw her swinging from a noose twenty or thirty feet up. It was pretty gruesome."

I swallowed. "Yes, I imagine it was."

"I guess my daddy wouldn't like knowing me and Jack were there."

"Miss Clarice! What you doin' in here? You supposed to be in bed, sick." Rose looked over at me. "I'm sorry, Miss Lyle." She turned to the girl, "Miss Clarice, you get yourself back to bed."

The girl assumed a stubborn expression, not unlike a puppy pulling at a leash.

"I feel better now. I was hungry. You didn't even bring me any breakfast, Miss Rose."

"'Cause your daddy say let you sleep. He say, 'If she don't feel well enough to go to school, then she has to stay in bed.'" Rose took the girl's arm and pulled her out of the chair. "Now you get yourself back upstairs and out of this lady's way, you hear?"

I could still hear the conversation and their steps on the stairs. The girl was resourceful; she'd managed to get food out of the kitchen without anyone noticing her. I wanted to talk to her again and also to her friend Jack.

"They are inseparable," Sister Adelaide said, pushing her empty cup to one side while I stood warming myself at the stove, "Thick as thieves too, even if Jack is a patient." I waited for the rest of the story.

Sister Adelaide clasped her hands together, elbows on the table. "He was left here about eight or nine years ago, at the age of four. A sad story."

"Certainly is."

"The pity, too, is, even after he had no more break-outs for a year," she paused, "that's the incubation period before a patient can be released." I nodded. "Even after that, his family didn't want him. I came here about that time. Sister Clara said he was from Kaplan. He had something like eight or nine brothers and sisters. Maybe more. She guessed they were very poor. Jack's always been Sister Clara's boy, if you know what I mean."

"So he wouldn't have to leave, there aren't rules about that?"

Sister Adelaide smiled. She stood and tested her shawl hanging near the stove. "I asked that question too. I never really got an answer to it."

"Have any patients stayed? After they've had no break-outs in a year?"

"There's not been many. But, no, most of them can't wait to leave here."

"I don't blame them. Oh, sorry, Sister. I'm sure you

all try to provide as good a life as you can under these circumstances."

"It's not a place I'd want to spend the rest of my life, that's for sure."

The irony was, given her chosen profession, she might just do that. We walked toward the front door. "So Jack can come and go as he pleases, that it?"

Sister Adelaide nodded. "He runs errands for us after school, or he's supposed to anyway. And, yes, it was Jack who came shouting into the fellowship hall to tell us they'd found Sister Gretchen."

The hard, driving rain had turned to sleet when we made our trek down the narrow dead-end street of four houses facing each other to the entrance to the hospital. A sign announced US Marine Hospital No. 66. We walked past a tall, black iron gate, flanked on either side by a massive growth of hedge trailing off in each direction. I shivered. Was this their prison, meant to keep the ill and suffering locked away from view? If so, then it seemed a cruel and unnecessary way to treat those who hadn't committed any crime. I looked in both directions. No guards. Well, that was a positive sign at least.

Sister Adelaide pushed the gate open and I saw several nondescript small buildings in front. They were built of wood and brick, each perched on its own footed pilings. It was hard to tell what they were used for, maybe a post office or a schoolhouse.

Sister Adelaide pointed, trying to be heard above the weather. "The patients' rooms are in the back buildings, and over there is our library, the little building next to it. That's our chapel in the middle of the compound. The Protestant chapel is against the tall hedge over there. Everything we need is here."

The grounds stretched out of my sight, past four long, rectangular buildings, all very institutionally similar, sitting side by side with the Catholic chapel centered between them. I assumed one of barracks had to be the hospital. Somewhere inside the dull, lifeless buildings was a community of people, even if this morning the whole place seemed devoid of life.

The Roman Catholic chapel stood out. It was lovely, even on a terrible, winter's day, though its steeple seemed to have no top to it, pummeled by sleet at the moment.

Naturally, no one would be out on a day like this if they didn't have to be, but the place, except for the chapel, gave the impression of a military camp, not a village. It was hard to fathom any patient choosing to stay here if they could leave. Suddenly, it dawned on me, *I am the same as them.* I couldn't imagine their suffering, but it was not hard to understand why the outside world was so terrifying to them. Weren't they branded forever to be stared at and talked about? Wasn't my courtyard a sanctuary to me as surely as this hospital was to them?

But at least my courtyard, my home was beautiful. It gave me a sense of security. I felt sad for the community of people here. It was as if their disease had thrust itself upon the landscape. How awful it was that the patients had to call these ugly buildings their *home*. If I hadn't known this was a treatment center for Hansen's disease, it would still have had the same impression. Sterile. Paint the color of sadness. Everything gray.

I frowned. For someone to create such a void, such a blank canvas in a place teeming with natural beauty, the curve of the Mississippi, giant live oaks trees situated just beyond the tall gate and its accompanying ten foot hedge. Whoever it was had worked hard to make this place as ugly as possible, to destroy all natural beauty, carving out identical barracks, presenting a sordidness so unnecessary. I despised whoever it was, the creator of this place and a design that equaled the wretchedness of leprosy.

The snakes. I remembered one of Gretchen's letters telling me about finding a knot of harmless snakes nesting up under the joists of one of the rooms. Now I pictured in my mind patients hiding in the same way, somewhere inside. Sick. Unhappy. Inexplicably sad. Yes, it might drive someone to commit suicide. All these thoughts and I had yet to meet a single patient.

We entered the side door to one of the buildings. A sign read Infirmary. "Did you want to see Sister Emily first?"

"Yes." Once again we tried to shake ourselves dry. Sister Adelaide disappeared with my coat into a cloakroom. At least inside it was warm.

"It's just down here," she said, reappearing.

CHAPTER SEVEN

THE DOOR TO SISTER EMILY'S office stood open. Sister Adelaide and I interrupted a conversation between Sister Emily and Sister Paul and a man in a white jacket, who I assumed was Dr. Mills. The three of them stood in a tight circle facing each other, heads close together. Sister Paul saw us first and raised her voice, indicating, I thought, to the other two they should cease talking.

"Oh, look, it's Catherine. With Sister Adelaide."

Sister Emily immediately came forward. "Hello, Catherine. I hope you slept well." I nodded, and she continued, "I know you're anxious to hear about the results to the test we ran last night."

"Yes, I am. What did you find?"

"It was blood. You were right."

I heard Sister Adelaide's quick inhalation of breath behind me and noticed Sister Paul looking askance. Why would she avoid looking at me? Was it embarrassment, or animosity? I couldn't tell which, but there was palatable emotion in this room, and I felt it was directed *toward me.*

"The sheriff has been called?" I asked. "Will he be here soon?"

"I recommended that Sister Emily not place that call." The man crossed the small room, stuck out his hand to shake mine. "I'm Dr. David Mills, Miss Lyle." The doctor reached across Sister Emily's desk, retrieved the report, and offered it to me. "It was blood, Miss Lyle. But it is the same type as your sister's, universal Type O positive."

"So you think it was her own blood under her fingernails?"

"Yes."

I turned to the nuns. "Did you see any scratches on my sister's body? I didn't." When they didn't respond, I continued, "Of course, it's possible she might have tried to free herself from the noose, but then there would have been scratches somewhere. And fragments of the rope under her nails." I looked at the doctor again. "Were there?"

"No. Just blood."

Sister Emily said, "Perhaps the blood came from an old wound, already healed, but with traces still under her fingernails."

Doctor Mills said, "That's quite possible. Sister Gretchen was a nurse in the infirmary, she dispensed not just medicines for the disease, but often first aid for cuts and scratches and bug bites. Isn't that right, Sister Adelaide?"

Everyone looked at the young nun. "Yes," she answered. The word was barely audible.

"And the other things ..." The doctor's voice had become authoritative, I thought of arrogance too, in spite of his expression, which continued to be bland and even, his words formed with only small movement from lips and mouth. His age, I judged to be somewhere in his late forties, hairline receding, a generous sprinkling of age spots on his hands. I suspended my examination, however, trying to force my mind to listen.

If these two thought our meeting was over, they were mistaken. I swallowed, pursed my lips, and concentrated on not betraying the emotion I felt rumbling through my body.

"Sister Emily," I tried to make the words even, when I wanted to shout, "you've struggled with a reason my sister would commit suicide, but it wasn't suicide. My sister was murdered. There's blood under her fingernails and unexplained bruises on her back."

"Oh please, Catherine. Don't do this to yourself. God has forgiven your sister for her sin, I know he has. She was too good for our Lord to turn away from her."

"You think this is about sin, Sister Emily? Well, it's not. It's about truth. And the truth is, my sister did not commit suicide. I think an autopsy on her body will prove it. But if I understand you both, you don't think finding blood under my sister's fingernails sufficiently important to inform the sheriff. Well, if you won't do it, I will."

Sister Emily exchanged a glance with Dr. Mills. "I'll call him, Catherine," she said. "But I'll have to also tell him everything Dr. Mills has said as well."

The doctor added, "I'm sorry, Miss Lyle. I truly am."

Was that sincerity? I looked at him. "There is still the question of the noose. Have you seen it, doctor?"

For the first time I saw hesitation, his eyes blinked. He took a moment before he said, "I have. I can't explain the noose." Then he shrugged. "If you say she couldn't have made the noose herself," his words trailed off like a ball of twine rolling across the floor, "perhaps she had someone help her make it."

"Oh, really?" I was incredulous. "Well, that's certainly something to inform the sheriff about also, Sister Emily."

The Mother Superior started to shake, the color in her face turned so pale I thought she might faint right in front of us.

"Sister Emily, are you all right?" The doctor led her to the chair behind her desk. She whispered something to him. He looked at me. "Perhaps you could fetch Sister a glass of water, Miss Lyle?"

"Yes, yes, of course."

I tore down the hallway to the first person I saw, a man wearing a leather bomber jacket. I blurted out, "Where may I find a glass of water? I think Sister Emily may faint."

He grabbed my elbow and directed me immediately into a ward room with six beds, of which three had patients in them. Sister Clara and Sister Edith stood talking over a chart. My guide said, "Sister Clara. Sister Emily is in distress, I believe. This woman was sent to get her a glass of water."

"What?" Sister Clara said.

"Dr. Mills sent me to get a glass of water for Sister Emily." Suddenly, I felt foolish. It was obvious Sister Emily and the doctor wanted to get rid of me. I began to shake with anger. I started to follow Sister Clara down the hall, but the man took my arm, rather forcibly.

"My guess is you'd be better off not going back into the Superior's office just now," he said.

"That's what you think, is it?" I shook off the hand, and rubbing my arm, took a better look at him. His jacket was zipped halfway up over a dark sweater, which he wore with blue jeans and boots. He couldn't be staff, I thought; more likely a patient. But where were his sores or scars from leprosy? I saw none, but the scarf he wore around his neck looked suspicious.

His mouth turned up in the slightest kind of smile. I

felt like hitting him, to wipe that infuriating expression off his face.

"Is something funny?"

"You are a bit of a calamitous guest, that's all. It doesn't happen much here."

"And you're just plain rude." I rubbed my upper arm where he'd held me from following the nuns. "Plus, you're a bully."

"Actually, I'm a patient. Maybe being a bully is excused?"

"Maybe not."

His jaw tightened. "Fair enough. But you ought to give her a minute to calm down. You dropped a big bomb in there is my guess."

I took a breath. Then two. I leaned against the wall in the hallway. He was right. "Were you eavesdropping on the conversation with Sister Emily?"

He pursed his lips. "No, I guessed. You're Sister Gretchen's sister. I heard about running some late-night blood samples from under her fingernails."

"Who told you?"

"Ah, now that's a good question, but a reporter never reveals his source." He took my hand. "I'm John Weller, Miss Lyle. Editor of *The Light*."

"The hospital's newspaper?"

"Yes."

"Am I a story?"

"You'd be a good story. 'Sister Claims Murder.' Quite a headline. I'd have to move the weekly dining menu to the back page for a story like that."

"Not funny."

"Oh? I kinda thought it was. About as funny as you creating all this mess for the nuns."

I looked at him. We almost stood eye to eye. "Excuse

me." I slid away from the wall and began to walk down the hall.

"Miss Lyle?"

I stopped but didn't turn around.

"We don't publicize the deaths at Carville. Obituaries don't exist in *The Light* for good reasons. Maybe you'd understand how the closer you are to pain and death the more you anesthetize yourself to it."

I walked on.

"You're hurting a lot of people just to give solace to yourself. Don't you think that's rather selfish, not to mention childish?"

I spun around and walked back to John Weller.

"I think you should reconsider the newspaper's policy, Mr. Weller. Let me write that story for you. How about this? 'Beloved nun found hanging from a noose, though no one knows who may have crafted it so perfectly, because she certainly didn't know how to create those knots I saw. Will the guilty please step forward?' And while you're at it, find out who put the bruises along my sister's back, why she had blood under her fingernails but no scratches anywhere else on her body, and why ..." I took a breath, "why is it that, in this place, the sheriff doesn't think it's necessary to at least examine the bodies of victims of violent death!

"Mr. Weller, I don't know much about the pain you experience here. I never will, I know. But I know my dear sister was murdered, and I'm going to prove it."

I turned on my heel, not toward the Sister Emily's office, but to the front door of the infirmary.

"Miss Lyle?" Sister Adelaide came running down the hall.

"I'll see you later, Sister Adelaide." I opened the door, and I realized I hadn't stopped to put on my coat. "Where's my coat?" I remembered the cloakroom and ducked inside to find it.

"Where are you going?" She now stood in the doorway.

"I'm going to my sister."

"Whatever for? You can't do anything for her now."

"I need to sketch her. It has to be done soon. It's important to save any evidence."

Sister Adelaide stared at me. Her eyes were huge. I passed her and reached for the doorknob.

"Wait. Please wait, Catherine!"

I stopped.

"Stay here. Please. Promise me you'll wait five minutes."

"Sister Adelaide, I don't need you. It's not necessary for you to come with me. I'll run back to the guest quarters, get my pencils and my sketch pad." She had already disappeared down the hallway.

Less than three minutes later, she appeared again, toting a pair of rubber boots. "You'll need these," she panted, holding them out to me. "I use them in the spring for the garden."

I nodded, sat down in the cloakroom, and pulled them on. "They're big but not bad." I looked up at her and smiled. "Thanks, Sister."

She held out a box of matches. "The candles are still there. Are you sure you don't want me to go with you? The door to the root cellar is really heavy."

John Weller appeared, standing in the doorway.

"Please, just go away, will you?" I said.

"I think you might be able to get some good photos of your sister's body with this. Better than a sketch pad." He pulled out a camera attached to a leather strap from inside his jacket. He took it off and handed it to me.

Sister Adelaide smiled. "What a good idea."

"I have a box camera at home. What's this?" I asked.

"A Leica. It's German. I received it as a gift a few years ago."

"It's beautiful." I turned the small camera over in my hands. I liked the feel of it, light, easy to hold, to see through a lens mounted, not inside like my box camera, but in a sleek, round aperture attached to the front. I handed it back. "I don't know anything about using a camera like this."

"Then I'll take the photographs. And open the heavy door."

The offer of the camera was tempting. I would need to be careful around him, let my first inclination toward mistrust not be minimized by his willingness to help me. I felt there was an ulterior motive behind John Weller's offer, perhaps to keep an eye on me for Sister Emily. Why else would he grab my arm so tightly, but with an automatic instinct to protect her? Yet the offer of photographs, whether for good will or ill, was something I needed. When choices must be made, I thought, sometimes the best way was not the perfect way.

I headed for the front gate, thinking to walk to the mansion by the road I'd taken the night before, but John Weller pointed to a path opposite the front gate, to a solid-looking wall of hedge behind one of the smaller buildings on the property. He led me through a small opening in the seven-foot-high hedgerow.

When I saw the misty outline of the mansion, a chill ran through me, not entirely from the wind and mist. No, it was more than that. I sensed danger here; a senseless idea, to create persona out of stone and wood, to tremble before the broken columns of a crumbling mansion ravaged by the vestiges of time, but I couldn't help it. Something mean was here. One had only to listen and hear pain howling like the wind from every crevice, every window. I wanted to run away but trudged behind John Weller, trying to put these thoughts away.

"So, I guess you've been filled in on the stories about this place," he said as we pushed our way through tall weeds and mud.

"Clarice Mills told me it was haunted." I stepped into a small, muddy hole covered by grass. Thank goodness for Adelaide's boots.

He glanced back. "Oh, you've met Clarice? Surely not without Jack?"

"She's home today. Sick."

"Ah." He took my hand to jump across a rivulet created by the heavy rain. "She's right, though." He gave me a sardonic smile. "The owner of the place still wanders about on the third floor sometimes."

I wrinkled my nose as if I'd smelled something unpleasant. John Weller laughed. "It's been renovated, you know. About thirty years ago. But the original family who built the place was running from Napoleon. The story goes, Madame St. John insisted on this building site, even though it was an Indian burial mound. The stories are juicy bits of legend, not the least of which comes with the property becoming the only hospital for Hansen's disease on American soil." He stopped. "Here we are."

He pulled the door open to the root cellar and went down ahead of me into the dark. I remembered we'd left candles on one of the shelves and told him so, following close behind. John pulled out a cigarette lighter to find and light two candles, then handed me one. I was curious to see what John Weller's reaction might be to my sister's body. His eyes widened in surprise, and he stared, drawing in his breath. The nuns had covered her again in the simple, white muslin gown. We stood for a minute, each buried inside our own thoughts.

"I had no idea she was so beautiful," he said in a low voice.

"Yes. She was. Papa always said Gretchie was the pretty one."

He looked at me and a different expression took over his face. "That was a bit cruel ... and also not true."

His words had trailed away into an off-hand remark that allowed me to ignore it if I wished. Which I did, but turned aside, feeling myself blush. "So, Mr. Weller, can we take those photographs you promised?

He smiled, seemed to hesitate for a moment, as though he had something more to say, but changed his mind. "Ah, yes. The photographs."

CHAPTER EIGHT

I TURNED FROM THE WALL TO the other side of a narrow bed, not immediately knowing where I was. I felt my leg throbbing and reached under the coverlet to rub it. I shuddered, suddenly remembering. I had fainted seeing the crowd before me, hovering there, and the man with an earless head.

I sat up in bed, pushed my back against the wall, legs extended over the side. *I'm in Gretchen's room.* I pulled the wool blanket up under my chin. It was more of a cell than a room. I rubbed the side of my leg where a bandage had been administered. Yes, I'd fainted. I thought, *You're an accident walking on two legs, aren't you? Fainting, stumbling over that gate made of barbed wire ... what else can happen?*

Outside Gretchen's small window, ice crystals had formed, like petals of white flowers shining against a bright moon. Someone must have brought me here. I'd lost the rest of the day, I realized with the moon up, framed so perfectly. But thank goodness the storm was gone.

The autopsy. I must get up. I needed to find the deputy coroner.

But I didn't move. Murder. Or suicide. Whatever had happened to my sister was preposterous. Insane. I leaned back against the wall speaking into the darkness. "I wish you hadn't come here, Gretchie." And I closed my eyes again.

I saw my sister's face; she was da Vinci's angel in *Madonna of the Rocks*. I'd said as much the first time I saw her in a veil and habit. She laughed at me when I pointed to the face in a book of ancient masterpieces. But now, how ironic it was, her face, from an artist whose paintings forced everyone to concentrate on symbols and mystery. Like Mona Lisa's smile. Or the two completely different landscapes da Vinci placed behind her. Why had he done that? Why was my sister found hanging in a deserted plantation house? Back then I'd concluded da Vinci wanted his subjects to confuse most of us, his answers saved for only one or two people in the world.

Sitting on my sister's bed, I imagined her presence, believed I caught her scent in the blanket around me. Maybe by concentrating on what happened today, in the office, and the fellowship hall, and here ... something. What did I miss? Conversations. Expressions. What had John Weller said so early this morning? Yelled, actually, over the wind outside the administrative building when we returned from the root cellar.

"It's the coroner's van," he'd said when we paused outside the front door. The vehicle was parked parallel to the front door of the hospital and covered in mud, which told me the road between here and Prairieville was dirt some of the way and probably hard going in good weather, since it was twenty miles, but certainly treacherous in a heavy rain.

No, not that. John Weller had said something else. I

remembered. He had turned to walk in a different direction when we reached the infirmary's door.

"You aren't coming in?" I'd asked.

"I'll let you handle what comes next. I'll find you after I develop these." He paused. "There's something else."

"Yes?"

"I'm a reporter. I would check into the other suicides. Maybe a pattern. Maybe not. Just a thought."

I'd watched him disappear between the buildings.

When I entered the infirmary, I nodded to Sister Adelaide, who sat at a desk behind a glass partition with a boy next to her. Jack, probably. He raised his head from a stack of mail but didn't speak. He wore an un-ironed white shirt buttoned to the collar; his black hair was in need of cutting and combing, and I could tell he assessed me even as I him. His face brimmed with curiosity and he sat straight on the edge of his chair. At another time I might have smiled, introduced myself, and engaged him in conversation because I thought him to be someone who knew things. Sister Adelaide spoke first, however.

"They're in Sister Emily's office," Sister Adelaide said. "All of them."

"Thanks."

The deputy coroner didn't have a winning personality. He attacked me as soon as I walked in.

"So it was you on the phone, working everybody up over a *murder* here, huh?" He said.

It was hard to stand in his space; his body odor was abominable. I backed away from the thin, spiny man with a young, black assistant standing behind him. The coroner must have interpreted my action as fear because he moved himself closer and stuck his index finger under my nose. "Do you really think all we got to do is run out here because you say so? It's sleeting on the road now; the bridges will probably be frozen up by the time we finish. And when we end up in the ditch, it's on you, young lady." I looked away. "Yes, and I'm positive it will be for nothing, nothing at all," he finished.

I had a feeling he might be right, not because I'd changed my mind, but because his pathology probably smelled as bad as he did.

"If it's all for nothing, sir, then why did you come?"

Sister Emily and Sister Paul went pale, their shocked expressions not unnoticed by the deputy coroner, who, when he smiled, displayed a nervous twitch at his mouth.

"Don't play that part with me. We both know why I've been sent to this godforsaken place on the worst day of the year, don't we? You and your friends in high places?"

"I don't know what you're talking about."

"Don't you now? Sheriff Doucet got a call early this morning from Judge Leander Perez." He looked meaningfully at the nuns. "Yes, and then I get my orders to autopsy the body at Carville. Just like that. So who called the judge, lady, tell me that?"

"I have no idea."

"As if you didn't know." But he did pause fleetingly to take in my statement. A brief change in his expression, something like, *She's telling the truth or she's a really good liar.*

"Where's Dr. Mills?" he said loudly.

Sister Paul answered, "I'll get him," and escaped out the door.

"Will you have to take her all the way to Baton Rouge?" I asked. I had no idea what the facility in Prairieville might be like.

"Hell no! I'll look at the body here." He turned to Sister Emily. "You have an operating room, don't you?"

The nun's eyes had widened at the doctor's salty language. Then she frowned. "Dr. Guidreau, I wish you'd reconsider. Our patients are vulnerable to this kind of tragedy. It's bad enough we lost one of our own, but to perform an autopsy on her body here, I just worry how it will affect our community. We live in a fragile place. The balance between coping and despair must be dealt with every day."

"Sister, I don't have any choice. I don't want to be here anymore than you want me here, so the sooner I get started the faster I can leave you with all your *fragile* lepers."

Sister Emily flinched and I bit my tongue. We both stood in silence while his assistant was dispatched to retrieve my sister's body, and as he left, Sister Paul returned to say she would take him to Dr. Mills.

I wanted to tell Sister Emily how sorry I was, how upsetting I knew this must be. But I let the moment pass. We stood in her office staring at anything but each other. She turned briefly to the window at the sound of sleet hitting the window pane.

Finally, I found my voice. "Are you feeling any better, Sister?"

She nodded. "I don't know what came over me. I'm never sick, but suddenly I felt so lightheaded. Thank you for your concern."

"I've brought you a lot of stress today. If I wasn't so sure ..." I let the sentence drop; our eyes met and she turned away.

"It's going to be a terrible day," she said. "Such unusual weather."

"I just want the truth, Sister."

After several beats she said quietly, "And now you shall have it."

"I wonder."

"Something else?"

"I'm not too confident in the coroner's ability to do anything but throw insults about."

She smiled slightly, walked to her desk, and sat down. "He's a horror of a man."

"Yes." I decided the chair across the room looked inviting.

Sister Emily said, "And, what's more, I'm guessing we'll have to put him up for the night."

I laughed. "A foul, smelly problem. I've read somewhere some people suffer with odors of the mouth or excessive sweating, but my opinion of Dr. Guidreau is that he flaunts it. And he does as little as possible otherwise."

"You may be right." Her attention left me and my inane comments about the coroner. Something else occupied her mind; she frowned as if she'd just had a piercing, worrisome thought, like a candle left burning or the oven not turned off. She stared at a paper in front of her on the desk. Something troubled her very much.

When I excused myself from the room, there was only a barely perceptible nod from her. I walked toward the front office, where I'd last seen Sister Adelaide. My encounter with the coroner left me a bit nauseous. Mind over matter. I took several deep breaths and stood quietly for a moment, alone in the hallway. There was nothing wrong with me, I told myself, except having to endure fifteen minutes with Dr. Guidreau. His hostility was directed toward me in particular, but I sensed most likely he hated all women, a misogynist of the highest order.

You can deal with him, I told myself, at the same time longing for my sunroom, my courtyard, where all was safe.

There was something I'd wanted to do since arriving the day before; it gnawed away at me so insistently it felt like Gretchen spoke to me, her voice in my head saying, "Something else is here. Find it."

I asked Sister Adelaide for directions to my sister's room, but I got lost in the maze of rooms and hallways, even finding myself once in a treatment room, empty, thank goodness. At the end of the hall, eight steps down, I entered the kitchen. "If you go through the kitchen, you can find our rooms easily," she'd said, "and there's a covered walkway between our quarters and the hospital, so you won't have to go out into the weather hardly at all."

Outside, sleet was blowing across the overhang between the buildings so thick I could barely see the walkway. *Such wretched weather,* I thought, and then slipped on the cement straight into a barbed wire gate. I yelled, feeling flesh on my calf tear.

I reached a door that opened to a common room sparsely furnished with a table and chairs. This had to be where the nuns ate. But why the wire fence outside? Was it a law that caretakers had to be physically separated from the patients? Strange.

"No one should be inside our quarters now," Sister Adelaide told me, and she was right. Their commons room was empty when I opened the door. "Sister Gretchen's room isn't marked, but it's the third door on your left when you go down the hallway."

It was a cell, not a room, with a single window so small, sunlight would have a hard time penetrating on the brightest day. Looking around, it was patently obvious the room had been scrubbed clean. It contained Gretchen's cot, a single ladder-backed chair, a small armoire, and a tiny lamp table with a copy of the Bible. I picked it up, leafed through it, and replaced it on the table.

What was it like, living here for ten years? I opened

the armoire. Inside hung two freshly washed and ironed habits. I wondered where her cornette was kept. The shelf above the habits was empty.

Gretchen wasn't here anymore. And what I'd been sure I'd find wasn't here either: my sister's journal and letters, which I knew she would not throw away. Where were they? A living person had occupied this space, slept here, certainly prayed here, but she was an artist, a good one. Where were her paints? Her charcoal pens?

"Miss Lyle?"

The woman in the doorway had the gravelly voice of long years and a face deeply etched in experience. She would not reach my shoulder if I stood next to her, and the habit she wore seemed to swallow her. She leaned on a cane. I sensed she did not wear a cornette because its weight might topple her. Yet she smiled at me, and it was an infectious kind of smile, one to return.

"You must be Sister Anne."

"I am. I'm sorry not to have met you yet. I was the logical one to stay behind, last night, though. The trek over to the mansion would have been a bit too rough on my knees, I'm afraid." She motioned for us to sit together on the bed. I heard the click of her knee when she lowered herself to sit down. I saw the sparkle of blue eyes also.

"I don't want to intrude, Sister. I just wanted to see my sister's room."

She reached out and took my hand. I could feel her pulse, see the brown, thin skin barely covering bony fingers. "You should have stayed here in Gretchen's room. This is where you need to be. I told them that."

I let out a sob. I couldn't help myself. It came from some deep intrusive place that surprised me because I wasn't one to cry. I was very good at not crying, in fact;

yet here it was, something almost primeval. I was shocked at what had happened, perhaps more than Sister Anne.

"Now, now, child. I understand. Cry it out. Scream if you want to."

I laughed even as tears ran down my face. "I'll try not to do that."

The nun said, "But I did. I certainly did. I stood right over there and screamed. Because I couldn't believe it. I still can't."

"Neither can I! Thank you, Sister. Thank you. When I think that my sister is in an operating room right now, that her body is being subjected to an autopsy. It's just so hard."

"Of course it is." Her voice was gentle, even calm, and if I wanted protection from my anxiety, I thought it might be found by listening to these soft words whispered in my ear. "It's not how she died that bothers me, dear, though I know it matters to Sister Emily. No, I'm suffering from the lack of her presence. You see, the most amazing thing was, I wasn't a burden to your sister. She had a gift for reaching out to anyone who felt pain, whether that pain came from excruciating illness or, in my case, infirmity of old age, She always had a smile or a story for me, a project to keep my mind from wandering into the Mississippi River. Oh, how I want her here with me because I miss her so much. I dream about her, you know."

"What's your dream?" I managed through my tears.

"Oh, my goodness, you're bleeding, Miss Lyle."

I looked down at blood oozing from the cut on my leg. "The wire gate got me. What is your dream, Sister?"

She stood up carefully, balancing on her cane. "I will tell you. But I think we should take care of your leg right away."

As I followed her out of the room, I asked, "Where

are Gretchie's personal things, Sister Anne? Letters, you know, and her personal diary. Shouldn't they be here?"

Sister Anne looked surprised. "Of course. Her case is under the bed. I saw it this morning."

"No, it's not."

"It's not?" She went back into the room, leaned over, and looked under the bed. "You're right."

"There's nothing that anyone but me would be interested in. I can't think who'd want letters I wrote to my sister. But I know she must have saved some of them."

"Of course, you're perfectly right, my dear." She touched my shoulder. "Now, don't worry. I know there's a simple explanation. Someone must have put them away for you."

"There doesn't seem to be explanations for much of anything here, Sister."

Her eyes looked kind. "I think it's because we don't often ask questions. We pretty much live each day. That's the way of this place."

"No questions so no explanations necessary."

"Something like that."

We walked into the commons room and I sat down at the table. Sister Anne gave me a clean wet cloth, then an antiseptic, which I applied. She helped me put a bandage on the cut. "That will do for now, but it's a rusty old fence. You'd better get Sister Clara to give you a tetanus shot, just to be safe."

I nodded. "Thank you."

"Sister Gretchen told me you're an artist. You shared that with her, didn't you?"

"We had a wonderful teacher."

"Oh?"

"Yves Antoine. Gretchie and I have known him many years. He was our teacher and now is a dear friend."

I saw Sister Anne's face light up. "Oh, I know what we must do to cheer you up. Why didn't I think of it before?"

I followed Sister Anne's rather shaky, tenuous lead into another building. The wind had subsided a bit when we stepped outside to traverse the wire gate and the overhang, but this time I was successful, and it was just a short distance into an adjoining building. We entered a very long hallway and passed rooms belonging to patients. Most doors were closed, only a few stood open. A woman sitting on her small bed glanced up at us from her reading and nodded when we walked by.

"Hello, Sister."

"Hello, Lillian, dear."

At the end of the hall was a set of double doors and a plaque that announced Fellowship Hall. I heard voices. Was she bringing me here to meet some of the patients?

As if Sister Anne read my mind, she said, "Miss Lyle, there will be a few of the community inside. They have access to this hall all day. They use it to play cards or read or just visit together with a cup of coffee. We always have our birthday parties here." She paused. "Some will have visible sores and ulcers. You may see deformity. Will it disturb you?"

"I don't know."

"I promise you it'll be worth it."

"Then I'm ready."

"Good girl." She opened the doors.

Only two groups were in the fellowship hall, one playing cards and another with cups on the table and in their hands. It was they who were laughing. Yet the moment we opened the door and entered the room, they silenced themselves, turned, and stared at us. I felt my cheeks burn.

"It's there, at the end of the room, Miss Lyle. At the back of the stage."

A painting glowed from the back wall of a small raised stage.

"Isn't it exquisite?" she whispered to me.

"Oh, yes."

"Go on, get close to it."

I walked past the two groups of men and women, not noticing whether they were deformed from the disease or not. I stared only at the painting, which was of a large body of water, a lake, with purple and gold flowers in full bloom along its shore. It could have been Lake Pontchartrain except for its background: jagged peaks covered in snow, thin, wispy clouds winding around them, and a blinding color wheel of sky bursting with joy in tones of white and yellow, red and orange. A day about to begin.

"We asked Sister Mary Gretchen to paint something to decorate the wall at the back of the stage, you see. It was more beautiful than any of us expected it to be. Magnificent, isn't it?"

"Yes, it is."

Sister Anne patted my arm. "Would you like to stay here for a while?"

I looked down at the nun. "May I?"

She smiled. "Of course. I have to open the library for two hours this afternoon. But you stay as long as you like. No one will bother you."

I stood next to the stage, close enough to see the words on the bottom of the painting, written in my sister's hand.

Lord, if you are willing. Matthew 8:2.

I began to relax. I sat at one of the long tables in the fellowship hall at Marine Hospital Number 66, but my mind was remembering being in New Orleans, in my sun-room, with Gretchen and our tutor.

🖎 🖎

NEW ORLEANS, 1921

Monsieur Antoine said, "Keen minds can create scenes, think of God and creation; did He imagine the world all at once?"

"I think He did," Gretchen answered.

"Well, then, Gretchen, so can you. That's how you will paint His world, even if you've never seen it. Tell me, what can you imagine?"

"Mountains. I've never seen mountains, except in pictures," she said. "But if I think about it, I guess I'd imagine them with tall peaks, covered in snow … yet how would I capture the coldness of them? What would that feel like?"

"Is it snowing?" her little sister asked. "I'd like to feel it snowing."

Gretchen turned to her. "Yes, Cathy, it is. I'm imagining snow on the mountains, and it's such a lonely place to be. Someone would surely get lost in the snow unless they knew the mountain well."

The teacher jumped out of his chair and held up a paintbrush, pointing at a blank canvas set upon an easel. "You can paint it. Your mountains will sit and wait for you until you decide to bring them to life, here, upon the canvas."

"I want mountains too!"

"Of course you do, little one," he said, suddenly tearing about the sunroom, setting up another easel, placing the canvas then handing Catherine a brush. "We'll paint our mountains, shall we?"

"WHEN YOU CONTEMPLATE HER WORK, Miss Lyle, what's the first thing, exactly, that speaks to you?"

It was Charles Bremmer. His words interrupted my thoughts, but his voice was soft, like a prayer. He might have been behind me for some time.

"Some of us thought you might want to eat. He put a plate and glass of milk in front of me."

"Peanut butter and jelly? I love it."

"I often wander in here during the day. Your sister's painting is like receiving good news from home."

I looked closer. "You're right. There is a sense of happiness there. I'm really amazed by her use of color."

"Oh?" He stared with me. "So am I. Her technique is also amazing. Those purple phlox look real enough to pick. My mother used to grow them in her garden."

I chewed a bite of the sandwich then washed it down with milk. "Most of Gretchie's work reminds me of our old sofa pillows, puffed and faded by the sun. She said it was the color of Louisiana to her, the too-short bright green of spring fading into unrelenting summer heat. Our summers melt everything to gray."

"No gray there, is there?" he said, pointing to the mural.

"No. It's just unbelievable color. And so real. Like a photograph. She must have been so inspired to have painted this."

"Do you know by what?"

"I think I do, Mr. Bremmer. I was just thinking about it. It was a painting lesson from a long time ago. I was still a child."

He smiled. "I wish you'd call me Charles."

"And I'm Catherine."

"Thanks for sharing something of your sister with me. I've only been here about six months, but she became a special person to me and the islanders."

"Have you always been a missionary, Charles?"

"You're going to laugh, but I'm actually a clown from New Orleans."

"What? But I thought someone said you came with the Samoans."

"My father lives in German Samoa. He's the mayor of a small town on the north coast. Right after I was born, however, my mother returned to her home in New Orleans and took me with her. At sixteen I decided I wanted to join a circus."

"That's amazing."

"I was one of the stake-and-chain gang putting up the tents. I was small; I could shimmy to the top with guy ropes. But everyone did more than one thing in the circus. I ended up being a clown too. It was fun."

"Why did you leave?"

"My father convinced me I had no future putting up and taking down tents or being a clown. He sent me to school in Berlin, but I wasn't very good at school. So I went back to his island. And I learned about the leper colony there. I wanted to help."

"Commendable of you."

"Thank you. It's odd how different I thought my life would be. First, I thought I wanted a career on the stage, then I decided I'd become a politician like my father. But this is where I end up. Geographically, I've made a full circle, haven't I?"

"But you seem to be happy with your decision. At least you're one of the few people I've heard laugh while I've been here."

"Oh, yes." He shrugged. "Well, most days I am. But—"

"Catherine?"

I looked around. It was Sister Paul. She was a dripping, wet mess. I hadn't noticed her come in.

"I've been looking everywhere for you!"

"Sister Anne brought me here." I smiled at Charles Bremmer. "Charles fed me."

I might as well not have said a word.

"You should have told someone where you'd be. I expected you would stay in your quarters."

Her trek to find me in the guest quarters had clearly wreaked havoc on her from head to toe.

"I'm so sorry, Sister Paul. Sister Anne—"

"I know. I've just come from the library. Sister told me where you were."

"It was the painting."

Her expression softened. "Oh. Of course."

My lunch companion stood. "We'll continue our conversation another time, Catherine," Charles said. He reached out to shake my hand. "It's been a pleasure."

I smiled back. "Yes."

He disappeared into the crowd of twenty or thirty people assembled behind us. When had they come into the room? I hadn't the slightest idea when they'd appeared or for what reason. They were so silent; no one uttered even the slightest sound. The news of an autopsy had traveled quickly I surmised. What must they think? Or see? The woman who brought a threat of murder into their midst? They stared at me in silence and with a complete lack of expression, which was more frightening than an unruly mob.

Sister Paul took my hand, the crowd parted like the Red Sea to let us pass. I could hear my heart beating like a current running from my body. Here were more people than I'd ever seen, and they were so close to me! *Too many people. Too many people!* I squeezed Sister Paul's hand, trying to not think. *Just put one foot in front of the other.* A man with both his ears missing and lesions all over his face stepped in front of me, his rage stared a hole right through me. Suddenly, I couldn't breathe anymore.

So that's when I must have fainted. And someone carried me to this cell. It was dark outside. I reached over to turn on the lamp beside the bed. Nothing. Just a click. Had the storm taken out the electricity? At that moment, the door opened just a crack.

"Oh, good, you're awake."

I recognized Sister Adelaide's voice. She closed the door again, but almost immediately Sister Emily came in and stood beside me, a lantern in her hand. Other faces hovered at the doorway. Sister Emily came close; she pulled the only chair up beside me, sat, put the lantern on the table, and stared into my face.

I said, "I'm fine. Really. I think it was the crowd. I've never been that near so many people."

"How are you feeling now?"

I rubbed my forehead. "Better. I'm fine."

A pale hand appeared with a glass of water. I drank it down. "It was just all those people were so close."

"You don't need to explain, Catherine."

I was grateful for that. "I'm in Gretchie's room, aren't I?"

"I hope you don't mind."

"No, of course not." I didn't mention I'd been there before, that afternoon.

"We've lost electricity. It's an ice storm, I'm afraid. And the road is probably impassable by now. I hope Dr. Guidreau got back to Prairieville safely. He left two hours ago."

My mind was clearing. "He's gone?"

"Yes."

"Did he finish the autopsy?" I pulled myself to a sitting position on the bed. I could see the faces of the nuns in the doorway, candles or lanterns in their hands. Sister Clara wore a worried expression, Sister Paul's lips were tight, her face taut. So I looked at Sister Anne and Sister Adelaide, whose faces seemed noticeably bland.

"What did he find, Sister?" I asked the question but was afraid to hear the answer. "What happened to my sister?"

"Dr. Guidreau has taken Sister Mary Gretchen's body back to Prairieville. He wouldn't say why except that he must 'run more tests.'"

I could barely speak. "What sort of tests?"

Sister Emily took a deep breath. "I don't know."

"I'm confused. So it's murder then?"

"It might be. But the coroner left without speaking to me. We'll hear something soon from Sheriff Doucet. After he left, maybe thirty minutes later, we lost our telephones. Then electricity. I imagine there's ice on the lines, even downed poles. We're very much in the dark, in more ways than one. I'm sorry."

"I'm not. I know Gretchie didn't hang herself. Someone murdered my sister."

"As hard as it is, we've got to wait for the authorities, Catherine. Can you do that?"

"I suppose I have to."

"Rest a little longer. We'll call you when dinner comes, and you can decide if you want to eat with us."

I slipped under the covers again and tried to think it through. Taking my sister's body to Prairieville didn't prove she'd been murdered. But it must mean something, to "run more tests." How long? Tonight, tomorrow …

until I would have the answer? I remembered what John Weller had said to me this morning, "I would check into the other suicides. Maybe there's a pattern." Simple to say, but how would I do that? And would it really make any difference?

Just then, the wind outside gusted against the window pane, and its sound was strange but beautiful at the same time ... because it sounded like my sister's voice.

CHAPTER NINE

"SISTER CLARA?**"**
She looked across the table to me. We'd just finished a cold dinner of ham and cheese, French bread, apples and red wine. I was getting used to dining by candlelight here. It wasn't the worst way of eating. Another time, another place, I might have thought it a very nice thing, but while sitting with a blanket wrapped around me and still shivering, dinner was rather dismal. I could hardly wait to return to my quarters, for good reason. Earlier, Sister Emily explained that my sister's trunk had been moved there for me. So I wanted to leave the sisters and return to my rooms, but I couldn't. Not yet. Something else needed my attention.

"Did I hear you say you are going to the hospital?"

"To relieve Sister Edith, yes. I'll spend the night there."

"Do you think I might need a tetanus shot, Sister?"

I was pretty sure the accident I had with the wire fence had been reported to her.

Sister Clara nodded. "Oh my. Of course you must have

it. I'm sorry. Sister Anne told me this afternoon you'd fallen and cut yourself on the fence outside. Then, with the storm and all … well, we'll tend to it now, won't we?" She pushed back her chair.

"It's no hurry, Sister. Really."

"No, no. I'm ready to go. Of course, it's only precautionary, but you should have the shot tonight."

Sister Paul said, "You mustn't put that off. You'd die if you catch that disease, and it's a terrible death. Horrible."

She must have seen someone with tetanus. Not a pleasant thought. Sister Paul was quite close to me, and her eyes evoked an image, looking down into a barrel of water the color of ink. I closed my eyes to erase the disturbing picture.

"Ready, Catherine?" Sister Clara said.

Once inside the infirmary, Sister Clara made quick work of my tetanus shot. "You should sit still for about fifteen minutes," she said.

I picked up the receiver to the phone on the desk. "Still dead."

"Hopefully it'll be fixed tomorrow. Anyway, I doubt anyone would work tonight." Sister Clara headed for the door. "I must relieve Sister Edith. You'll be fine here, won't you?"

"Oh, yes. And you're just around the corner in the ward, aren't you?"

She smiled. "That's right."

"Sister Clara, may I ask you for a favor before you go?"

"Of course."

"I wonder, well, it's a bit odd, but if I could, I'd like to read the records of the other people who committed suicide this year. May I?"

"My goodness, Catherine."

"I know it's a strange request. The thing is, John Weller suggested it to me this morning, but I think I should do it before we hear from the sheriff that my sister was murdered." I took a breath and dove in again. "The point is, the more information we have about what's happening here, the better, isn't it? I actually agree with John Weller on that point."

Sister Clara flinched. She took a moment to compose herself. "I can't believe anyone would murder Sister Gretchen, Catherine." She sat down at the desk. "But even if she was murdered, why would you want to look at those records, and now you're telling me John wants to know about those poor souls?" She saw my expression and her jaw dropped. "You couldn't possibly think all the suicides were murder?"

"Please, Sister. I really don't know anything. It's information I'm after. I'm sure there's nothing in them to point to murder. But reading the facts of their deaths can't hurt now, can it?"

"I'm not in charge of the records."

"But you know if I made this request of Sister Emily, she'd probably have me locked up or sent away in a straightjacket. I know it's Sister Paul who keeps all the records, but she'd never let me see them. Not without Sister Emily's permission."

"With good reason. The records are private. Sister Paul keeps the records cabinet locked."

"Yet I'll bet you know where that key is, don't you?"

"It's not my place ..."

"Sister, it's not as if I wanted to expose anything. I have no interest in anything about those victims except how they died. But what if there is something, I don't know what, but something that was missed before. How they died. Was it all hanging? John Weller is right, don't you see?"

"I'm afraid I don't see."

"What if the sheriff calls us in the morning to tell us they know now that Gretchen was murdered. He'll tear this place apart then."

"No, I can't do it." She leaned across the desk, the lines on her face deep and furrowed. Her sober expression stirred a response in me. She must know suffering in a most personal way.

Sister Clara continued, "Poor lost ones. We couldn't save them, or even take away pain, much less their whole tormented existence on this earth."

"Awful," I said quietly.

In the silence that followed, it was obvious I had stirred something inside the woman, something awful. She suddenly blurted out, "I pleaded for Sister Gretchen to be buried in consecrated ground, you know." Her face went pale. She took her rosary beads in her hands, clinging to them.

I found my voice after several moments. "Thank you for that. I'm sorry, Sister Clara. I was wrong to ask for the records." I began to put on my coat. "I hope I haven't offended you. You of all the people here. I couldn't live with myself if I've upset you. You cradled my sister's body in your arms when she was lowered on the rope. You loved her as much as I did, I know. Please forgive me."

"There's nothing to forgive, *cher.*"

I heard the Cajun accent in her choked voice. She nodded at me and said, "I must go now. I've got to relieve Sister Edith. She must be starving for her dinner." And she was gone.

When I entered my quarters across from Dr. Mills's

house, I saw wood had been placed in the potbellied wood stove and one of the twin beds moved from the bedroom and placed near it. A stack of quilts and another kerosene lantern would provide enough warmth and light for me, and I was sure the sisters had seen to it that my cupboard in the kitchen was stocked with food.

My eyes found the trunk placed at the foot of the bed. My hands shook when I snapped the latch and opened it, pulling out several neat stacks of letters tied together. Underneath was one of Gretchen's favorite books, Poems by Emily Dickinson. I picked it up and flipped the pages. She'd underlined one:

> I went to heaven—
> 'T was a small town
> Lit with a ruby
> Lathed with down.

I replaced the book and picked up a crucifix attached to a mother-of-pearl rosary. Yves had given it to her when she joined the order. There were other things, several embroidered handkerchiefs and a woolen shawl wrapped around what I most wanted to find, her journals.

I wrapped the shawl around my shoulders while examining the journals. They were different sizes. She must have acquired whatever was available when she needed a new one. I flipped the pages of one dated 1934. It was filled with words and drawings and remarque in the margins next to watercolors or sketches or prose she'd written. Sister Adelaide, as a postulate, dressed all in white and smiling from ear to ear. I would have to show it to her.

In another journal, an earlier one, Gretchen had painted the old mansion over and over, in many different styles; realism, but also impressionism and cubism. I laughed at the abstract rendering she'd done of the old house and her comment in the margin, "My Picasso!"

She sketched many of the patients too, or used watercolor. One woman in particular stood out as I flipped through the different pages and saw her likeness several times. She wrote the name "Eleanor" at the bottom of one of the pages. I could see why Gretchen might choose that patient as a subject; her flaming red hair and almost translucent white skin would be a challenge. I'd like to find her and paint her myself. If she was still here. It would be nice to think such a pretty woman had recovered and went back to another life.

I poured over the journals, forgetting the time. I was with my sister in these, hearing her voice again, laughing with her about all sorts of wonderful things and discovering art as I'd never thought of it, as a pathway to finding myself, what I wanted to do in my life, where I wanted to go, who I could be.

NEW ORLEANS, 1921

"Do you see?"

"What is it, Gretchie, you want me to see?" It was dark and the two girls were lying in bed staring at the ceiling that wasn't there. Not in the darkness.

"A song."

"You can't see a song. You're so silly, Gretchie." Catherine snuggled up against her sister in the bed. She put her cold feet on Gretchen's legs and made her jump and giggle. It was so safe there that she wanted time to stop.

"Sing one to me."

She laughed. "I would ruin any song I tried to sing. And it's so much more beautiful in your mind." She reached out to pull Catherine close, into the warmth of her space, and Catherine closed her eyes, imagining a song. Before it was finished, she was fast asleep.

⟡ ⟡

I TURNED A JOURNAL OVER in my hands, remembering my sister's face. I clutched one to my heart, breathed in its worn leather binding, and placed it with the others in a row on the bed. Inside these was her life here, people and scenes, even objects. I paused to look at Sister Adelaide's portrait again. She couldn't be more than fifteen. The same age I was when Gretchen left me to join the order.

On another page was a drawing of the Protestant church under construction and on another page, the river, then a paragraph she'd written describing a new priest's first homily, with a small remarque on the edge of the page. He was a fat man with bulging eyes and a tight collar. I laughed. "For your eyes only, Gretchie." It was a glimpse into her life that her letters hadn't given me.

I didn't hear a knock at the door, if Jack even knocked. He was in the room before I was aware of it.

"Ma sent me with more wood for the stove. It'll be cold tonight." He was staring at the contents of my sister's trunk on the bed. "I put them on the porch."

"Thanks, Jack. Please thank ... who's Ma?"

"Sister Clara."

Sister Adelaide had told me this morning Jack was "Clara's boy."

I nodded. "Can you sit for a while?"

He opened his coat and took three folders from inside where he'd belted them against his body. "From Ma." The gangly boy filled the chair uncomfortably when he sat down.

"Oh. Thank you, Jack. Thank Sister Clara for me, will you?"

"She says I'm to stay here with you till you finish with them so's I can bring them back tonight."

"Oh. Yes. Certainly." Hastily I replaced my sister's journals into the trunk and sat down on the bed to open and read the first folder. I glanced up to see the boy staring at me. "Would you like something to eat or drink?" I stood up and walked over to the icebox." I'll bet there's something in here. Oh, look," I said, opening the door, "here's milk and also a pitcher of orange juice. Would you like some?" He nodded, and I found a glass in the cupboard, also some crackers. I put some on a small plate for him, poured his juice, and set it before him on the table. He accepted the food silently.

I sat down on the bed again to open the first folder. "*Laurence Dunn. Death by hanging.*" I read the notes. "*Mr. Laurence Dunn, admitted March 27, 1940.*" I looked at the date on his death certificate. "*April 13, 1940.*" Mr. Dunn had been here only two weeks. I read from one page:

> The disease was in an advanced state on the patient's stomach and lower regions. Intense chaulmoogra oil therapy by capsule does not relieve pain. Prolonged vomiting. Patient may respond to intravenous treatment.

Another note in Gretchen's hand, stated:

> Mr. Dunn is a quiet man, very gentle, affable, and

soft spoken. He is quite worried about his wife and children and asked for assistance to prepare forms for a veteran's stipend that would, in his words, "carry them through."

I picked up a small piece of lined note paper, the handwriting almost illegible.

> I'm not goin to get pas this so I will go and love you Ma and Little Lo and Bess. Yours Very Truly, L. Dunn

Dr. Mills signed the death certificate. *"Self-inflicted."* Sister Paul wrote:

> On the morning of April 5, Mr. Dunn did not appear for his treatment. Three hours later another patient reported Mr. Dunn's body. He was found hanging from a hook in a supply closet. He used a man's tie. A note was found near the body. Attached. Sister Paul.

I closed the folder. Had someone told him the treatments wouldn't work on him? Then again, did they work on anyone? Or had Laurence Dunn discovered this was just a place where one would stay forever.

The next folder was a young woman, seventeen years old. Jessie Mae, no last name, though the last name had been there once and now it was blacked out. Did the family have the right to do that? I looked at the death certificate. Dr. Mills had written *"Jessie Mae ███████ ███████ died of complications following blood poisoning."* Blood poisoning? I chose one of the notes written in Gretchen's hand:

Jessie Mae was sent to us three months ago. She was a simple girl with no education and worked as a maid for the ████████████████ family in New Orleans. Jessie confided to me that she had a baby boy which she had given up to adoption by the family before she was admitted to Carville. They promised to take care of him. Her mental state started to deteriorate when she didn't receive any letters from the family. She was found dead lying on her cot. Both wrists were cut. May God have mercy on her soul.

I closed the folder. *How could you cope with this misery, Gretchie?*

I opened the last folder. His death was dated June 22, 1940, less than two weeks after the Samoans had arrived. I recognized the name as Samoan and the handwriting as Gretchen's. *"Enoka Noa. A male, approximately twenty-five years."* I turned to the next entry. The first page announced *"US Government/Western Samoan Leprosy Project."* It was at least twenty pages in length, but the first paragraph explained that patients from the Samoan leprosarium in Falefa were to be part of a pilot project for a proposed drug called sulphanilamide, initiated by the United States Public Health Service. In addition, this test group of islanders would be compared to mainly Caucasian patients whose reactions to the drug had included some success but also fever and other symptoms. Sister Paul had filled in the patient information including:

Enoka Noa, admitted June 13, 1940 from German Colony, Western Samoa. In a test group of eleven males and four females. Patient displays no mutilation or deformity. No skin lesions. His file from

Falefa describes tuberculoid leprosy, a benign type that presents itself in the patient through numbness in his fingers.

I read through the death certificate.

Enoka Noa, death assumed by drowning. The body was not recovered.

On another page:

Enoka Noa lived with the other Samoans separately from the regular patient quarters. This accommodation was created by request of German Samoa, funded by US Public Health Service. Sister Mary Gretchen and Sister Adelaide discovered Enoka Noa missing on June 22 when he did not present himself for treatment at the Samoan camp. Members of the Samoan group explained Noa had "gone out fishing" the day before and had not returned. A spokesman for the Samoans, Reverend Charles Bremmer, discussed a letter written by Bremmer for Noa, to his family, in which the man expressed his sadness in being so far from home. It is assumed that Enoka Noa probably drowned in the Mississippi River while fishing, but suicide cannot be dismissed. Another search for the young man produced nothing. Mother Superior Marguerite Emily, D.C.

"Them was the ones killed themselves like Sister Gretchen," Jack said.

I stared at the boy. *How to imagine his life here*, I thought. Impossible. I closed the folder and put it back on the stack, my mind still trying to process the hopelessness of this place.

"Jack, Clarice told me the two of you found my sister's body in the mansion." He nodded. "That must have been horrible for both of you."

"Sister might still be hangin' if we hadn't found her, I guess." He stood and walked to the pitcher of orange juice on the table. He seemed remarkably calm, as though he was discussing the weather outside. When one was so surrounded by suffering, did it numb the senses completely? I'd noticed more people other than Jack for whom death just didn't seem to register. Was everyone in this place in denial? Young teenagers talking about death in the same way they discussed what they ate for dinner?

"Clarice said almost the same thing to me this morning," I said.

"Almost nobody goes in that old house, I guess."

"I've heard. It's full of history, not all of it good."

"Hanted. That's for sure. But me and Clary ain't afraid of ghosts."

I smiled. "Well, I'm glad you found my sister, Jack. I think you and Clarice must see quite a lot of what goes on around here, don't you?"

He narrowed his eyes briefly then tapped his fingers on the table before answering. "Why do you think Sister was murdered?"

"It's more than a thought, Jack. I know an autopsy will prove she was murdered."

He raised his eyebrows and, leaning in, said "Tell you the truth, I can't believe Sister Gretchen would do that to herself. Everyone here loves Sister." He paused. "Well, maybe not everyone."

My heart skipped a beat. "Who doesn't like my sister?"

He took a sip. Just the hint of a smile crossed his face. If I didn't know he was thirteen and still a child, I'd have thought I was being toyed with.

"Somethin' I heard. The day before she hung herself. It made me wonder."

"What did you hear?"

"Mr. Tom. He works for Sister Gretchen. He's got the disease really bad. His own ears have come off." Jack frowned. "My guess is he's pretty close to dyin'. If you look around at all them that's here, I guess you'd have to say he's about the worst."

I swallowed. "Yes. I think I saw him in the fellowship hall."

"Sister Gretchen told him he needed to be put in the hospital. But Tom blew his top. He got really mad." Jack's eyes were dancing. His cheeks flushed. "I heard 'em talking in the office on Sunday."

"And? What about it, Jack?" Did this upstart boy know that very same person had presented himself to me just a few hours ago? How I'd panicked then fainted?

"For sure Mr. Tom didn't like Sister's idea."

"But, Jack, if Sister Gretchen wanted him to move into the hospital, wouldn't that have been a kindness on her part?"

"Not if you got a wife like he does, and your wife is going to have a baby soon."

"He's married?"

Jack grinned. "Last year. First time here. I helped them get one of the shacks down by the swamp put back so they could live there. That was fun, that wedding. The priest married them but Mr. Tom and Miss Penny still wanted to jump the broom too. Away from the nuns, you know? We stayed up all night, me and Clary. It was a real good party, that."

"Jack, why did you want to tell me this? About Tom yelling at Sister Gretchen? Do you think he hated her enough to kill her?"

He shrugged. "I dunno." Then he said defensively, "I could tell you somethin' else too, if I wanted."

"So tell me."

He seemed to relish the idea. "Mr. Tom, he yelled at her, 'I know you did it,' he said. And, 'You better stay away from us 'cause nobody's goin' to mess with me. Or mine!'"

"Just those words?"

Jack shrugged. "Something like it." Jack pursed his lips together and spit out, "I think he had it in for Sister Gretchen. I really do. And I don't think it had anything to do with him being put in the patients' ward." Neither did I. But did I want to trust the words of a thirteen-year-old boy?

I asked, "Who else heard him say that, Jack?"

He jumped up and grabbed the folders off the bed. "I ain't a liar! He said it all, all right, and the next day, me and Clary saw her hangin'!"

"Calm down. Calm down. If it's true, then tell me who else might have heard him threaten my sister. The Infirmary is a busy place. Was someone else in the hallway?"

Jack grabbed the folders from my bed. "I gotta go."

The biting cold air brushed across me when he opened the door and disappeared, slamming it behind him.

I had the urge to follow him, but decided not. If his story was true, I would soon find out. In just a day I'd learned nothing here was kept secret for long. Word had spread throughout the hospital that I suspected murder and that an autopsy had been performed.

I picked up the copy of Emily Dickinson and began

reading. My favorite writer. Not only for the words on the page. She'd proved to the world how one could live in seclusion, even be called a recluse and still be an important voice in literature.

Sweet hours have perished here;
This is a mighty room;
Within its precincts hopes have played,—
Now shadows in the tomb.

Staring at the words, I thought about how strange that poem appeared at random. It could be Carville itself her poem described. Life for all the sufferers, but the shadow of death always so near. I closed the book and retrieved Gretchen's journals from her trunk. Tomorrow the sheriff would arrive and tell us she had been hatefully murdered by someone, surely an insane killer. John Weller had suggested I look for similarities in the suicide deaths. There were none, as far as I could tell. Except each one of them had a clear motive to commit suicide. And Gretchen didn't.

I spoke out loud, "You'll lead me to your murderer, Gretchie, I know you will." I picked up one of the journals in the stack and began reading it.

CHAPTER TEN

THREE, FOUR, AND FIVE O'CLOCK. *Enough of this sleep-less night.* I got up, added some more wood to the stove and dripped myself some coffee. I'd thought all night about what to do next. Maybe nothing. The telephone lines would be repaired today and the sheriff would call. The coroner had said as much when he tore out of here to get back to Prairieville, taking Gretchen's body with him. The sheriff would come, and he'd begin an investigation into Gretchen's murder.

I took a sip of the hot, dark roasted coffee, which burned my tongue. "Cripes," I muttered to myself. If I could only talk to Yves, I thought. What would he advise me to do, sit and wait? Hang around the hospital just taking up space? Join Sister Anne in the library? Yves would say no. He liked to solve problems as much as I liked to avoid them.

I took another sip. The coffee stirred my senses, and like a jolt out of the blue, I knew exactly what I wanted to do.

I dressed as warmly as I could, layering a shirt and sweater under my heavy coat. I still had Sister Adelaide's boots and added an extra pair of socks. It was very cold outside, very early; the sun hadn't risen yet, but I could see enough that the heavy clouds had lifted and there was promise of a better day. I stuffed my hands deep into the pockets of my jacket and listened to the icy crunch under my feet as I walked down a path next to a field, worn, I imagined, by a century of slavery working a large sugar cane plantation. It was so quiet during this hour before sunrise. Even birds slept.

I knew of an actual road leading away from the compound; Sister Adelaide said it had been laid out when the Samoan village was built. But this trail I followed must lead to the old slave quarters. During my sleepless night, I had reasoned the shack Jack spoke of where Tom and his wife lived had to be part of the original plantation.

Something rustled inside tall grass near the path. A rat, perhaps, or raccoon. *Let us keep to our own agendas, please,* I thought. Mine was a bit hazy, though I wanted a morsel of information from Tom Langlinais, as dearly as the nearby varmint searched for food. I wasn't at all sure how to approach him with Jack's information. Maybe it would come to me. One thing was for certain: I must know whether Jack invented the whole dramatic story. But how to discover the truth? Ask directly? Given my experience meeting Tom in the fellowship hall yesterday, I wasn't sure if the direct route was best.

Then again, what actually happened yesterday? The crowd of people triggered my dizziness as much as Tom's face staring at me. Was it an expression of animosity or my revulsion to his missing ears? I remembered something Yves had said, staring at a canvas I'd repaired. "You can see the very brushstrokes that the artist intended, Catherine. It's a rare gift." But I knew it was much harder to read a real face. It would have been better if Jack hadn't told me what he'd heard, for I knew I couldn't let it go until I looked at Tom again and asked him to his face.

I'd been walking for about fifteen minutes and stopped to look down the trail. The landscape was flat, a light breeze blew against the tall grass, and something dark like a grove of trees inserted itself into my line of sight. If a house or a shack, as Jack had described it, was there, I couldn't see it yet. Perhaps it was hidden under the trees. I hoped my hunch hadn't failed me. Maybe I should have waited for the sun to rise before setting out.

I did prefer the dark, though. Everything was equal then. Whatever meanness lay beyond a closet door was invisible if one was invisible too. It never found a person in that dark hiding place.

After another five minutes, I stopped, trying to decide whether to trudge on to the tree line or not. This was surely a wild goose chase. I rubbed my gloved hands together, blowing into them.

I heard it then. A noise. It wasn't the rustling of another varmint, but footsteps. I spun around and saw a person approaching on the path. Whoever it was stopped when the person saw me. I took a few tentative steps forward. It could have been a man or a woman wearing a shawl or long coat of some kind. Like my teacher, Yves. He sometimes wore a cloak around his shoulders. Or perhaps it was a nun's habit, without her cornette. Or one of the patients out for an early morning walk. Were they free to walk the grounds? The person stood there, a shadow against the lightning sky.

"Hello?" I moved, but whoever it was disappeared

suddenly. Gone. The figure vanished. I was thunder-struck. I'd passed some tall grass, not as tall as a grown person, though. Was there another path I'd missed further back? Or was the mysterious figure hiding in the grass, out of my sight? I was amazed. I had another thought. Could whoever it was have been following me? I shook off the notion. No, whoever it was must have an errand of their own and didn't want company. Whoever it was decided things for me. I would follow this trail as far as it took me. And in the daylight, I'd see a lot better.

I found the cabin hidden near some giant water oaks leaning into a bayou. Smoke rose from the chimney and a lantern suddenly glowed from the small window. Good. Someone had just gotten up.

Maybe they would see me standing under the tree and so give me an excuse to approach their house. Perhaps Tom would come outside to fetch water from the well I saw in the side yard.

As the minutes ticked by, I decided I must act. I approached the front door, walked across a dry brown bit of dirt that might have been swept with a broom, and climbed four steps up onto the planked wood porch. I walked heavily to make some noise, to announce myself. The first knock on the door met with silence.

Knocking a second time, I said, "Hello? I'm Sister Mary Gretchen's sister, Catherine Lyle."

I heard steps. The door opened slightly. She gazed out at me with huge eyes.

"Mrs. Langlinais?"

"Yes, I'm Penny Langlinais."

"I'm Sister Gretchen's sister, Catherine."

"I know who you are." She opened the door a bit wider.

What a pretty face, although right now her brow was knotted into something registering a bad surprise.

"I apologize for just showing up like this. I couldn't sleep." What to say to this woman with a beautiful, innocent face twisted into a solemn expression and tightly pursed lips staring back at me? "I wanted to speak to your husband, if I might."

"He's had a bad night."

"Oh, I'm sorry. But it's so important. He knew my sister, didn't he? Worked closely with her?"

She nodded. "I don't want to wake him up."

"Oh, oh, please don't worry." I moved to the porch swing and sat down. "I can wait as long as I need to. I think he has an answer to something I heard last night. I couldn't sleep thinking about it. That's why I'm here at the crack of dawn. If you'd just let me ask him one question. That's all. When he wakes up."

They say you think she was murdered, that she didn't hang herself."

"I know she didn't kill herself, Mrs. Langlinais."

"How do you know for sure?"

"I'm her sister. I know she wouldn't kill herself."

Her expression changed. Softened. "You're right. It doesn't seem like Sister Mary Gretchen would do that to herself."

"Thank you for saying that."

Our eyes connected. Those large pools were as black as night. "I'll come get you when Tom wakes up." Penny Langlinais closed the door.

As the sun rose I could begin to see the road, the wild grass that created a skirt of brown ribbons up to the house and dead stalks of wild sugar cane growing in the field about fifty yards away. The porch swing whined from new rope adjusting to its load. But it was very well crafted, carefully knotted and big enough for two people to sit upon.

I had no idea what time it was. I felt warm out of the wind with the sun on my face. I closed my eyes. When I opened them again I saw Sister Adelaide on the trail coming toward the house.

"Good morning," I said as she entered the yard.

She carried a black bag at her side. "This is a surprise," she said and sat down beside me on the swing.

"So you didn't come here looking for me?" I said, thinking of Sister Paul's concern yesterday.

"No. I've come to give Thomas his chaulmoogra oil I didn't think he'd be up to coming to the clinic today." She glanced sideways, briefly averting her eyes. "I've given it to him before, but Sister Gretchen was always with me."

"Is it difficult?"

"We have to insert it into the muscle. It's quite painful," she said, sadness written on her face. "There was a sister in the pharmacy here many years ago who came up with a shot instead of taking the chaulmoogra oil by mouth. No one seemed to be able to keep it down taking it that way."

"So the oil is tolerated better in a shot?"

She looked upset. "It doesn't seem like it to me. People still get so sick. I just hate it sometimes. I don't think what we're doing makes any difference."

"Sure you are. You give comfort, hope, even if the medicine doesn't seem to work."

"I guess you're right. I just wish he'd been approved for the sulphanilamide."

She must be referring to the clinical trial project I'd read about in the files last night. "Why wasn't he?" I asked.

"I don't know. Dr. Mills didn't give us a reason."

I didn't want to say the reason might be because he was too ill, with no chance to recover from the disease, no matter what the treatment. It seemed cruel, if realistic. Sister Adelaide rose and knocked lightly on the door, then suddenly turned back to me, as if a thought had caught at her. "Why are you here?"

Penny opened the door, allowing Sister Adelaide to enter before I had a chance to answer.

Ten minutes later, the door opened again and Sister Adelaide motioned me inside. "Penny tells me you want to question Tom about something?"

I let my eyes adjust to the dark room, noticing the table and a few chairs, a potbellied stove in the corner, a small cradle, and an empty bed. But no Tom. My confusion registered with Sister Adelaide.

"Penny took him to the outhouse. He'll be back in a minute. He wouldn't let me give him the chaulmoogra oil this morning. He said he was too sick to his stomach. He'll come to the hospital later, he said, and get Dr. Mills to give it to him. She lowered her voice, "Why did you come here?"

"Oh. Yes, well it was something Jack said he heard, an argument between Gretchen and Tom in the pharmacy." I lowered my voice. "I'm not sure if Jack wasn't just making the whole thing up."

"When did you see Jack?"

"Last night. He came to my quarters. I gave him some orange juice and crackers."

"Why would Jack be coming to your quarters?"

I paused. "I expect Sister Clara wanted him to check and see if I had everything I needed."

"That's strange. Sister Clara asked *me* to lay a fire and bring you breakfast food."

I didn't lie well. I glanced away. "I don't know then, unless she thought I might need something else. Like wood."

Sister Adelaide said softly, "Yes. That's probably why." Of course she didn't believe me. Another question brought her eyes back to mine. "Jack said Tom argued with Sister?"

"Yes. Sunday morning. Saying he knew she 'did it,' whatever that means. Then warned her she better stay away from them. Very much like a threat."

Sister Adelaide looked shocked. "Do you have any idea what Tom might have meant?"

I said, "None. Well, there was the question of putting Tom into the hospital."

"But Tom refused. He wanted to be with Penny when the baby is born."

"Would saying he should be hospitalized make him angry?"

Sister Adelaide thought. "No, I'm sure it wouldn't."

"Why are you sure?"

"I was with them when they talked about it, and that was at least a week before Sister's body was found. Tom wasn't upset and neither was Sister. I heard her tell him if he could help Penny then he should."

"Then what were they arguing about Sunday morning?"

"I have no idea. I certainly didn't hear them arguing."

"Was Jack lying? Would he do that?"

Sister Adelaide pursed her lips, offered a half smile. "He's been known to stir things up. He and Clarice are usually in the middle of it when something happens."

"Two children?" I couldn't put two young teenagers into something as sinister as murder. The back door opened and Tom leaned on his wife as she led him to the bed. He sat down, looked at the floor, his breathing labored. Sister Adelaide used the dipper and brought him a cup of water from a pot on the side board.

After drinking, he raised his eyes to me. "You want something?" he said.

"No. I mean, I did want to ask you a question, but Sister Adelaide answered it for me."

"I'd still like to know," he said almost inaudibly.

"All right." I moved toward him. "I heard last night you might have been the last person to see my sister alive. I wanted to know if that was so. It would mean a lot to me to know what she was doing before ..."

"Before she hung herself?"

I was stunned. "No. She—"

"You think somebody strung her up?"

"I do."

"You got any proof of that?"

"Not yet."

He stared at me, transfixed by something racing through his mind. And I stood there in front of him, a cold shiver running through me.

"Just tell me, when's the last time you saw my sister?"

"Tom ..." the words were from Penny. Her hands were clasped tightly in front of her. Tom looked at his wife. He shrugged.

"She was fixing the doses," he said, "like she always did. Nothing different."

"I see."

"She asked me to fetch some of the Samoans because they hadn't shown up for their treatments when they were supposed to."

"Why do you think that was?"

"Dunno. But it wasn't the first time. Maybe they

didn't understand. Most of them don't know any English at all."

"So that was all? You left her to go to the Samoan camp?"

He glared at me. "That's what I said, didn't I?"

Penny spoke rapidly, "Sister Adelaide, did you see what Tom made for the baby?" She pointed to a small cradle at the end of the bed.

"It's beautiful, Penny."

I looked at it. It was beautiful. Handmade, the smallest of beds set on two rockers, with a pointed wooden hood on one end where Tom had carved leaves and trailing vines into the soft cypress. I knew he'd built the swing outside as well.

"It'll be used by the end of the month. Maybe sooner," Penny laughed nervously.

"Do you have names picked yet?" Sister Adelaide asked.

She faltered, the brave smile vanished. "No, not yet."

Tom rose, balanced himself on the bed post. He towered over me. His expression felt threatening. But I knew it wasn't his appearance that rattled me. No, it was a seething anger that permeated every inch of his body, most obvious in his eyes. He was a man ready to explode.

"You better go. Time you left my house."

Sister Adelaide and I walked back together.

"Does the disease cause that kind of anger in patients, Sister Adelaide?"

"It affects everyone differently. But I can't say I've seen Tom like that before. He's always been a quiet sort. It's strange."

"Something's not right in that house."

"The disease is killing him. That's the truth, but I don't think either of them want to admit it."

After we'd walked in silence for a few minutes, Sister

Adelaide sighed. "I wish Dr. Mills would have let him start the new treatment with the Samoans last June. We have several of our patients on it, and Sister Gretchen put Tom's name on the list, but Dr. Mills said no. I mean, what difference would it make? That's what Sister said, but Dr. Mills wouldn't do it."

"No wonder Tom's so angry."

"I did wonder about Penny," Sister Adelaide said.

I stopped. "Why do you say that?"

"She was really upset."

"About Tom?"

"Of course, she's so worried for him. But, no, this is different. I might as well say it, she was afraid of *you*. She whispered as much in my ear."

"What?"

"'I'm afraid of her.' That's what she whispered. I can't figure out why she'd say that. What has she to fear from you, Catherine?"

"I felt it too. How she looked at me. I knew she was scared. I never dreamed it was of me. I thought maybe she'd had a hard pregnancy."

"Her pregnancy has been fine. In fact, we've all laughed about how easy her pregnancy has been. 'Like my mother,' she says. 'She had fourteen children.' No, it was you she was afraid of. And I can't for a minute think why."

"Well, I must pose some kind of threat to her, to Tom, or maybe, she might be thinking, to her baby. Why else would she say that to you?"

"I don't know. I wish I did. I feel so bad for both of them. Penny is in remission, thank God, but poor Tom. He may not even live to see his baby born."

I suddenly remembered something in one of the reports I'd read last night. It was written by Gretchen, about the young woman who committed suicide because she had to give up her baby when she came here.

"What's the policy on mothers and their babies, Sister Adelaide?"

"Policy?"

"Are they able to bring their babies with them if they have the disease?"

"I don't know of any who have."

"There's bound to have been mothers committed who have children. So what happens to those babies?"

"I guess the family takes care of them. That would make sense."

"And do you think Penny and Tom will have to give up their baby to someone?"

In the lengthening silence between us, I glanced up at the sky. A solitary Mississippi kite circled the field, and I could hear monotonous croaks from frogs as we passed them. The smell of rotting leaves nearby was all about us. When I looked toward Sister Adelaide, I saw she understood.

"Penny must be afraid her baby will be taken from her," she said. "But nobody's said anything, no one I know of. Do you think Sister Gretchen might have said something? Is that why she's afraid of her sister? It doesn't make sense."

"I think she's afraid of anyone who walks across her doorstep right now, Sister. She's about to have a baby, and she may not be able to keep it. I don't blame her for being afraid."

"But how could that have anything to do with you?"

I couldn't answer her question. Yet maybe the hateful job of telling the couple they couldn't keep their child fell upon my sister's shoulders. And if it did, could it be a motive for murder?

CHAPTER ELEVEN

M Y QUARTERS WERE STILL WARM when I returned from the Langlinais's cabin. I shed my coat and sweater, pulled off one pair of socks and settled down to read. I wanted to study the rest of Gretchen's journals. I was sure of one thing, something there would offer a clue to who killed her. She would tell me herself if someone or something made her feel threatened. I was more certain of that than anything I'd encountered since I arrived.

I picked up her most recent journal. Flipped to the final entry, dated Saturday, December 7. My hands shook. I stared at the last words my sister had written.

> Father O'Quinn in high form today. Isn't laughter better than tears? I could swear I saw him pinch Lillian. She squealed and poked him in the chest with her finger. Laughter is contagious. We all enjoyed ourselves in the fellowship hall following Mass.

My sister was in good spirits. She seemed amused over the priest's peccadillo, absent any criticism or judgment, only that he brought fun as well as spiritual guidance to the community. Saturday. On that the following Monday, her body would be discovered by Jack and Clarice, hanging in the old mansion. Just two days after she'd written those cheerful words, Gretchen would be brutally murdered.

I turned back to the first page.

I noticed several watercolors and written paragraphs about the islanders.

She'd drawn their quarters, still under construction, four small houses. They looked very bland and reminded me of the institutional architecture I'd encountered here already. Each was set diagonally, facing one another. Odd not to have windows in sight. The houses were in different stages of completion in my sister's drawing, and Gretchen also described them that way, with something I assumed was a fire pit in the center. Was this to resemble their native village in some way? It was a pathetic attempt if that was the case. Washington, DC, needed new architects.

On another page she had taken her pencil to draw portraits of several of the new Samoan patients. I was struck by the fact they wore Western clothes rather than native garb. Who had insisted on that? Gretchen had done some remarkable charcoal likenesses of the men and women in profile while they cooked, rested, or worked. One man looked like he might be cleaning a bucket of fish.

Then a series of pages were landscapes. I recognized the river, the ferry crossing, and a watercolor of a woman sitting beneath a tree sketching the river; a dark bank of clouds looked ominous. Was it an interior painting of herself? In the margin she wrote, *"Not always at peace by the river."* I turned the page. She had painted a watercolor of a canoe of natives fishing on the river. In the margin she'd written, *"Too many."* What did she mean? And another question entered my mind, why were the Samoans allowed to fish outside the grounds when other patients were interned unless they had special permission? This federal project must have had a different set of rules. I smiled, remembering Sister Emily's frustration at the dock when I arrived. It made sense now.

As I read the entries, I could sense my sister's anticipation growing.

June 7, 1940

I'm so excited to start the clinical trials with the Samoans and some of our patients. Dr. Mills says he has heard such good things about sulphanilamide. Maybe this is the breakthrough we've been praying for. Let me describe these islanders. They do not smile, or speak for that matter. Their leader, whose name I have yet to learn to pronounce or spell, speaks little English, mostly Samoan and German. I know that is strange, but their islands have been occupied by Germany or America following the war. I hope in time we can establish friendships within our community and bring them closer.

June 15, 1940

Mr. Charles Bremmer arrived today and announced he is the liaison to the Samoans. Sister Emily told me she had not been informed of his arrival or his position. His credentials are in order, however, so it seems someone just forgot to tell us. When I asked Sr. Em what his role would be, she said he told her he would be in charge of their "spiritual needs" (???) and their tangible needs. He would leave us to administer the treatments." Beneath the entry Gretchen had drawn a sketch of Charles.

June 19, 1940

Well, at last the Director General has approved our treatment regimen. While men and women are dying of leprosy, the starched white coats in Washington, DC, "debate" about the program. We've been at wit's end waiting for a decision. *(She'd drawn a remarque of herself in the margin, hair standing on end.)* Our clinical trial has started on some of our patients and a group of Samoans. The antibiotic is called sulphanilamide. Praise God! Anything will be better than chaulmoogra oil. I agree with Sr. Em that intermuscular injection is safest way to begin even if the Director General suggested we use oral doses because tests cured the leprosy bacillus in a petri dish. So what? Without use of animal experimentation first, it's too risky and dangerous. Intermuscular injection is best, I think. We can limit the dosage. We proved injection with chaulmoogra oil was much less painful, but with this drug it's not the pain we're afraid of, but whether it could be lethal. I'm going to be very careful and pray they can tolerate it. Thank goodness for Dr. Robert Cochrane. His research is going to find the cure, I know it. I pray for that night and day.

So we proceed. Tests to begin tomorrow. Intramuscular low doses first, monitoring each patient's reactions. Then, if all goes well, perhaps oral doses can begin as early as January.

The journal entries went on interspersed with Gretchen's duties within the pharmacy. My sister spoke of many patients by their first names, like they were family. Then I stopped. My eyes landed on one name in particular, Tom Langlinais.

June 30, 1940

Dr. Mills still refuses to give sulphanilamide to Tom Langlinais. I understand the treatment may produce harsh side effects, but Tom has begun to run out of options. He and Penny are expecting their baby in December. Poor sweet things, my heart breaks for both of them. What's to become of the child? Discussions with Sr. Em and no one knows at this point. The family has written that they will adopt the child. It is too sad to contemplate!

July 11, 1940

The treatments are not as toxic as we feared. Good news! Bad news is Tom Langlinais needs them. Why does Dr. Mills keep saying no? I had a letter today from Cathy. She's going to restore a Whistler portrait for the New Orleans Museum exhibition in December. I'm so proud of her!

I had to smile. I continued to flip through the journal. Most pages were filled with sketches followed by a small entry. She hadn't dated any of them, but as I studied what were mostly the same landscape, I followed the changes, a spring dress of green across the fields. Wildflowers. Replaced by greenish gray, withering leaves. A summer dress upon the trees surviving the sultry humid air. She'd picked out a plantation across the river, where rooftops from a row of old slave quarters were just visible between the trees. As the season changed again, the trees lost their leaves or turned orange and red, or bare branches revealed the silent sentinel of deserted shacks in the middle of ripened sugar cane, their stalks extending taller than a man could reach with his machete. I remembered the French painter Claude Monet's fascination with painting the same landscape captured at different times of the year, how light and space, depending on the time of day or season in the year, but changed dramatically whether his subject was a church in Rouen, a garden, or a sunset. How wonderful Gretchen painted her own Giverny, right there at Carville on the banks of the Mississippi. Except, several of the watercolors on the last pages of her journal were scratched out with charcoal pencil. I had no answer for that. Perhaps she hadn't captured just the right light or something.

November 11, 1940

Samoans fishing. Fascinating to watch them.

She'd used charcoal and only a few quick strokes to capture the small fishing boat, almost swallowed in the current of the river. What did my sister mean, *"Fascinating to watch them"*? I made a mental note to ask Charles Bremmer if their fishing techniques were somehow different.

I flipped several more pages until a date made me stop.

November 15, 1940

Cathy's thirtieth birthday. I called Yves and asked him to find her something lovely, maybe pearl earrings. That was my plan when I gave her Mother's pearl necklace at twenty-one.

I miss my sister. The life I've chosen is the one I want and my only regret is Catherine."

Somehow the sentence sounded hollow. I knew my sister didn't "regret" me. Did she? I was sure she regretted our not being able to see each other, to stay close to one another. I grieved over that too. I didn't like her choice of words.

I didn't like the watercolor portrait of me either. She had used a different painting style, not unlike the Renoirs I'd studied. I was standing against scarlet azaleas in full bloom, staring directly out from the canvas. My blue eyes and short black hair glowed from an unknown source of light. It was pure impressionism. I was dressed in one of my favorite painting smocks, with Mama's pearl necklace around my neck, but in my hands I held ... I blinked. It was a doll.

Why would she paint me that way? No longer a child, yet clinging to something I had destroyed when I was nine years old. What did she mean to say through those light, lovely colors, my cheeks tinged with pink, my expression smiling, happiness written all over my face. I didn't understand. The doll represented all my anger, my guilt, the meanest time of my whole life, when my mother was suddenly taken from me. When I'd felt so deserted.

Were my cheeks rosy or flushed as with fever? Was my expression a smile or something else? Guilt? Embarrassment? The set of my mouth drawn into a smile made me look like the doll.

I hated it. Gretchen had painted an impression, not of me, but of a child in a woman's body.

"... And my only regret is Catherine."

My hands trembled. Had I uncovered something from my sister's private, innermost thoughts in her journal? What was her regret? We'd been as close as two sisters could ever be, hadn't we?

I slammed the book shut. Of course we had! Her regret was she had to leave me if she wanted to join the Daughters of Charity. What other possible thing *could* she mean? I felt the roll of my empty stomach curl into a painful knot. I stood up, paced the room, but lightheadedness made me grab the back of a chair. Another fainting spell? This was silly. *Get hold of yourself!*

The room felt too hot. I opened the door to a freezing wind blowing hard against me. The cold breath of air jolted my senses, like waking up from a bad dream. Suddenly, I had an overwhelming desire to speak to Yves.

I threw on my coat and stepped outside. I crossed the street and knocked on the doctor's front door.

Rose answered almost immediately and ushered me in with, "Ah, Miss Lyles, come on in here."

"I wondered if the phone has been repaired."

She led me into Dr. Mills's study again. "I dunno. It sure hasn't rung."

My heart sank when I lifted the receiver and found no dial tone. I needed to speak to Yves. I wanted him in the room with me, to explain away my shock, the words *"my only regret is Catherine."*

I caught Rose staring at me. "That's too bad," she said, immediately shifting her eyes away. "Miss Lyle, will you come with me, please, ma'am?"

In the dining room, she motioned for me to sit at a place set for one.

"You look like you ain't et, have you?"

"I'm not hungry. Really."

But her back was almost out the door, her voice trailing after her, "Well, there's times when we need to eat somethin' anyway, and I'm hoping you will try."

She sounded like Grace.

The taste of slow-cooked chicken in thick roux over rice was unbelievably good. Her cabbage mach choux so delicious. I couldn't remember the last full meal I'd had, and when Rose offered seconds, I didn't hesitate. I hardly noticed her setting the table for someone else until I heard the front door open and Dr. Mills's footsteps.

"Ah, Miss Lyle. Joining me for lunch?"

"I seem to take my nourishment from anyone who offers. I'm going to blame it on Miss Rose if there isn't enough left in the pot to feed you."

She set a heaping plate in front of the doctor. "Never you mind about that. They is always plenty in Rose's kitchen to feed an extra person." She disappeared again.

The doctor ate a few bites, lifted his napkin to his mouth. "How are you feeling today?"

"Oh, yes, that. Well, I've never fainted before. It was a shock. I think I may be claustrophobic. The crowd sort of overwhelmed me."

"Oh?" I didn't hear that part of the story. Of course, you've been under considerable stress since you arrived."

Shall it be called "stress"? I thought. Maybe. Certainly, the last two days had shocked me beyond belief. And add to that the fact my sister might have had secret thoughts about me gave me pause to wonder if I'd always been so paranoid. Or was it the stress of knowing someone murdered her? Or was that irrational too?

The doctor and I continued to eat in silence. I remembered that yesterday the coroner asked for Dr. Mills. Did that mean he had assisted him in Gretchen's autopsy? At the very least, he must be privy to information. He must know why the coroner tore out of here with her body.

"Dr. Mills … I—"

Our voices overlapped.

"I wonder if I might have your company for dinner tonight."

"What?"

"It's last minute, I know. Father O'Quinn dines with me on Fridays, with Sister Emily, and Charles Bremmer. Of course, my daughter, Clarice, will be here too. I'm sorry my Eleanor, she's my wife, is away at the moment. But maybe some company might help pass the time. Does it appeal to you?"

I wanted to decline. My dinners were in the kitchen with Grace or sometimes on a tray with Tante. But it would be an opportunity to speak to Charles Bremmer. One that might not come again. Gretchen's journal entries showed her great interest in the Samoans and the sulphanilamide trials. Maybe it was just a casual interest, curiosity about their culture, but she had drawn far too many sketches of them for it to be unimportant. Beyond that was the note, *"Don't trust the Samoans."* What did that signify, if indeed it was meant for Gretchen at all? I needed to meet them, and probably Charles Bremmer was the only one who could arrange that meeting.

"Thank you, Doctor, I accept. I can hardly pass up another chance to sample Rose's remarkable cooking."

He smiled slightly. He didn't seem like a man who would ever smile broadly, but clearly he had something on his mind. "Good. Father O'Quinn comes over from Brusly to hear confessions on Fridays and say Mass on Saturday. Would seven o'clock suit you?"

"Yes." I rose from the table. "My errand here was the phone. It's still not working, is it?"

"I don't know. Let's try it again." He stood, removing his napkin from his lap, and led me into the study, closing the door behind us. As I stood in front of his desk, I studied the woman and child in the small photograph. It was of Mrs. Mills and Clarice. She couldn't have been more than four or five years old in the photograph, but her pensive look told me Clarice had a story to tell, and perhaps not a happy one. A child growing up in a leper colony. I recognized his wife as the beautiful woman in some of Gretchen's earlier journal sketches. She'd been a favorite subject of my sister's.

"I have something important to tell you, Miss Lyle."

The words riveted my whole attention. "Yes?"

He motioned for me to sit on one of the chairs. I declined. Standing on my feet, I felt on a more equal footing with him. I wanted both my legs under me.

"I sent someone for you yesterday afternoon, but Sister Emily said you'd fainted. We decided to give you a night's sleep."

"I'm perfectly well. What is it you need to tell me?"

He frowned briefly before his expression returned to what I deemed to be his professional doctor look, benignly calm, practiced over time. I wondered if others could see beneath that face. He was a tired man. His hair could stand a washing. There were bags under his eyes, adding years to his age. His light gray eyes were as round and hard as river stone. My hands began to shake, so I clasped them together in front of me.

"I assisted Dr. Guidreau during Sister Gretchen's autopsy. You knew that, didn't you?"

"I heard him ask someone to find you."

"Are you prepared to hear some devastating news?"

"My sister was murdered, wasn't she?"

"Probably."

"The autopsy proved it?"

"The autopsy proved she didn't die from hanging."

"What then?"

Dr. Mills swallowed. "Sister Gretchen drowned. As irrational and unbelievable as it sounds, that is how your sister died. She still had the water in her lungs."

CHAPTER TWELVE

"I KNEW MY SISTER WOULDN'T TAKE her own life."

"Miss Lyle," he hesitated, tightening his lips. I was reminded of a Roman statue, a sterile whiteness to his coat and not a crease anywhere except on his face. The face gave us all away, and his couldn't hide the agitation he obviously felt.

"Oh, please, Dr. Mills, call me Catherine. I'd prefer it."

"Catherine." Was there also fear in his eyes? Did his dilated pupils mean that? "I'm keeping this quiet for now. Only you, Sister Emily, and I have this information. Of course, we both wanted you to know, but I can't stress enough, we must say as little to as few people as possible."

"But it's only a matter of hours before the sheriff arrives. Everyone will know then."

"Sister Emily and I still need to decide how to tell the community. Until then, I must ask you to say nothing. Yes, I know a full investigation will begin when Sheriff Doucet gets here, but I think we have today. I've heard the roads are impassable between here and Prairieville. The sheriff might consider crossing the river in Baton Rouge, driving all the way around to the ferry at White Castle. The ferry is still running. But I doubt he will do that. My guess is he'll wait until they've cleared the road from Prairieville, which means tomorrow, or even the day after." Then, an afterthought, though his words sent chills down my spine, "We're quite cut off from everything, you know. I suppose it was like this at the beginning. A sanctuary for lepers." His eyes narrowed. "An invisible place for the unclean. Can you imagine what conditions patients had to endure at first? And here we are, just like they were, cut off from all civilization. It gives one an unsettled feeling."

An understatement. "With a murderer walking around? Yes. Quite unsettling."

Dr. Mills peered down at his desk. He was staring at the photograph of his wife and child. "The fact that Sister Gretchen was already dead before she was hung is very disturbing." He lifted his gaze to me. "But I think we're quite safe, for now, especially if the killer hasn't an idea we know about him. It's another reason we must be discreet."

I sat down, feeling my legs might actually give way after all.

"Do you want something, Catherine? A glass of water?"

"No, thank you. I've expected to hear this. I knew Gretchen was murdered. But it's still a shock. I need a moment."

"It's a lot to take in. I'm sorry. The sheriff will certainly find out what happened to Sister Gretchen. You must believe me."

"I do. Of course I do. And I won't say anything. But why, why hang someone who's been drowned? It's unbelievable!"

"I don't have an explanation, Catherine. It's what Dr. Guidreau told me. Of course, I also saw it for myself."

"It doesn't make any sense."

"I know it doesn't."

"It almost sounds sadistic, insane ... why kill her twice?"

"I have no answers for you. Speculation is what I'm most concerned with. We mustn't get ahead of ourselves. Let the sheriff sort this out."

"I have to tell one person. My partner, Yves Antoine." I picked up the phone, then replaced the receiver. "As soon as the phone is fixed, of course."

I saw his facial muscles twitch. His eyes focused on me. I thought I could read his mind: *Did she not hear me?* A heavy sigh, then internally counting to ten perhaps. He composed himself. He must stay in control. Nothing must show. Calm. A bland expression. He was the authority figure in this place. When he spoke, it must be in that practical, everyday tone, which I was sure sometimes covered a rage burning inside his head. Never mind that. I would call Yves, whether the doctor liked it or not. I stared at him and took my own deep breath. I felt like we were two fighters coming from opposite corners of the ring.

"No. Even if the phone is repaired before the road opens, you can't say anything on our telephone. I insist on that." He stood on the other side of the desk, spread his hands flat upon it, his eyes fixed on a piece of the wall behind me.

"I know about the party line," I said. "I can tell him in code. I won't go into detail. My sister has been murdered! And Yves is like family, not just my business partner. I must let him know!"

The doctor stayed in his own space, saying nothing. The silence stretched to a minute or more.

I was impressed. Papa would have yelled right back

at me. Yet here was the doctor, winning with silence, not words. *Round one goes to you, Dr. Mills.*

"I'm sorry, Doctor. You're right. Your patients don't need to worry about a deranged killer in their midst until some kind of protection is here, like the sheriff. The patients already have more than enough to be concerned with."

When he spoke, his tone, as much as his words, sucked the breath out of me. "Thank you." He looked out the window. "I wonder if it will make any difference at all. I've been here eighteen years, and what I've learned is that Carville is not a hospital to save lives, but a place to learn how to face death. I've witnessed a few apparent successes, yes. I count them on one hand. And we keep hoping 'the cure' is just around the corner. The next drug always brings hope. Our patients must live in the present. Each day for them is precious because thoughts about tomorrow are too painful. Living just today can give you a certain kind of tranquility, not religious, in my opinion, though the nuns would have you believe the Holy Spirit provides their peace of mind. I disagree. Carville's just a holding place until death comes."

"Not everyone accepts death from the disease as inevitable, do they? Surely some hope to recover."

He turned his gaze toward me, eyes glazed over as he nodded slightly. "Yes, of course."

I had the most uncomfortable feeling about his last sentence because I knew he didn't mean it.

I decided to walk to the river. The distance from the doctor's house to the levee wasn't far. I followed the gravel road outside the hospital, then took a narrow path to the top of a ridge. The river was beautiful from there; my eyes followed it to the bend, where it disappeared. I sensed the world with its cities and people lay only a few miles beyond that bend. Baton Rouge wasn't far. Yet here the road ended and the river melted away. Still, I loved what I saw. I wanted to find a quiet place and think about my sister. I worked my way down the river bank, pushing aside weeds and bare vines clinging to leafless scrub trees. I was rewarded at river's edge by a path that ran several hundred feet before ending at a large live oak tree whose massive roots and low hanging branches made any further forward movement difficult.

Clouds had almost vanished from the sky now, a north wind created white caps rolling into shore, and trees were whistling like music. *It's playing a hymn for Gretchen,* I thought. It pained me to think she might have died here on this beautiful river. The roots of the ancient oak tree were big enough to sit upon. Its branches touched the water. I closed my eyes and tried to think. Murder. Why would anyone want to murder my sister?

But my mind didn't cooperate. The words from her journal came back to me. *"My only regret is Catherine."*

I forced my mind away from her words. Someone killed my sister and I must find out who and why. I tried to tick off a reason, any reason, a murderer would commit the act twice. Perhaps she wasn't quite dead from the drowning so he finished it with a rope? But the murderer had only to hold her down until she was gone. Let her body float down the river. Done. Gretchen would have vanished. Later, if ever she was found, the bruises on her body would mean nothing. A simple explanation would be stated, partly true, that the body had brushed against rocks in the river. No "murder" the coroner could rule. *An accident.* Gretchen slipped and fell into the river and drowned.

So why stage the suicide? I watched rivulets of water brush against the bottom of the roots on the tree. A breeze shook melting ice crystals from its branches. I shivered and stilled my mind. Might it be that whoever was responsible for Gretchen's murder *needed* us to believe she committed suicide? Did the murderer also want the nuns to find her body? All I could picture was a deranged mind, a killer who craved the attention and who would revel in the horror brought to the nuns. But a nagging thought wouldn't let go of me. What if it wasn't insanity, but an enraged patient bent on revenge? Someone whose plight was overwhelming, whose rage turned violent. It wasn't enough that he drowned a nun. That might be construed as an accident. No, his mission would be to wrench as much horror and fear as possible.

Then I had another thought. What if her murderer *was* a nun? One of the five women I'd met. Did one of them harbor bitter feelings toward the Daughters of Charity of St. Vincent de Paul, or even the whole Catholic Church?

I shivered, closed my eyes. It could have been ritual. And the purpose: to humiliate the nuns.

It made sense in a way and explained the pristine way the noose was constructed, so perfect. The murderer wanted us to question that, to see it as staged. But why the mansion? If the premise was correct, it would have made more sense to find her inside the church. But maybe he or she had to be expedient. The mansion was deserted. Interruptions were more than likely inside the church. He ... or she. Maybe more than one person was responsible.

"No one can prove it ..."

I heard the words over the wind and recognized the voice of Sister Paul. She walked on the ridge toward me, with John Weller. I was quite hidden by the large tree but still scrunched my body down between two large roots, my back against its huge trunk.

The words of the editor of *The Light* floated past me as they approached. "Come ... not ... leaving with or without you on December 21."

They had stopped right above me. John Weller grabbed both of Sister Paul's arms and shook her. "You made a promise to *me*. Have you forgotten that?"

She pulled away from him. "No, of course I haven't. I wish ... I just wish it wasn't so furtive. I want it to feel right. It doesn't. Not now."

She turned and began walking away from him, along the same path I'd followed.

I could hardly breathe. John Weller watched her until she was out of sight, then he walked slowly, in the same direction, his head down, shoulders slumped, clearly crestfallen.

He followed the top of the ridge toward the hospital. He would pass not too far from the old mansion. Perhaps John Weller would return the same way he led me into the house to photograph Gretchen's body, through the hedge. *The photographs!*

I felt an urge to follow, to intercept him and ask if he'd printed the photos. Surely he had. But this wasn't the right moment. He and Sister Paul! It wrangled me, inexplicitly. Why should I care one way or another? I stood, angry with myself. It wasn't any business of mine.

I retraced my steps up the bank, pausing to look back at the river, this time in the opposite direction. In the distance I thought I could make out the ferry dock.

I walked down the levee to the dirt road running beside it. The natural barrier shrank to a small rise, easy enough for travelers to cross. The ferry crossing came into sight. It had to be a place where Indians and early settlers crossed the river. Now it provided automobiles or walkers with a ferry crossing to the plantation and village called

White Castle and, more importantly, a highway leading north or south.

Just beyond the dock, the road made a sharp left turn. *It must be the road to Prairieville,* I thought. Straight ahead was the village of Carville. Something else surprised me. The dirt road I followed offered a small wooden bridge across a bayou.

The bridge was damaged; one of its side railings lay on the ground, blown there by the storm, perhaps. But it was still passable. I stood in the center of the bridge and, with my eyes, followed the bayou inland as far as I could see it. Trees and tall weeds grew along its bank.

Now some other things made sense. This bayou was bound to flow a good ways into the leprosarium's property. Who knew how far it went? Its source was the Mississippi, so it might go inland for miles. And this was how the Samoans fished. If I followed the bayou, which must be impassible on foot, I'd find the Samoan camp Gretchen described in her journal.

Something else caught my eye. A boat. A small sailing schooner. I could see just a section of its mast from the side of the bridge. I crossed over, finding a kind of path through the brush.

Two heads popped up over the hull, and I jumped. It was Jack and Clarice.

"Good heavens!"

"What you doing here, Miss Catherine?" Jack asked.

"Taking a walk. What are *you* doing here?" I observed that Clarice was red in the face and that her hair was tangled, but her companion carried off a bravado as cool as ever.

"We decided to clean up the doc's boat. It got sort of messed up in the storm. Didn't it, Clary?"

"Yes.

"This boat belongs to Dr. Mills?"

"Yep." The teenagers jumped out of the boat onto the bank. They scooted past me up the narrow path.

"Now we got to meet the ferry."

"We have to carry Father's bag to the church. Bye!"

I stood there staring at the boat. Like dead leaves from a tree, one thing after another seemed to be piling up around me. How was I ever to make sense of it all? I looked up through the trees at the sky. Dr. Mills wasn't just a doctor. He had a hobby that included ownership of a sailing boat. Anyone who sailed also knew about knots and ropes, didn't they? I sighed, starting to climb up the embankment. If finding out who fashioned the hangman's noose would lead me to Gretchen's murderer, then there were several I could point to already. A missionary who'd worked in the circus; Tom Langlinais, who could tie up a rope swing; or maybe, maybe the doctor himself. And how many of the patients were also capable?

I slipped down to my knees and had to start up the bank again, hanging on to weeds and roots to keep my footing. I would be a complete mess walking back into the compound. Then I laughed ruefully. But not as messy, perhaps, as the situation brewing between John Weller and Sister Paul.

CHAPTER THIRTEEN

"MY DEAR GIRL, HOW AWFUL for you." Father O'Quinn took both my hands in his. His eyes were gentle, his expression sincere. I guessed he was past seventy; his white hair gave an impression of someone laden with life experience. In his black suit and white collar, I remembered the remark about him in Gretchen's journal, his bulging eyes and too-tight collar. Well, the description was accurate, to a point. He did have a bulbous nose and was quite fat. But Gretchen hadn't captured the soft, benign face attempting to telegraph his concern to me.

"Thank you, Father."

Rose served our dinner almost immediately after I arrived. We ate by candlelight, of course, a beautiful candelabra in the center of the table with oil lamps set out on the buffet. It really was rather nice, I had to admit. How she had been able to put together such a feast without electricity I couldn't fathom, but it was delicious, as was the wine. David Mills might live on the outskirts of civilization, but he hadn't suffered for it.

We sat at the doctor's dining table, Dr. Mills on my right, Clarice on my left, then Charles Bremmer, and Sister Emily, with Father O'Quinn at the foot of the table. All of us were dealing with emotional crises, I thought, but because the priest engaged his host in lighthearted, banal conversation, I assumed Father O'Quinn, Charles Bremmer, and Clarice didn't know anything yet of my sister's autopsy.

Truthfully, I was glad. I didn't want that conversation now.

Clarice answered only direct questions and kept her eyes on the bowl of crab bisque set before her. The rag-tag girl from this afternoon looked almost angelic in a white woolen dress, her red hair brushed until it glistened in the candlelight. *What a strange life she has, living here,* I thought. She attended school in Carville, the village down the road, but didn't she have friends? Surely not many. Jack must fill that role. I wondered if Clarice's mother and father approved of Jack. My guess was that neither parent paid much attention to this only child. The father was consumed with too many patients, and her mother was gone. For how long, I wondered?

I hoped my tone was gentle when I leaned over next to Clarice and said, "I understand your mother is away. I would have loved to have met her." My words produced the weakest of smiles. It seemed Clarice didn't much care where her mother was. I thought it possible she'd been away a long time. But I was wrong.

Overhearing my comment to Clarice, Father O'Quinn asked, "Yes, where is our hostess tonight, David?"

It prompted a bemused smile on the doctor's face. "Eleanor is stuck in New Orleans, I'm afraid. She was just going for a couple of days for the opening of the James

McNeill Whistler portrait exhibition tonight, but there's no way she can get back tomorrow. Not on the Prairieville road, anyway."

Inwardly, I remembered. How normal had last week been when I concentrated on repairing the Whistler portrait?

My eyes found Sister Emily's. She looked so sad, so tired. We shared a secret soon to be revealed. I caught my breath. My sister. Murdered. Suddenly, I wanted to jump out of my seat and run from the room. I wanted to scream, "Why?"

Instead, I stilled myself, clasping and unclasping my hands in my lap, and pretended to be interested in the conversation between the men at the table.

"So, what you are saying, Father, is that President Roosevelt is an idiot?"

"Don't put words in my mouth, Charles. I'm certainly not in favor of Germany's aggression. I want America to help the Brits. No, what I'm saying is the Lend-Lease bill was his idea. I don't want Congress to just rubber stamp it, that's all."

"But you called it 'idiocy.'"

The priest narrowed his eyes at Charles Bremmer. "I'm afraid of America being dragged into another war. I wonder if we don't have other alternatives, that's all."

Charles smiled coldly, "It's a dilemma, isn't it? On the one hand, if Britain and America want to rule the world, then they must be allies. It's all politically expedient, I suppose, to send American soldiers into a war against the will of the people."

Sister Emily grimaced. I guessed from her expression that she neither knew nor really cared about a 'lend-lease' with Great Britain. Perhaps she should, but it wouldn't be fair to chastise Sister Emily. She must focus on her war right here. Every minute of every day.

We needed to talk, just she and me together. A horrible act had been committed inside a sanctuary of safety for lepers, where the shadow of death should not include fear of a murderer stalking them.

Rose refilled my wine. "Thank you," I whispered. She smiled and moved silently around the table.

I let my gaze follow her as she moved past a painting hung on the wall behind my host. It wasn't a Clarence Millet but certainly inspired by his painting of the Mississippi at a bend in the river called Batteur *Shanty at Riverbend.* And, like it, the artist had depicted that no-man's land between the land and the river, where shanties appeared and squatters dared the tax man and the river to make them move.

"I see you admiring my painting, Catherine," Dr. Mills said.

"It reminds me of Clarence Millet."

He took a sip of wine. "Really?"

Father O'Quinn said, "What was that, David?"

"Catherine is admiring my new painting." To me then, "I'm intrigued you know of the painter Millet. He's not that well-known."

Father O'Quinn smiled. "Yes, indeed. Very impressive. Good schooling, I'm sure."

Charles smiled and asked. "Have you studied art, Catherine?"

"Not formally. Just at home."

Sister Emily raised an eyebrow. "Catherine is being modest. She and Yves Antoine have built a reputation in New Orleans as the best art restorers in the city, if not the whole state."

I felt myself blushing. "Perhaps Yves, certainly not I."

"Yves Antoine? You work with Monsieur Yves Antoine?"

"Yes, Father. Why? Do you know him?"

He pounded the table, his wine glass teetered. He caught it from spilling and raised it in the air like a toast. "What a stroke of luck, an absolute amazing stroke of luck!"

A small voice beside me asked, "What's a *restorer*?"

"Hush, Clarice," her father said sternly. Then to the end of the table, "Why is it so lucky, Father?"

I leaned over to Clarice and whispered. "I'll tell you later, okay?"

"Okay," she said with just a hint of a smile.

"Because I've written to that very person, Monsieur Antoine. That very person. What a coincidence, yes?"

"It is."

The priest downed most of the rest of his glass of wine, "Let me tell you all a most interesting story." He pursed his lips together, set the wine glass down carefully, then glanced meaningfully at Clarice. "A mystery. Would you like to hear it, my girl?"

She nodded her head and clasped her hands together tightly in her lap.

"Then here it is. Last week I decided to search for more suitable luggage. You know I'm to attend the ordination of my nephew in Rome in March. I told you that, didn't I, David?"

Dr. Mills nodded. "Yes, of course."

"I thought so." He looked at me. "Our storage room is not on church grounds but located in a private home in town, given to us many years ago. From time to time, some of our church women go through the articles given to the church and distribute them to the poor, as you might well expect." When I nodded he continued, "I hoped to find a decent suitcase because mine's pretty shabby at this point. But I wasn't prepared for the amount of things inside the house. Stacks of chairs and tables and a huge armoire stuffed with linens. Bookcases full of mostly religious volumes, and clothes! Oh my, we must have received a whole estate, lock, stock, and barrel to have so much crammed into that little house."

Father O'Quinn took his last sip of wine, savoring it as much as our attention, I thought.

Rose had begun to serve us a dessert of crème brûlée, but she listened intently. I smiled into my napkin. We all liked a spinner of tales.

"Well, in one of the bedrooms I found exactly what I was looking for. A rather large leather suitcase, with leather straps too. Fairly new, I thought, or if not, then well taken care of through the years. I took it and lifted it onto the bed to open it, hoping it wasn't locked." He smiled at Clarice. "That would be a hard piece of luck, wouldn't it? But it wasn't. Inside was a package, wrapped in brown paper and tied with string. Can you guess what it was?"

"A painting?" Clarice whispered.

"Yes. But not just any painting. Do you know what an icon is, my girl?"

The girl shook her head. "No, Father."

The priest looked meaningfully at me. "Would you like to explain what it is, Catherine?"

Not really, I thought. But I acquiesced anyway. "From what I've read, icons were early paintings or mosaics of saints. The word means 'image.'"

Clarice said, "You found an icon, Father?"

The priest grinned broadly. "I did!"

"And is it old?"

"Well, my girl, there's the mystery."

Charles Bremmer said, "You know, there's a legend that Pilate had an image of Christ done. It's been written about by some of the earliest church historians."

I asked, "You've read those?"

"Oh, heavens no. They were written in Greek or Aramaic probably. No, I read about it in an article I expect, but isn't it fascinating to think about? I mean, fascinating how the historians say Christ was depicted."

"Did the history tell us?"

He smiled at me. "I'll never forget it. Pilate's icon supposedly depicted Christ as a young man, beardless, with short, frizzy hair. That's not the image we have of Him today in our paintings, is it?"

Clarice looked at Father O'Quinn. "Is your painting one like that, Father?"

"No. It's of Saint Mary."

Charles said, "Ahh. So I can add more to our conversation. Because I also read that Saint Mary's image was first painted by the Apostle Luke."

"And when was that?"

"Dunno."

Sister Emily spoke haltingly, "In the fifth century, an icon of Mary was written from a cave painting and sent to the emperor in Constantinople. Sent there but moved somewhere else." She looked at Clarice. "It's lost now."

Clarice asked Father O'Quinn, "Is your icon of Mary as old as the fifth century, you think?"

"I don't know! But I know it looks very old."

David Mills chuckled. "Father, there are lots of copies of old icons. Thousands. When I was in Europe, every antique shop had 'original' icons. My guess is that suitcase of yours has been to Rome before you."

The priest shrugged. "Maybe. But maybe not. It's so

beautiful." He smiled at me. "That's why I'm in desperate need of an art expert, Catherine. That's what I wrote to your colleague just the day before yesterday."

"I'm sure Yves will contact you very soon."

"But you are *here*. Wouldn't you have a look at it?"

My glance took in the doctor and Sister Emily before I answered. "I'm afraid I can't help you right now."

"But why? Why not take a small journey across the river with me tomorrow, after Mass? If nothing else, it might take your mind away from your sadness for just a bit."

Dr. Mills rose and moved to leave the table, so we all followed. "Why don't we have a cigar in my study, Father? And a cognac, Charles?" He looked down at his daughter. "Time you went up to your room, Clarice."

Candles on the table flickered like the atmosphere in the room had changed, from a warm glow to a terse chill. I pulled my sister's shawl close around me.

Sister Emily stood. "I must be getting back. I still have work to finish tonight." Her breath was now noticeable in the semi-dark room." Did I detect a tremor in her voice also? I wondered if she'd sat through our dinner worrying that I would want to discuss my sister's murder. Perhaps.

Father O'Quinn put his arm around me. "Why don't you think on it tonight, Catherine? I'm hoping you'll change your mind." Then turning to his host, he said, "Thank you, David, but I, too, must say goodnight. That 'unfinished work' of Sister's is me!"

We laughed hesitantly. I knew Sister Emily wasn't looking forward to tonight's conversation with her priest. It seemed, incredibly, that Sister Emily had shrunk since the last time we met. The slumped shoulders made her carriage different, as if she was carrying a dead weight around on her back. I shuddered. What a horrible way to think of it. But there it was, wasn't it? If I tried hard, I might imagine my sister hanging around Sister Emily's neck.

Charles stood near me. "May I walk you to your quarters, Catherine?"

"Thank you."

Charles took hold of Dr. Mills's hand. "Then I'll also say goodnight, Doctor. Thank you for a stimulating evening. Please tell Miss Rose she outdid herself tonight. How she created this meal without electricity is nothing short of magic itself."

We murmured our agreement, and very soon the company filed out the front door.

"I was so pleased to see you at dinner tonight," Charles said.

Charles put his hand on my elbow protectively as we walked slowly across the uneven ruts in the road. I'd been conscious of his staring at me several times during dinner. What was he thinking? His expression had intimated some thought I couldn't read.

I pulled Gretchen's shawl closer. "So cold."

"I'm sorry. I should have given you my coat."

"Not at all." We had already arrived across the street at my door. On the doorstep, I paused. "Miss Rose's dinner was wonderful, wasn't it?"

"Yes. I'm fortunate that Dr. Mills has added me to his Friday dinner party. Miss Rose never disappoints. But having you there was a special treat."

"Thank you, Charles. I'm not at all social and I was really dreading it. It turned out to be quite bearable."

He laughed. "Only bearable? We've got to work on that." He smiled. "Goodnight to you."

"Charles, might I have a word?"

He only hesitated briefly. "Of course."

I opened the door and offered him a seat at the table. "Would you like some coffee?"

"Thank you, no." He opened the door to the stove. "I think the fire's too low." He moved at once to the front door, picked up two logs, and deposited them onto the glowing embers. "It'll catch in a minute."

We sat across from one another. "Thanks." *How to begin,* I thought. I rose, "I'd like to show you something. My sister's journal."

He accepted it without opening the cover.

"I've been reading the journals today. That's her last one."

He didn't look at the book but at me.

"I want you to take a look at some of it. Not all, of course, because it's too personal, but at some of her sketches of the Samoans."

"Sketches?"

"The first few pages." He turned to the pages where Gretchen had drawn the Samoans. "You can see she seemed to warm to the newcomers."

Charles flipped back a few pages, then forward again. "They are remarkably accurate. Very nicely done." He returned it to me.

I closed the journal and put it back on the stack, turning, "I thought, from these, it looked like Gretchen was very fond of the islanders. Would that be so?"

"Oh, yes. Yes indeed. And the feeling was so reciprocated. Not just by the Samoans but by me. Your sister had a gift. Truly."

I felt hot tears on my face. "I'm sorry. I'm so emotional since I've been here. I apologize."

He stared at me, rose from the table, and took my hands in his. Something passed between us for a second. "I'm so sorry, Catherine."

"I'm fine now. Thank you for saying that."

"What can I do to help you? Anything?"

"You've guessed I want something from you."

"Yes. And if it's in my power to do it, I will."

"Thank you. If I might go with you to the Samoan's camp. Meet them. Would that be possible? I don't want to intrude ..."

"You wouldn't be intruding. We're suffering the loss of Sister Mary Gretchen as much as everyone else. I think if the people met her sister it would be a good thing." He smiled. "A very good thing. Not just for you." Then he frowned. "But the sheriff will come tomorrow, won't he? To begin a murder investigation?"

I was startled. "How did you know? Dr. Mills said no one knows anything of the autopsy yet, except Sister Emily and me."

"I guessed it as soon as the coroner pulled away from the hospital with Sister Gretchen's body."

"Really?"

"Yes. Of course, I have no idea how the murder was committed. Do you?"

"Actually, I do. Though I've been sworn to secrecy by Dr. Mills and Sister Emily. They'll tell everyone tomorrow."

Charles exhaled slightly, placing his lips together to form an O. His gaze left mine briefly. "Murder. How horrible. So now we must worry about these other so-called suicides. Perhaps we have a serial killer in our midst."

"From what I've learned about the other deaths, I doubt it. Except ... and this has just occurred to me, Charles, didn't one of the Samoans disappear mysteriously right after they arrived?"

He pursed his lips tightly before speaking. "Do you mean Enoka?"

"Yes. That was his name. I heard it was assumed he drowned while fishing. His body was never found, was it?"

"My, you've been busy in the short time you've been here. How did you learn of other deaths?"

I'd said too much. I couldn't let on I'd read their files. "I'm not at liberty to tell you. But people do talk, don't they?"

Charles crossed the room, and opened the stove. He used the poker to make the wood flare, and I sensed the same going on inside his mind. He poked at the logs, staring into their flame. Closing the stove, he turned around, avoiding my eyes, an angry tone to his voice. "Samoan's don't drown. They are born to the water and the sea. A river is not a threat to them. Enoka Noa didn't drown."

"So what happened to him?"

"He ran away. That's the only explanation."

"Someone drowned my sister. That's what the autopsy showed. She drowned and then was hung!" I felt like my voice belonged to someone else. "Why would someone do that?"

Branches from a tree outside the window trembled and a sound like shards of glass hitting the side of the house startled both of us. Charles went to the window and looked out.

"There's ice on the branches." He turned back to me. "I suppose there are reasons," he said quietly. "But it doesn't make sense at the moment." Our eyes connected to the fear he voiced finally. "You must be careful, Catherine. Until we know what's happening here."

We promised to see one another the next day and I locked the door behind him. There was something he hadn't said but wanted to. I had a terrible feeling I wouldn't like knowing what that might be.

When I heard a knock a minute later, I wondered why Charles would return. But it was John Weller standing in the doorway when I opened it.

He walked past me uninvited, turned, and stared at me. "Why in hell would you invite Charles Bremmer into your house?"

I was so shocked I couldn't speak for a few seconds. Did my mouth also fall open?

"I'd begun to give you credit for being able to read people. But it looks like I was mistaken." He withdrew an envelope from inside his jacket and threw it on the table. "Your photographs." He turned back to the door.

"Wait a minute!" I said, finding my voice at last. "Why are you so angry? Why should you care whom I choose to entertain?"

"I guess it's because I can't abide idiots."

I was appalled. "How dare you!" I tried to slap his face, but he grabbed my wrist. "Let me go!"

He did and I said, as contemptuously as possible, "It's not idiocy to ask the person in charge of the Samoans to take me there."

"And what possible reason would there be for that?" He screwed his mouth into an incredulous smile. "You think the Samoans murdered your sister?"

I ran for my bag under the bed, found the note inside, and threw it at him. "Here. Read that. Sister Adelaide found it inside my sister's desk."

He studied the note for a few seconds, his forehead furrowed. When he spoke again, his voice seemed slightly calmer. "Samoans is spelled wrong."

"I know that!" He was so infuriating. "I don't even know if the note was left for my sister or not. But if you were me, wouldn't you want to at least look into it?"

"Maybe. But my advice is to go to the village on your own. Or get Sister Adelaide to go with you. And stay as far away from Bremmer as you can."

"What do you have against Charles? He's been nothing except nice to me. He hasn't called me an 'idiot,' not once, and if he does have something to hide, what difference does it make? I'm not asking to be his friend, just for him to introduce me to the people he brought here."

He stood still, looking at me but not seeing me, then turned on his heel. Gone in a second, not even the decency to say goodnight! I should have thrown the words I'd heard between him and Sister Paul in his face. I didn't know why I held back.

I undressed and got into bed, but sleep wouldn't come. What a hateful man! What was it I did that ignited that sort of anger? I rolled about in bed, unable to get comfortable. Why would he not take anything I said seriously? Why did he insult and offend me with every word? It had almost become physical again, in the same way he held me back from going into Sister Emily's office. How did we arouse such spit in each other? I had no answer for that. And I couldn't sleep for thinking about it.

About midnight, I remembered the photographs left on the desk. I crawled out of bed and took them to the light of the stove. Gretchen looked serene, but there were also close ups of her fingers, the bruises on her arms and back. It was good work. Thorough. As I flipped to the last picture, I started. It was of me leaning down looking at Gretchen. He'd written, *"Two beautiful sisters,"* beneath. It was a thoughtful thing to do. Was there another side to the furious man I'd seen earlier? As I crawled back into bed, I admitted to myself that I hoped so. And I slept.

CHAPTER FOURTEEN

BABY HOPE CAME IN THE early morning hours. I didn't find out about her until Sister Adelaide arrived about seven, with bread, jam, and butter. She told me the news while preparing *café au lait,* placing a spoonful of ground coffee into the upper cavity of the small enamel pot and pouring boiling water over it, then mixing the dark, strong brew in a cup with warm milk she'd prepared on the wood stove.

"A little girl. Almost seven pounds!"

"How is Penny?"

"Pretty tired. But so happy. And a funny thing, Catherine. She asked me, twice actually, if you would visit them."

"So she's not afraid of me anymore?"

"Apparently not. I've heard it said expectant mothers can have moods sometimes. Shall we put Penny's fear of you down to that?

"I don't know anything about that, Sister. And I don't know what I could possibly have done to frighten her. But when I see her, maybe she'll tell me."

"They're in the hospital. We've put mother and child in a vacant room, away from the ward. It's best."

"Hope. What a perfect name."

Sister Adelaide nodded, rose, and cleared the table, and deposited our dishes and cups in the sink. "I wish we could celebrate. Everyone's so happy for Penny and Tom. If only ..."

I guessed what she left unsaid. If only Tom could live to see his daughter grow up. But he might not even get to hold her. The question of whether the couple would be able to keep their baby here at the hospital was still in my mind. But, surely, whatever the policy of the past had been, Sister Emily would not separate a mother from her child. Yes, I knew what Adelaide left unsaid. Sister Emily was a stickler for rules.

"Well, if I've been invited to see the baby, I don't want to waste any time. I want to do exactly that."

Sister Adelaide dried her hands on the dishtowel. "Good!"

I hugged her. "And whatever happens, we must be happy for Penny and Tom at this very moment, right?"

Sister Adelaide chuckled. "You give consolation better than I do, Catherine. You'd make a good nun, I think."

I laughed. "No. Trust me, I definitely would not."

I wasn't prepared for how small a newborn baby was. Her little head fit into the palm of her mother's hand. Penny looked genuinely glad to see me. When I entered the small room, I could see preparations had been made. An improvised baby bed was nestled next to the mother's single cot. Stacks of white cloth on a washstand indicated diapers. But what I liked best was the light from tall windows. And though the sky looked gray and heavy with clouds, I could imagine mother and child bathed in sunlight. I grinned at Penny. They were a masterpiece I would love to paint.

"She's beautiful."

"Thank you, Miss Lyle."

"Please, I'm Catherine."

"Do you mind if I nurse her while we talk?"

"Would you rather have privacy? I can come back later. It's no problem."

"No, no. Stay. Hope and I would like some company."

I sat on a small chair in the corner. "It's really a pleasant little room."

She smiled. "Yes, it is. The sisters are so kind, aren't they? I didn't know they'd done this for me. Sister Adelaide said it's been ready for weeks."

That meant my sister had a hand in these preparations. "It's very nice."

She said, "We both have sorrow in our lives, don't we?"

"Yes, we do." I thought it a strange thing to say, holding her little baby in her arms. It should be the happiest day of her life. Yet it wasn't.

"Tom won't come into the room. He stayed with me until Hope was born and then he left. He stood outside the window until I told him it was too cold and he needed some sleep." She had tears in her eyes. "I understand why he won't hold her."

"It's the most beautiful declaration of love I've ever heard."

A wistful smile crossed her lips. "You're right, it is." She rearranged Hope to nurse on the other breast. "Tom was so rude to you at our house ..."

"Never mind that."

"He's not like that."

"He had reason to not like someone barging in like that. I was the rude one."

"There's something I want you to see, Catherine. It's in my bag under the bed. Would you mind getting it for me?"

I placed the bag next to her on the bed and she began to fiddle with its string, but with the baby in her arms, it was difficult.

"Here, let me do it for you." I got the knot untied and pulled the strings apart so that it stood open.

Penny loosened Hope from her breast. The baby was asleep. "Would you mind putting her in her crib?" She lifted her to me.

"She's a little chunk, isn't she?" I whispered, carefully putting her down into the crib.

I remembered the first time I'd seen my little brother, Joseph, sleeping so quietly.

NEW ORLEANS 1913

"He sleeps all the time, Mama. I want to play with him"

"Right now he wants to sleep so he can grow to be as big as you are, my girl." She picked Catherine up and sat her on her lap. While they rocked, Catherine watched her new baby brother through the slats of his crib.

"But I want to play with him now." Then Mary Louise Lyle started to sing to her, low and pretty, and soon Catherine closed her eyes, just before drifting off, thinking she could decide about her brother later.

"Here."

I was jolted from of my memory and turned to accept a piece of paper from Penny. It was crudely folded twice. I opened it, recognized the school tablet lined paper again, like the note Sister Adelaide had found in my sister's desk and given me. Same paper, written in the same childish print.

A stranger will steal your baby.

I looked at Penny. "What's this?"

"I don't know." I handed it back to her but she waved her hand. "No. I don't want it. I was afraid it was you. But after you left, Tom and I talked about it. He said I should show it to you. Maybe you've come to help us, not hurt us." She paused as I read the note again. "Miss Lyle, I mean ... Catherine. Will you help us?" She glanced at her sleeping baby, then with tears in her eyes looked at me. "Who sent us that note? Who would do that?"

I stuck the note into my pocket. Did I want to voice my own fear that their child would probably be given over to a family member? Surely the couple had to know what the rules were in this place. Hope couldn't be the first baby born here.

"I can't imagine who would send you such a note. But if I can find out, I'll tell you. I promise." I stared into the crib. Hope wasn't sleeping. Her round, blue eyes were focused on me, questioning what it was that towered above her. I smiled at her then looked again at Penny. "I'd really like to paint a water color of you and Hope before I leave. May I?"

Penny's face softened. "Of course." Her sentence trailed off. "Tom would love that, I know. I could give it to him ... to keep." The question returned, spreading itself like cancer, replacing her soft expression from before. "It's hateful, isn't it? Cruel. For someone to send us that."

"I want to help you, but Penny, I can't promise anything. Any more than I can find out who murdered my sister."

Her voice cracked as she spoke, "You still think you're sister was murdered. She didn't hang herself?"

"I know she didn't." What did it matter if I told her? Soon everyone would hear the truth, wouldn't they? This business of secrecy was loathsome to me.

"How do you know?" Silent tears fell down Penny's face.

"Because Dr. Mills said water was found in Gretchen's lungs. She died from drowning, not hanging. Someone hanged her to make it look like suicide."

Penny gasped, and her hand flew up to cover her mouth. Her eyes were filled with fear or terror, I thought.

The room was suddenly very warm. I moved to crack a window to let in a bit of the cold December air outside and then I saw Tom. He moved close to the window, pressed his face against the glass with an expression holding more sadness than any I had ever witnessed in my life.

CHAPTER FIFTEEN

I LEFT PENNY AND WALKED ACROSS the compound grounds toward the Protestant church, a small clapboard building, its three wooden steps bound by a white, wooden railing. When I tried the door, it opened into a diminutive sanctuary with pews set in a square, facing each other. It was a meeting room. A Franklin stove sat at the end of the room, and two small windows provided a tiny bit of light. Long wires with electric bulbs hung naked from the ceiling. They were useless, at least today.

As I stood there, sadness swept over me. The empty room reminded me of how my home used to be, after Gretchen left.

I examined the white walls thinking how much this place would benefit from color. It was how I put some life into my house, painting every surface with portraits. Paint would liven up this place because right now it looked stark and cold.

Waiting for Charles Bremmer, I thought of all the portraits in Gretchen's journal. Each one displayed her curiosity but also her affection and compassion for all who were forced to come here.

Charles came through the front door waving a hand, "Catherine. My apologies. I completely forgot I had to complete monthly reports on the Samoans. They're already a week overdue. Sister Paul cornered me in the fellowship hall during breakfast."

I stood. "Oh, I completely understand. We'll do this another time."

He touched my arm. "No, no, no. I'm trying to say that's why I'm so tardy. But now they're done and I'm quite ready to go." He took my elbow, turning me around. "Let's use the back door, that's the trail I take usually."

We let ourselves walk leisurely on the small path lined with weeds and scrub bushes.

"This is so nice of you. Not an imposition, I hope," I said.

"Not at all. I go down to the camp every day. It's really a pleasure to have your company." He blew his breath on the cold air. "I like to check on them, so if problems arise I can step in and mediate."

"Problems?"

"They're always problems, aren't there?"

"I guess it's been hard for them to relocate from everything that was familiar."

"Yes. You probably aren't aware that Falefa, their leprosy station, is closed now."

"I'm sorry. I've never heard of, what's it called?"

"Falefa. It's one of the oldest leprosaria. But lately some Mau chiefs have led an uprising against the people, right on the streets of Apia. My father wrote to me that political reasons made it necessary to abandon it."

"Political?"

"You've heard of the Nationalist Socialist German Workers' Party, haven't you, Catherine?"

"The Nazis?"

He nodded. "For about five years now, our islands have seen many converts to the party. We have a Samoan Nazi Party headquartered in Apia."

I was surprised. Everything I'd read in *The Times-Picayune* said Hitler wanted a "pure Aryan" race of people. It didn't seem to me Samoan natives fit his agenda. When I expressed that, Charles studied me for a moment.

"I've read the articles too," he said. "And it's true. The survival of mankind depends on a pure Aryan race. But studies by a German anthropologist explains the difference between the Samoan and colored Negroids. He's proved Polynesian natives actually descend from pure Aryan blood. Not everyone believes that, of course, and for now the natives must be content to belong to the Party as part of a non-Nazi group. My father is convinced the designation is only temporary."

"Your father?"

"He's the mayor of Apia. Didn't I tell you that last night?"

"Your father is a Nazi?"

"Yes." He looked sideways at me. "And so am I."

I was stunned.

"You're surprised. I don't wonder that you are. Nazis only live in Germany, isn't that right? It's what most people think, for sure. Sorry, but it's not true."

I had to let it sink in for a minute. "You support Hitler? The occupation of France? I admit I don't know much about Nazism, shame on me. But I've asked myself what's the difference between black or white or yellow skin. My answer is nothing. No difference, really. So why are they so repugnant to Nazis? Why is a pure Aryan race so important?"

I received an indulgent smile. "It's really a good thing, Catherine. I know your government has propagandized the Nazi Party as a giant monster. It isn't that at all. We want everyone to succeed."

"Yet it would seem not all the people in your father's town agree with you."

"Yes. But I don't think the uprising is against the Nazi Party. It's more about self-governing themselves. This independence notion has been going on for decades now, but recently, it's gotten nasty. They destroyed several buildings, my father's office, and Party headquarters."

Good for them, I thought.

"The worst part is that some of the dead are related to my community here." He bit his lower lip. "Yes, close relatives. Fathers, brothers. It's really been hard for all of us. The leprosy station, even my own father, has been attacked by a gang of insurgents. He survived, thankfully."

What had I read about the Nazi party in *The Times Picayune*? Mostly the ranting on of a strange man who seemed to be intent on taking over other countries, who had invaded Austria and Poland. Yet some of the stories told of his hatred of Jews and the goal to create a perfect Aryan race of men and women. Fuzzy photographs in the newspaper pictured a small man with a funny mustache, eyes bulging, a shock of hair across his eyes, his mouth open as if shouting, and an arm extended like he was waiting for a returning bird to land upon it. I thought him comical. Surely that was how he must seem to others too. I turned to glance at Charles Bremmer. I was next to one of his followers, who looked pretty normal, who had a completely different perspective than mine. And now I understood why John Weller had warned me against him.

"Here we are."

The Samoan camp looked bleak and lonely on this cloudy, cold morning. Smoke rose from the chimney of their round house in the center of the clearing. And it was just a clearing, as though whatever had been here before was erased. Stalks of wild sugar cane or other tall weeds, trees covered in poison ivy, the watery wet land, all lay just beyond the four small cottages with its community house in the middle. I assumed it was where their kitchen was and where they ate their meals.

"Let me show you this first." He led me to the small, sweet gum tree near one of the cottages.

"This is the fish tree."

"The what?"

"Fish tree. Don't you see the fish? Only two today. It's not a good season to fish."

I shivered and pulled my coat against my body. I stared silently at the tree and several ropes hanging from its branches. "Why would anyone hang their fish on a tree?"

"They're very good, I'll tell you. Once a fish has been gutted and then hung for a few days, it gets rid of all the blood. It really tastes better that way."

"So they've tied the fish with that hemp rope around its tail and hung it out to dry?"

He glanced at me then said drily, "Not something you'll see every day, is it?"

"No, indeed."

"Polanie. This is Miss Catherine Lyle."

One of the Samoans stood at the entrance to the round house. His brown, weathered face looked like a leather book cover, his expression lay in straight lines, lips tightly bound, aquiline nose of high straight proportion, slanting eyes half-shut, standing straight and tall next to the building. My mind saw a George Caitlin painting. Polanie's Samoan face reminded me of those stoic Indian faces he'd immortalized. Polanie even wore a homespun blanket wrapped around his shoulders. It was printed in black and white and yellow checks; however, not in a Native American pattern. No feathers either, but a woolen cap pulled down over his ears.

We entered a large, dark room where an open fire pit with its wood fire emitted as much smoke as heat. It was as thick as fog too so that when I sat next to and across from the men and women of Samoa, I saw their features indistinctly.

Charles Bremmer introduced me as Sister Gretchen's sister, "Miss Catherine Lyle," then spoke their names, none of which I'd ever heard before, "Hoanui, Viali, Unutoa, Malu," on around the circle; shadowy men and women in the semi-darkness of daylight, firelight, and smoke. "Setoa, Popo, Kekona, Lale." I knew I would forget every one of those names before I left the building. They sounded so melodious when spoken, different from the hard English sounds of a Jack, Joan, or George. Did the softness of a name like Lale, broken into two syllables, the "e" extended like a musical note, signify the personality of the individual? It would be nice to think so.

Charles explained that he conducted an English lesson each day, just a few words and phrases meant to make a transition perhaps from the island to being able to talk to the other patients. "It was Sister Gretchen's idea. A good one, don't you think?" I nodded, watching as he went around the circle with a phrase they were to repeat after him, "Good morning. Hello. Good evening. Good night." The English words sounded strained, quietly spoken, so that sometimes Charles would ask them to speak up. His students were shy in front of me. Perhaps embarrassed. It was impossible to tell if their reticence was caused by my presence or something else, because I couldn't see their faces clearly. I decided it had been a mistake to come here, to invade their privacy like this. What had I hoped to gain from visiting the Samoan camp? What had Gretchen written in her journal ...

> They do not smile or speak very much ... I hope in time we can establish a relationship with them.

And there I was, another white woman come into their midst, but one without any authority or reason to, except selfish curiosity. No, I had a reason. A *good* reason. Still, I had broken the rules, and these patients didn't deserve to be on display to anyone, least of all me. Didn't I feel the same way about my neighbors with their prying eyes?

"I really must go, Charles," I said, rising.

"What?" He seemed taken aback. Following me into the yard he said, "I've got to check on a patient who didn't come for treatment this morning. I'm told he's too ill to leave his house."

"I can find my way back alone. But I must go ... now." I was on the path. How stupid I was and how ridiculous. I turned around. "Thank you. I mean that. But I can't be here."

He looked alarmed. "What's wrong? Have they done something to offend you?"

"Oh, no. No, of course not. It's I who have offended. I shouldn't be here. I am someone who cherishes privacy. You should know this is the farthest I've ever been away from my home, and I'm very uneasy about being here, but even more than that, I realize I have no right to intrude upon these people."

"I see."

"I hope you do. I guess the sketches Gretchen made were so beautiful I thought I should witness what she did. I wanted to be next to her ..."

"... By being next to them."

It was good enough. He need not suspect another reason. He must believe what was acceptable. "Please apologize for me, Charles."

"No need."

"I would appreciate it if you would."

He pointed out the main road back to the center then disappeared into one of the nearest houses. I still had the acrid smell of smoke in my nostrils, on my jacket; it clung to me like syrup. I stuck my gloved hands into the pockets of my jacket and listened to the silence. How odd not to hear a bird singing or the wind rustling dead sugar cane stalks nearby. Sounds of nature or of human conversation were not here, nothing except my breath, air escaping from my mouth, forming its own kind of smoke into the freezing air.

I walked to the road and passed the fish tree again. Reaching out to it I grasped one of the frozen fish in a gloved hand, stretched it out as far as possible, not staring at the fish, but the greenish hemp rope.

It was the same rope as the hangman's noose, that horrible circle of rope I'd found on the dirt floor inside the root cellar. I had recognized it immediately when Charles Bremmer pointed out the fish tree.

I pulled hard on it. A jagged burst of pain shot up my arm, then it fell into my hands. My eyes did not deceive me regarding its green color or how hard and ugly the rope felt in my hands.

I wrapped it around my hand and stuffed it in my

pocket, at the same time looking back at the camp. Polanie still stood like a guard at the door to the meeting house, but he wasn't looking in my direction. He was staring at the house into which Charles had gone.

I set off down the road, my purpose clearly etched in my brain. I needed to be sure, to know if it was actually the same rope, then I needed to find out if it was a plentiful commodity imported from Baton Rouge or, as I suspected it might be, a special kind of rope brought here by the islanders. And what else? I trembled, letting my fingers rub the rough texture of hemp threads in my pocket.

It was something I'd read in Gretchen's journal. All those sketches of the Samoans. Yet a note she'd scribbled in the margin of a sketch with the natives fishing in the river had jumped out at me. I didn't understand it. She'd written *"Too many."* Whatever could that mean?

I knew it might turn out to mean nothing at all. Regardless, there was the rope. Finding out if it matched the noose might lead somewhere. I felt the hemp rope again in my pocket. I couldn't help but think finding it in the Samoan camp had not been accident, but that Gretchen was leading me, closer and closer to whoever was responsible for her murder.

I began running. Each breath I took floated in front of me like smoke. There was effort in running: the heart beat faster, one could hear pulsing in the ears, perspiration trickled down the back. The sensation was remarkable. I was alive for the first time since I'd arrived.

CHAPTER SIXTEEN

I DECIDED TO TAKE JOHN WELLER'S shortcut to the mansion, through the tall hedge. When I reached the entrance to the hospital, however, I was completely out of breath. I leaned against the massive iron gate for a couple of minutes, not ready yet to push its heavy iron bars open.

I held up the rope, examining it again, my mind churning with the possibility that I'd found a clue to Gretchen's murder. If the hangman's noose was still in the cellar, it would be easy to match to this sample. Were the Samoans guilty of murder then? Collectively or just one? And for what reason? My sister's journal seemed so positive about their arrival; though, she was worried because they continued to segregate themselves from the rest of the patients. Did a secret exist that Gretchen had somehow discovered? Would it be so dire it led one of them to murder her?

Shoving the rope back into my pocket, I pushed open the gate. As I passed the infirmary, I saw there was still no electricity; the buildings looked dark and cold, much as the Samoan camp had. Surely we couldn't be so far removed from civilization that the village down the road couldn't repair these things by now. How long had it been since the storm? Thursday night, wasn't it? Two days before I'd gone this way with the editor of *The Light*.

"Where are you going?" John Weller said softly from behind me.

I jumped. Speak of the devil. He was standing in the shadow of an aperture on the building, still wearing the same calculating look I remembered. His bomber jacket was zipped up tight against the cold, a scarf rigid round his neck.

"You look out of breath, Miss Lyle."

No apology. "I've just taken a long run, so yes, I'm out of breath."

"How was your outing with Herr Bremmer?"

"You could have warned me he's a Nazi."

"As I recall you didn't give me a chance to tell you."

"As I recall you called me an idiot."

"I thought you were smarter than that. But it was a poor choice of words."

"It certainly was."

A cloud of irritation passed across his face. "Your sister was murdered. The autopsy proved she drowned."

"And hung afterwards. To appear as suicide. Does everybody know?"

"Pretty much." He took a pack of cigarettes from his pocket inside the jacket. "Smoke?" I shook my head. After he lit up, he raised his cigarette, inhaled deeply, slowly expelling the smoke into the air. "Did you have a chance to read the other suicide reports?"

"I did. Two victims, a man and a woman. They were

found in their rooms by other patients. They also left suicide notes."

"Pretty straight forward. I'm sorry to say I didn't know either of them well."

"I think their notes are proof they did take their own lives. I question Enoka Noa's cause of death, though. The report called it a 'presumed drowning or suicide.' But neither of those reasons hold up since his body wasn't found. Charles Bremmer told me he thinks Enoka ran away. That he couldn't have drowned in the river. Samoans know the water too well. They're born to it, he said. And even if he drowned himself, his body should have been found down river by someone." I paused. "And something else. I could see something in Charles's face as he told me those things. It was as if he was afraid of something. I wondered for a moment if it might be that Enoka Noa *was* still alive. Hiding out somewhere. But why?"

John frowned and said quietly, "I may have underestimated you."

"In what way, Mr. Weller?"

He was about to say something but stopped, threw his cigarette on the ground, and scrunched the butt into the wet grass. "Never mind."

He tossed that last remark behind him as he walked slowly away toward the hospital, without looking back.

Why did he never finish a conversation? His habit of just walking away without a word was infuriating. The man appeared to be in a perpetual state of bitterness. Yet I guessed it wasn't aimed primarily at me. He'd been forced to come here. Maybe he had a good job. Now he was nothing but an outcast, imprisoned for life, perhaps.

I continued around the chapel, passed the hospital, and pushed myself through the hedge to a path that led toward the mansion. As I shuffled along in Sister Adelaide's boots, I berated myself. I'd never walked in a leper's shoes. The little I knew about the disease, though, the word "fickle" seemed to fit. Maybe "capricious." Their blood tests must be like opening a present each month, to find a butterfly or a black widow spider. No one knew if they would ever be "clean" for twelve months. Of course, if that happened, they were free to leave, to go home to their families. I shuddered, thinking of Jack, a thirteen-year-old boy whose family didn't want him. It might not be an unusual thing. Still, it was better to be free of disease than the alternative, wasn't it? To suffer and die in so much pain.

No wonder John Weller wasn't planning to stay around here much longer. What had he said to Sister Paul? That he was "leaving with or without you December 21."

But the question was, where could they go? Was there a place anywhere where he could live and be happy? At least here there was treatment. There was a chance. At the end of every month.

Reaching the root cellar, I struggled to lift the heavy wooden door, letting it fall noisily to the ground. Stepping down into the small room, I wished for a flashlight or a lantern because, though it was afternoon, once underground, I couldn't see much. Of course, I knew exactly where the hangman's noose was, where I'd thrown it in the corner. I hoped no one had moved it. I wanted to take it into the daylight to compare the rope strands.

I inched my way along the shelves, my back to them, until I reached the corner of the small room. With my foot, I felt around on the floor until I nudged something. I bent down to see just enough to know it was the hangman's noose.

Suddenly, the door crashed on top of me, banging like a thousand cymbals.

I couldn't see a thing at first, not even my hands holding the noose. I dropped to my knees, skin scraping against the rope under me. Tipping sideways to steady myself, I gripped the noose, then shoved it away, tears springing to my eyes, unable to catch my breath.

I sat there on the floor wondering what had happened, staring at the door. It wasn't complete blackness around me. I could see bits of daylight through the wooden slats in the door. Then, after a few minutes, my mouth curled into a tight-lipped smile.

I've been here before, I thought. A long time ago. Not in this cellar but in a place where darkness enveloped me except for a tiny bit of light under the door. Moments of terror long buried in my subconscious mind rose again. I rubbed my head, ran my fingers through my hair, pushing it back behind my ears. It wasn't as short now as it was when I was eleven and had tried to cut it all off ....

NEW ORLEANS, 1922

Catherine sat in the dark place, letting its warmth protect her. She pushed her body fast against the wall, covering herself with wool sweaters and coats. At first she squeezed her eyes shut to hide the faces in her mind, but gradually she began to realize that if the light in the hallway stayed as it was, then she was safe. Holding her legs up under her chin, Catherine felt very small, like a snail or a bug, so tiny it would not be seen or discovered.

Her hiding place in the woolen closet on the third floor seemed far away from the rest of the house. Unfortunately, it was not far enough, for she heard their voices. Not distinctly. The words were muffled, but she recognized who was speaking. Gretchen was crying again, her sobbing louder this time, even when Catherine covered her ears with another wool sweater.

She prayed and listened. She was waiting for the silence to begin. The split seconds when she suspended breathing to listen felt like hours. She had to shake out her hands; they'd become numb.

Her head ached with worry. He was hurting Gretchen. The fear she tried not to think of was what her own fate would be. Gretchen would have to tell him soon where she was because in Catherine's mind, she believed that was what they were arguing about. Papa wanted to know where she was. She shifted herself slightly, listening.

She knew her sister wouldn't tell him willingly. But maybe this time she would, she thought, squeezing her eyes with silent tears. This time he would kill her sister. Oh, please, Gretchen, don't die! You can tell him. No … please don't tell him!

Her mouth was so dry. Just a sip of water would be good. Her mind raced. What to do? Maybe she should find another hiding place. A possibility struck her, to get out of the house. It was better than a hiding place. Go out to the street. Escape. Papa couldn't do anything to her if she ran away.

She felt a tingling course through her body. First, she must sneak down the stairs, to the second floor, then slide down the banister to the front door. But how to do it without being seen? It depended on where Papa and Gretchen were. Catherine's heart raced. Were they on the balcony? She was sure to be caught if that was the case. She must take a peek down the narrow third-floor stairs before going down.

Catherine had begun taking sweaters off herself, to open the closet door, when she realized something. The silence had begun. That meant Papa had passed out. Gretchen would come for her now.

She shouldn't have worried. It was always the same, wasn't it? Gretchen said Papa always passed out because he was falling-down drunk. Afterwards, when all was quiet again, Gretchen always came.

Catherine's head hurt so bad she rubbed the heels of her hands across her forehead like she'd seen their maid do sometimes. It didn't help. She rearranged some of the sweaters around her again. She could lean into them and cushion her head. Some nights, in fact, she fell asleep in the closet; at least, she thought, it was sleep. Only when her big sister touched her on the shoulder, put her finger to her lips, did Catherine know she could go downstairs to her room.

She held her body still, clasping her hands together like prayer. She must believe that Gretchen would come soon. Not Monster Papa.

Strange to think she had loved her papa once. Before Mama and Joseph died. Coming in the front door, he would hold his arms out wide, waiting for her to run to him. His big mustache tickled when he picked her up and gave her a kiss. When they walked to Mass, he held her hand and admired her dress. She and Joseph sat on his lap sometimes, Joseph on one knee, she on the other, to read the Sunday funnies in *The Times Picayune*. "Joseph," he'd say, "has my eyes," which made her sad because she didn't have them. "But you, Miss Cathy, have your mother's beautiful blue eyes, and I believe you'll be the image of her when you grow up." She loved her papa then.

Not now. After Mama died he sat in his study with a bottle of whisky. He sat silently at dinner, not listening to Tante when she spoke to him, but studying Catherine with his dead eyes. He stared at Gretchen the same way. He usually rose from the table early, put on his hat, and grabbed an umbrella, announcing as he left he was going out with his friends or to the opera or just out. Somewhere else. Catherine knew why he didn't like her anymore, at least she thought she did. It was because she had her mother's blue eyes, and when he sat at the table, he had to look at them, but they were not Mama's. And they weren't Joseph's.

Catherine stared ahead, whispering, "If the light under the doorway stays that way, with no dark spots, I'll be okay."

The footsteps on the stairs were heavy. They weren't her sister's. Catherine raised her hand to her mouth to stifle an uncontrollable sound. "Please, God," she prayed, "let it be Gretchen. Please, please, please, God."

Her eyes flew open in time to see two dark spots under the door. She heard him breathing hard because the stairs were steep and narrow and Papa was a big man.

The door opened, and for one fleeting moment Catherine thought he wouldn't see her, that she had melted into the winter wool stacked around her.

Two hands reached out and touched her. He pulled all the wool sweaters from her then, with a crushing grip on her forearms, pulled her from the closet as Catherine screamed in pain, "I didn't do anything! I didn't do anything! Papa, you're hurting me!"

His voice was beyond understanding. Some rage in him produced only grunts, spitting out profanity, his eyes as red as blood.

He pulled the small girl by the hand behind him. But Catherine kicked and squirmed like she was fighting for her life. Had he spoken to her to scold her for something she had done, some incident for which she was responsible? She would have melted into submission, but this was not her papa, nor anyone she'd ever seen before. She was seeing the monster she had imagined. He was real.

Catherine bit his hand, hard. He yelled, letting go of her momentarily to rub the wound. She wiped his spittle off her face, running down narrow stairs to the second floor balcony.

He was right behind her, but something told her she would escape. She just needed to get to the balcony, to the stairs leading to the ground floor and the front door.

Suddenly, her head was jerked backwards. Her father was holding on to a handful of her long, black hair, spinning her around, stuttering something, choking on his words.

Catherine screamed in pain, "Help me! Help me!" She was fighting for her life, writhing under him, beating against his body with her hands, yelling at the top of her voice, kicking toward his groin. He released his hold on her, and suddenly, like a ghost, his body was gone. Her father had disappeared.

CHAPTER SEVENTEEN

Slowly, my eyes adjusted to threads of light from cracks between the boards on the cellar's door. The mind didn't rest; it enjoyed playing tricks. How could a cold, musty, underground room bring back the smell of wool and mothballs? Yet it had. My eyes couldn't let go of the light between the old wooden slats slanted above me at the top of earthen stairs. I was searching for shadows.

It was so cold in the cellar. I rubbed my legs, which were stretched out before me, and felt around the floor. Yes, the noose was still beside me on the floor. I shivered. So damp. The air was like a solid mass of darkness pressing against me, trying to bury me deep inside an underground tomb.

I raised my hands in front of my face. I could see them, barely, in the dim light emanating from the cellar door. Hands that were real, if unseen. I asked myself, *Could it be the same way with memory?* The same dream that always ended with my father disappearing? Why? I touched my head. When was it I cut most of my hair off? Eleven? I remembered very well when I did that. But not Papa pulling part of my hair out. My memories were like shattered mirrors, their splintered fragments inside my distorted mind. I could see some pictures through its cracks, follow the edge of events, but not enough to really know if my dream was real and had truly happened to me or if it was some nightmarish fear imbedded in my mind since childhood.

My father was murdered in the spring of 1922. He'd been attacked, robbed, and beaten to death. Left in an alley off Bourbon Street in the French Quarter. Someone had torn most of his clothes off him. In fact, until identified, he was thought to be a vagrant. His body was discovered behind his club. One of the women who worked there identified him. He must have bled to death before the sun rose.

It has remained an unsolved case. Unresolved. Like my dream.

I stood up shakily. I needed to get out of this cellar. I went toward the slats of light. If I used all my weight against it ... I sighed, grabbed my shoulders, shaking all over, frozen in that spot.

Sunlight.

The cellar door was thrown open. It landed with a bang and light streamed through it into my tomb as cold air hit me in the face.

I didn't move. My mind said, "Get out of here. Escape." But my body wouldn't move.

"Catherine?"

Hearing my name gave me a jolt. I took tentative steps toward the stairs. A face peered down at me.

"Are you in there, Catherine?"

Sister Adelaide stood above me, her eyes huge behind

her glasses, her brows wrinkled in puzzlement. She extended her hand, I took it, and she gave me a pull up the steep stairs. "Why were you down there, Catherine?"

"Someone shut the cellar door on me. How did you know I was down there?"

She glanced away, to the road. Something had crossed her mind, something worrying. I could see it written on her face. Then, looking back to me, she answered, "You were screaming for help."

"Was I? I don't remember doing that. Well, thank goodness you heard me."

She looked somewhere beyond the house, toward the road.

"What are you looking at?"

"I saw them ... just as I was coming through the hedge." She turned back to me. "Jack and Clarice. They were running down the path, around the side of the house." She stumbled over the words, clasped her hands in front of her, then began rubbing them together.

I stared in the direction the children had run. "It had to be them."

Sister Adelaide's eyes widened as she comprehended what I was saying. "They wouldn't do such a thing, ... shut the door on you? Why, then you couldn't breathe, could you?" Beads of sweat appeared on her forehead, and her overly bright eyes behind her spectacles stared back at me.

"It had to be them. No one knew where I was going. No one knew I would be going down into the cellar. They were hanging around here, saw me, and decided to play a hateful prank."

She whispered, "But that's more than hateful."

I nodded. "Let's go," my heart raced inside my chest. I walked around the house with Sister Adelaide following me. I could hear the scrub grass scratching against her long robe.

There wasn't a sign of the children. I almost doubted Sister Adelaide's statement, except she was sobbing now, in real distress. I pulled her over to the front porch of the mansion, encouraged her to sit on the steps, then sat beside her, taking her hand in mine.

"I can't believe they would be so cruel. How could they do such a thing?"

"We're not positive it was them, Sister Adelaide."

She turned to stare at me. "Then who?"

We sat together, shoulders touching, side by side. I had a brief image in my head from long ago, when this house was new, of a family sitting there enjoying the crisp air of winter, the wind dancing among the branches in live oak trees that grew on the wide slope toward the road, the levy, and the river.

There must have been a time when the people who lived in this house were happy.

"Who? I have no idea," I said. "I suppose anyone could have followed me from the Samoan camp." I paused, thinking. "Did you see John Weller, Sister?"

"Only for a second. He stuck his head in the office asking for Sister Paul."

Of course, I thought. Taking in a deep breath, I said, "Sister, there's something important you can help me with."

Sister Adelaide wiped away her tears with the back of her sleeve. "You want help from me?" Her chin trembled. "Ask me anything."

"I know you were the closest one to my sister. You worked together every day. She's bound to have shared things with you. Maybe when tempers flared or people made threatening remarks."

Sister Adelaide fingered the long crucifix necklace she wore over her habit. "I'm sorry. Everyone loved Sister Mary Gretchen. They did."

I shook my head, "Not everyone. Someone murdered her, and even worse, they humiliated her, a Catholic nun, by trying to convince everyone it was suicide."

Sister Adelaide pulled back from me and studied the folds of her robe. "I know," she said finally. "Sister Paul told me about the autopsy. I can't believe it. Drowned. Then hanged. I can't believe it." She was crying.

"We can't wait for the sheriff to make up his mind to come and find out who did this, Sister."

"What else can we do?"

"I believe there is something." I opened my book sack and took out Gretchen's journal. I have all of my sister's journals. I wouldn't ask you to read them all, just the last one. I think we'll find a clue in there. Maybe she wrote something that would help you remember. Anything different, a bit off balance, not normal. Unusual. Would you do that for me?"

She raised her head, took off her glasses, and smiled. "Oh, yes. Of course I will." She laughed shakily. "But please don't count on my remembering anything, Catherine. I'm really the dumbest nun there ever was."

"I know that's not true, Sister Adelaide. You were there with her most of every day. She trusted you above all the others to help her in the pharmacy."

"But I don't remember anything different. They were just normal days. Sometimes patients got upset; they always got over it, don't you see?"

I gave the journal to Adelaide. "Read her words. Study the sketches. Something may jump out at you, something you saw or heard, anything out of the ordinary. Maybe you're right, maybe nothing's there. But maybe you'll read something that will make you pause and question it. That's all I'm asking."

Sister Adelaide hadn't moved. With soft tears still in her eyes, she said, "I just hope I don't disappoint you."

I stood up and took her arm to walk back to my quarters. "There's no failure in this, Sister Adelaide. It's a long, long shot at best. But I really believe the clue to whoever did this to her and why is there, somewhere inside her journals. If I only knew what it was."

It didn't occur to me at first to ask Sister Adelaide why she was looking for me or, for that matter, how she knew I had walked in the direction of the old house. It was not until we reached my quarters' front door that she gave me the answer.

She said, "Mass. Oh no. Sister Emily sent me to tell you it's time for Mass because she saw you walking toward the mansion." She glanced at her watch. "Oh goodness, we don't have much time."

I wondered how many other people besides Sister Emily had seen me walk past the hospital. My actions seemed to have been witnessed by several people, but who among them would want to lock me down in the cellar?

It seemed incredulous to suspect Sister Emily. What possible reason might she have? Except … she *was* the most adamant that Gretchen's death was suicide. She fought any idea blood was under my sister's fingernails, or even if so, she was positive the blood was Gretchen's. And the bruises on my sister, she dismissed those as well. I was fairly certain she'd also faked a fainting spell in her office to get rid of me, for no other purpose than that I raised questions she didn't want to answer. Could she have also faked a suicide?

I stared at Adelaide. "Someone hated Gretchen enough to

kill her and then try to make it look like suicide. Maybe they wanted to humiliate not just her but the Catholic Church."

Sister Adelaide looked shocked. "What?"

I said, "I'm sorry. My mind takes off in so many directions. But nothing else makes sense, does it? Gretchen's journal must contain a clue. Someone had it in for her, or for all the nuns here and used Gretchen as an example. At first I thought it might be Tom, but now I'm doubting that. He's so ill and the act of drowning her, holding her under the water, well, I don't think he'd have the strength."

Adelaide touched her crucifix as though finding strength in its touch. "And then, whoever it was had to hang her in the mansion."

"Yes." I studied the front door of my quarters, for a few seconds. "I heard today that the Samoans are rioting in their home villages. That note, the one you gave me said, '*Don't trust the Samoans,*' didn't it? Do you remember anything Gretchen said about them? Was she afraid of any of them?"

"No, I don't think so. I do remember she said she noticed they didn't seem to like Mr. Bremmer."

"Neither do I. But if they also disliked her, wouldn't my sister have written about that in her journal?"

"I never saw anything like that." Sister Adelaide held the journal in both hands. "I can't miss Mass. I want to help you, truly I do, but I must get back. Please come with me."

"I'll attend tomorrow."

"No, you don't remember. Father O'Quinn is here only today. This is our only Mass. Today. He catches the last ferry across the river. I really must go."

I watched her bunch up her robe in front of her, still holding the journal in the other hand, and run toward the church.

Second thoughts ran through my mind. Wouldn't it be a prudent thing to attend Mass? Everyone would be there, all the nuns, the patients, probably outside staff, like Dr. Mills, his daughter, cleaning people, gardeners, whoever kept the place.

I put my hand on the door knob, hesitating, then stepping inside. Maybe I should go. It dawned on me Sister Emily might want me there because it was where she planned to announce to everyone my sister's murder, not suicide, and the anticipated arrival of Sheriff Doucet from Prairieville.

I would go. I turned around then noticed the yellow sheet of paper, folded twice, on the desk. Was it the note Penny had given me this morning? No. I put my hand into the pocket of my jacket, felt the paper, drew it out, and laid it next to what looked like it was on identical tablet paper as the other. Was it the note Adelaide had given me, the one she found in Gretchen's desk? I went to my shoulder bag on the bed, found it, and placed it beside the other two on the desk. And I knew, without looking. This was a new note, left here for me.

Leave or you will die.

I jumped at the sharp stab of pain over my heart, fell against the desk chair, sending it thudding across the floor behind me. Bile rose in my throat. A step back and I fell over the upturned chair. On my hands and knees, I reached for the edge of the desk, not trusting myself to stand without support. I placed one hand over my heart, feeling it race, trying to pound itself right out of my body.

I picked up the note and read it again. My hands shook so that the words blurred before me. A wave of lightheadedness suddenly overtook me, but I somehow managed to right the desk chair and get myself into it. *I will not faint,*

I thought with a fleeting image of my body crumpling to the floor. Taking one deep breath after another, my heart slowed down, and though it was probably but a short few seconds, it seemed to take forever to get control again. I rubbed my temples and it seemed to help.

My mind reeled, asking questions. Why would someone want to kill me? I knew nothing about Gretchen's murder. If only I did!

I fingered the notes on the desk. Should I take them to Sister Emily? Dr. Mills? Was there no one besides Adelaide whom I trusted? Maybe Sister Anne. I sighed. The youngest and the oldest. One whose naïveté and innocence would overwhelm and Sister Anne, whose experience was marred by age and dementia. Truthfully, I probably trusted both of them because of their shortcomings, and the determination in each to see the glass half-full even when faced with the wretchedness of a situation.

Who then? I heard Yves's voice in my mind. *You have the strength to do anything, Cathy. I'm here if you need me.*

Yves. *Oh, that I could put you in this room with me now. Something is happening, so quickly, and I'm so afraid. Why can't I at least call you on the phone? Hear your voice?*

Another thought occurred to me. What else had my intruder done here? My bed, hastily made this morning, looked the same as I left it. My eyes traveled around the room. My small suitcase was next to the sofa, next to Gretchen's case with her journals. "Oh God," I said, taking quick, jerky steps to where the small trunk lay closed on the floor. Hadn't it been left open this morning when I took Gretchen's last journal and put it in my book sack? I reached down and pulled the top open. The journals looked untouched. I turned back to the notes on the desk. Staring at them, I whispered, "Think. What should you do?" I folded each note and stuck them into the pocket of my coat.

Sitting on the sofa, I let the silence surround me, my shaking subside. I could picture Yves working, though his mind would not be on his work. Even as he stared at a painting, paintbrush in his hand, he would wonder what I was doing, if all was safe here. I must have shocked him with my allegation that Gretchen had been murdered, then my emotional outburst on the phone. Yet he listened, was patient, like always.

Yves knew me, knew no arguing would work. I must arrive at the truth in my own way. But hysterically? I glanced at the clock on my bedside table, then out the window. Almost five o'clock. Already the sun sat low, just above the trees. No, I didn't handle surprises very well, but who would? I knew it was murder, and now there was proof. Too much was happening to stop and think rationally.

I sighed, pressing my hands on the window sill, trying to think straight, staring at nothing. I was positive Yves had tried to call me many times the day before. Then, perhaps, the previous night, even this morning; he would start calling other places, like the telephone company. He'd learn of the devastation left by the storm. A call to the state police eventually and the sheriff in Prairieville. Somehow, my partner would glean the truth about Gretchen's autopsy, though no one would want to give him that information. Yves had ways. He would know by now.

I straightened, suddenly alert. A thought. A feeling that was so strong. Yves wasn't working in New Orleans. *Yves was coming here!*

I looked through the window focusing on the deserted road, at the pitch-black windows of the doctor's house across the street.

Then I paced around the room, my mind reeling with excitement. If Yves was coming, he would have taken the

River Road on the west side of the river and crossed over at White Castle on the ferry. I could meet him across the river. Or if he wasn't there I could find a telephone and call him, tell him where I was. No matter what, I'd be out of here.

I grabbed my small suitcase and stuffed my few clothes into it. I closed it with shaky hands, frowning, and then felt a bitter smile form on my face. "Are you sure you want to do this?" My lips tightened even as I slammed the nearby dresser drawer. I was running away. I should stay put, wait for the sheriff, and give him the notes.

"Yves is coming. He's coming to you. Stay where you are." The sound of my voice rang in my ears. Was I losing my mind? I opened the dresser drawer. I began to unpack my suitcase.

I heard a tap at the door, and I jumped, an involuntary "Oh!" on my lips.

I opened the door to Father O'Quinn and Sister Adelaide and a young man standing next to a small cart with the priest's suitcase.

"Oh my," Father O'Quinn said, a chuckle in his voice. "We've surprised you, haven't we? But I hope this means you've changed your mind." He smiled broadly at my blank expression. Sister Adelaide even offered a tentative smile.

"What?"

Sister Adelaide and I looked at each other reading each other's thoughts. She must still be reeling from an hour ago. If she only knew how much more dangerous than just a prank the threatening note in my pocket was. It changed everything. I think she saw the panic in my eyes, yet had no idea how the words scribbled across a yellow tablet, *"Leave or you will die,"* had had a devastating effect. I was shaking all over as I walked back to the bed and began to pack again. Did she see in my eyes how frantic I was at this moment? At the same time, I knew it would serve no one to say anything to Sister Adelaide or the priest.

I felt her hand on my shoulder. "Are you going to Brusly?" she said softly.

"I think I must. I must call Yves and tell him what's happened."

"Yes, I think that's what you should do."

Father O'Quinn stood just outside the open door. "Good then! But we must get a move on. It's past time. The ferry will already be docked." He motioned to the young man to fetch my suitcase while I reached for my coat and gloves. I followed him out the door.

Sister Adelaide stood beside me. "Maybe it's for the best." I tried to smile, failing miserably. Her chin trembled but she smiled back. "Call him right away."

We stepped onto the small porch. "I will. Are you going to walk with us to the ferry?"

"No. I'll stay here for a while. I'll make sure Sister Gretchen's journals are safe."

"Thank you." I grabbed her and hugged her close. "Thank you for all your help. And if you read anything in her journal ..." I stepped back, our eyes questioning each other.

She nodded, then whispered in my ear, "I'm afraid I won't ever see you again!"

I turned my head to hide the visible panic in my eyes at her words. I muttered, "No, I'll be back tomorrow. The sheriff will come. We'll get to the bottom of it all."

Her anxiety was as raw as mine and she didn't know about the note left for me. Yet she had sensed I was in danger from the moment she lifted the cellar door. She took my hand; her eyes seemed to glow with an inner light. "God bless you, Catherine."

CHAPTER EIGHTEEN

A TEAM OF MULES PULLED A wagon up to the gang-plank as we approached the ferry. The animals were being quite resistant to the urging of the owner, a gray-whiskered black man whose angry outbursts at them seemed to fall on deaf, obstinate ears. I wondered aloud if the frightened mules had ever been aboard a boat, but was assured by Father O'Quinn they had indeed, probably once a month, and also that they never failed to act this way. Well, it *was* a slick, steel gangplank prepared for automobiles, not mules. The wagon was empty except for a large crate, yet it took both boat hands pushing and pulling to get them on board. Finally, the mules broke for the deck in a bit of a jerk, a jump, to stand stonily as the gangplank was lifted, their owner still cursing them at the top of his lungs. Inwardly, I found a smile. The mules couldn't have cared less how angry their master was.

The ferry had a couple of automobiles at the front and several people on foot like us. It was in that group that I saw Charles Bremmer, who waved and began to make his way across the deck.

Above the drone of the engine, Charles yelled, "Are you going to Brusly to examine Father O'Quinn's icon?"

"Yes, indeed she is," the priest yelled back. "Excuse me, children, I'm going to try and get out of this spray if I can." He moved forward, near the engine room.

The cold water blowing across the boat stung my face but revived me at the same time.

"Father O'Quinn told me his telephone was working when he left yesterday. I really want to call home."

Charles laughed. "What a coincidence. It's the same with me. Today's my mother's birthday." He shrugged when I smiled. "No, I'm not such a good son, and my mother reminds me of that regularly. But I'd drive the last nail in my coffin if I failed to call her on her birthday."

"Well, I'm impressed, even if it sounds like your mother may not be."

I looked out at the river, at the fast-approaching shoreline. Just a few lights, probably waiting motor cars, were visible. Night came quickly at this time of year. The river was black and churning, its smell overwhelmed by the oil from the engines whining around us. I felt Charles's eyes staring at me intently. What was he thinking? Did he sense the panic I felt inside? When I turned to meet his gaze, he seemed caught off guard, harboring some secret thought, but he quickly recovered, smiled, and looked away.

I pointed to the wagon. "Do you know why that man wanted to get his mules across the river?"

"Oh, that's old Jacques. He'll spend a few days in the cypress swamp around Morley. He picks up scrap lumber then brings it back to Carville to sell to carpenters or cabinet makers. I think he's got a good business going, except his mules are about as cantankerous as mules can be."

"You seem to know him."

"Everyone knows old Jacques. He's the entrepreneur of the parish. I gather he's interested in just about anything that will pay him a few dollars. A crusty old guy."

"Isn't that one of your crates in the back of the wagon?"

Charles started. His voice registered surprise. "How did you know that crate belonged to me?"

"They were on the barge. When I arrived Wednesday, remember? I sat all the way down the river between twenty crates like that stacked around me. Your church pews, right?"

He paused, speaking again, measuring his words. "You've a good eye for detail. Yes, it is one of mine. An acquaintance in White Castle wants it." Another pause. "To build a coffin."

"A coffin?" Now it was my turn to look surprised.

"Yes. If he's satisfied with the wood, he'll buy all the crates from me." His eyes darted back and forth, blinking with nervous excitement. He swallowed then laughed. "I suppose you could say I'm picking up some of Old Jacques's tricks, couldn't you? Next thing you know, they'll be calling me an entrepreneur too."

I didn't believe him. He'd made up the story on the spot, I'd have sworn it. The question boiling inside me was *why*? What else had he said that wasn't true. His mother's birthday? Or the story yesterday about his being a Nazi? Was Charles Bremmer just a pathological liar? Or more dangerous, perhaps. A murderer? My whole body shivered. The ferry slowed down, pulling into the dock with a loud banging of the gangplank. We bumped against the dock and I caught the railing just in time before losing my footing. The boat hands tied us off to posts at the front and rear. I was glad. I wanted to get away from Charles Bremmer.

"I must get over to Father O'Quinn."

"Take my arm. The boat rolls, sometimes."

"I can manage. Thanks."

"Something wrong?"

"No. No. Just a little queasy." We made our way to the front of the ferry. The two automobiles left first, along with the wagon. I watched it, the mules moving off quickly, glad to be on solid footing. When the wagon was clear of the boat, Charles climbed up next to Jacques, and two black men got into the back. Charles turned and waved at us once more.

"We could easily have taken him to town. It'll be a rough ride with old Jacques," Father O'Quinn said. "Our transportation is a bit better."

A few old automobiles of questionable vintage sat at the top of the hill waiting for foot passengers. None of them resembled Yves's smart, little black coupe, though, the car he bragged was a "dream to drive." It had not been of interest to me when he offered me a Sunday drive, but at this moment, I would have liked nothing better than to see it parked out there with the other waiting vehicles.

"He told me Jacques is going to Morley to collect scrap wood. But Charles is only going to White Castle. He's looking for a telephone to call his mother in New Orleans. It's her birthday." I didn't mention the proposed business with the crates.

The priest's eyes widened. "Good heavens. Why didn't he say so? He'll probably have to pay for a hotel. He could have ridden to Brusly with us; we certainly have room."

"Maybe he has a friend in White Castle."

"Maybe. At least he doesn't have to go all the way to Morley riding on that bouncy wagon. Jacques will have to sleep in the back of his wagon because Morley is an old lumber company town, but the company left the area years ago. It's more of a ghost town than anything else now." Father O'Quinn waved at a middle-aged black man leaning against a car. "William! Here we are!" The man came running down the hill.

William and I were introduced as he collected our suitcases and walked ahead of us.

Father O'Quinn said, "If we're lucky, Catherine, Mrs. Duggan, the housekeeper at the rectory, will have made a chocolate meringue pie for supper. Let's keep our fingers crossed!"

We drove on a dark stretch of road with William in the driver's seat, I next to him, and Father O'Quinn spread out in the backseat with his eyes closed. I held my book sack on my lap. Only our headlights illuminated what was ahead of us, shadows bouncing off the trunks or branches of trees, and a blackness ahead. I knew we were traveling on what was called the Great River Road, from an article I'd read in *The Times-Picayune*. Two years before, this section, on both sides of the river, was dubbed the last leg of a scenic highway stretching all the way down the river to New Orleans. There was nothing to see tonight.

I grabbed the door handle when the car swerved against loose gravel, skidding sideways. William righted us quickly.

"Slow down, William. We're not in a race, you know."

William turned to the backseat. "Yessur, Father." He grinned at me. "Sometimes old Bessie here speeds up and I don't notice."

Father O'Quinn said, "You're a fine driver, William," then dismissed both of us to close his eyes again. Ten minutes later, William hit another bump, but a paved road opened up before us, and so did some light. We passed Nottoway Plantation, its gleaming white columns standing like sentries in the darkness. I'd read somewhere it was the largest plantation house in Louisiana.

Twenty minutes later, the empty landscape vanished. There were houses and fences, headlights of oncoming cars, and a church steeple in the distance. William pulled into the grass next to the rectory and parked, then proceeded to remove our suitcases from the trunk. In spite of the fact Yves couldn't possibly know I was now in Brusly, I found myself looking again for his shiny black coupe.

"William will show you where the guest room is, Catherine. Get settled and then I'll see you for supper. Shall we say thirty minutes?"

"I'm really anxious to speak to my business partner, Father."

The priest directed William to take me into a small sitting room to the telephone. My fingers trembled. I could hardly hold on to the receiver my hand shook so. I gave the operator the number and waited what seemed an interminable interval. Finally, I heard the connection, the phone ringing. But no answer.

I wasn't about to give up yet. I gave the operator my home number, letting it ring more than ten times. I was on the point of giving up when I suddenly heard Grace's voice, "Miss Lyle's residence."

"Grace? It's me, Catherine."

"Oh my Lord Jesus!" She paused. "I'm hardly able to breathe. Is that really you? Are you safe? We been calling and calling and can't get no answer from nobody!"

"I'm safe. I'm not in Carville."

"What do you mean?"

"I'm at the rectory of a Catholic church in Brusly. Across the river from Carville."

"What you doing there, Miss Catherine?"

"The storm. We lost all our phones." It was explanation enough for now. "Oh, Grace … there's more to tell you and Yves. Do you know where he is? He didn't answer his phone."

"Because he's not there. We been so worried about you. He said he was going to find out what happened, why you didn't call us. He coming to get you he said."

I felt warmth pulse through my body. I wanted to scream, to jump up and down, but settled on laughing. "I can't tell you how happy that makes me."

Grace went off in a peal of laughter also, then a stream of words, not all of which I caught, "Tante ask for you yesterday. I thought something must be happening to you if your Tante come up out of her dream world and remember who she is … and you is. Like it's God speaking, I thought, cause you know that woman ain't remember nothing even how to go to the toilet sometimes …"

"Grace, Grace," I interrupted, "I want to hear all about Tante, but it's long distance. I can't stay on the phone too long. Will you hear from Yves, you think?"

"I dunno. He call me this morning to say he leaving and if you call to tell you he coming to get you."

My mind was churning. *He won't know where I am.* "If he calls you again tell him I'm in Brusly. At the Catholic church in Brusly. St. John the Baptist Catholic Church."

Grace repeated the words back to me.

"Tell him not to go to the leper colony until he talks to me."

"Why is that? Is there something tormenting you, Miss Catherine?"

Why lie. "Yes, Grace, I'm afraid there is."

"Oh Lord Jesus."

"But I'm quite safe here with the priest in Brusly. Remember that. Brusly."

I was sitting, staring at the phone when William appeared in the doorway. "Dinner's ready, miss. Father say to tell you we got chocolate pie, so get ready for the best thing you ever et!"

CHAPTER NINETEEN

SOMETIME AFTER MIDNIGHT, I HEARD muffled voices in the hall. I jerked awake immediately, listening but unable to identify who William was talking to. The bedroom door opened just as I switched on the bedside lamp. It was Yves.

"I'm sorry to wake you. I wanted to make sure you were really here."

Was my smile as huge as his? I threw off the coverlet, not bothering to reach for my robe, and fell into his arms, into a huge hug so long I gasped, and stepped back, taking a breath and laughing. It was not in character for either of us. Gretchen always compared our teacher to me. "You're both so solemn. Neither of you laugh enough." Then she'd muss my hair, continuing, "But being an introvert isn't a bad thing. I love you both just the way you are."

I understood what she was saying and thought being an introvert described me perfectly. Sometimes, though, I did burn inside while staying quiet. Yet it seemed the best way. My life needed quiet, order. Control. Monsieur

Antoine, not Gretchen, understood that because he acted in the same way. Not shy, only quiet.

Yet at this moment we were out of character, both laughing. I wiped tears away with my hand. Our words ran over each other's. "I'm so glad to see you. I'm so glad." "Are you quite all right?" "I told myself last night you were coming, but when I got here and talked to Grace, I began to worry you would go first to Carville. I've been dreaming of opening doors to empty rooms."

I reached for my robe. Pulling it around me, I stood and looked at my closest friend, at his lean, sculptured face, and the few thin lines of age on the edge of his enormous brown eyes. Eyes that glistened with tears. Such kindness I'd seen in those eyes. He'd tried to protect two lonely, abused children.

"A malleable young man," was how Papa described him. *"He has a degree in fine arts from Tulane … and an impressive pedigree. Born in France, the son of the principal tenor with the New Orleans Opera Company."*

Yves voice brought me back. "I'm so glad I've found you."

I smiled and asked, "You must have called Grace. She told you where I was?"

"No, I talked to the Mother Superior."

"They have phone service? The telephone has been out for three days. That's why I couldn't call you."

"She told me they'd only had it restored a half-hour when I called. I didn't tell her I'd been calling several times a day for three days." He smiled. "I'm starving. And a cup of tea would warm my bones. How about you?"

"I'm sure I can find the kitchen somewhere, but we may wake Father O'Quinn," I said as we walked down a narrow hallway in single file.

"The caretaker, William, let me in. He volunteered a

cot next to him on the enclosed sleeping porch and a sandwich in the refrigerator. My guess is he's left us something to drink as well."

"What time is it anyway?" I switched on the kitchen light and spied a tea kettle on the stove. A large kitchen clock on the wall showed 12:44. I busied myself with water for the kettle, while Yves opened the icebox and found a sandwich on a plate. "I wonder you could wake William up. Did you ring the bell several times? I didn't hear it if you did. I woke up hearing voices."

He had already sat down at a large kitchen table and taken a bite of his sandwich. Swallowing, he said, "Actually, I think he must have been awake. Or my headlights woke him up. He was beside the car before I had turned off the motor. He seemed very glad to see me and even pointed to the window where you were sleeping." He looked between the two slices of bread.

I smiled. "What is it?"

"Mystery meat. And cheese. Not the best thing I've ever tasted."

I found the tea canister on the counter and the tea pot and cups above it in the cupboard. Mrs. Duggan kept an organized kitchen.

With cups in front of us, the tea steeping in the pot, I sat down across from Yves. "Good?"

He chuckled, swallowed, finally saying, "The more I chew the bigger it gets."

I poured tea, and he took a long sip then pushed the rest of the sandwich aside. "Enough of that, I think." He grinned.

So did I.

His expression changed, his voice sober. "Now, please tell me what's happened. Can you?" I nodded. "Then tell me everything. Don't leave anything out."

"It's hard to know where to begin, to put the past four days in any kind of order that makes sense."

"Start at the beginning. I want to hear it all. You believed Gretchen was murdered. Were you able to get the sheriff to order an autopsy?"

"Yes. It seems like that was a lifetime ago. What I couldn't tell you on the phone was why I suspected she was murdered. I found bruises along her back that shouldn't have been there. And blood under her fingernails. But what was strangest to me was the noose. It was so perfect. As if a professional had made it or at least someone very familiar with tying knots. Gretchen couldn't have made it."

He dropped his head, staring into his cup, saying quietly, "No. You're right, she'd never be able to make a noose."

I explained to Yves how neither Dr. Mills nor Sister Emily wanted to inform the sheriff, but that when they did agree to call, the deputy coroner arrived amazingly fast. "He was angry. He accused me of calling someone to whom the sheriff couldn't say no. Who would I know?"

"It was I." I looked at him, dumbfounded. He spoke quietly. "I painted portraits of Judge Leander Perez and his favorite granddaughter. He has a lot of influence around here, I think."

"I didn't know that."

"Judge Perez was pleased with my work. Pleased enough I thought I could ask if he could help me with a strange situation." He shrugged. "I didn't know if he would help, but he said he knew Sheriff Doucet and volunteered to give him a call."

I stuttered, "It was murder. Gretchie was murdered. She didn't die from hanging. She was drowned, then hung!"

Yves's cup rattled as he set it upon the saucer, spilling

a few drops of tea on Mrs. Duggan's spotless tablecloth. His face contorted as his mind seized the significance of what I'd said. He pushed back his chair, stood, and paced the room, his hands rubbing the sides of his head as if he wanted to wipe away the words I'd spoken.

I knew this reaction from Yves. It was his way of somehow staving off screaming or cursing, to quell rage or whatever was going on inside him. In our house, he'd exhibited this same kind of behavior, especially on mornings when he learned from us how Papa had come home drunk again.

Tears ran down my face even as I tried to keep my voice steady. "Dr. Mills told me. But I've had no official word since the deputy coroner took Gretchen's body back to Prairieville."

"I'll be back in a minute," Yves said, disappearing into the hallway.

The minutes stretched on. I wiped my tears away and finished my cup of tea and poured another. My guess was Yves was vomiting in the bathroom. I had experienced that, bile rising in my throat, being unable to swallow or breathe until the body reacted violently to pictures my mind couldn't erase. But perhaps with Yves the sandwich he ate didn't help.

When Yves reappeared and was sitting across from me again, another cup of tea in front of him, I noticed how pale he looked, how his body seemed to have shrunk, compressed against the chair.

Quietly, he said, "We'll find out who did this."

"I know. It would be so hard to lose my sister to suicide. But the idea of someone drowning her then hoping to pass it off as suicide is atrocious. I'll find the murderer."

My throat constricted as I thought of the note I carried in my book sack. "Or I'll die trying."

He was astonished. Staring across the table, his eyes wide, he said, "I'm barely holding it together, but look at you."

For the first time I realized something. I *was* holding on. And when I looked at my dearest friend with only the ticking of the kitchen clock filling the space around us, I knew it was I who, in this moment anyway, was the stronger of the two of us. And I knew very well why.

"Gretchen is with me. I've felt her everywhere at that place. She's in the very air I'm breathing. I've read her journals. You should see the beautiful mural she's painted in their fellowship hall." I sighed. "I can see her in some of the expressions on the faces of the nuns. Especially one, Sister Adelaide. My sister is leading me to her murderer, Yves."

His wilted smile encouraged me.

I rose from the table. "I must show you something." I went to my bedroom and returned with the three notes, laying them out side by side on the table.

He read them then looked up at me. "What are these? Were they sent to you?"

"Not all." I pointed. "Just the last one."

Leave or you will die.

"That was the last note and it was left on my desk yesterday afternoon."

Yves asked, "And the other two?"

"'*Don't trust the Samones*,' was given to me by Sister Adelaide. She found it in Gretchen's desk and didn't know what she should do with it."

I pointed to the last one.

A stranger will steal your baby.

"This one was given to me by a patient, Penny Langlinais. She's just given birth to a baby girl. Yesterday. She and her husband, Tom, first thought I might be the stranger."

"Yet she trusted you with the note?"

"I went to their cabin to talk to Tom because I was told he was the last person to see Gretchen alive. The meeting didn't go well. In fact, Tom all but threw me out of his house, or would have if he wasn't so ill. Yet something I said or did must have convinced them I didn't come to hurt either of them. That my search for a killer might be tied to whoever is threatening them and their baby. Penny said maybe I'd come to help them, not hurt them."

Yves studied the three notes. I stood behind him looking over his shoulder. The words made me shiver. I pulled my robe tight over my pajamas.

I said, "I think the first one was meant for Gretchen, although Sister Adelaide said perhaps it came into her possession like the second note did to me. Someone gave it to her and asked her to find out who sent it."

"But the third note was definitely left for you, wasn't it?"

I sank into the nearest chair. "I'm afraid there's no doubt of that. And I'm wondering why. It must be that the murderer thinks I know who he ... or she is."

"And do you have a suspicion?"

I took a deep breath. It was so frustrating. "Do I? I'm afraid I have too many suspicions. A young boy, Jack, told me Tom Langlinais was yelling threats at my sister the day of her death. But I don't trust Dr. Mills or Sister Emily either. Sister Emily continually puts roadblocks up against everything I've uncovered, although that might just be her personality. She's a strong-willed, I'd have to say, inflexible woman. Sometimes you have to believe what your instincts tell you, don't you? I really think Dr. Mills is hiding something. The question is, what? I've turned that question over and over. Someone must have hated Gretchen or what she represented. The Catholic Church, perhaps? It might be Dr. Mills. I told you about the noose. So perfectly made. Gretchen couldn't have done that. But Dr. Mills has a boat. He must know a lot about knots."

Yves nodded, his eyes still on the notes in front of him. "And you think Dr. Mills might hate the Catholic Church?"

I studied the tea grounds in the bottom of my cup for a minute or more. Yves knew my mind was weighing his question's pros and cons. I looked up, saying, "Probably not. When you think about it, the reasonable answer is one of the patients. A leper who blames God for his disease, and the nuns represent God to his twisted mind. Because, if they just hated my sister, why stage her suicide?"

Yves nodded. "And someone there knows enough about knots to fashion a noose."

"Could it be one of the Samoans?" I pointed to the note. "Or even Charles Bremmer? He's not a native, but he came with them from German Samoa six months ago. The fact that he told me he was a Nazi makes the hair on my neck stand up."

Yves's face jerked toward me. He blinked. "What?"

"Charles Bremmer. He's at Carville as a liaison for the Samoan patients who are in the clinical trials of a new medicine. He calls himself a missionary. He seems very charming on the surface, smiling all the time. At first, I was taken in, I admit. Now, though, I don't trust him. Sister Adelaide said Gretchen didn't think the Samoans liked him at all. One of the only natives who spoke English, who the nuns could have spoken to about Charles Bremmer, disappeared soon after they arrived. It's suspicious, isn't it? I read in Gretchen's journal the nuns knew nothing about him coming. He just appeared with papers they accepted. Odd, I think. And Gretchen thought so too."

Yves slammed his hands on the table so loudly that I jumped. He rose and walked around the table, his hands slapping his thighs. "I'm reeling from this, Catherine!"

"Sister Adelaide told me things at Carville were not always what they seemed."

"And she was right! My God!"

I took our cups and saucers to the sink and turned on the tap water to rinse them out. Turning back to Yves, I said, "There are others who might have a motive to do harm to Gretchen. I overheard a conversation between a nun and one of the patients. I think they're planning to leave the center together. Soon."

Yves raised his eyebrows. "Gretchen might have discovered their plan?"

"Yes. Murder seems a bit excessive, though, doesn't it?"

"Who knows what the criminal mind might conceive."

I nodded. "Or what secrets they may be hiding." I took a dishtowel from the drawer and began drying the cups. Yves studied the notes again.

When I'd finished, I folded the dishtowel, placed it on the counter, and sat again at the table. Yves asked, "Could the Nazi missionary have murdered Gretchen?"

I thought for a minute. "I can't imagine why. I was much more suspicious of the head man, Polanie, when I went into their camp yesterday. He made my skin crawl. Supposedly, the islanders don't speak English, yet I sensed Polanie understood every word I said.

"The note sent to Gretchen tells her not to trust them." He picked up the paper. "Did you notice 'Samoans' is spelled wrong?"

"Do you think it means something?"

"Yes." He stared at the three notes again. "The printing is almost childish, unless they have been written to appear so. If I had to guess, I'd say the writer of these notes has not had much schooling."

"Which would lead us to one of the Samoan natives. Maybe warning Gretchen against Polanie?"

"Yes, that's possible if it were only the first note. The second note tells me it's probably not an islander. You say they are segregated away from the main building. What would prompt writing to the Langlinais that their baby would be stolen? But your note is another thing. Taken altogether, they seem to form a pattern.

"Do they? I can't think what. Those words are terrifying and they certainly sent me running. I know it's exactly what the murderer wants, just as I know I have to go back. But my first thought was to run, as fast as I could."

"Of course. It would be anyone's reaction. The main thing is, I'm convinced the same person wrote all three notes.

"So what is the pattern you mentioned?"

A tiny smile appeared on his face. "Honestly, I think you may have misread these."

"I don't understand."

"He read them aloud, *'Don't trust the Samones.'* *'A stranger will steal your baby.'* *'Leave or you will die.'* I don't think these notes were meant to be threats at all. But warnings."

I stared at Yves, letting what he said sink in. It made sense.

Yves said, "Have you met anyone who may not have much education but who you think sees and hears much of what's happening at the hospital? It would have to be someone who comes and goes pretty much at will and who is the curious type. Have you met anyone like that?

I nodded my head as it dawned on me. "Yes, I have, as a matter of fact." I picked up the notes, reading them once more. "And now I think I know who wrote these," I said quietly, "but it isn't one person. It's two."

CHAPTER TWENTY

WHEN I WOKE LATER THAT morning, I looked from my bed out the window. A thick layer of fog blanketed the grounds and the levee across the road. It was like being inside a cocoon, with my bed floating on a calm sea. Except I wasn't calm inside my head. I pulled myself to a sitting position and stretched my arms over my head. I looked at the clock and realized I'd slept four hours. It was enough.

I would confront Jack and Clarice today. Why had they written those notes? Were they indeed warnings as Yves believed, or just practical jokes of young teenagers with too much time on their hands? I threw off the homespun quilt, reached for my robe, and tiptoed into the hallway toward the bathroom. I was looking forward to a hot shower.

Afterwards, I found my clothes, washed and ironed, in a neat stack on top of the bureau. Mrs. Duggan again. My how that slight blond-haired woman managed the rectory perfectly. She'd mentioned to me as she was leaving after dinner that she lived in town with her husband and three children. What an impressive lady.

I dressed in gray slacks and a black turtleneck sweater, pulled a comb through my hair, dabbed a bit of lipstick on, and decided I might pass for a living person today.

I entered the hallway and heard Father O'Quinn and Yves talking. They were in the dining room hunched over the table examining the icon.

Looking up, the priest said, "Ah, it's Catherine. See what we're doing, don't you?"

Yves acknowledged me with a nod and resumed studying the small, framed canvas on the table with his magnifying glass.

"I do indeed. And I see you've replaced me with the real expert."

"I prefer to think it is God's will or at least blind luck that you've both landed in my house when I needed your experience and knowledge"

Yves said, "Come take a look, Father. Look at the craquelure on the face. Around the eyes."

Father O'Quinn said, "What does that word mean? Cracks? Is it really an old piece?"

"Probably," Yves answered. "It's a combination of things that will tell us how old it is."

The priest bent over to have a closer look. Yves handed him the magnifying glass and grinned across the table at me.

Father O'Quinn said, "Well, would you look at that. And all those cracks in the paint mean something? What did you call it, cracks something?"

"Craquelure. But you're right. It's just a fancy word for cracks."

I left them, walked into the kitchen in search of coffee,

and returned with a cup in one hand and balancing a croissant on a plate in the other.

"Is that enough food for you, my dear? I think Mrs. Duggan is in the church arranging flowers, but William can fetch her and she'll fix you a hot breakfast."

I shook my head. "This is perfect, Father. Thanks."

"All right then."

I placed the cup and plate on the table and pulled out a chair to sit. "Father O'Quinn, may I ask you a couple of questions?" He nodded. "I've been thinking about Charles Bremmer since last night. I'm wondering when he's had time to get to know Old Jacques?"

He rubbed his chin. "Yes, I wondered about that too, but I only see Charles on Friday nights at Dr. Mills's house for dinner, so it's possible he's extended his acquaintances beyond the hospital and into the village of Carville."

"Has he shared anything about his background during all those dinners?"

"Oh, yes. We've discussed his upbringing. So unusual I think. Did you know he worked in a circus before returning to Samoa? Then he joined the church. I don't know of another minister in any church who's had that kind of background." Father O'Quinn warmed to the subject. "Yes, I'd have to say I think of him as an odd sort of fellow. Not that he isn't a superb conversationalist. Certainly more informed than I am about much of the world." His voice dropped, "But mostly I find he wants to discuss politics, and some of his information I've found to be ... shall I say, excessive?"

Yves looked up. "Anti-Jewish ideology?" Glancing first at me he continued, "He told Catherine he's a member of the National Socialists German Workers Party."

"A Nazi?" The priest frowned. "I've not been told

that." He paused. "But now something he said when we were introduced for the first time makes more sense. He said he was a missionary to the Samoans, and I asked to which denomination he belonged. I was surprised at his answer. He said he belonged to 'The Reich Church.'"

"Has he mentioned his mother living in New Orleans?"

The priest pursed his lips together. "No. No, not that I can remember. Of course, my memory isn't as good as it used to be." He paused as though searching for a thought. "You need to ask Eleanor. She would know if Charles mentioned a mother living in the city."

"Eleanor?"

"Mrs. Mills. Oh, that's right, she's been in New Orleans. But she's usually at dinner on Fridays, and between her and Sister Gretchen they would know ..." The priest blushed pink. He stood up and stepped around the table to take my hand, staring down at me. "I'm so sorry, my dear. How insensitive of me."

"Oh, please, Father. It's fine. I'm interested. So my sister was invited to Dr. Mills's dinner parties on Fridays?"

"Always. She and Eleanor were close friends. They had their passion for art in common, I think." He shook his head. "Dr. Mills told me his wife is going to be devastated when she gets home. I know she will."

Yves said, "So Sister Gretchen sat at dinner with Charles Bremmer on Fridays and listened to his opinions on the 'master race'?"

"Politics has squirmed its way into the conversation often." He chuckled. "But just as often, Eleanor has prompted Charles to regale us with his experiences in the circus. Do you know he professed to love a trapeze artist who specialized in *corde lisse*? None of us knew that term."

"Neither do I."

"It's someone who hangs upside down from a rope. Doing poses of some kind, I think."

Yves said, "Oh, yes. I've seen those acts but didn't know what they were called."

"Charles was madly in love with her and told us he always double-checked her rigging, afraid she might fall. It was sweet but unrequited love. The girl shunned him for the circus manager."

The priest turned to check the time and patted my hand again. "I've got my first Mass in ten minutes. Did I help you at all?"

"Oh, yes, Father. And we won't forget the icon. Yves will examine it closely."

Yves said, "I'll take samples of the wood panel back to New Orleans with me. I can test it there."

"That will tell you how old it is?"

"Yes. But it takes more than the age of the wood to determine if it's authentic. I wish I could test the pigments in the paint as well, but that would mean taking it with me."

"But that's what you must do. Take it to your laboratory. Do all the tests."

Yves laboratory was a shelf with a few tools, some chemicals, and a workbench, in a shed in the backyard of my house. But regardless, the praise he'd received in the field of art documentation was real.

Yves said, "Are you sure, Father? Do you really want your icon out of your sight?"

The priest picked up an old leather valise in the corner of the room. "Put it in here. It seems as though it may have been inside this suitcase for a long time."

"Protecting it."

"Yes indeed." The priest headed for the door but

paused, turning around. *"Protecting.* I remember Sister Gretchen using that word at dinner several weeks ago. Speaking to Charles. I thought it was a strange thing for her to say."

"She wasn't talking about your icon?"

"No, no. She was talking about the Samoans. It was an awkward moment between Charles and Sister Gretchen. That word bothered me when I heard it. The whole conversation seemed odd."

I held my breath.

Yves asked, "Why, Father?"

"Protecting them. That's what Sister Gretchen said. She wanted all the Samoans moved to the main building to *protect them.*"

"Did she say why they needed protecting?"

"Actually, she didn't. I got the feeling she'd said something to him earlier because of the way Charles jumped in on top of her words, saying she was wrong and that it would be a tremendous mistake to move them. And, as I recall, Dr. Mills said he wouldn't approve such a move because the hospital had put a tremendous amount of expense toward building separate quarters. Then Charles ended the conversation by telling Sister Gretchen she was wrong about Enoka."

I explained to Yves, "Enoka was the Samoan man who disappeared shortly after they arrived. The one whose body was never recovered. Father O'Quinn looked at the kitchen clock. "Oh, I've got to go. Now I'm late." Shaking hands with Yves he said, "Please take my treasure back to New Orleans with you, Monsieur Antoine, and bring me wonderful news on my discovery!"

Yves smiled. "I'll do my best." He rose to take his hand. "Thank you for your hospitality, Father."

"Of course, of course." He turned to me. "Catherine, what are your plans? I hope you will travel with your friend."

"Yes, but I must return to Carville and wait for my sister's body to be released to me. I want to take her home."

Tears rose to the old man's eyes. "Of course. And, please God, soon we will know who did this horrible thing." He made the sign of the cross on my forehead, blessing me. "You will take care, won't you?"

The look on his face froze the words in my mouth.

"I'll be with her," Yves said.

"Good. Watch out for her, Monsieur Antoine." He turned and headed for the door, but I heard him mutter to himself, "A terrible, terrible business."

Yves wrapped the icon in white muslin tea towels borrowed from the kitchen, then packed it into the suitcase and fastened the leather straps.

"Are you ready to go?" he asked.

"Not really. But I will be. I'll have a stern talk with myself about fear while I'm packing my case."

CHAPTER TWENTY-ONE

THE ROAD WAS A NEEDLE we threaded through the fog, rolling along comfortably in Yves's sleek, black roadster. He turned on yellow fog lights, driving slow beside the indefinable earthen levee, toward the ferry. I felt an emptiness to the beginning of this day, like one feels at a funeral. Staring at nothingness. At a hole in the ground waiting for the dead. I swallowed, leaning back into the seat, closing my eyes. A little more than twelve hours before, I was running for my life and now I was heading back to the same place.

After crossing the river and descending down the gangplank of the ferry, Yves drove cautiously on the gravel road. We sat silently. He turned off his fog lights and continued until we saw an outline of the iron gate. He pulled over and parked.

"No sheriff's car," he said. "What in the world's keeping them, you think?"

"I don't know, but I don't think you should park inside the gate. Not if you're still bent on doing some exploring on your own. I'm sure once the sheriff gets here, the rules will change about anyone walking about. I'll show you where my quarters are. You can park around the side."

He nodded, drove slowly, allowing the vehicle to submerge itself within the thick fog. He parked the car in the grass, between the two guest houses. The car would not be in anyone's direct view, though I was sure it wouldn't be long before Jack and Clarice discovered it. I must make sure it was locked securely.

"I'm not sure we weren't seen or heard by someone," Yves said as he stood and stretched.

I opened my door, grabbed my satchel from the backseat, stood, and hung it with the strap slung across my body. "If they did hear us, then I'll explain why you came with me. You might have been so tired from your drive from New Orleans you decided to take a nap in my quarters, right?"

He grinned. "You're getting more devious by the minute."

"Are you still bent on going to the Samoan village? I wish you'd reconsider."

Yves opened the trunk to the car, taking out a sketch book, a small leather shoulder pouch, and a camera on a strap. He said, "Why write that note to Gretchen if there isn't something going on there? Father O'Quinn's story about Gretchen wanting to move the natives for their own protection sent a chill down my spine."

"Me too." I paused for a few seconds. "I need to come with you."

He walked around the front of the coupe to where I stood. "I would feel so much better if I knew you were safe inside the hospital with the nuns and the rest of the staff nearby." He smiled as I nodded, acquiescing. "But I will need your help on how to find their village."

I listed the paths I knew of, the main road that started at the side of the nuns' quarters on the hospital grounds, and the path Charles had shown me, next to the swamp. But both of those, I explained, would necessitate his walking near the main building.

"I think the best way is right behind my quarters. It's not a road, I think, but a worn path. It's how I found Penny and Tom Langlinais's cabin. It follows a fallow sugar cane field and some woods. The bayou is right behind the house; I don't think you can miss it. If you follow it, I think you'll come to a boat landing. It can't be too far from the Samoan village."

A raised voice called, "Miss Clary, is that you?"

Yves put a finger to his mouth and took a few steps to the corner of the house, to peer across the street. I followed, standing behind him.

"It's Rose, the doctor's housekeeper," I whispered. "You'd better go before she sees you."

I pointed the direction of the path I'd mentioned, and nodding, he adjusted the straps around his neck, then disappeared into the fog.

I still didn't know what Yves thought he would find at the Samoan village. Something hidden? Would a new pair of eyes catch something I didn't see? What if Polanie saw him? Drawing my jacket around me, I prayed silently, *Protect him, Gretchie.*

I stepped from the side of the house and into the road. I was going to the hospital to wait for the sheriff's investigation to start. I guessed that every single person, patient or staff, would be interviewed. How many people was that? Fifty? Probably more.

I crossed the road to Dr. Mills's house. Rose was standing on the porch.

"Miss Lyle? Why you in the road?" She was flustered, her arms crossed. I took the bottom step and looked up at her. She continued, "We thought you gone away."

"No, Rose. I don't think I can leave for good until I know who murdered my sister."

Her arms came up to cover her face with her hands, then flailing them in the air, her body shook as she let out a loud gasp. "It's an evil here, for sure!"

I took another step up toward her, but she backed away. "Rose, I'm going to the hospital. If you're afraid, come with me."

Her eyes found mine. She sighed. "It ain't me the devil want, Miss Lyle. I'm pretty sure of that." Her eyes looked warily beyond me.

"Who is the devil interested in, Rose?"

She looked stunned. "I said more than I should. You go on now, Miss Lyle. It'd be better for you to get over there."

I didn't move. "I'm wondering why you were calling Clarice? Today's Sunday, she can't be truant."

"No, miss. She just run out of the house like nobody tell her nothing! But I thought I heard her and Jack talkin'. This fog so thick." Her face changed. "Was that you talkin' to Jack?"

I evaded her question. "No, I don't know where they are, but I'd like a conversation with them myself."

"That child don't mind nobody! She say she's going to find Sister Adelaide, and I tell her no, 'cause her daddy say she's not to leave the house at all today. So what do she do but run out the door anyway. Now her daddy goin' to have both our hides for this 'cause it ain't safe out there today with Sister missin'!"

"What are you talking about, Rose?"

"You don't know? They can't find Sister Adelaide

nowhere. They's said she disappeared ..." Tears began to stream down Rose's face. "It's the devil! He come to take away all the nuns!"

I put my hand out on the porch's post, trying to comprehend the words. I thought, *Steeling oneself to hear or see horrible things. Is that the test?*

"I must see Sister Emily," I said, steadying myself to walk.

"Please send Miss Clary back home, you see her."

"Yes, I will." I tasted bile as it rose in my throat. I walked down the road. A steely sun appeared, burning away the fog. I pushed open the iron gate and the front door and walked into the hallway, where an unnatural quiet hung in the air.

Sister Emily sat behind her desk. Her eyes widened in surprise when she looked up and saw me. She shook her head. I didn't need to ask.

"We didn't miss Sister Adelaide until this morning. We started to leave for chapel and Sister Anne asked where she was. She wasn't in her room. Her bed was made, but whether she disappeared last night or this morning we just don't know." There was visible perspiration on Sister Emily's forehead.

Her office was too hot. I saw that the space heater was still churning out heat, in spite of today's rising temperature. Sister Emily had forgotten about the heater. Everyone had forgotten about whether rooms were too hot or too cold. Sister Adelaide was missing.

I sat down on a small chair near the door. She said softly, "Some of the more able men wanted to walk the grounds. I spoke to everyone in chapel this morning. I told them it's very possible Sister Adelaide just wanted to find a quiet place to pray. But they wanted to do that ..."

She moved a paper on her desk and mumbled, "I let them. Sister Adelaide should not frighten us like this."

"They should look in the root cellar first."

"Why would they do that?"

"I was trapped down there yesterday. Someone followed me, and when I went down into the cellar, they shut the door."

"Why ever would you be down in that cellar, Catherine?"

I laughed slightly "That's not quite the point, is it? If you must know, I went to fetch the noose used to fake my sister's murder. I had it in my hand when someone slammed the door on top of me."

"How did you ..."

"Sister Adelaide came along. But, actually, I have you to thank, because she said you saw me walking toward the mansion on the shortcut path through the hedge. She said you sent her to remind me of Mass."

"Yes."

I stared at her. "Anyway, they won't be able to use the suicide ruse again. The game's up on that business."

She winced, rubbed her hands together, trying to still an involuntary tremor, asking, "What do you mean? You can't believe she's been murdered?"

I wanted to scream into her face, "Of course she has!" but I looked away, taking a deep breath. The silent moment stretched out between us. I stood and moved over to her windows. The fog was gone. A blue sky provided a backdrop to a view of the tall hedge and the top of the mansion.

Sister Emily said, "We really have no reason to think anything has happened to her ..." Before she could finish, a coughing spasm took hold of her.

I turned around. "Sister ..."

Sister Clara appeared at the doorway. Sister Emily waved her away. "I'm fine, I'm fine," she croaked.

"Sister Clara," I asked, "when did you last see Jack? Did he go out looking for Sister Adelaide?"

Sister Clara threw me a look of annoyance as she poured water into a glass, placing it on the desk. Her comment was to Sister Emily. "We're so worried about you. You've got to go and lie down."

"Not until Sheriff Doucet arrives."

"Have you talked to him recently?" I asked.

"He'll be here soon." She took a long drink of water, swallowed, put her hand around her throat. "I'm a bit hoarse ..."

Sister Clara said, "You've a nasty case of bronchitis and there's no need to be here in this office now." She turned, her expression angry, her voice raised at me. "And all your questions don't help her!

"I've as much right to ask questions as anyone! My sister's been murdered and what's being done about it? Nothing!"

Both of them looked shocked, but I didn't care. Though I did lower my voice. "I'm as upset about Sister Adelaide as you are. I'm going right out of here and looking in every place I can think of. But please, *please* tell me if you hear from the sheriff."

A couple of minutes later, I stamped out into the hallway, past the pharmacy. The information had been terse. "The sheriff is on his way. Any minute now. A bridge is out on the Prairieville Road, so they must take the long way around, over the Huey Long Bridge in Baton Rouge. They'll take the ferry at White Castle.

"Catherine?"

I heard the small voice and knew at once it was Penny

Langlinais. I turned away from the front door to see her standing in the hallway.

"I recognized your voice," she said.

"I'm sure it was loud enough to be heard by everyone in the building. What are you doing out of bed, Penny?" I hastened to walk her back into her room behind the pharmacy's office and helped her into bed. Her face was red. Whether it was from crying or the temperature in the room I wasn't sure. I cracked both windows. She held the sleeping infant in her arms and tried to smile.

"How is Hope today?"

I had said the right thing. Penny's face suddenly softened, and with a smile, she answered. "Oh, she's fine. She's such a good baby." She held out her hand and I took it. She whispered, "Sister Adelaide came to see me before daylight. She left something for you; if you should return, I was to give it to you, but if you didn't, I was to give it over to the sheriff," she said.

"Really?" I closed the door then sat on the chair next to her bed.

"It's under the mattress."

With my hand, I felt between the mattress and the box spring of Penny's bed and withdrew Gretchen's journal.

"Sister said to tell you, you were right. She did find something unusual in the Sister Gretchen's journal."

"Did she tell you what it was?"

Her eyes averted, she said, "Just that she needed to check on something."

"Where was she going? Didn't she tell you?" I saw her lips tremble. She readjusted Hope to her other arm, her eyes focused tightly on her baby. "Penny?" I thought maybe she didn't hear me, intent as she was with her baby.

Penny looked at me. "To our house. She wanted to talk to Tom."

I was confused. "So whatever was unusual in Gretchen's journal, Tom has the answer? What could that be?"

I saw fear in her eyes. "I don't know."

"You don't know why Sister Adelaide has gone to talk to your husband?" My tone wasn't exactly unkind, but Hope squirmed, opened her eyes, and looked at me with growing concern.

Penny studied the wall behind me. "It's nothing, really. Dr. Mills has Tom on the new medicine now. The sulphanilamide. Sister Adelaide said she was going to ask Tom why Dr. Mills started him in the trial six months after it started. But I told her, why did it matter anyway? Dr. Mills knew how bad Tom needed it and decided to give it to him. That's all."

"Who's been giving him the injections, Penny?" A good question, I thought, since Gretchen and her assistant, Sister Adelaide, obviously didn't have a clue as to Tom's treatment. "Which nun has been giving Tom his injections?"

Penny avoided eye contact, stroking Hope's hair. "I'm not sure."

I swallowed hard. "All right. Then tell me when Tom was put into the trial?"

She looked up at me. "Monday."

I thought, last Monday? The day my sister's body was found? I studied the cover of the journal in my lap, opened it and flipped through its pages. I remembered something. Gretchen's entries. Five or six of them complaining that Dr. Mills wouldn't put Tom on the experimental drug or in the test group.

I recalled those entries for six months, in her tiny, neat

handwriting, of confrontations again and again with Dr. Mills over Tom being left out of the medical trials. I wondered aloud, "Why didn't Sister Adelaide go and ask Dr. Mills directly? Isn't his office just a few doors down the hall?"

Tears welled in the young mother's eyes. "I begged her not to. I was afraid for Tom."

"I'm so sorry, Penny. I didn't mean to upset you. It's just me. My head doesn't feel screwed on very tight right now."

"Hold Hope, Catherine. Hold her for a second." She held out the infant to me to take into my arms. I didn't want to. I had to go to Tom and Penny's cabin. Sister Adelaide needed me *now*. I didn't have time to hold her baby. The real truth was, there was something about this tiny little thing that frightened me. I didn't want to hold her. But of course I accepted her into my arms.

Hope examined me with her round, blue eyes. I imagined there was no gaze in the world like that of an infant whose eyes were seeing life around her for the first time. She should have screwed up her face because I was not her mother; that's what my brother, Joseph, always did. It was a strange sensation to feel her curious eyes on me.

"She loves to be held."

I rocked her gently in my arms. *Such a small, innocent thing*, I thought.

"You get over being afraid of them," she said.

I smiled at Penny. "Yes, I guess you would."

"You learn they're not going to break."

I flinched. *Everything breaks.* I handed the baby back to her mother. "I've got to go. I've got to find Sister Adelaide and tell her everyone is searching for her."

Penny put the baby down on a pillow next to her, reached up, and took my hand. "Please. Please, Catherine, I might not see you again. Just one more thing. I know it's important for you to talk to Sister, but may I ask you for a tremendous favor?"

"A favor?"

"Yes." She composed herself for a few seconds. "I just hope you understand why I'm asking you." She paused, setting her chin before spilling out, "Would you take Hope with you when you leave here? It wouldn't be forever. Oh no. I'm a little over six months clear of disease right now; I've only six more to go before I can be discharged. Forever." Her tears made rivulets on her cheeks, but she held her voice in check. "Of course, I couldn't leave Tom. Even if I'm clear. I don't know how long it will be, before he ... well, you know. Anything can happen. I know miracles can happen. But you wouldn't have to take care of Hope that long. I know you wouldn't. Tom wants me to leave here when I'm clear. I've told him no, I won't, but, well, one of us needs to raise our baby. We've made up our minds. God will decide if it's both of us, or ..." she turned away and whispered, "or just me."

I was stunned. "Oh, oh, Penny. You can't mean it. I can't take care of a baby. I'm such a mess I can't take care of myself." I struggled for the words. "Besides, both you and Tom have family. Family to love and cherish little Hope."

She squeezed my hand and with the other one wiped away tears. "Oh, sure. My family has already decided, you see. Hope will be adopted by my sister. I've told Mama over and over I'm going to be discharged, but she says it will never be." She swallowed. "She said, 'Wouldn't it be a blessing to Hope to have a healthy family?' Oh, yes, my family knows what's best for my baby, all right!" She pointed to a folder on the chest across the room. "Adoption papers. They want to take her away from here next week."

I closed my eyes. "Oh no."

"I'm not going to give my baby to anyone. Not to my sister, not to anyone."

"Tom surely must have family."

"No. No one. His folks were sharecroppers somewhere in Oklahoma. They've disappeared from his life. The last letter he had from anyone was one paragraph from his sister saying they were going to California to make a new life." A deep wetted sigh. "So you see, there's no one to help us. And then you came. The minute I saw you I thought you were the answer to my prayers."

"Not to Tom's. I'm pretty sure of that."

"He's not feeling too good lately. He really thought the new medicine the doctor gave him would help, but so far it hasn't. But it's less than a week. Maybe it takes a little longer." Her eyes got bigger. Tears ran down her cheeks. My hand was almost numb she held it so tight. Seconds passed in silence. "Please, Catherine. You've got to help us. Otherwise, they're going to force us to give our baby away."

I wrenched my hand free and stood shaking my head. "There must be someone else, Penny. Forgive me. I wish I could help you, I do." I wanted to run. "I'll tell you what. Let me go and find Sister Adelaide and we'll both come back and talk about this. It's not a problem that can't be solved. We just need to think some more. I'll see you in a little while. And I won't say no, not yet. We'll think of something. Will that do?"

"All right."

But clearly it wasn't all right. And I feared I couldn't ever make it that way.

CHAPTER TWENTY-TWO

HE PUT TOM INTO THE program *the day after my sister was murdered.* I wanted to know why. A moment of hesitation and I might have changed my mind, but I ignored my trepidation. I walked the few steps to Dr. Mills's office and knocked on his door. If anyone knew why a patient had been moved into the Public Health Service's special experimental program six months after the trials had already begun, it would be Dr. Mills. Penny might be afraid and may have convinced Sister Adelaide not to confront him for an answer, but I was not.

The doctor answered, "Who's there?"

I opened the door, stuck my head inside, surprised at what I saw. David Mills held a woman in his arms, her head on his shoulder. She turned toward me, tears on her face. Her chin quivered.

Heat rose quickly to my cheeks. "I'm sorry, Dr. Mills. I didn't mean to interrupt …"

The woman moved a couple of steps, and with a hand as cold as ice, shook mine. "You must be Sister Gretchen's sister. I'm so happy to meet you." She spoke in a quiet voice, tilted her head then, and glanced back at the doctor, as though uncertain what came next.

Coming forward, he put his arm back around her shoulders. "My wife, Eleanor, Miss Lyle. She's just got off the ferry. I was telling her about Sister Gretchen."

Standing there in a full-length hooded traveling cloak, Eleanor might have been beautiful or not, but her eyes took one in and wouldn't let go. They were green with brown and gold specks, startling against her porcelain-white complexion.

She said, "I'm so sorry. So sorry. Sister was my closest friend. It's terrible. Terrible!"

Dr. Mills whispered, "It's all right. It's all right, Eleanor. Here, sit down. Take deep breaths."

Eleanor's body went slack into the cushions of the chair. She said, "We must talk, Miss Lyle. She meant everything to me. What will I do without her?" Her words slurred, "David? Let me talk to her ..."

"You'll have plenty of time to talk to Catherine, dear, but I've given you a sedative and it's making you sleepy." He shrugged then motioned that we step outside the door. "Sorry, but she's going to sleep a few hours. It's for her own good. Sister Gretchen and my wife were very close, and this is too much for her right now. But it would do her good to talk to you about their friendship. Just not until later."

"Of course. I'm sorry to have barged in like that."

"What was it you wanted?"

I hesitated. "Nothing that can't wait."

"In that case, look in on Eleanor tonight. She'll be stronger by then."

Heading for the front door, I turned the corner into the main hall and collided with a lanky young man in uniform, gun strapped to his side, rushing, or at least moving with purpose.

"What the hell?" rang in my ears as we both regained our balance. Through the windows on the front door, I caught a glimpse of a police car, St. Gabriel emblazoned on its side.

"Excuse me. So sorry," I said.

The confused, surprised expression on his face quickly turned to agitation. I saw a perplexed young man struggling to regain composure or credibility, probably both. My fleeting thought, if this was Sheriff Doucet here to lead an investigation into my sister's murder and Sister Adelaide's disappearance, we were all surely lost. Just as quickly, though, I knew he was not the sheriff. His eyes looked too innocent.

Inanely, I found myself staring at the young man's hat. What was the protocol for officers of the law and hats? Were they supposed to take them off inside buildings, like other gentlemen? Or was his hat a part of the uniform, part of the mystique of being in law enforcement? Any mystery this gangly boy could muster would be a plus. I would have welcomed something more than his cockiness, shuffling feet, hunched shoulders, and wrinkled forehead. Then I noticed he was lame.

"Are you in charge, here?" he asked in a thick country accent.

"No. That person is Sister Emily." I pointed. "Her office is at the far end of the hall."

"Staff?"

"No. Nor patient either."

He nodded and, dismissing me, turned away, taking a few steps. He was pigeon toed or crippled. That's what gave him such a strange gait.

"I'm nobody. The murder victim was my sister."

He stopped in his tracks and turned around. At that moment Sister Clara and Sister Edith appeared from the hospital ward.

"Kevin, what are you doing here?" Sister Clara asked.

The officer straightened his back saying to the nuns, "Follow me." He then pointed at me. "You too."

I needed to get out of there. Whether Adelaide needed my help or not, I wanted to find her, see her standing in front of me in one piece. But it seemed I wasn't going to be allowed to do so.

Inside her office, Sister Emily sat behind her desk, but Sister Paul also was there and Sister Anne, both sitting on straight chairs in front of her. The officer pulled three more chairs from a room across the hall and arranged them in a semi-circle around the desk. He motioned for Sister Clara, Sister Edith, and me to sit on them.

"What's this all about, Sister Emily?" Sister Clara asked.

"Sheriff Doucet called this morning. He wanted me to know he was calling the police department in Carville to send a deputy. Officer? Sir, what's your name?"

"Deputy Kevin Cormier, ma'am." He cleared his throat. "Sheriff Doucet ordered me to protect the nuns till he gets here. Is this all them, ma'am?"

"All except Sister Adelaide."

"The missing one?"

Sister Emily nodded.

I stood up. "Well, I'm not a nun. You've no reason to keep me here." I spoke with more vigor than I felt.

"He said you too, yes, ma'am. If you're Miss Catherine Lyle." I sat back down.

Sister Clara said, "We can't all sit in this room until the sheriff gets here! Who's going to be on the desk in the ward?"

"How many are in the ward right now?" Sister Emily asked.

"Six. We can't leave them unattended." Then, "And there's injections today."

Kevin said, "I'm sorry, Aunt Clara. I got my orders direct from Sheriff Doucet. He said I was to protect all of you till he gets here." He opened the door. "I'll be right outside. Lock it from the inside and don't open it to anyone but me."

Sister Clara was on her feet. She grabbed his arm. "Kevin, that won't do. It simply won't do."

Sister Emily's voice sounded quite hoarse, but she managed, "Deputy Cormier, Sister Clara is right. We can't leave the hospital ward unattended. There are very sick people in there."

"What about Lillian?" Everyone turned to Sister Anne. I loved her eyes. So blue and bright one forgot her shrunken little body and wrinkled face. Her eyes always danced.

Sister Clara weighed the suggestion before answering, "Yes, that would be all right. She was a nurse before she contracted the disease. She's helped out before." Sister Clara stared down Officer Cormier. "As long as we don't ask her to sit all day, Kevin. How long is our confinement going to be?"

"Just till Sheriff gets here. Maybe an hour. Two. Not long."

The group of nuns nodded, agreeing silently, and Sister Edith was dispatched to Lillian's room along with the officer.

We were a silent group when Sister Edith returned ten minutes later, the cook behind her with a tray of sandwiches and a pitcher of water. "Lillian was happy to sit in the infirmary. She'll come get me if there's a problem.

And I thought we might need something to eat since we don't know how long it will be."

Sister Edith took her seat again. We were silent as we ate, except for Emily making odd noises in her throat. I rose, walked to the back of the room, and turned off the space heater and cracked a window before sitting again.

"Don't you think you should have asked Sister Emily before you turned off the heat?" Sister Clara said.

Sister Emily waved her hand. "It's fine."

I looked over at Clara, her fingers at work in her lap, clasping and unclasping, in nervous agitation. "Officer Cormier is your nephew?"

She looked at me. "What?"

"He called you Aunt Clara."

She pursed her lips, "My sister's child."

It wasn't hard to picture Clara as a nun, her back stiffly erect against the back of her chair. Her demeanor reminded me of several teachers I'd had at the academy in New Orleans. But the fact she was from the small village just down the road was interesting. As a child she must have heard horror stories. How could she not? A disease so misunderstood. Yet Sister Clara chose to devote her entire life to the sufferers. As I watched her fingers working her rosary beads, she seemed bigger, taller, stronger.

"Deputy Cormier is very professional. You must be proud of him."

Her expression softened. "Yes, I am. He was born with a club foot, but he hasn't let that stop him."

I looked at their worried faces. And even without their lips moving, I sensed they were praying. There was no murderer here. Secrets, yes. Behind their flowing dresses and huge headpieces, I saw frightened women, a thin veneer of courage ready to crack like fissures on wood planks.

"Sisters, I need your help," I said.

Fingers that had been moving across the beads in their laps stopped. Each pair of eyes focused on me. I took Gretchen's journal from my satchel and passed it to Sister Paul. "Sister Adelaide was in Penny's room before daylight."

The group around me burst into spontaneous sighs, smiles, clasping their hands to their chests, covering their hearts. It forced me to smile back at them, not wanting to go on, but knowing I had to. "That was before daylight, Sisters. It's now past eleven."

Sister Edith asked, "Why did she visit Penny?"

Would this be the right time to tell them about Dr. Mills changing Tom's treatment? I decided to wait. "She left my sister's journal with her and a message telling me she had found something in Gretchen's journal. 'Something unusual,' she said. She wanted to ask Tom about it."

Sister Paul flipped the pages. "These are wonderful watercolors. She's captured how beautiful the Samoan people are."

"May I see?" Sister Paul handed it to Sister Anne. "It's Lale."

Sister Emily asked, "May I see it?"

Sister Anne handed the journal across the desk to Sister Emily who turned the pages slowly, as though trying to absorb every stroke of Gretchen's brush or pencil.

Sister Edith spoke up, "Enoka Noa and Lale were lovers, I think. At least Sister Adelaide told me she thought so, and when Enoka Noa disappeared, Lale seemed inconsolable."

"Everyone was," Sister Clara said.

"Yes, I know. But Sister Adelaide told me Lale took it the hardest." Sister Edith slumped in her chair, spreading her hands in front of her, "Of course, you're right, Sister. Everyone was sad to lose Enoka Noa."

Sister Clara nodded. "It was too bad. He seemed to be the one in charge. After he was gone, Sister Gretchen told me the group became disjointed, lost somehow. She mentioned it more than once. There was little we could do. They spoke so little English, and none of us understood Samoan."

"But surely in the six months Charles Bremmer has been teaching them English they can communicate to you, in simple ways?" I said.

I received blank stares from the nuns.

Sister Clara said, "We know nothing about English lessons."

Sister Emily closed the journal and handed it across the desk. Quietly, she said, "Sister Gretchen was right."

Thunderstruck, I leaned across her desk. "What? What did you say, Sister?"

"I need a glass of water, Sister Clara. Please?"

After taking a sip, then placing it carefully on a napkin, Sister Emily said, "Sister Gretchen told me she thought food supplies were being stolen from the Samoan camp. She was replenishing too often. She worried the Samoans weren't getting enough to eat." She paused. "Since these drawings and watercolors were completed six months ago, most of the men and women have deteriorated into shadows of themselves."

My brain raced, remembering the first night I saw Polanie and another man unloading the church pews from the barge. "Those men, the ones unloading the crates the night I arrived. They looked fine."

"That's true. I told Sister Gretchen it was the medication, or depression, or both affecting some of the patients. But not all."

"My sister disagreed with you?"

"Sister Gretchen tested over and over. The disease was either in remission or actually improving with the new drug, in everyone but one poor soul. Sister Gretchen was so hopeful this was the breakthrough we'd been praying for." Sister Emily frowned, pointing at the journal. "I suggested to her it was depression. They were so far from their home. But I can see in her sketches they seemed happy when they arrived."

Sister Clara said, "Who could deprive patients of food?"

Sister Emily nodded. "That's what I asked Sister Gretchen. Who would want to steal from the Samoans?"

Sister Clara added, "Besides that, it's not possible. Someone would notice."

Sister Anne said, "And someone did. Sister Gretchen. Isn't that right, Sister Emily?"

Silence permeated the group as all eyes looked at the old nun.

Sister Emily spoke first. "You're right. But I didn't believe her." Her eyes focused on me. "I hypothesized with Sister Gretchen; if we discovered food and other supplies missing, then we had to ask for what reason." She paused. "Neither of us could answer that. Perhaps some of the Polynesians had a vendetta against others. But it didn't ring true. They all came here from Falefa. They knew one another before. Remember the welcome party in the fellowship hall?"

Sister Emily took another sip from her glass. "They listened to Enoka and obviously looked to him as their leader, but I didn't see jealousy or animosity toward him, and I didn't see it between the others. I know Sister Gretchen knew them all."

"But how much did anyone really know them?" I asked

"The scene Charles Bremmer played out for me two days ago was a lie. They aren't getting English lessons. I'm sorry, but I think the Samoans or Charles Bremmer must have had something to do with my sister's death. Maybe she discovered a secret so threatening she was murdered for it."

Sister Paul raised her hand. Every eye turned toward her. "There's something you all don't know." She took a breath. "It involves John Weller." She cleared her throat, and I wondered if she about to tell them she was leaving the order to run away with John Weller. When she spoke his name aloud, I looked away. How painful for her. Sister Paul and I might not agree on many things, but I wished I was not in the room. Such personal, private matters did not need to be shared with outsiders.

"As you all know John's real name is Adam Wolf. Recently, some of his reporter friends have convinced him German spies may be trying to infiltrate our Gulf coast and along the Mississippi River."

"What?" My startled reaction was mirrored on other faces around me. I certainly knew who Adam Wolf was, had read his byline on stories in *The New York Times*. But did I question when it no longer appeared? No. Adam Wolf had disappeared and no one asked why. How sad.

Sister Paul continued, "John came to me after Enoka Noa disappeared six months ago. He said he believed the native man might have been murdered because he suspected one of the patients wasn't sick at all but just playing a part. At this point, John is positive Charles Bremmer is a point person behind an infiltration of German spies."

Sister Clara spoke first, reflecting the incredulous expressions appearing on our faces. "What? But that's unbelievable. Here? How could anyone have an idea like that?"

"Why Charles Bremmer?" Sister Emily asked.

"Nazis. Remember, Charles has been very open with his politics."

I was stunned. "Sister Paul, one of Gretchen's watercolors had the words, 'too many' written in the margin. What did she mean?"

Sister Paul shrugged. "I don't know. But John might have an idea." At that moment, we all heard muffled voices behind the door.

Sister Edith stood and put her ear to the door. Sitting down again she whispered, "It's Dr. Mills."

Several knocks. "This is Deputy Cormier, Sisters. Please open the door."

Sister Edith obeyed, to reveal the young officer and an angry-looking Dr. Mills.

"I must ask why our entire hospital is now void of anyone to take care of patients. May I ask why you have decided to hold this meeting?"

"Hardly a meeting, Dr. Mills," said Sister Emily. "We and Miss Lyle were ordered to remain in my office until Sheriff Doucet arrived." She looked at the red-faced young officer. "Deputy Cormier, do we know yet when that might be?"

"No, Sister, but I know it won't be long now. My orders were to protect the nuns."

"In the meantime," the doctor said, "we've a patient on the desk in the ward, a line of patients waiting for injections, cook asking me what the menu for dinner is, blood tests unanalyzed, and several men and women out of the gate searching for our missing nun!"

I wanted to add, and a distraught wife for him to take care of.

Sister Emily raised her voice, answering, "Dr. Mills,

this young man, excuse me, Officer Cormier, has his orders. We intend to obey them. Please try to cope with the situation for an hour, at most!"

With tight, pursed lips, the doctor stared at her, finally saying, "Very well." He turned on his heel and left.

Sister Clara's lips twisted into a tight smile, "You may shut the door, Kevin. We'll lock it from the inside."

"Yes, Aunt Clara … Sister."

A couple of minutes later, I broke the silence. "Sister Paul, I heard you talking to John Weller on the levee. Sorry I eavesdropped on a personal conversation. I thought you were making plans to run away together."

Sister Paul blushed a deep red. Her laughter lightened everyone's solemn expressions. "How wonderful you are, Catherine." She laughed again. "We're talking about murder and you can make us all laugh in spite of it."

"He mentioned December 21. He's leaving on that date and he wants you to go with him."

"Yes, well that's true. When he found out Sister Gretchen was murdered, John said he had to get word to the Coast Guard and let them know about Charles Bremmer. He's in remission and has received a pass to visit his parents in Philadelphia over Hanukkah. But now he's changed his mind about going there. He's going to 'borrow' the doctor's boat and go to the Coast Guard station. I say borrow because he doesn't intend to tell Dr. Mills what or where he's going. It's important, he says, to tell them what he suspects here."

"He wants you to go with him?"

"Yes, he's afraid he'll lack credibility because he's a patient. He wants me there for that reason. I've been hesitating because," she motioned with her hands to the other nuns, "like you, I wasn't ready to believe him. Except for his hatred of the Nazis and therefore Charles Bremmer, he couldn't prove a single thing." She stopped for a moment and turned to me. "He's very impressed with your tenacious determination, Catherine. You wouldn't back down from proving your sister was murdered. He says his people call that chutzpah."

Now it was my turn to blush.

Sister Emily said thoughtfully, "You know, John is still connected with what's happening outside. I suppose it's because he still has so many friends in the newspaper business."

Sister Anne offered, "He receives lots of mail. So many books."

Sister Emily nodded. "I'm sure John's information has provided him with more than just a passing suspicion about Charles Bremmer."

Sister Paul said, "Oh, yes. He's sent photographs of Charles to some of his contacts. But they've not discovered anything. Not yet. Have any of you heard of someone called Derwent Whittlesey?

No one had. Sister Paul explained he was the author of *German Strategy of World Conquest,* of the Nazis' plan not only to dominate Europe, but beyond that, to control of the entire world.

"But how on earth can the Germans do that?" I asked.

"The same way they've done it in Austria and Poland and now France. I don't remember all his points, but a main one is destroying sea power. It begins with infiltrating enemy bases with spies and sending the information to Nazi Germany. The next step is to send in their submarines. John says they're called U-boats."

It was hard to digest. But at the same time, I had a burning desire to talk to John Weller, to somehow try to put my head around such ideas. Suppose it was true? "How would they do it?" I asked.

"That's just it," Sister Paul said, "They couldn't. Not here. I told him. We see what's happening every day. Sister Gretchen and Sister Adelaide had the closest contact with the Samoans."

"And they saw too much perhaps." It was Sister Clara.

I said, "On this huge piece of property, it wouldn't be hard to hide someone like a spy, would it? I think that's what my sister meant. *Too many.*" The puzzle pieces in my mind were coming together. Too many men in the canoe as it crossed the river. If my sister questioned Charles, then she became a threat. It would be necessary to eliminate her. Yes, both she and Sister Adelaide had access to the Samoans every day, and it put them both in grave danger, didn't it?

I stared at the faces of the nuns, stopping at the Mother Superior's. "I don't think Sister Adelaide would have any notion about an espionage scheme. Penny told me Adelaide was going to Tom to talk to him about being placed in the clinical trial for sulphanilamide. My sister fought for him to take it before the program started, but Dr. Mills refused. But six months later, on the day my sister was murdered, he acquiesced. That's why Sister Adelaide was going to Tom's cabin. It was unusual." To say the least, I thought.

Sister Emily's face drained of its color. A coughing spasm took her close to a minute from which to recover. Finally, she croaked, "I insisted on Tom's treatment. It wasn't anything unusual. He's a dying man. Of course we knew it wouldn't help. But he wanted it and I insisted he have it. It hasn't anything to do with Sister Gretchen's death. If Sister Adelaide had come to me, I'd have told her. She'd have saved us all a lot of grief today."

The nuns nodded in agreement. Poor Adelaide, I

thought. She was in for at least a tongue lashing, if not more, when she got back. Still, at the back of my mind, a nagging worry about the young nun wouldn't leave me. If John Weller was right, then my sister may have been murdered because she stumbled innocently upon whatever subterfuge Charles Bremmer was intent on carrying out. Like Enoka Noa.

I shuddered. "Thank you for explaining that for me, Sister Emily. Yet listening to Sister Paul, I'm wondering if Sister Adelaide is in danger. Did Charles Bremmer kill my sister because she stumbled into information he had to keep secret? Would they wonder whether Adelaide also knows too much?"

"Oh my goodness. I'm afraid for her." It was Sister Edith. "That's why the sheriff is protecting us. We're all in danger, aren't we?"

Sister Paul spoke rapidly. "But the sheriff doesn't know it's Sister Adelaide who's had the most exposure to what's happening at the Samoan village. She's the most vulnerable."

I stood up. "Sister Emily, I've got to get out of here. I've got to find Sister Adelaide."

"You can't," Sister Edith said. "We have to stay here until the sheriff comes."

"By then it may be too late. It may already be." I was adamant.

Sister Emily nodded. "Go. Go now. Hurry."

At the back of the office, we raised the window, and two nuns took my arms and lowered me, leaving a jump of only a foot or so to the ground. Sister Paul handed down my shoulder bag. I was behind the building and headed toward the path I'd shared with Charles Bremmer, behind the Protestant chapel, ironically, his secret way into the Samoan village. Now it was mine.

CHAPTER TWENTY-THREE

ICLEARED THE LAST BUILDING AND ran between
spreading branches overhead, through a heavy stand
of woods, where it looked like earth and water tried to
coexist. Bald cypress, sycamore, and water oak pushed
their branches high above me.

The path was fast disappearing in front of me. What
had happened to solid ground? It hadn't been the case
when I followed Charles. Truthfully, though, I hadn't
paid much attention to what lay around me then. His
announcement that he belonged to the Nazi Party
shocked me so much I'd focused much more on what he
was saying than where he was leading me.

My sense of urgency increased with each step. Mud
almost pulled the boots off my feet, forcing me to take one
deliberate step after another as the path tried to give up to
the water on each side. Was it possible a swamp actually
flowed like the sluggish bayou near the Samoan camp? I
stepped into a hole, water knee deep, and my mind suddenly filled with the possibility of snakes. Even an alligator.

Taking a deep breath, I stopped to study the path. Yes, it was there, if just. Anxiety aside, it really was a stunning landscape to look at. No wonder Gretchen was inspired to paint it. The bald cypress tree to my right was glorious, sunshine filtering through its rope-like branches down to exposed roots. Beneath its branches, protected from the cold, a few woody plants popped colors of red-spiked flowers. Their scent was thick, sensuous, like the swamp itself. A lone wood duck perched on a branch nearby, his iridescent chestnut and green plumage drawn more carefully than my brush could ever capture, though I'd certainly have liked to try. Portraits were where I'd focused all my energy, but this scenery was worth doing. My sketch book was in my bag.

No. Find Sister Adelaide. I trudged on, hoping I'd come upon the Samoan village soon, see the dead tree with its drying fish hung about its branches and Polanie guarding the round house. Following the bayou would lead me to Tom and Penny's house.

This swamp must be connected to the bayou and the Mississippi River. Somewhere behind this curtain of trees, where sedge, woody plants, and water grass grew, was the bayou, that is, if my sense of direction was correct.

I stopped. Turned around. The path behind me was almost indistinguishable. But I'd been so careful, I couldn't have veered away from it. Thank goodness for Adelaide's boots.

Another few steps and I paused once more. Strange. The forest had stopped singing. No sound of birds, no wind blowing dead leaves off the branches of trees. No slithering noises of things I didn't want to think about hidden or, heaven forbid, of four-legged animals. The only sound I heard was someone walking. Yes, it was that.

Rhythmic, steady, a person walking, or rather sloshing, along the muddy path.

Charles Bremmer. He saw me at the same time I saw him.

"Catherine. What a surprise!" A pasted smile. He narrowed his eyes against the sun, raising his hand to shade them. He stepped closer, invading my space. "Why are you out here?"

"Sister Adelaide has been missing since last night. It occurred to me she might have come this way and possibly gotten lost. The path is hard to follow, isn't it?"

"It gets easier when you turn toward the camp." His lips tightened into an appropriate look of concern. "I heard Sister Adelaide missed church. Wasn't that it?"

"Yes, everyone's worried about her. She should have been back hours ago." I stood there, trying to keep eye contact with him. I smiled, shrugged my shoulders possibly not so convincingly. "It may be a wild goose chase, but it's better than not looking at all, isn't it." I started to step around him but he reached out and took my arm.

"She's not at the Samoan camp. I've just come from there."

My mind was spinning. "Oh. Well, I'll visit with some of the Samoans then. Maybe one of them saw her today. And I left in such a hurry the last time I was there; I feel I owe them an apology."

"Don't you remember? Their English is so limited. There's no way you can carry on a conversation." He had not let go of my arm. If anything, his grip had tightened. "Besides, today they get their injections. Without Sister Gretchen or Sister Adelaide, they had to go to the hospital."

"Can't another nun administer their medicine?"

He delayed his response. "I don't know. Can they?"

Did he also know the nuns and I were locked in Sister Emily's office? I pulled his hand away. "That hurts a bit."

He frowned. "Oh, sorry." He was staring a hole through me. "You've no reason to go to the village today, Catherine."

I took a step back, raising my voice. "Where I go or don't go is no concern of yours, Charles."

His eyes narrowed, and he gave me a hard, strange look. *He's making a decision,* I thought. Then the moment passed. "Of course it isn't." He frowned and through compressed lips said, "No one's told me why Sister Adelaide's run away. Do you know?"

I hesitated a bit too long. "No, I hoped she'd have turned up by now."

I had never lied well and it was obvious he didn't believe me. Was it a test? But just as he was about to say something else, a great sound in the air caused both of us to look up at hundreds of white birds just above the tree tops.

"Good God, what's going on?" While I was looking up at the birds, Charles extracted a pocket watch and looked at it briefly before putting it back in his pocket. I caught a slight frown, immediately registered and gone. He was late for something or someone.

"Egrets!" In spite of being with Charles in the middle of nowhere, I was thrilled watching hundreds of white-winged creatures spacing themselves along the branches of trees. "This is the most beautiful thing I've ever seen."

He gave me an indulgent smile. *What an actor he is,* I thought. Only a few fissures in his façade. Most people wouldn't catch a thing unless they were looking for it.

"Let's hope nothing bad has happened to Sister Adelaide," he said. "That would be so dreadful. There's been too many deaths here."

A shiver ran down my spine. Was that a warning to me?

But he looked worried and sounded worried, even to the small crack in his voice. He shifted from one leg to the other.

He asked, "Will you continue on then? On your own?"

"Yes. Maybe." I quickly opened my shoulder bag and pulled out my sketch pad. "I'll decide after I sketch these birds. They're so wonderful."

For a fraction of a second I saw indecision in his eyes. "Well, then, I can only warn you not to veer away from the path," he looked quite serious and concerned. "Be careful. It's not an easy path to follow. Please don't get lost."

I assured him I wouldn't and watched his form move away.

I should follow him. With the racket of the birds, he wouldn't hear me trailing behind him. No. Whatever his errand had been to the camp, he'd completed it. And that had to be to cover up something, to get rid of evidence, or to give Polanie and his men instructions. Were the rats running from a sinking ship, covering up whatever it was they had going on in the village before the sheriff's men found it? I looked at the path ahead.

Restoring the sketch pad to my shoulder bag, I set out again. My mind was like a storm at sea, waves of fear rolling over me. Had Charles Bremmer followed Sister Adelaide? Would I even find her at Tom's house? She had had plenty of time to go and return to the hospital by now. Unless, unless that had been Bremmer's errand. A cold chill ran down my spine.

Then, suddenly, without any hint, my path appeared firm beneath my feet. I began to run as fast as I could. *Please be safe, Sister Adelaide.* "Dear God," I whispered, "let her be safe!"

CHAPTER TWENTY-FOUR

THE SUN OVERHEAD WAS QUICKLY giving way to a low bank of gray clouds moving up from the south. I stopped to look across the yard. The small, dead catalpa tree's branches were bare, absent now of any hanging or rotted fish. Past its skeleton was a deserted camp with its four huts and communal round house. Charles hadn't lied. The place was as lifeless as a tomb, except for a wispy trail of smoke coming out the top of the round house.

The smoke led me to open the door and peek inside. Still no sign of life. Just a small, burning fire in the pit. Folding chairs formed a circle around the stove, with four tables set against the wall behind them. A row of shelves held an empty cracker tin, some water glasses, a stack of china plates. An icebox stood in the corner. I looked inside the pantry for food on the shelves, and in the icebox there was just a pitcher with what looked like milk.

So Gretchen was right. Had voicing her concern made her a threat? Why? I tried the water faucet over the sink, cupped my hands, and drank some water. As if on cue, at that moment, my stomach growled.

No food. Not here, anyway. And no people. But surely they were at the hospital.

Sick, threatened people who had no means to defend themselves. Today, however, they were being fed and kept warm. I could take solace from that fact. I was so deep in thought I didn't hear the door open.

"Catherine!"

I jumped and swung around to see Yves, followed closely by John Weller.

"What are you doing here?"

"I'm looking for Sister Adelaide."

Yves came forward and put his arms around me. I saw the face of John Weller over his shoulder. John looked surprised, then looked down and brushed past us to the fire pit.

I stepped away from Yves, my eyes trailing after John. He had knelt beside the fire.

Yves said, "I thought you were safe at the hospital. You shouldn't be out here."

"Sister Adelaide disappeared this morning. I know where she is, at Tom's cabin, but I had to take the long way around not to be seen by the sheriff."

The scraping of a stick drew our attention to John. He was intent on pulling a few bits of unburnt paper from the fire.

I asked, "Is that why you're here, John? Looking for Adelaide?"

He didn't turn around. In a husky tone he answered, "No. You're the reason I came here. But you may have sent me on a wild goose chase."

I stepped across to him. He looked up, studied my face. His eyes were intense. They seemed to see right through me. I said, "What you're talking about. I sent you? Here?"

"The note."

I gasped and turned away.

"What's wrong?" John said, rising. Then it dawned on me, he wasn't talking about my note, but the one sent to my sister about the Samoans, which I'd shown him the night he warned me about Charles Bremmer.

Shaking my head I said, "Nothing's wrong," and walked back to where Yves stood. "How is it the two of you are together?"

Yves said, "I stayed hidden in the woods and watched as everyone left. I decided to take a look around and ran into Adam Wolf." He raised his voice to include John. "I recognized you from *The Times*."

John grunted, still studying several scraps of paper. "I'm John Weller here. There's not much left of Adam Wolf."

Yves quizzical expression turned to one of embarrassment. He'd just realized this wasn't a famous reporter in search of a story but a patient here.

"John was kind enough to make photographs of Gretchie's body for me. He also warned me about Charles Bremmer." I turned back to John. "You were right, you know. I met Charles on the path coming here. I really think he's a dangerous man and capable of murder. I don't trust him for a minute."

I'd shocked Yves. "My God, Catherine! What are you saying?"

John walked toward the door, saying "What she's saying is true."

We all stepped outside into the daylight, Yves and me standing over John as he spread the paper fragments on the ground and studied them. This happened while I described my exit from Sister Emily's office and then my encounter with Charles Bremmer.

"He was in a hurry, I'm sure of that. Not his normal

obstreperous self. But nervous. He looked at his watch and shifted his feet all the time. I think he was late for something." I peered over John's shoulder at the pieces of paper. "Is that a map of some kind?"

"Of some kind," John said. "Maybe a road map. Or not. It's hard to tell." He stood and put the pieces in his pocket. "Can you show me the path he took?"

I led both men to where the path started, asking John, "Are you going after him? I wonder if that's wise. He may have a weapon, you know."

John unzipped his jacket to reveal a hand gun stuck in his belt and bit down on his next words. "I found this in his quarters last night. It's a German Luger. Maybe that's what has him in a panic. It's missing."

I clutched at my book sack. A lump rose in my throat. "You think my sister was murdered ... because she discovered what he was doing?"

Yves asked, "Do you really think there's an espionage plot taking place here? Under everyone's noses? It just seems a bit farfetched to me." His voice had a nervous tremor in it. He was looking hard at the gun John held.

John's silent scowl spoke louder than his words. "It's possible Bremmer murdered two people."

I jumped in. "No. No, John. Sister Adelaide is on an errand that I'm unfortunately responsible for. I was on my way to Tom Langlinais's house. Penny told me she was there."

"Not Sister Adelaide. I believe Enoka Noa was Bremmer's first victim. Then Sister Gretchen."

The mention of the Samoan man I'd read about in the files jogged my memory. "I remember him. Wait a minute. I remember sharing his disappearance and suspected suicide with Charles. He got very angry when I brought it up. He said Enoka Noa ran away."

"Bremmer is an excellent actor. He hides everything in plain sight. Then no one will suspect him of espionage or murder."

It was what I had concluded about Charles Bremmer myself.

John continued, "I just wish I'd paid more attention to the Samoans when they arrived. Yes, it was clear they all looked up to Enoka Noa. He was a handsome, tall, talkative guy. In Samoan. But he could also speak a little English. That probably made him important to the group. I'm afraid I didn't form any opinion of him after that, and I could kick myself for it."

He paused and looked at me directly. "I'm off then." He turned to leave us but stopped when I spoke again.

"John, wait. I think I have something that might be important to you." I took the journal out of my book sack again and started flipping through the pages to find what I wanted. "Here it is. This is what Gretchie wrote on June 15:

> "Mr. Charles Bremmer arrived today and announced he is the liaison to the Samoans. Sister Emily told me she had not been informed of his arrival or position. His credentials are in order, however, so it seems someone forgot to tell us.

"... And it goes on from there."

He seized the journal out of my hands, studying the words as if they were a sacred text. When he looked up from the page, his eyes were wide and glowing. His face beaming. "I knew it! The man's a complete fake."

Yves asked quietly, "May I see the journal?"

John handed it over to him then put his hands on my shoulders. I couldn't help but smile back. The man looked joyous. And speechless.

"The famous reporter with no words? I'm surprised."

His eyes were dancing. "You really are radiant when you smile, you know." He paused. "Or blushing."

Yves broke the moment between us. "I don't see that this proves Charles Bremmer isn't who he says he is. Aren't you just jumping to a conclusion because you want to? This isn't proof. Not really." He handed the journal to me and I put it away. I was sorry to see the scowl return to John Weller's face.

"You forget I'm a reporter. Research is my business. And if there truly was a liaison sent here with the colony from Samoa, I'll find out." He touched my shoulder lightly. "Thank you, Catherine. I mean it." And he loped away from us in a trot.

"Wait!" It was Yves. John stopped and waited as Yves ran over to him. They exchanged but a few words. Yves reached into his pocket and handed him something. What was it? John disappeared before Yves made his way back to where I was standing.

"What was that about? What did you give him?"

"The keys to my car."

I was shocked. "Really?"

"Yes. I think he's going to have to get to that marine station sooner rather than later."

"That was generous of you. I didn't read your expression clearly. I thought you didn't trust him."

Pulling in, he slowly released his breath. "I don't know if I do." He pursed his lips and sighed. "But you do. And Gretchen didn't trust Charles Bremmer. If both my girls had doubts about him, it's worth investigating. And Adam Wolf is the right person to investigate."

"You don't even know if he can drive."

"And I didn't bother to ask. Oh well. I'll try not to

think about it." He took my hand. "But I'll tell you truthfully, what might happen to my car is the least of my
worries at the moment." And with that he turned and led
me away from the camp, toward the stand of woods and
the path he'd found from Tom's house.

CHAPTER TWENTY-FIVE

YVES AND I HAD BEEN walking about ten minutes out of the Samoan camp through some thick woods. A carpet of leaves crunched beneath our feet. We walked slowly, with no conversation, lost in our own thoughts. Climbing a slight rise, we stood on the bank above the bayou and looked down to a boat landing with a canoe pulled on shore. A line of old trees on the opposite side leaned into the still, opaque water.

"We could borrow the canoe, Yves. If it's any distance, it might be faster than on foot." When he didn't answer, I said, "Yves? Did you hear me?"

"What? No, we won't need the canoe."

"Yves, what's wrong? You haven't said a word since we left the camp."

Facing me, his jaw muscles tightened. "We shouldn't have come back here. We should have gone straight back to New Orleans from Brusly. Let the sheriff sort all this out. I'm kicking myself for bringing you back to this place."

Surprised, I answered him curtly, "You had nothing

to do with it, Yves. Do you think I'd have left here not knowing what happened to my sister? I would not!"

I went ahead of him, down the slope, through an aggressive amount of grass and weeds, which seemed destined to take back the makeshift boat landing.

He followed me. "It's a dangerous place, Catherine. You must know that. I'm very concerned. We don't know what we're doing, and running around here seems like a fool's errand."

"I don't care." I kept walking, picking my way along the bank, making slow progress, but he was right. My mind told me Adelaide wasn't at Tom's cabin. Either she'd taken him back to the hospital for treatment or she'd gone back on her own. Being out here was ridiculous at best and maybe dangerous if a murderer was wandering about. But I wasn't listening to my head anymore. I stopped and turned around. "I promised the sisters. I know Sister Adelaide's probably back at the hospital by now. But I promised them, don't you understand?"

He said quietly, "Yes, I think I do." A few seconds later he pointed and said, "All right. I cut across the fallow sugar cane field about there. It comes out almost directly in the cabin's backyard. You want me to lead?"

We walked along in single file. When the path led out into open space, Yves veered away from it, next to stalks of wild, uncultivated sugar cane. We kept the path to our right. Fog was rolling in fast. It felt wet and slimy on my face. A chill ran through me. I pulled my jacket closer, sticking my hands deep into my pockets, shrugging off my fear. When we reached Tom and Penny's cottage, a gray shadowy pall hung over it.

"Wait," Yves said. "Something doesn't seem right. When I came by here earlier there was smoke in the chimney."

Standing behind foliage of tall, rotted cane stalks, we waited, hoping to see a sign of life coming from inside the house. The top of a tall water oak tree nearby swayed; its whispering breeze seemed to announce our arrival. If rain came, it would not be like the winter storm we'd had earlier in the week. I knew too well what a wind rising from the Gulf was capable of doing. Sheets of rain and incredible thunder and lightning. But perhaps not this time. Just as often, winter brought a misty, warmish fog like this, spreading across the landscape. Gretchen and I had called it southern snow. We'd get lost inside it sometimes, losing sight of everything, the house across the street. Even each other.

Yves and I stood silent for a few minutes until I whispered, "I think you should stay here. Let me check. If Tom is in there, and I doubt he is, he would expect me to be looking everywhere for Adelaide, so he would understand my barging in on him and no harm done. Or if the situation turns ugly, I'll just leave and join you back here."

"What do you mean, 'ugly'? If the man is dangerous then I'm going and you can stay."

"It turned ugly when I was here before, but it was my fault. Tom's not dangerous. The disease is killing him. It's the worst case I've seen in this place. What's so torturing is that he and Penny probably have the most to live for of anyone here."

"What if you run into one of the native men? Or Charles Bremmer? We don't know where he is. No, you shouldn't expose yourself." He laid his hand on my shoulder. "We'll both go."

"The Samoans have no reason to harm me either. And I think I'm much less threatening than a stranger would be."

"I make friends easily. Let's go." It was unequivocal.

We stepped onto the brushed gravel walkway, opening

the front gate of the picket fence surrounding Penny's garden space. I checked for movement or light from the coal oil lamp Penny had placed in the window when I was there last time. Black as pitch. Nothing moved behind those panes of glass. The only sound was a rustling of branches in the tree. Not even a bird called. I looked back at where we'd hid, at the dead stalks of wild sugar cane. The fog had almost obliterated them.

"At least let me go in first," I whispered.

"I'm right behind you."

The door creaked as we opened it and looked inside. I could see a bed dominating the space and outlines of a table and chairs next to the kitchen counter. My mind flew back to the day Sister Adelaide had come to administer Tom's chaumoogra oil and he'd refused. His reaction to me. I was a stranger, yet somehow I had angered him as much as he'd frightened me. But not more than now. Then my eyes locked on Tom's crumpled body slumped next to the potbellied stove.

"Oh no," I said, stumbling across the room, catching my foot on the rung of the rocking chair, then righting myself before kneeling down beside him.

"Tom!" He opened his eyes, a bewildered expression on his face. *He must be in shock,* I thought. He was bleeding from his face and neck and through his shirt. Someone had clawed at his face. He had stab wounds on his arms and to his chest. Bloody pus ran down his cheeks. I started to rise, but he reached out to stop me with a hand missing three fingers.

I looked up briefly at Yves, who was white as a sheet. "My God," he whispered."

I nodded. "We've got to get him to the hospital."

Tom's face was gruesome, but I was sure it didn't end

there. The wounds didn't seem deep but there were many, and without attention, he could bleed to death. I placed my hand over his, and he opened his mouth, grimaced, then tried but failed to speak.

"It's Catherine, Tom. My friend and I will help you."

He opened his mouth again, trying to voice something, using one finger to point to the back door.

Yves ran to the door, pushed it open. "Is there someone out there?" The door slammed behind him. I heard him going down some steps.

I needed to stop the bleeding. I rose and found water in a bucket in the sink, a dipper resting inside, sticking out of it. Searching frantically through the cabinet, I found some dishtowels.

With the bucket on the floor beside me, I wrapped his wounds with dishtowels. Then I lifted his shirt. The stab to his chest didn't seem as deep as those on his arms. It had congealed and stopped bleeding. He must have warded off his attacker with his arms. I used a compress of dishtowels to clean his chest as best I could. Then I offered him water from the dipper, but he refused and closed his eyes.

The door creaked. Yves stood just outside on the doorstep. Without looking at him I said, "He's still breathing, but he's lost a lot of blood." I paused. "I need some light. Would you light the lantern?"

When Yves didn't answer, I looked over at him. He stood in the doorway holding a white cornette in both his hands. His face was ashen.

I couldn't speak. It had to be Adelaide's.

"It's just this. She's not out there."

I got up and stumbled across the room, touching the headpiece that so reminded me of birds' wings, like those beautiful egrets I'd seen earlier in the swamp. I pushed past Yves onto the porch, looking across the yard toward the trees along the bayou, almost hidden now in thick fog. I strained to see anything. Tears stood in my eyes. My mind roiled in turmoil. Why was her headpiece in the yard?

"She's not out there, Catherine. I looked … everywhere."

"I've got to find her!" The words strangled me. I started coughing, walking toward the bayou, unable to breathe. Yves ran after me to the tree line at the water.

The fog had filled the bayou like steaming soup poured to the top of the bowl. I had to stop, let a spasm of coughing pass.

We kept our eyes on the ground. What were we looking for? Sister Adelaide's body? I shivered. I didn't notice when Yves bent down and stared at something on the ground. But I ran when he called my name.

"Catherine! I've found something."

It was a knife. Not a large knife like a butcher knife, but a kitchen knife like one Grace used for paring fruit or vegetables.

"I don't think we should touch it. There may be fingerprints."

I nodded. My hands shook as I lifted my sweater, tore off a piece of my undershirt, and wrapped the knife carefully.

He stared at me. "If she's not here, maybe she got away."

I nodded numbly. "I hope so." I looked into his eyes. He didn't believe it any more than I did. Sister Adelaide was somewhere on the road or in the cane field, dying of knife wounds, and there was nothing we could do. Except tell the sheriff and start looking everywhere.

Once inside the cabin again, I put the knife into my book sack, hardly noticing when Yves returned or the lantern he lit. Its light spread across the room to Tom's unconscious body. I sat on the floor beside him; the bandages seemed to have stemmed the bleeding.

Yves shook his head "Poor soul. He needs help. He's lost a lot of blood. We've got to get him to the hospital. We need the sheriff. Form a search party for the nun."

"Yes." My mind didn't want to process what I was thinking.

"We can't both go. We shouldn't move him." Yves temper flashed. "Damn whoever did this!"

"You must go, Yves. Let me stay here."

"I'm not leaving you alone out here."

"I know we're much safer if we stay together. I'm ashamed to say it, but if I could leave Tom, I would. I'm afraid. But I can't leave. Because he may be dying. And I'm cruel and petty enough to want to be here if he wakes up and says anything about Adelaide. I think he'd tell me before he would you."

Yves stared at me for a moment. "It's a long shot he'll even wake up, much less be able to talk to you."

"But he might! I need to stay just in case he does. Please, Yves! I know how much you want to protect me, but I have to do this."

He said slowly, in a low voice, "I don't know this Catherine. The young woman I know doesn't want to walk down St. Charles Avenue or take supper at the Pontchartrain Hotel. She prefers the safety of her morning room, the company of her portraits."

Tears sprang to my eyes. "Well, you encouraged me to come, didn't you? You and Grace?"

"I'm sorry. I certainly regret it now."

"No! It was the right thing. I needed to come. For Gretchen's sake."

His mouth twisted in a sardonic smile. "If I'd known what I was throwing you into though ... well, I—"

"I know. And I'll fuss at you for it too ... but not now."

We sat in silence, lost in our own thoughts.

Yves spoke first. "You're right. I should be the one to go. My guess is whoever did this won't be coming back here." He knelt down and looked closely at Tom. At his swollen face, closed eyes, labored breath. "Poor boy. Whoever did this to him is through with it now."

I thought, He's right. Tom's been left for dead. I stared at him, my eyes full of tears.

Yves rose and walked to the window. "This fog is getting thicker." Turning back to me, he said, "All right. I'm going to get help. I can make it there in ten or fifteen minutes if I run." I could read his worried expression. "Don't try to be brave. If you hear anything, no matter what, hide. Or run away. Even if it means leaving Tom. Will you promise me that?"

I nodded. "Absolutely."

Tom raised his hands in front of his face. "No, no, don't!" His words stunned us both, a yell, receding to a low moan.

"He's reliving what was done to him. Please go, Yves. Oh, please hurry!" Taking a step backward, he seemed uncertain again. I cried out, "We can't just let him die!"

Yves nodded and was gone.

I counted the seconds, a minute, two. I took a pillow from the bed and wedged it carefully between Tom's head and the stove. His eyes opened and he stared back at me. "Will you try to drink some water, Tom?" When he blinked, I took that as a yes. I held the dipper against his lips, pleased he could actually swallow. "Tom, who did this to you? Was it Charles Bremmer?"

He whispered, "No more." I removed the dipper. He moaned.

"No more water, Tom. See? I'm putting it here on the floor."

He was agitated, trembling, trying to grab my arm struggling with the words, "Murdered ..."

Oh my God, no! "Tom, did they murder Sister Adelaide?" I felt beads of sweat on my forehead.

Tom's face took on a feverish, spongy glow, his eyes red with blood, darted around the room. "Where is she?" He made an attempt to grab my arm.

"Tom! Tom, tell me! What happened to Sister Adelaide? Did she get away from them? Did she run away?"

"My baby." Tears streamed down his cheeks.

He was delirious, clearly out of his head. Maybe he was thinking about the note. The stupid note written by two insufferable teenagers.

"Your baby is safe, Tom. Don't worry, Hope is with Penny. She's in no danger."

"Stop her!" Tom grabbed my arm with a strength I didn't expect. Rivulets of tears had obliterated his eyes."

I was about to lose my mind. "Stop who, Tom? Sister Adelaide? Was she here with you? She was coming to see you, Tom. Try to remember. Sister wanted to ask you about your new medicine. Remember?"

He groaned in mounting pain. He started shaking. "No. No! Hiding ..."

"Sister Adelaide? You hid Sister Adelaide? Why, Tom? Why did you have to hide her? Was it because someone was trying to hurt her? Was it Charles Bremmer? Tell me."

He fell back against the pillow, his breathing erratic, alarming. He managed only, "God forgive ... me!"

"God forgives you, Tom. He does." Finally, his eyes

found mine with a recognition I'd not seen before. Maybe my voice sounded like Gretchen's.

"Sister Gretchen ..."

"Yes, Tom. I'm Catherine. Sister Gretchen's sister." I tried to smile through my tears. "Don't be afraid."

Tom stirred. Recognition enlarged his eyes, and a look of acceptance imbued itself upon his diseased face. Quietly he said, "Over." Then his body sagged from its semi-sitting position. No more moaning. His breathing, though shallow, was slowing down. I put my arms around him and cradled his head and shoulders in my lap. His eyes grew vacant again as I listened to one breath, then another.

He was slipping away and there was nothing I could do to stop it. The tug of war that was Tom's body had lost. "Oh, Tom!" I whispered, knowing it was his last few breaths.

But in a clear, measured voice, he said, "Find her ..."

"I'll find her, Tom. I promise."

I sat on the floor holding Tom as his life drained away. In those moments I knew, whatever part he'd played in this horrible mess, he'd still been an innocent pawn, terribly ill-used by someone. I would find out who. I would! He took another breath and it was over. I closed his eyes with my fingers. He was gone. Then my body reacted. I began to shake, rocking back and forth, still holding Tom in my arms.

"It's not fair! Not fair! Never to see your daughter again. Someone stole the tiny amount of time you had left. Why? Hadn't you suffered enough? How could there be such evil in the world?" I couldn't stop my racking, uncontrollable sobs. I looked to the ceiling. "Gretchie, will you put in a good word for Tom? Please, will you do that?" I took a deep breath, allowed the deep silence around me to permeate my mind. Was there even a God? I thought. And in that moment, a voice inside my head answered me.

I suddenly knew Tom was in a better place. Yes. I smiled. Had that been Gretchen's voice I heard? A validation from my sister? I didn't know, but when I closed my eyes, I saw Tom's face. No more pain. He was a handsome young man. He was free.

CHAPTER TWENTY-SIX

TOOK A QUILT FROM THE bed and covered Tom's body, repeating over him the only words I could think of, a Bible verse—"Peace be with you; my peace I give unto you." At the end, I think he did die with some peace on his heart. I walked to the window and stared out at a palpable layer of fog, its density like a blanket covering the cabin. Concealing it.

Questions rolled around in my head. Had Sister Adelaide walked into something here? She must have. It was the only thing that made any sense. And Tom tried his best to protect her. But what then? He'd been stabbed and then whoever it was took Sister Adelaide somewhere, or tried to. "Find her … ," Tom had said.

Was it a Nazi spy? But that was crazy, wasn't it? Yet parts of what John Weller said could be true. I racked my brain. What scheme would involve Tom? Why would he ever agree to hiding someone here?

I stepped out on the back porch. To my left was a set of stairs leading up to what I recognized as another room, commonly called the stranger's room. Most creole cottages had them. Travelers, whether priests or doctors or peddlers coming down the bayou, could spend the night and move on before the sun was up the next morning. I'd been told it was a courtesy the Acadians brought with them from Canada the century before last.

I retrieved the lantern from the house, climbed the steps, and peered into a windowless room, at the bed, nicely made with quilts and a homespun coverlet. A candle had been used recently, burned down to half. A tray sat beside the bed on a small table with the remains of bread on a plate and wet tea leaves in the bottom of a china cup. I picked up a spoon, then a white napkin off the floor, putting them back on the tray. It was a nicely furnished room, recently used by a stranger. *Or a Nazi spy.* Did Sister Adelaide accidently discover him? If so, she'd be a threat that must be eliminated. But Tom fought for her. The question was, did Charles Bremmer or Polanie or someone else take her away from here, or was she able to run and hide? A shiver ran up my spine. The knife next to the bayou had had blood on it. Was it only Tom's? If the blood was Adelaide's, then where was her body? I began to tremble. Was her body thrown into the bayou? *Oh dear God!*

Extinguishing the lantern, I left it in the room and retraced my steps, hanging on to the railing, taking one step down at a time. I couldn't think she was dead. I mustn't.

Inside the cabin again, I stood at the window, straining to see the road. Yves was taking too long. I must have misjudged the time for him to get there and back.

But now, was there any need for me to wait for him? I wanted to get out of this place. It was time for the authorities to take over. To make sense of the room above the cabin and who'd been staying there. I must find Sister

Adelaide. She must be hiding somewhere. Maybe she got to the mansion, to the root cellar. Suddenly, I thought, *Why not?* She would know I'd look for her in that cellar, even if no one else did.

A noise interrupted my thoughts. I couldn't see movement with my eyes. The fog had blotted out the day. Its swelling veil of cloud seemed to have a physical presence, somber, as if warning me of something. I squeezed my eyes shut and listened. Was someone coming? Yves would call my name. If it was the sheriff's deputies, wouldn't they at least have a flashlight? No, whoever this was didn't want to be seen. I moved away from the window, stood with my back against the wall. My palms were wet.

I tiptoed across the room; the floor boards creaked. I opened the door to the back porch then saw my book sack lying next to Tom's body. I retrieved it quickly, stepped outside to the back porch, listening for movement again. It had stopped.

I walked down the back steps and ran as quietly as I could to the tall stalks of rotting sugar cane at the side of the house. No one came after me. I stood for a time, well hidden, watching, waiting to see if it was Yves, or an animal out hunting,

I heard a door open and close. No animal there. Steps on the wooden stairs. Two of them. They were checking the stranger's room.

I pulled my jacket close, looked in both directions, trying to make out the path we'd come along from the Samoan's camp. I paused. If this was Charles, he might guess I'd be on this path. I readjusted my book sack in front of me. A cold mist covered my face.

I took off walking across the field. The dead stalks of sugar cane were taller than me, standing like sentinels.

I started walking in the deep ruts between rows. If I cut across the field, I was pretty sure I'd connect to the new road leading from the hospital to the Samoan camp. I just had no idea how big this field was: though, I felt my direction was right, fog or no. It would be easy to get lost out here, I thought.

I tried not to push against the sugar cane but to step around each plant. For a few quiet minutes, I trudged on. There was an absolute absurdity to all this. Lost in the middle of a cane field? I ducked under dead leaves holding the stalks for balance, stepping into the soft, mushy ground. If I was going in a straight line horizontally, I would reach the road. But I might be going around in circles.

I stopped to catch my breath. I felt like shouting obscenities at Charles Bremmer, at everyone, especially those who called themselves Nazis.

After thirty minutes, maybe more, I was still in the field, still surrounded by cane. My sense of direction was completely gone. Everything looked the same. I might have been going right back to Tom and Penny's cabin.

I stumbled several times over things on the ground. Little noises disturbed me, something like a stick pulling itself through the dead leaves. My heart roared its beating in my ears.

I clapped my hand over my mouth to stifle a scream when a small hare feeding on a tuft of grass appeared in front of me. It disappeared, as frightened of me as I was of him.

Something else was happening. Not the mist or the wind or the leaves rustling. Was it a motor running? I walked carefully in its direction.

Another step and I was out of the sugar cane and in brush that came to my knees. In another few steps, the plants felt more like grass. Then I stepped onto a firm surface and I could see it was a road. I looked in both directions, but the fog hung like heavy drapery around me and I saw no headlights. It was a car, wasn't it?

A low, dense rolling sound of thunder filled the still night.

Not a motor. I walked away from the sound of thunder. A storm was rising out in the Gulf. I hoped I had the direction right to the hospital. Thunder and lightning were still behind me. It seemed the right way. *Follow your instinct*, I thought.

Lights glowed in the distance. At first they all ran together in a streak cutting through the fog. I knew it must be a series of windows. The whole complex was ablaze with light. And well it might be. Safety inside the light. Most people trusted in that. Just a few of us felt differently, I thought, and believed darkness was the better protector.

Lightning struck then. Its glare helped me see the building in front of me, the broken barbed wire fence where I had fallen and cut my leg. Like all the buildings, it sat on four-foot piers. But I knew this was the nuns' quarters. A lighted window above me might be the window in Gretchen's room.

Standing with my back against the clapboard siding of the quarters, I tried to make out where the hospital might be. Suddenly, into my line of vision, Sister Clara walked toward me with the young deputy, her nephew, Kevin. I dropped down onto my stomach and rolled between the pilings to hide under the building. If I saw Sister Clara and Kevin, surely they also saw me. But perhaps not. They were having an intense conversation.

"... And put an end to it! Except we still don't know where Sister is, do we?"

Kevin answered, "Don't worry. If she's to be found out there, Sheriff Doucet will get him to tell where. When I was working for him in Prairieville, I saw him question suspects. He gets answers. You don't want to mess up around him."

"Who is the suspect anyway? Did you hear?"

"No. I been out here, guarding all of you."

"It was better we sequester ourselves out here, Kevin. Sister Emily isn't well. She needed to lie down. Besides, her office gave the sheriff a place to question everyone."

"We're all coming apart, Kevin! Why is this happening to us?"

"Now, now, Aunt Clara. It's going to be okay. Sheriff will get to the bottom of it. Soon."

"Not soon enough for me. Oh my dear Jesus!"

They were just above me, on the porch. Sister Clara's crying subsided as though she was trying to compose herself before opening the door. She said, "If they've really caught the man who took Sister Adelaide, we should be told where she is. Somebody should tell us, Kevin! Can't you find out? And what about Tom Langlinais? He hasn't come for dinner or to see the baby. Penny's hysterical. She found me in the ward. 'He must be missing too,' she says. 'Is Tom missing too?' Kevin, is the man they've arrested responsible for doing something to Tom too?"

"If he is, then he's a murderer, Aunt Clara."

Sister Clara gasped. "What?"

"I spoke to James and Vilmer while I was waiting to bring you back here. They went to his cabin and found him dead."

Sister Clara's anguished voice cracked. "Tom is dead? Oh, the poor soul!"

"Not from the leprosy."

"What?"

"He was murdered. That's all I'm saying. You don't want to know how. And, Aunt Clara, you can't say anything to the others. You got to promise me."

"But I've got to tell them! I must!"

"Only that the deputies found him dead. Nothing else. I could lose my job for telling you. Promise me, Aunt Clara."

After a long pause Clara blew her nose then whispered, "I see. Yes. Sheriff Doucet will tell us soon enough. I won't get you into trouble."

A stream of light ran across the ground when she opened the door to go inside.

The dirt under me was sticky. Its thick, rancid smell made me nauseas. The wind came on in a rage at that moment, obliterating the fog in great drops of rain water. I pushed my body back another foot.

The door opened again. Sister Clara said, "You'd best come in with me, Kevin. You can as soon protect us from inside as out here in the rain. I'll get you something to eat. It's long past dinnertime."

After the door shut behind them, I turned over on my back and closed my eyes, trying to think, jumping out of my skin when a loud clap of thunder seemed to shake the whole building above me.

I stared upwards at the two-by-fours holding the floor boards. The suspect was Yves. It must be Yves the sheriff was interrogating. He was a stranger to everyone except me. Yet surely in a matter of minutes a telephone call to Father O'Quinn would establish who he was and why he was found on the grounds alone. I knew I should make sure. I could go into the nuns' quarters and tell Kevin. And what would happen then? Kevin would take me to the sheriff. I'd tell them what happened. The sheriff would want to question me. But how long would that take?

Looking in the root cellar would have to wait. Tears stung my eyes even as I felt wind driven rain spray my face. *No!* The thought clamored in my brain. What would Yves have me do? If a choice had to be made, I knew Yves would want me to look for Adelaide and to let him deal with the sheriff. I turned onto my side, watched rainwater running down a furrow next to a pile of dirt.

It was time to decide. The thought that kept rushing at me was that Adelaide might be waiting for me in the root cellar. I must find out.

A flash of lightning illuminated the building on the other side of the compound. If memory served me correctly, it was where patients lived. A row of tall hedge ran along the other side, up to the Protestant chapel. It had been through an opening in one of the hedges that John Weller had led me to the back door of the mansion.

I could find it again. And I could check on the cellar quickly. Then run back if she wasn't there. Right or wrong, I must go there.

The overhanging roof from the patient's quarters would keep at least some of the rain off me. But now my best protection, the fog, had been swept away by the rain. I rolled out from under the building, ignoring the mud clinging to my jacket, my slacks, and my hair. Rain sprayed my face, washing the mud off me as I ran across the courtyard. Suddenly, the night lit up as if by a beacon from above. I tripped across a tree branch lying on the ground and rolled like a ball on the grass. "Oh God! What next?"

Taking a deep breath, I stood and took a few tentative steps. My leg ached, but I could move and hadn't been struck by lightning.

Moving as fast as my aching leg would let me, I ran between buildings and found the hedge. Lights from the windows of patients' quarters above me offered a view of the path but gave little protection from my being seen if someone came this way. Beyond the hospital offices, I saw the Protestant chapel outlined in front of me.

The church was dark, unlike every other building in the compound. Charles Bremmer must be elsewhere. But something made me stop and turn and stand on tip-toe to look into a window of the church. What did I expect to see in there? Sister Adelaide tied up in ropes, gagged, thrown into a corner? Maybe. No, but I did see something. Through dim candle light, the Samoans sat in the pews facing each other, huddled into a small mass of yellow and black plaid. I fell to my knees, afraid I'd been seen.

Underneath the pilings I saw several large wooden crates I recognized. They were the boxes the pews had been shipped in, that I'd sat beside on the barge. So, was this simply a convenient place to get them out of the way? Or to hide something?

Crawling on my hands and knees, a sense of dread came over me. Why save these boxes if not to hide something? I pushed on the top of one of the crates and it gave way easily. It was full, and I took a deep breath. It wasn't a dead body, but food. Bags of rice and sugar, cans of something. Here was the missing food. When I pushed open the next box a shiver went down my spine. Rope. My hands felt the same hemp as before when the cellar door had crashed down above me.

The thought of Sister Adelaide then ... entombed ... the other boxes could wait.

Crawling out from under the church and pushing up to a standing position, I felt a blow to the back of my head and fell to my knees, bright spots jumping before my eyes. Then a sudden sharp blistering pain seared through my brain. The world was spinning. I heard a voice, "Hey, hold on there! What you doing?" Then the craziest thought went through my head. My assailant was Papa!

I waited for the next blow, knowing it would come, seeing my father's face so clearly in my mind ... before losing consciousness.

Like a missing key unlocking the vault of memory buried in my brain, or a tornadic wind whirling around me, those tormented moments I'd buried for so many years returned.

ॐ ॐ

NEW ORLEANS, 1922

Avery Allen Lyle dragged his child out of the closet where she'd hidden, down the steps to the balcony, to the second floor, to the landing with bedrooms where she and Gretchen slept. Catherine struggled against him, screaming, seeing his eyes red with blood. Her screams hurt her ears, but she couldn't stop them from coming because all at once she knew it wasn't just her own screaming she heard. It was her father's voice that filled her ears after she bit his hand.

She pushed against him and watched as he tried to get his balance, how he reached for her, but clawed only air with his hands, screaming, "Help ... me."

His body arched backwards over the banister, arms extended, falling twenty feet to the marble floor below. Strangely, for a moment, Catherine imagined him flying up to her again, his eyes gaping, mouth wide open, the scream so loud Catherine put her hands over her ears. Her father's head hit the edge of the round French pier table standing in the center of the foyer. A large Ming dynasty vase on it fell and shattered into a thousand pieces. Blood spewed across the white marble floor. When his screaming stopped, Catherine grabbed hold of the banister and leaned over it, mesmerized by his twitching body. Then he became quite still. His eyes glazed over. She was like a spectator at the movies, with Bela Lugosi lying in a pool of his own blood, a horrific expression on his face, staring out at the audience.

At some point, she became aware that her sister stood behind her. Gretchen whispered very soft, "He can't hurt us anymore."

Catherine couldn't take her eyes off the body. "Is Papa dead?" She stared unblinkingly at him, at the red blood stain seeping like syrup around him. Only then did she feel tears on her face. "Why was Papa was so mean to me? He pulled my hair out."

Gretchen pried her fingers off the banister. "Don't look at him. Come to bed."

The soft voice made her turn around, released her from the blood and the body below. She looked into her sister's eyes. "Why didn't you come for me, Gretchie?" Her hand and fingers that had gripped the bannister felt numb as Gretchen led her away from the balcony, into her bedroom.

Gretchen's body shook involuntarily, in spite of her will to stop it. She pulled back the mosquito netting, then the coverlet, lifting her sister into the four-poster bed.

Catherine still had questions, "Why wasn't it you? Why was it Papa who found me?" Anger began to build inside her. "How did he find me?" she demanded. "Gretchie? How did he know to look in the woolen closet?"

Gretchen sat on the bed, staring at the floor, her voice almost inaudible. "Yes. I told him. I'm so sorry."

Catherine stared at the trickle of blood from her sister's nose, at her right eye swollen shut, a noticeable bruise on the cheek. Catherine studied those things, the visible wounds on her sister's face, and realized she'd not seen such things before. Yes, her father had beat her sister. He must have bruised parts of her body many times, but not her face. Until now. The answer suddenly came to Catherine. Terrible, bad things had happened to her big sister. Things that were too unspeakable. Her big sister was right; he couldn't hurt them anymore. Because Catherine had pushed him over the bannister and killed the monster for both of them.

"I'm glad Papa's dead," she murmured before turning away from Gretchen, pulling the blanket well over her head.

CHAPTER TWENTY-SEVEN

"MISS LYLE! MISS LYLE!" JACK'S voice penetrated my dream. I tried to shield my eyes from a garish beam of light.

"The light. Put it out. I can't stand it."

"You got a bad gash on your head, Miss Lyle. But these folk going to help you."

Struggling to sit up, a wave of nausea swept over me. "I'm going to be sick," I said before vomiting on the ground.

Jack's voice sounded far away. "Can a couple of you help me carry her?"

Soundless bodies dressed in yellow and black plaid picked me up and began to carry me. I pleaded with them, "The cellar. I need to go to the cellar and passed out again.

I woke up in a black sea of sadness. Spots still sparked behind my eyelids. But it was warmer and my mind had stopped churning. My body jerked upon hearing a piece of wood crack. A fire? I opened my eyes and saw a flame nearby. Had I been unconscious for minutes or hours? And where was I?

I smelled wool. It chafed my skin. Damp wool. I chanced more pain trying to focus. A wood stove glowed with wood cracking. Jack lay near it on a pallet of quilts. I heard him snoring lightly.

"Jack?"

At once he was awake and standing over me. "I guess we should have taken you to the hospital. Maybe somebody needs to take a look at that bump."

I felt a sticky substance on the back of my head. "The floor was covered in blood."

"Miss Lyle. You going bonkers or something? What you talking about?"

I tried to focus, make my mind work. Jack handed me a soaking wet towel. I put my face into it then placed it over the wound on my head. "Jack. The root cellar. I think Sister Adelaide may be there."

"Is that where you were going?"

I whispered, "Yes." My head hurt terribly; a pain as hot as fire affixed itself above my ear. I closed my eyes again. "The Samoans. Where are they now?"

"I guess they're still in their church. Couple of them and me carried you here." He took the cloth back to the sink, rinsed it out, returned, and placed it on my head. "I'm guessing maybe they were hiding out from the cops." He laughed lightly. "I didn't hang around either."

"Charles Bremmer?"

"He wasn't with them."

"I saw the Samoans inside the chapel." I remembered how their bodies were so still, deliberate as statues. "My mind was clearing, slowly. I remember. Two of them. Standing over me." Such sorrowful eyes staring at me.

"Yeah, that's right. Well, at least you ain't lost your mind. Somebody sure gave you a wallop, though."

I wanted to ask Jack who it was. I would do that. Soon. Right now I just wanted to go back to sleep. The towel on my head was cool. "I need to sleep a few more minutes. But I must talk to you then." And I drifted away again, even as Jack stared down at me. I didn't know or care about anything but sleep.

And dreams floated through my subconscious. I dreamed I was at my father's funeral and Polanie was down in the hole that was my father's grave, I assumed. He looked up at me. Or was I looking up at him? Another scene. A new vase stood on the table in the foyer. Jack and I were laughing, throwing my dolls off the balcony at it. Many dolls. One after the other, until one hit the vase and it shattered all over the floor.

My eyes flew open. "Jack? Where am I?"

He rose. "Hey, you're finally awake. I told you. Don't you remember? At your place. Me and the native guys brought you here." He studied me hard a few seconds. "How you feeling? You were kinda moaning a minute ago. Maybe I ought to go get one of the sisters to come take a look at you."

"No. No, don't go. I feel better. Really." It was the truth. I looked around at my quarters. My coat hung up on the hook next to the bed, my suitcase on the floor next to the window. "You did the right thing bringing me here."

He moved to the sink, filled a glass with water, and brought it to me. "The bump on the back of your head wasn't so bad. So we brought you here."

I sipped, thankful not to throw up. The warmth of the wood fire wrapped itself around me. Touching the bump behind my ear, I said, "Well, I'm glad it's not so bad. It feels like a boulder fell on it."

"Naw, but a pretty big piece of wood. I found it next

to you." He stood up. "I can boil some water for tea. You want some?"

Handing the glass back, I said, "I would. Thank you." My mind kept trying to remember. There was something I had missed. Something important, but what was it? Had I seen the person who hit me? I touched the sticky mess on the back of my head again.

I took the warm cup of tea with both hands from Jack and took a sip. I was feeling better by the minute. My shaking had stopped. Jack sat on the edge of the bed with his own cup.

"Jack, did you see who hit me?"

He shrugged. "Nope. They ran off before I could get a good look."

"But it was your voice, wasn't it?"

"I yelled at him 'cause I could see him raise that piece of wood. Tell the truth, I didn't know what was going on. It was like somebody was on their knees. "

I smiled. "I was."

He tipped his head to one side, "I sure was surprised to see it was you."

"Well, I'm glad you came along when you did. Otherwise, I might not be here, I think." I thought a few seconds, then asked, "Why were you on that path? Were you going to the mansion too?"

He paused, turning his head from me. "Clary needed me to do something for her."

"Clary? So Clarice isn't missing anymore?"

He chuckled, his eyes on me again, a grin on his face. "You got a knot on the head for sure. It's Sister Adelaide that's been missing, not Clary."

"This morning, when I went to talk to Clarice, Rose told me she'd run off somewhere."

"Well, she ain't gone now." He bent down suddenly. "I found something I bet is yours."

He pulled my shoulder bag out from under the bed.

"Oh, Jack. Yes. It's mine and I wouldn't want to lose it. Thank you." He took my cup and put it on the sink. I opened the bag. My sketch book and pens and Gretchen's journal were still inside. And under a flap, I could see my under-shirt, hopefully still hiding the knife we'd found.

I smiled. "You're a boy of many talents, did you know that?"

His face lit up. "I can save people!"

He was enjoying himself now. Humble he was not. I'd known that from the first time we'd met. But at that moment, I was in love with this thirteen-year-old boy, and I'd have given him a big hug if he'd have allowed it, which I was sure he would not. I hugged the book sack instead.

"Thank you for finding this. And me."

We sat with our own thoughts for a few minutes.

I said, "Before I got waylaid, I was looking for Sister Adelaide. I was hoping to find her in the root cellar next to the old mansion."

Jack stood, walked over to the sink, turned on the water, and rinsed out the cups.

When he turned to me again, he looked thoughtful. Something was on his mind. "You need to find her?"

My heart skipped. What did he know? "Yes, I really need to."

"I wasn't going to say anything yet ... I sort of promised Clary I wouldn't."

"Jack, please, if you know where Sister Adelaide is, you must tell me!" I could feel my head throbbing again.

He hesitated a moment or two before speaking, then it seemed he made up his mind. "Clary might know something. I can take you to her, but if I do, you got to promise you won't get her into any trouble with the sheriff."

I wanted to yell at him, "Stop playing games! Don't you realize how important this is?" But I didn't say that. I couldn't have yelled if I tried. Instead, I said, "If she knows anything, anything at all, I promise she won't get into trouble if I can help it. Will that do?"

He nodded. "Okay. Do you think your head's better now? Enough to leave here?"

"Yes. Where are we going?" I wasn't quite as ready as I thought. I had to steady myself for a few seconds when I stood up. I went into the bathroom, cupped water from the faucet and applied it to the sticky dried blood in my hair. A splash of water on my face helped. Then slowly I removed my damp woolen sweater and put on a dry one. I didn't look in a mirror. I didn't dare.

CHAPTER TWENTY-EIGHT

WE WALKED ACROSS THE ROAD from my quarters to Dr. Mills's house.

Jack tapped me on the shoulder, pointing to the front porch. "You knock on the door and ask to see Clary. Get her alone, upstairs if you can." Then he disappeared quickly to the other side of the house.

I had no idea of the time but sensed it must be very late. Or very early. I kept knocking on the door and ringing the doorbell. Finally, Rose responded. She stared through the glass panes. She clung to her robe pulled tightly around her, a terrified look on her face. Then, recognizing me, her face changed. Opening the door to me she said, "Oh, it's you, Miss Lyle. I thought it might be the sheriff." She held the door open.

"Rose, it's unforgivable of me to wake you this time of night. I know Dr. Mills and Clarice must be asleep."

"Doctor Mills hasn't been home all day. He had to stay at the hospital to be close to the patients until the sheriff finished. I think the sheriff must be talking to every single one."

"What about Clarice? Did you ever find her?

She frowned, averting my eyes when she spoke. "Oh, she here. She came home when she got hungry. Maybe I shouldn't, but I do worry so about that child."

"I understand why you would. I'm so glad she's here because it's really important that I talk to her."

"The child is sleepin'."

"Would it be okay for me to wake her up? Just for a few words?"

The housekeeper didn't like the idea at all, and from the set of her mouth was about to tell me politely but positively no, when a small voice from upstairs said, "Rose, who is that? Is it Daddy?"

"No, Miss Clary. It's Miss Lyle. Remember her? She had dinner here a couple nights ago."

Clarice came down several steps. She wore a white flannel robe over printed pajamas and had dark socks on her feet.

"Oh, hi, Miss Lyle. Why don't you come up? I've just been reading a book 'cause I can't sleep. I've been waiting for Daddy to get home so he can tell me what the sheriff is going to do about the murder. It's horrible, isn't it? I really loved Sister Gretchen."

"Your daddy won't like it, Miss Clary," Rose said.

"Really, it's all right, Rose. Maybe you could bring us some warm milk?"

Rose sniffed, "Well … I suppose I could do that."

I started up the stairs.

"Oh, thank you, Rose. We'd like that." Clarice's voice was a little too polite. Our eyes met and she threw me a bit of a smile and then turned, signaling me to follow her.

I stood in Clarice's doorway to catch my breath. The small lamp on her desk allowed just enough light for me to see Adelaide lying on Clarice's bed, covered up to her neck. I suspected Jack knew Sister Adelaide was there, but it was still a shock. It took me a few seconds to recognize her face. Brown hair clung to her head like a wet mop. As I moved to the bed and stood beside her, her blank expression made me grab at my throat to repress a gasp.

In a trembling voice I said, "Adelaide … it's me."

Clarice touched my shoulder, put her finger to her lips, turned, and went to the door. She must have heard Rose coming.

She closed the door behind her, saying, "Thank you so much, Rose. You can go back to bed. Miss Lyle is leaving in a few minutes. She'll let herself out. You know Daddy will be home soon."

Clarice brought two glasses of milk to the bedside table offering me one and holding the other out to Sister Adelaide. "Do you think you could try to drink a little of this, Sister?"

The blanket covering Sister Adelaide was rumpled, half on the floor, as though in a feverish act she had tried to throw it off. She opened her eyes at the sound of Clarice's voice and recognized me standing over her. She uttered a low moaning sound and moved her hand toward me. I took it. Her eyes were filled with fear. Was it fear of Clarice? Surely not. I leaned over when she tried to speak.

"No," I said, "don't try to say anything. If you can take a few sips of the milk, it might help you, though."

I was rewarded with a weak smile and a couple of sips from the glass Clarice held to her lips. The effort seemed overwhelming. In seconds, her eyes closed, and she had slipped away from us.

Clarice set a glass on her dresser, offering the other glass to me. I held it in my hand. She asked, "How did you know Sister Adelaide was here?"

"Jack told me." She nodded and glanced across the room to the partially open window. "How did she get here?"

She swallowed, her expression pained, her eyes still on the window. In a low voice she said, "I found her out on the road. I asked her if she wanted to go to the hospital, but she said she wanted a place to hide. I asked Jack, and he said if she wanted to hide from anyone, then the safest place would be in my bedroom. They'd never think of looking for her here." Then she hesitated. "Don't you want your milk? You look like you need it."

I looked down at the glass of milk in my hands. Then I looked hard at Clarice. "You're a terrible liar."

My words had the desired effect. She looked frightened then quickly regained her nerve. She scowled, saying angrily, "Liar? I'm not lying about anything. That's not a nice thing to say, Miss Lyle. We found her and wanted to help her. You can ask Jack."

"I will. Where is he?"

Clarice peered out the window, and in a moment Jack had raised it and crawled through from a tree branch. "Miss Lyle doesn't believe me, Jack. I did find Sister on the road when I was going to the library, didn't I? I asked you where to take her, and you said this would be the safest place. Tell her."

I stood facing them. "I'm so tired of this." My words were acknowledged with silence. I raised the glass of milk. "You drink this, Clarice." She shook her head. "Rose put something in the milk, didn't she? Sister Adelaide's been drugged. Your father's orders? You thought to do the same thing to me, didn't you?" I placed the glass back on the dresser.

Jack's eyes widened, his body stiffened. I was positive he had no idea what had been going on all day in this room. After eye contact with Clarice, however, he said, "What she said is true."

"No, it's not. Here's the truth, Jack. At some point during the day you came up that tree to see Clarice and found Sister Adelaide here. Why didn't you go to the police? Because Clarice said no?"

I raised my voice more than I wanted. "You're quite a pair. Where do you draw the line, anyway?" I stared at Clarice. "How did Sister Adelaide actually get into this room? Was it one of the workers? Or your father?"

"My daddy won't let her die! She's safe here. He told me. And he's coming back soon."

"So wherever he found her, he brought her here, instead of the hospital." The question was *why*, and searching the faces of the two teenagers, I knew they had no answer. But Clarice knew something. She was terrified and I desperately wanted to know why.

I made a stab at the answer. "You saw your father minister to Sister Adelaide. He left you and Rose with orders to keep her sedated. He told you not to tell anyone, but naturally, you told Jack. That wouldn't make Dr. Mills happy, but he actually might not have an idea how much time Jack spends coming in and out of that window. When your father gives you an order, he believes you obey him. However, I'm sure most of time," I paused, "you don't." My words had the right effect. She looked shocked.

Her face changed suddenly, anger took over. Clarice turned to Jack, spitting out, "You promised me you wouldn't tell anybody. I hate you, Jack. I hate you for doing that! I want you both to leave right now!"

I said, "I'm not going anywhere, Clarice." I turned to

Jack. "But you are. You're going to run as fast as you can and get the deputy standing just inside the nuns' quarters and bring him back here. His name is Deputy Cormier. Tell him you know where Sister Adelaide is. He'll come running. And you better be back in ten minutes!"

Jack hesitated. His eyes darted back and forth between Clarice and me.

I said as forcefully as I could, "Jack, Clarice says her father is coming home soon to take care of Sister Adelaide. You must believe me when I tell you she's in grave danger anywhere but with the nuns. Protected by a sheriff. Someone on the grounds of this place is a murderer. I was meant to be their next victim and would have been if you hadn't come along. Do you understand, Jack?"

As Jack turned to leave, Clarice grabbed for his arm. "No!"

He shook her off with a frown. *Thank you Lord,* I thought. He climbed out the window onto the tree branch. Then I turned back to Clarice, whose body shook with rage. I was pretty upset too.

"Those notes you wrote. Was my sister's the first? No, it must have been Penny and Tom's. *'A stranger will steal your baby.'* Wasn't that it?

Clarice crumbled before my eyes. She began to cry. "We wrote the note to warn them. A woman from some-place in New Orleans came to talk to my father. Jack and I heard everything. They were going to take their baby! They needed to run away!"

"Oh, really? How far did you think Tom would get before he was stopped, or dead? And what's your explanation for the note to my sister, warning her to watch the Samoans. What information do you have, Clarice?" I had to stop myself from grabbing and shaking the living daylights out of her. "Tell me. You didn't tell her, so tell *me* now!"

She collapsed in the window seat, sobbing. "I loved Sister Gretchen. But I heard her telling Daddy he should send Mama away."

"Your mother? Away?"

Her eyes blazed as she said, in a raised trembling voice, "Yes."

I was confused. "Explain to me what your mother has to do with the Samoans."

"Nothing. But Sister needed to mind her own business, that's all! So when Jack said he didn't trust the new people, that he thought they were up to no good 'cause he'd seen Polanie loading boats with groceries and taking off down the bayou, we decided to warn Sister Gretchen. Let her worry about the Samoans, instead of my mama!"

I could only shake my head, stare at her in disbelief. How incoherent, how silly. And how *childish*. Jack had witnessed Polanie stealing supplies and food and said nothing? Had he spoken to Sister Emily at once maybe the whole game being played by Charles Bremmer and his henchman, Polanie, would have been unearthed, discovered and dealt with by the marines. My guess was Jack probably would have told Sister Clara, at least, but Clarice had other ideas. Her mind seemed obsessed with fear for her mother. Why?

Sister Adelaide's eyes opened. She was drifting in and out of consciousness, but I thought she'd understood at least part of our conversation. Her mouth opened. I got down on my knees next to her. I now saw stab wounds where a knife had penetrated, wounds now held together with sutures. I trembled, whispering, "Oh my God, Sister Adelaide, who did this to you?" I took the top of her sheet and wiped away the sweat on her brow. I could tell she wanted to say something. I leaned in as close as I could.

She whispered one word close to my ear. But it was enough. I turned to see Clarice's whole body stiffen. She'd heard what Adelaide told me.

I knew everything now.

CHAPTER TWENTY-NINE

ROSE PUSHED OPEN THE BEDROOM door, holding a candle in her hand. I looked beyond her into the dark. It wasn't an electrical outage. The single lamp on Clarice's dresser glowed steadily within the bedroom. Its light was dim but bright enough to see Adelaide and Clarice. No, the lights must have been turned off on purpose.

Without moving from the doorway, Rose said, "Miss Eleanor wants to see you, Miss Lyle. She just come into the house." Clarice gasped and her hand flew across her mouth.

Rose said quickly, "No, Miss Clary. She's fine. She's real calm. Your mama just wants to talk to Miss Lyle, that's all. She said she's got to tell her somethin'."

"Does Daddy know she's here?"

"I don't know, child. But you stay here while Miss Lyle and me go downstairs."

Pointing at Adelaide, I said to Clarice, "I'm trusting you won't upset her. The deputy will be here in a few minutes." I waited for her silent nod then followed Rose downstairs into the blackness of the center hallway, where we entered the dining room, which was illuminated by a candelabra on the table and another on the sideboard.

The woman at the head of the table didn't speak or move while Rose held out a chair for me, opposite her. Eleanor sat in the same chair where Dr. Mills had sat at his dinner party on Friday. I thought I knew why she'd chosen that place. It was her painting on the wall behind her. Candlelight brought its scene of the river to life. The impasto technique used gave a textual dreamlike quality, layer upon layer of pigment. The painting seemed to frame Eleanor's head and shoulders into it. It was mesmerizing. Together, the artist and art glowed, encircled in candlelight. I had to shake my head back to reality as Rose leaned over to pour me a glass of wine. I studied the maid's expression, her hand trembling as she poured. She was terrified and hurried back into the kitchen.

A half-smile on her lips, Eleanor took a sip of her wine and motioned I should do the same. The white dress she wore glowed in the flickering candlelight. Her long, slender fingers coiled themselves around the wine glass in front of her. They were the fingers of a pianist. Or a painter. She'd been covered by a long cloak the last time I saw her, though I had seen her beautiful face, sculpted and white, with enormous eyes above hollowed, high cheek bones. What had been covered was her red hair cascading to her shoulders.

"Your sister told me so much about you, Catherine."

"And I was told very little about you, Eleanor. Only that you were away. Yet I suspected you couldn't have been gone too long. The paint's not dry on the painting behind you. That's your own work, not Millet's, isn't it?"

"Are you comparing me to Clarence Millet? I'm

honored, truly. But when were you here in my dining room?"

"Friday night. At a dinner party. It's imperceptible now, but that night I could smell paint and knew it wasn't dry yet. It's very like Millet's work. You've captured the children very well."

"We owned land across the river too. I watched the different families, squatters they called them, come and go, live in those shacks, all during my childhood. I confess, I envied those children playing together every day. Maybe I even hated them."

"This plantation belonged to your family then?"

"To me, actually. My father spent only one night here. And my mother left less than a year later. It was all so sad. Three years renovating this place and my father suddenly died the day after we moved in." She paused. "My poor mother seemed to go mad. She said she saw him walking and moaning night after night. My nanny told me it wasn't the ghost of my father, though, but that we were all cursed because the house sat on an Indian burial mound." She sighed.

Her story, told by rote, didn't match the pain in her eyes. And at that moment, she chose to shut them. A few seconds later, when she opened them again, they were glassy, staring into space. I could see her story had taken her back to another time.

She continued, "True or not, I've come to believe something must haunt my house. My father had a heart attack and Mother went away nine months later to a sanitarium in Baltimore. I think she planned to send for me, but she died there." Eleanor took a sip of wine, expecting a question, I thought. But impatient as I was at that moment, the questions I wanted to hurl at her might put her off. I wanted her to keep talking.

She sipped her wine. Searching for something else in her mind? Something forgotten? Finally, she asked, "Did you know I was there, when you had dinner with the sisters? My studio is on the third floor, in my old nursery."

My surprise must have registered. She chuckled. My hands were clenched together in my lap as I spoke. "It was your face I saw above the second floor balcony. I thought it was my imagination."

Eleanor laughed. A short, spiky sound, a flash of power in her eyes. "I was hiding from you in plain sight!"

Was this just a game to her? I felt a prickly surge of anger run through my body. "My imagination runs away with me sometimes. I imagined my sister's hanging corpse. But your face was real. What I didn't know then was that my sister was murdered. And I didn't know I was looking at the face of my sister's killer."

Eleanor's face contorted. She set her wine glass down, some of its contents spilling out onto the table. "Oh, Catherine! How could you accuse me of that! I didn't kill Sister Gretchen!" The anger in her voice shook me. She continued, "I was there when she died, but it was an accident. I loved her. I wouldn't hurt her!" Her voice changed to a high-pitched whine, like a child's. "Ask anyone. They'll tell you how much I loved her. She was the sister I'd never had. Of course, I hated it when she had to work. She was always so busy! 'I must see to the patients,' she'd tell me. I was so jealous of them! They had so much more of her than I did. You must believe me, Catherine; I'm devastated by her death."

Silence filled the room while I studied the woman at the end of the table. It was odd how one minute she spoke calmly, rationally, then in the next flared out of control. I watched her expression change yet again, as though she were fighting some inner demons. Her hand trembled when she held the wine glass. As she sipped, a false smile rose to her lips. Eleanor's eyes were strangely fascinating, darting from me to the door behind me, to the walls around us, but I felt she really wasn't seeing anything, that she was trapped inside her own mind, desperately trying to make sense of her thoughts.

I jumped when she spoke again. The sound her voice had become deep and husky. "Don't say those things. And don't make such a face, Catherine. What happened to Sister Gretchen was tragic, but it was an accident." She uttered a small sigh. "A horrible accident. Someone should have explained it to you. I'm sorry no one did.

Through gritted teeth I said, "I'm here now." I wanted to scream in her face.

"And I'm so glad." She took a small sip and straightened herself against the back of her chair, taking another moment to exert what seemed rigid control over her voice. Tonelessly, as if practiced, she continued. "Your sister knew how sad I was. But I don't think she felt sorry for me. We painted and sketched together. That's when she told me how the both of you did the same thing." A small smile appeared. "She talked about you so much. What I wouldn't give to have been in your shoes!"

So Gretchen had left out the horror. Perhaps for good reason, I thought. "Our lives weren't as nice as you might believe. But, yes, I have my sister to thank for any happiness I've enjoyed."

"Were you devastated when she took her holy orders? I would have been."

I said quietly, "I've missed her every day she's been gone."

Eleanor's eyes gleamed intensely, "Your sister taught me so much more about painting than I ever learned studying in a class. We sketched and painted with watercolor under the trees at the bottom of the levee. Sister loved it there, even if I didn't. I told her the river didn't hold the same magic for me as it did her. She kept saying it was important to get in touch with my feelings. I tried. I really did! And as hard as it was, I think the painting behind me is the best thing I've ever done."

I could feel my heart throbbing. Her eyes told me everything. Eleanor was sick. Did it go as far as insanity? I said, in as calm a voice as I could, "It's beautiful. Haunting."

"Haunting? You have your sister's artistic eye, don't you? You see beyond the surface, into memory. The shacks have been gone for so long; I had them all removed. Yet I had to paint them in. I saw them as clearly as I saw the children." Through pinched lips she continued. "I hate that painting, really. I won't look at it again. It needs to be destroyed, along with all the memories."

Suddenly, I remembered. One of the last pictures in Gretchen's journal. The purple sky setting over the river, a small house hidden behind the trees, and then the whole page scratched out. My sister would not have treated any sketch with that much anger.

I said, "Maybe my sister was wrong. Not everyone should be encouraged to remember their past."

Eleanor nodded. The gleam in her eyes was replaced by something else. Loss? Sadness? Guilt? I couldn't tell.

"I shouldn't have lost my temper with her. If I could take back what I said ..."

"What happened, Eleanor? How did she die?"

"Words!" She yelled angrily. "I didn't need any more words from anybody!"

She shut her eyes again, remembering perhaps, or trying to erase the memories flooding in upon her.

"Didn't you bring me here to tell me what happened? What happened at the river?"

Eleanor threw a glance of irritation down the table at me. Would she continue? Or blow apart? Remarkably, though, when she spoke next, her voice was calm, the words sincere.

"I wanted to die. I've wanted that for some time, and it seemed like the right time, you see. It would be so easy. Just let the water cover you. Everything gone. But when I waded out into the river, Sister Gretchen was there. With all her words! But I was stronger than she was. We fought. She couldn't swim. It was over before I knew what had happened."

Alarm bells started going off in my mind. I stood and reached for the light switch. The chandelier cast a reality I suddenly wanted.

"Did you also lose your temper with Sister Adelaide? And Tom?"

Her eyes darted around the room. "That was all so unfortunate. But, honestly, I don't know if I'm to blame for any of it. I told David I didn't want to stay in that place. It reminded me of the shanties across the river. Tom was in constant pain, stoic though, sleeping when he was there, but thankfully not there much. David told me Penny would be lying in at the hospital. I just had to stay until you left."

"Then Sister Adelaide showed up and you were discovered."

The soft lines of her mouth turned downward, scowling. "Stupid of me. Most likely she'd never have searched the room above. And, really, I don't think she was looking for me but for Tom. I'm afraid I made a mess of things, telling them about Sister Gretchen. But I wanted to tell someone, you see. I wanted to tell *you*."

"Tom is dead. Eleanor, why is Tom dead?"

Only her hands showed her distress. She twisted the wine stem between them. Her face remained placid. "He was dying of his disease. All lepers die. Isn't that obvious to you?" The sad smile she offered wavered, her eyes left mine and searched the top of her glass, a thought uttered almost to herself, "What a stubborn man."

"Why do you call him stubborn? Because he wouldn't get out of your way when you tried to stab Sister Adelaide?"

Her disdainful expression changed to an intense, fevered stare. When she spoke, I felt a sudden chill. "He was so unreasonable ... they both were. There was no reason for it. Sister Gretchen's death was an accident."

"Did Sister Adelaide tell you she was going to the sheriff? And you had to stop her? You stabbed her with a kitchen knife. But Adelaide got away from you, didn't she? After Tom intervened."

She narrowed her eyes at me then looked aside, her voice agitated. "David will be furious with Tom. He was supposed to protect *me*."

I thought our conversation might end at any second, in an uncontrollable outburst.

"Tom was insufferable. He grabbed me from behind and wouldn't let me go! He had no right to do that. A squatter on my land, and he thought to touch me!" She paused throwing me a furtive glance. "Lately, I've had an aversion to anyone touching me, Catherine." She frowned, "It's that awful medicine your sister made me take, I think."

I waited a moment or two, tried to make eye contact, which was useless. I knew she'd hear me, however. She couldn't ignore my voice. "But Tom is dead. And we don't know if Sister Adelaide will survive. You did that, Eleanor."

Eleanor's wine glass broke between her fingers. She stared at it, at the blood on her hand. The child-like whine again in her voice. "This is your fault, Catherine. It was my mother's best crystal." She took her napkin and wrapped it around her bleeding hand.

A minute passed in silence. I studied her facial expressions, her eyes darting from one place to another, like a storm being waged inside her head. The childlike pout upon her lips, the whine in her voice changed to a twisted smile, her thoughts taking her to some darker retreat exploding inside her mind. When her eyes found mine again, there was an accusation of some inner transgression I'd committed, of an explosion yet to come. I imagined her jumping up and coming at me, the broken wine glass her weapon.

When she spoke again, her voice was like a jolt of lightning, and there was a hard, fixed smile still on her lips. "If Tom is dead, it isn't because of anything I did. He died from his disease. Sister Adelaide got in my way. I had to get away from them. I've told you, Catherine, I've never killed anyone. That would be a horrible sin. I couldn't live with myself."

I was amazed. How was it possible to inflict such horror on three human beings and not know it? Where did that kind of madness come from, I wondered. At which point did her love and obsession with my sister cross a line into insanity?

We both heard the front door open. "Who's at my door?" she said, her eyes suddenly round, searching the opening to the hallway behind me.

By his gait, I knew Deputy Cormier had entered the

house. But I heard more steps behind him. Then Jack said, "She's upstairs."

"Is it David?" Eleanor whispered.

"It's a deputy sheriff."

"Why is he in my house?"

I searched for some semblance of recognition, but her eyes only looked round and frightened. Suddenly, she pushed her chair back and stood. Was she going to run out of here? I stood up, not knowing if I could stop her. But she turned around, her back to me. She was staring at her painting. She walked next to it, placing her face and body against the canvas.

It didn't strike me as terribly odd. I thought immediately of my woolen closet on the third floor, of the darkness inside it, making me invisible to everyone. It must be the same for Eleanor. Once she'd put herself inside her painting, she'd crossed the river to play with the squatter's children. She'd found a sanctuary where she could disappear from the rest of the world.

I heard Jack say, "Sister's upstairs in Clary' room. You want me to show you?"

Deputy Cormier answered, "Yes." I heard their footsteps on the stairs.

"There's a light in the dining room. I'm going to check on it." I jerked my head around. It was Yves's voice.

The deputy answered, "Suit yourself."

Seconds later, when Yves appeared at the dining room door, he stopped, started to speak, but I put a finger to my lips. I would wonder later what had made Yves come down the hall. Had it just been the light? Or Rose's muffled crying, barely audible through the thick pocket doors between the dining room and the kitchen. Or did he sense

I was in there? When I asked him later, he said for some unexplained reason he felt compelled to walk that way.

Oh, the questions, the answers I had for him! But it was not the time. When I put my finger to my lips, he understood how imperative it was the silence not be broken. I motioned to him I was going upstairs and for him to wait for me there. He nodded, touching me on the shoulder as I passed him into the hall.

I climbed the stairs to Clarice's bedroom and told Deputy Cormier Eleanor confessed to me she had stabbed Tom and Sister Adelaide. That was enough for now. I'd tell the sheriff what she'd done to my sister later. He needed to get downstairs and help Yves before Eleanor decided to run away again.

He said, "Okay, I'm going. But Sheriff Doucet wants all of you to get back to the hospital. He'll send one of the nuns to sit with Sister Adelaide." He turned at the doorway, "I'll give you a call when we're ready to leave with the lady down stairs."

It wouldn't do to argue with him, but I knew I wasn't going anywhere just yet. I certainly wasn't' going to leave Sister Adelaide. Still, I nodded. "I understand." And he was gone.

Clarice stood against the wall, her head down. Looking at her, a stab of guilt touched my heart, but nothing could be covered up anymore.

I looked at the two children. They stood shoulder to shoulder, like two stoic soldiers.

I couldn't keep the accusatory tone out of my voice. "Who closed the door to the root cellar on me? Was it the two of you or Eleanor?"

In a small voice, Clarice answered, "It was just to scare

you. To get you to leave." Her face was red, streaked by incessant crying.

Jack's shoulders seemed to curl into themselves. He mumbled, "We wouldn't have let you die. It was just so we had time to write the note. We were coming back to open the door, but Sister Adelaide found you first."

I glanced at Adelaide. She suffered. Her eyes were red, filled not just with pain but with sadness too. I could see she was listening. I knew these two children had participated in their own conspiracy to protect Eleanor as surely as others must have done. Sister Adelaide didn't know how far they'd gone. She didn't know Tom was dead. No, she saw two frightened children, terrified of the consequences their actions might incur. But she didn't see meanness. She saw love as their motive; at least it was for Clarice. And I knew Jack would do anything Clarice asked of him.

A weak smile crossed Sister Adelaide's face as I said to them, "Well, I guess I must thank you both for your odd sort of protection, mustn't I?" I saw Clarice's pained stare then surprise. Her expression told me how confused she was. I continued, "Today will be hard for you, Clarice. You're going to hear some ugly things. Not just about your mother, I'm afraid." She flinched and her tears began again.

I continued, "I'm going to tear up the notes. I don't think it's necessary to discuss them with the sheriff or anyone. What do you think, Sister?" Sister Adelaide nodded and motioned both the children to her. It was a sweet moment, seeing them holding hands. Unfortunately, it didn't last long. We all turned to listen to the long, incessant screams coming from downstairs. "No! No! Don't touch me, don't touch me!"

Deputy Cormier and Yves were removing Eleanor from her house.

CHAPTER THIRTY

YVES AND I SAT IN Clarice's bedroom. He'd returned to the house when I refused to leave Adelaide in anyone's care but my own.

"No, Officer. Tell Sheriff Doucet I'm not leaving this room until Sister Adelaide is in the ambulance." I set my chin so stiffly it hurt. I had glanced at Jack. His eyes were round as silver dollars. "Take the children. I'm not moving. And I don't want to make a scene right now with Sister in such pain."

"He's not going to be happy about it, miss."

"I know that. But he'll just have to understand."

Yves sat on the small stool next to Clarice's dressing table, a dim lamp casting his shadow across the room. I sat on a chair next to the bed, stroking Sister Adelaide's hand. We allowed the silence to fill the space around us as minutes on the small alarm clock ticked on.

I jumped at Yves voice, though it was just above a whisper. "Jack and Clarice are with the nuns, in their quarters."

"I'm glad. Better they are away from what's happening

inside Sister Emily's office." I watched Sister Adelaide's breathing. Was she asleep or unconscious? I hoped for the former. Glancing over at Yves, I saw he'd closed his eyes. No wonder. We'd had no sleep for almost twenty-four hours. Through the window, a gray light of day appeared.

I rose to switch off the lamp and Yves opened his eyes. He said, "The ambulance will be here soon. When they take Sister Adelaide to Baton Rouge, I want you to go with them. You really need to get that bump checked."

We'd had the same conversation earlier, after I told him what had happened to me. But I didn't want to leave here. The bump on my head hurt when I touched it, but the headache was bearable now. I shook my head. "I hope Sister Adelaide will understand, but I can't leave until this thing is over. It wasn't all Eleanor's doing. She had help. We know it was Tom who hid her in the spare room above his cabin, but what else did he do for Dr. Mills? Poor Tom. He'd have done anything to get that treatment, and Dr. Mills knew it."

Clarice's bedside clock registered near seven o'clock. Night was gone, but no sun had appeared. The sky offered only a thick sheet of steel gray. Nature seemed to have postponed the beginning of this day.

There were beads of sweat on Sister Adelaide's face. "I think her pain medicine has worn off. I stared down at the unconscious girl and pulled the blanket away from her, leaving only the sheet. I looked at Yves. "Sister Adelaide got away from Eleanor. Tom intervened. But when did David Mills find her and bring her here?"

"Maybe he found Sister Adelaide at the bayou when he went looking for his wife."

"Yes, I think that's right. And brought her here to hide her. Not to protect her."

Yves nodded. "Sister Adelaide knew too much."

At that moment, Adelaide's head twisted from side to side. She seemed agitated. I stroked her head, whispering, "Everything's all right now, Sister. You're safe now. You're going to the hospital in Baton Rouge. I'm here and so is my friend, Yves. Don't worry." My hands were trembling and surely she heard the fear in my voice. She opened her eyes briefly then seemed to sink back into unconsciousness again. I took a breath. "I hope she understood me."

Yves looked at his watch and frowned. "Where's the damn ambulance?"

The ticking of the clock filled the ensuing silence between us, letting my mind go to a place I dreaded to think about. But it needed to be said. The dream I'd had; I couldn't let go. Should I tell him? I didn't even know where to begin. How would he react? My dearest friend. I didn't want to hurt him, and yet if I didn't tell him now, when would I? It was festering inside me.

I tried to speak as normally as possible. "Yves, something happened to me after Eleanor hit me." When he looked up, I took a breath, letting the words spill out. "I remembered what happened to Papa. I remembered pushing him over the bannister."

I expected shock to register on Yves face. It didn't. He didn't speak at once but regarded me from his chair. He nodded. "You were bound to remember it all someday."

"Why did you and Gretchen cover up what I'd done, Yves?"

He sat still for a minute or more. I listened to Sister Adelaide's breathing. When he did speak, there was a hoarseness in his voice. "You say you remember, but if you do, then you know it was an accident. Gretchen saw all of it. Your father fell. And if you hadn't been able to get free of him, he'd have pulled you over the bannister with him. You're lucky to be alive."

I wasn't prepared to hear that. "If I didn't push him, then why take him away? Why take his body out of the house and make it look like he'd been beaten to death?"

His expression changed, his mouth tightened around a grim memory. "Gretchen asked me that same question. I'll tell you what I told her that night. I wasn't going to let the police question either one of you. The horror in your house would become newspaper fodder. Gossip throughout the city. I wasn't about to let that happen." His voice cracked and tears appeared in his eyes. "Do you know how helpless I felt, knowing what was happening to Gretchen and never being able to help her!"

"Oh, Yves. The nuns couldn't help us. Gretchie was so afraid you might say something and he would fire you! We couldn't lose you too."

"I know. That's what Gretchen said. She begged me to be quiet." Yves coughed, choking on the words he said. "How could he do that to her? An innocent girl?"

"I know my father blamed Gretchen for Mama's and Joseph's deaths. He was a vicious, horrible man who stayed bitter and angry when he was sober and turned into a monster when he was drunk." The room suddenly felt hot. I felt a bead of sweat run down my neck. The next thing I said was the thing I dreaded knowing. "Did he rape my sister? Do you know?"

He stared at me. I didn't think he was going to answer, then in a low voice he said, "I asked her that. Had he molested or raped her, I could have reported it to the police. But she said he only hit her. She said, strangely, it seemed to relieve him after he'd beat her. He'd use the words 'you killed them,' over and over." Yves covered his face with his hands. "Oh God! I should have gotten you both out of there. I failed both of you."

"You didn't. When we needed you most, you came and took Papa's body out of house. You protected us and let me put that horrible memory away until I was old enough to handle it. You saved me, and I think your encouragement to Gretchen when she wanted to become a nun saved her."

A sad smile appeared on his face. I could see something still troubled him. I said, "There's something else, isn't there? Please tell me."

Tears ran down his cheeks. "I've wanted to tell you … I'm sorry. All these years I've watched and wanted to explain what happened that night. But then I worried, and so did Gretchen, if we brought the whole thing back, would it hurt you more? Your mind closed off the memory of his fall. We didn't want to make you remember if you didn't have to."

I stood and went to him, taking his hands, staring down at his face contorted in grief. He looked up at me. "It was a mistake, Catherine. Not my shielding you and your sister from all the gossip and meanness. I'll never say that was a mistake. But not telling you the truth. I've watched and regretted not telling you. You couldn't heal."

"That's what Gretchen meant in her journal. She wrote, 'My only regret is Catherine.'"

"We should have told you. Your whole life would have been so different if we had."

I thought about it for a few seconds. Then walked to the window, felt a coolness from outside. Finally, I said, "No, I really don't think it would. I think I'd have lived exactly as I've lived no matter what."

"Even if that's so, I'm glad you've remembered the

truth." He cast that same sad smile at me. *Perhaps,* I thought, *because something inside me didn't believe him entirely.* My dream was so real. I had pushed my father and he was dead. I shook my head, ran fingers through my hair. I thought, wasn't it right to put Yves's and my guilt behind us? Move ahead? I knew if my sister were alive, she'd be happy for it.

I stared down at the road leading to the hospital. "I think it's the sheriff walking this way. He's got a different deputy with him." I turned back to Yves. "And you'll never guess who else."

CHAPTER THIRTY-ONE

SHERIFF ALCIDE DOUCET LOOKED SLEEPY, red-eyed and badly in need of a shave. The gray stubble on his pouchy cheeks and chin looked like a Brillo pad, the thin line of his lips a fuse ready to explode any second. I lowered my eyes to study the veins on the top of his hands, which he'd placed on his knees. Yes, he was furious, but then so was I. He'd ordered I meet him in Sister Emily's office, where I gathered he'd been conducting interviews since yesterday. But I wasn't about to leave Adelaide until we put her in an ambulance to Our Lady of the Lake Sanitarium. I told the deputy I'd come to him as soon as that happened.

But instead, the sheriff had decided to come to me.

The deputy he called Vilmer stood next to the door. The only person in the room I didn't want there was Sister Emily. Her body, straight and erect in the window seat, was like a wooden post, her back glued against the wall. When she'd first appeared at the doorway, her eyes met mine, then she'd stepped directly to the bed and kneeled beside Adelaide and begun to pray silently. I turned my head, clenched my teeth. After a few minutes she rose and sat down.

The sheriff glared at me. "My deputy told me you've got some accusations to make, but first, I'm going to ask you some questions about you and your friend there."

"What? I have to identify Yves? Surely you've talked to Father O'Quinn, Sheriff. We found Tom barely alive. Yves came to you to get help. Why didn't you come?"

The sheriff's eyes flared, and he pointed a finger in my face, his gravelly voice contemptuous. "Don't tell me my job, missy. You answer *my* questions. Understand? There's criminal trespassing and a man murdered in his home, and the both of you up to your necks in all of it. I'm pretty close to running both of you into Prairieville and letting breaking the law sink in on you while you sit in a cell."

"Yves and I were trying to save Tom's life, not kill him! Sister Adelaide will tell you, Eleanor Mills tried to kill her. And if you hand me my satchel, I can prove Eleanor murdered Tom Langlinais."

Sister Adelaide's glassy, fever-filled eyes had opened when our interrogation began. Well, no wonder. I was shouting.

Yves handed my shoulder bag to me. My hands were shaking as I retrieved the bloody knife, still wrapped in part of my undershirt.

"We found this near the bayou. It was used on Sister Adelaide, but now I'm positive you'll also find Tom's blood and Eleanor Mills's fingerprints on the handle."

The sheriff's bushy eyebrows rose, he glanced over at his deputy, who immediately came forward to take it.

The sheriff turned to where Adelaide lay. She was conscious. Just.

"Sister? Can you confirm any of what Miss Lyle has

said? Did Eleanor Mills attack you with a knife? Just a simple yes or no or a nod of the head will do."

She winced, I thought from her pain, but more perhaps from the memory of what happened to her. She nodded, shutting her eyes.

"And you were in fear for your life?"

Her lips and chin trembled. "Yes," she whispered.

I thought I saw something akin to an expression of relief cross the sheriff's face. It lasted only a second before he shook it off and replied to her, "Thank you, Sister. Let's leave it there for now."

I stood up at that moment hearing the wail of a siren. "They're here, Sister Adelaide!" I was rewarded with a weak smile.

Sister Emily lowered her head. Yves ran out of the room before anyone could stop him. The sheriff's interrogation was interrupted. His questions would have to wait a few more minutes.

As Adelaide was prepared by ambulance attendants and then placed on a stretcher, I held her gaze. When the attendants left with her, I started to follow, but the sheriff's voice stopped me.

"We've got unfinished business, Miss Lyle."

"She's afraid. Someone needs to be with her. I can reassure her she's not in any danger."

From her seat at the window, Sister Emily murmured in a flat monotone voice, "She's not alone. Sister Edith is going with her."

I stared across the room. "Oh. Well, that's good."

The tension in Sister Emily's body hadn't gone away. She angled herself toward the window again, her expression blank, mouth tightly drawn.

The sheriff pointed to a chair, then sat opposite me.

Our knees almost touched as he glared down his nose at me. His black, coal-like eyes were impressively intimidating. It was hard to look at him directly. I had had a father like that, with terrifying eyes. But my father's voice was clipped, with staccato jabs of words that stung. Sheriff Doucet's voice, hoarse or not, was compelling to listen to.

He continued. "If it's the knife that stabbed Sister Adelaide and Tom Langlinais, and Mrs. Mill's prints are on it, then there's proof she's guilty of murder and attempted murder of Sister Adelaide. He challenged me. "And I'll know soon if you're lying about the knife or not."

"I'm not lying, Sheriff."

He stood and flicked the stub of his cigarette out the window. Everyone turned as Yves came back into the room, nodding at me, a tiny smile on his lips. He sat again next to the dresser.

Sheriff Doucet said, "If it's true, then I'll be satisfied you and Mr. Antoine didn't have a part in the man's death."

Anger made my voice quiver. "Eleanor Mills also murdered my sister, Sheriff. Don't forget that."

He waited, took another cigarette from his pocket, lit it, and inhaled deeply. "Doctor Mills claims he examined your sister's body and didn't find anything that would signify an altercation took place. His wife is sorry for the accident. He shouldn't have tried to cover it up as suicide, he knows that, but he wanted to spare his wife any additional pain. She was upset enough knowing Sister Gretchen drowned." The sheriff stepped closer, got in my face. His smoky breath made me flinch. Just above a whisper, he said, "You've got your murderer, Miss Lyle. With the knife and her confession as to Tom Langlinais and Sister Adelaide. Mrs. Mills will be put away for life. Let it go. You got no proof of anything else."

My cheeks were burning. "Didn't the coroner see the bruises on Gretchen's back? The blood under her fingernails from when she fought Eleanor Mills? "There's an autopsy. Blood evidence. Eleanor Mills confessed to me that she and my sister fought at the river because she wanted to commit suicide and Gretchen went into the river after her. They fought. Gretchen was held down in the river, Sheriff, until she drowned!" Shaking with anger, I turned to Sister Emily. "Dr. Mills is covering up murder! Did you help him do that, Sister?"

The sheriff said, "Now you're accusing Mother Superior? Where's it all going to end? What do you want? Should I arrest the whole damn leper colony!"

I couldn't speak. Then I heard Yves behind me. "She wants the truth, Sheriff."

The words tumbled out of me, "The truth! Yes, and the truth is," I gasped, "Eleanor Mills killed my sister. Dr. Mills knew it was murder, otherwise why hide his wife? From you. From me. He concocted a scheme to make it look like my sister committed suicide!" I thought of Tom. "Maybe someone helped him. Maybe not. But his wife told me the whole story, downstairs, in her dining room while sipping wine from her mother's best crystal!"

The sheriff looked hard into my eyes. "Take a deep breath." He stared at me in silence for a few seconds. "One thing at a time, okay? You've got a bump on your head. A good one. You want to tell me how that happened?"

"Yes. All right." I felt Yves hand on my shoulder, his breath on the back of my neck.

"After Tom passed ... well, I thought I'd find you or Yves on the road. Except someone was coming, and it wasn't either of you. So I hid."

"When was that?"

"It was turning dark; you couldn't see much with the fog so thick. I suppose I left there around six o'clock? I didn't take the main road. I cut across the field. Then I found a path leading into the hospital. I must have ended up under the Protestant chapel around seven." I thought for a second. "It had started to rain."

"You ended up *under* the Protestant chapel?"

I nodded. "It's built up on piers."

"And why were you under there?"

"Between the pilings I saw that Charles Bremmer had stacked all his pew bench crates. I crawled under to look at them. I thought it might be a hiding place," I glanced at Sister Emily, "for a body. For Sister Adelaide's body."

Sister Emily's eyes closed.

The sheriff looked behind me, at Yves, then at me again. He said, "All right. You were under the Protestant chapel somewhere between seven and eight o'clock. Then what happened?"

"And when I was just getting up, someone hit me."

"And knocked you out? Is that it?"

"Yes. I didn't see who it was. It was dark. And raining. Thank goodness Jack came along. I don't know what might have happened if he hadn't."

"You can't identify who it was?"

"Maybe it was Dr. Mills. But I know now Eleanor had been looking for me for hours. If I had to guess, I'd guess Eleanor. Someone stronger might have done a lot more damage."

He gave a heavy nod before saying slowly, "Given that time frame, it wasn't Dr. Mills. He was in the hospital all evening, seen and vouched for by Sister Emily and others."

I looked over at Sister Emily. Her face was turned

away, staring out the window. I wanted her to turn around. Could she lie to my face?

Sheriff Doucet waited until I gave him my attention again. I felt tears well up in my eyes. I couldn't cry! Yves grabbed me, turned me around, and I sank against his shoulder, sobbing.

Sheriff Doucet grunted. "Take her out into the hall."

We returned several minutes later. I sat on the bed. The sheriff looked down at me, "It's almost done, Miss Lyle. Can you finish it?"

I looked up at the old man and saw something in his eyes. Admiration? Surely not. "Yes," I said, trying to keep eye contact.

He nodded slightly. "I've already explained to you we only have Mrs. Mills's side of the story. And her husband, the physician, confirms it. She claims Sister Gretchen drowned trying to save her from taking her own life. Your sister went in after her, even though she didn't know how to swim."

"Sheriff, someone took her body from the river and hung it in the mansion!"

The sheriff scowled. "Dr. Mills has admitted doing that. But it was a cover-up to an accident, given his report. And, unfortunately, I can't charge anyone with murder for hanging a dead body. It's strange. It's crazy. But it's not a crime." He turned to look out the window. Or was he staring at Sister Emily sitting in the window seat? When he walked over to her, she raised her eyes to his.

She nodded and said in a low, hoarse voice, "I hope it wasn't murder, Sheriff."

I didn't move. She gazed at each one of us with eyes lost somewhere in the past. "I did what I did for the community of souls for which I'm responsible. They are so fragile! Their lives have been put on hold, at best. At worst, they've received a death sentence. I had to protect them, don't you see?"

Her voice was pleading, "Sister Mary Gretchen would have understood. She would have approved. Suicide happens here. All the time. I wish it weren't so … . It's so incomprehensible to outsiders. It was to me too when I first came here. Not now."

The sheriff said, "What do you mean, Sister, you did it for them? Is it the lepers you're talking about?"

A bitter smile appeared on Sister Emily's face, her voice cold as ice. "You'd call them outcasts, the living dead, wouldn't you? To be locked away like prisoners forever! Each day these patients live with so much suffering and death." She paused as if to make what she said next more important. "At least they've been spared murder! Even the suspicion of murder would frighten them so much!" Her eyes pierced mine. "Try to understand. Murder would tilt whatever view of normal we've managed to give our patients. For them to believe a murderer was running loose somewhere would be devastating."

The sheriff said, "So you helped Dr. Mills hang the dead body?"

"Dr. Mills came to me, took me to the mansion where Sister's body had been laid out. He explained what had happened. I accepted his explanation and we both thought to say her death was a suicide was the best course to take." She paused. "It wasn't to protect Eleanor! I wanted to protect *everyone else.* Perhaps Dr. Mills had a different reason, but I decided to say Sister Gretchen died by an act of suicide to protect the community. The police would come and go and leave us in peace. It was a small lie I knew God would forgive. I brought some dry clothes for Gretchen and left Dr. Mills there with her body."

The tension in the room was palpable. The sheriff stared at Sister Emily with an unfolding frown that gave his face unexpected strength. "So you told a small lie to cover up what you were told was a tragic accident. And look where that 'small lie' got you, Sister? One man murdered, another nun nearly murdered." He pinched the butt of his cigarette with two fingers then flicked it away through the open window. "A small lie? Not so good, Sister. You should have stuck with the truth."

I spit the words out, "Sister Emily couldn't tell the truth because she knew my sister was murdered! It wasn't a small lie. You knew Eleanor murdered my sister." I screamed, "Tell him!"

A gust of wind lifted muslin curtains that briefly covered the nun's face like a shroud. Sister Emily raised her hands pushing them away, and I saw her chin quivering, her taut face breaking apart like a china cup smashed onto the floor. When she spoke, it came in an agonizing outburst.

"Sister Mary Gretchen was an excellent swimmer, Sheriff. The minute I heard Dr. Mills's story, I knew Eleanor had probably drowned Sister Gretchen." Sister Emily stopped talking and pulled her arms tightly around her body in an effort to stop shaking.

"Take your time, Sister." The sheriff's voice was remarkably kind, but I noticed his eyes had not left hers, not for a second. After a minute had passed, she continued. "Eleanor is not well. She needs to be in a sanitarium, but both Dr. Mills and Sister Gretchen thought they could take care of her here. Just recently, though, Sister Gretchen mentioned to me she thought Eleanor needed more evaluation. She was 'more tense' was how she put it."

"Did Eleanor Mills and her husband know Sister Gretchen could swim?"

"Yes. There's no way they could not." Her voice constricted and she grabbed her throat as though willing the words to be said. "Sister taught many of the patients how to swim in the shallows of the river during the summer months. Yes, Eleanor knew."

"Both you and Dr. Mills knew?" Sheriff Doucet asked. Sister Emily nodded back at him. He continued, "Sister, you've just confessed to being an accessory to murder, then covering it up."

The nun looked exhausted. Her expression registered brief surprise, then acceptance. "If you say so, then I guess I'm guilty." She looked around the room. Her eyes lingered on me, as if saying, "Now you have your truth." Then continued on, taking in not just me, but everyone. And strangely, perhaps, others who weren't there. She was looking for my sister's face.

Her voice was choked by tears. "You'll never understand. Any of you! No one can unless they live here. I went along with a lie knowing Sister Gretchen could swim but praying what Eleanor said was true, that it was a horrible accident. Because it was the best way. I did it for every soul here. In my heart I thought I was doing the right thing. May God forgive me!"

I turned my back on her. In that moment I understood why the sheriff had brought Sister Emily with him to hear my statement. He hoped to get the full story by bringing us face to face. My admiration suddenly rose for the crusty old man, who, it turned out, was smarter than any of us.

In the next few hours, I watched Sister Emily, Eleanor, and Dr. Mills placed inside the sheriff's cars and driven away. But before Sheriff Doucet left, he pulled me aside to say, "I don't know about arrests for your sister's murder. It'll be up to the DA. Your sister's murder is going to be hard to prove, even with Sister Emily's testimony. The wife has a history of mental illness. What she confessed to you may not hold up. The best thing we've got is the murder of Tom Langlinais and attempted murder of Sister Adelaide. Her testimony and the knife should be enough for a conviction."

I said softly, "I see." Was there nothing more I could do? If no charges were brought against Eleanor, would it mean I'd failed my sister? Absolutely. Yes. And yet, in that same moment, I questioned if the answer was really *yes.* Sister Emily, Eleanor Mills, David Mills. These were people my sister lived and worked with and even loved, especially Sister Emily. And I had what I wanted, didn't I? The truth about her death. Reluctantly, I had to admit to myself some of the anger driving me was dissipating. I couldn't forgive them, even if deep down I knew my sister would want me to. I felt my stomach turn over. I swallowed and looked up at the sheriff again. "I'd like to bury my sister. May I at least do that?"

"I'll see to it her body is returned."

Yves took my hand. His expression said it all.

Or was it Gretchen's voice I heard in my head? *"Imagine a place you've never been, Cathy. Paint what you see in your mind."*

How to paint forgiveness? That would take some time.

CHAPTER THIRTY-TWO

BEYOND WHERE THE GUEST AND administrative quarters had been built, at the end of the gravel road, lay a piece of land from which the nuns had created a cemetery. An ancient live oak tree, its branches so heavy they touched the ground, seemed to stand sentinel over many white wooden crosses, symbols of life and death, of human joy and sadness, and over an everlasting stillness punctuated only by the sound of moving water flowing to the same rhythm of human life. The river.

The place was visible to any barge or steamboat or small canoe moving up or down the river's course. Thus, the cemetery gave not only a peaceful resting place to the departed, but also offered a surprise to travelers on the Mississippi, a place that inspired a silent prayer or just a sigh captured on the breeze as they passed by.

I sighed, pulling my coat around me. Looking back, I could see the hospital, not etched against a clear sky but faded and dismal gray. Yet, I thought, even under a clear blue sky, sadness would cling to this place like those low winter clouds. Sadness but also surprising happiness sometimes. For many it was a sanctuary. Guilt and shame and self-loathing weren't needed here. We were given permission to live our lives without those things.

We? I thought, then nodded my head. It was true. I needed this place as much as my sister had.

I looked down at the simple white cross in front of me:

Sister Mary Gretchen, D.C.
1903–1940

Would she approve of my decision not to take her home for burial, to leave her here? I thought so. A few hours before, every person who worked or was treated here had walked the short distance, holding hands, in twos and threes or more. Father O'Quinn, Sister Paul, Sister Clara, and Sister Anne led everyone. I watched them approach as two young men continued to diligently dig the grave in the cold, hard clay. Everyone encircled my sister's grave. No one spoke but let the men finish their task. Finally, their shovels laid aside, they lowered the plain wooden box with my sister's remains down into a six-foot hole. It was a dark place. Dark places had brought me a sense of protection. I prayed that my sister's soul was safe now with God.

My voice carried across the vacant cemetery. "We're leaving today, Gretchie. I think this is where you want to be, isn't it? Not inside a mausoleum in New Orleans. This is such a beautiful spot." My eyes misted over. "I'll miss you every day of my life, you know." I knelt down and touched the cross, its paint still drying. "We're taking Jack home with us. Yves isn't sure it's the right decision." I laughed lightly, remembering my conversation with him earlier this morning.

Yves had looked at me skeptically, saying, "I hope

you're sure about this, Catherine. I know you said Clarice is being sent to a cousin in Baltimore. Is that the reason you and Sister Clara came up with this idea?"

I'd looked at his earnest expression, answering, "Sister Clara's heart is breaking, but she wants Jack to go to a proper school. Jesuit accepted him. What could I say? I agree with her. And without Clarice, Jack's world would crumble, in spite of all the bravado he spouts continuously. Now he's off on an adventure, isn't he?" I'd smiled at Yves, at the adroit expression he wore across his face.

"He's going to get an education just walking through your house, looking at your walls."

My mouth fell open. "Oh my gosh! I'd forgotten. My paintings ..."

With a wry smile then, he'd said, "I would say it's time to whitewash the Roman Polyclitus you've painted in the hallway."

I smiled through my tears looking at Gretchen's name and the dates of her birth and death on the simple cross. "I think Jack will love his new life, don't you, Gretchie? And I won't forget Sister Adelaide, I promise. We're stopping off in Baton Rouge at the hospital." In my mind, I knew all these words were unnecessary. Gretchen was watching over Adelaide. The doctor told me she was lucky to be alive. One of the stab wounds had come within an inch of her heart. The doctor had told me, "She's going to heal physically, but her spirit is another thing. And, yes, I think a visit from you would help a lot. She's mentioned you several times."

"It will help me too, Doctor. More than you'll ever know."

I stood, reluctant to leave my sister's grave, hearing her voice so clearly in my head, *Don't be afraid, Cathy.*

I began to walk slowly back to the hospital and saw Penny standing near my old guest quarters, a small bundle I knew was Hope in her arms. Penny had cried throughout the funeral, holding her baby close, wrapped warmly against the chilly morning. As I got closer, I saw how sad her face was, a mother, a widow, and hardly more than a girl. I walked down the path to where she stood.

Her cheeks had traces of tears, her breath white as smoke in the cold air as she spoke. "I wanted to thank you. For everything. And tell you how sorry I am for lying to you. I'll never forgive myself for what happened. I was to blame for everything."

"Oh, Penny, you thought you were protecting Tom! You had no idea how dangerous Eleanor Mills was. If I'd been in your place I'd have done the same thing. Truly."

"Tom said all he had to do was keep Mrs. Mills out of sight and in return he'd get the new treatment. They would put him into the trials. When he asked me, I said he should do it. I made up the bed for her in the spare room. I cooked her meals and brought her tea. She didn't act dangerous. I didn't know!" Shaking her head she continued, "Why did I ever say it?"

"Why wouldn't you? It was the only chance left open to both of you."

"Sister Adelaide asked me who was giving Tom his injections. Who put him into the trial? It was all Dr. Mills. I was afraid to tell her." Penny looked away, crying, "So I lied."

"You wanted to protect Tom, whatever you had to do." I bent forward, touching her arm. "The reason Sister Adelaide was so curious about Tom's being given the new medicine came from my sister's journal."

Penny gasped, her eyes wide. Hope squirmed in her arms. "But why did she want to know?"

"My sister's journal contained entry after entry, week

after week of aggravation and frustration that Dr. Mills wouldn't put Tom into the test group. Gretchen kept asking him, for six months. He kept refusing. Sister Adelaide couldn't figure out why he'd suddenly changed his mind."

Penny's eyes widened in surprise. "I didn't know. Tom ... we thought it was Sister Gretchen who wouldn't recommend him."

"Quite the opposite. I'll show you her journals someday. Penny, you're not to blame. I asked Sister Adelaide to look for something unusual in my sister's last journal. If anyone's to blame for what happened to Tom and Sister Adelaide, it's me."

Penny spoke, her voice hoarse, "You know that's not true."

"Oh, I think so. I asked Sister Adelaide to do something that I knew might put her in danger. So whatever guilt you want to carry for what happened to Tom and Sister Adelaide doesn't come close to mine." I reached out to put an arm around her. "But I think Sister would be the first to say it's okay. That we should put it behind us. I'm going to try. Can you?"

Penny began to cry again, tears running down her face. "I'll try. But please, Catherine, don't hate Tom"

"Hate Tom? What do you mean?"

She spurted words in a rush, "He made the hangman's noose! He didn't think I knew, but I saw him doing something with the rope, and then it was gone the next day when I looked. When I heard Sister had hanged herself, I thought he'd done it for her! Then later, after I knew it was murder, I got so scared. I didn't know what he'd done!"

The news shocked me. I'd eliminated my suspicion of Tom making the noose, even if I'd filed away his porch swing, his familiarity with tools, with rope and tying knots. I'd moved to suspect Dr. Mills, a boatman, or Charles Bremmer, who'd worked with rope for a living once upon a time.

I touched Penny's shoulder. "She was already dead. Tom had nothing to do with her death."

"I know."

"And now you know it was Dr. Mills who ordered him to make the noose, don't you?"

Penny nodded, sniffing. "Yes. Tom wasn't a bad man. He was just hurting so bad!" Penny's infant daughter cried out, afraid. Penny uncovered Hope's face and soothed her. "It's all right, baby. It's fine. Don't cry. I'm not upset." She looked at me, "Even if I am. I'm so sorry! Please forgive us."

"There's nothing to forgive. Sister Adelaide will tell you that. Who knew what Eleanor Mills was capable of? Or why she thought she had to attack Tom and Sister Adelaide? But we can thank Tom for stopping her long enough it allowed Sister Adelaide to get away, can't we?"

I reached out and touched Hope's cheek. She stared up at us, so innocent. Life wasn't complicated for her, I thought. Nourishment and a warm bed.

"Penny, I need to tell you how at peace I think Tom was, even when he knew he was dying."

It took her a few seconds to find her voice. "Thank you for saying that." In another moment her expression softened and she kissed her baby lightly on her forehead before looking at me again. "I've decided to have Tom's body cremated. Hope and I will take his ashes with us when we leave." She cast an eye toward the cemetery and its rows of white crosses. "It's beautiful, but I know Tom wouldn't choose to stay here, without us."

I said, my voice a thread upon the cold breeze, "It won't be much longer."

She smiled. "Five months, twenty-two days, but who's counting?" A pause. "I suppose you know Sister Paul has decided that Hope and I can live in your old quarters as long as my tests come back negative each month."

"She told me. That's wonderful. And in five months, twenty-two days, I'll be expecting you."

Tears filled her eyes again. But this time she was smiling. And so was I.

Looking across the cemetery, I said, "I've also struggled trying to decide if I've made the right decision burying my sister here. I hope I'm right.

"You are. I'm glad all the patients who loved her so much can visit her here. She'll always be remembered for the wonderful, caring person she was."

Fifteen minutes later, I had walked down the road past the hospital to the old mansion near the river. I wanted to talk to John Weller before we left. He'd looked at me quizzically when I said I wanted to meet him inside the house, in the front foyer. John was waiting on the front steps as I approached. He opened the door, its squeaky hinges warning of the interminable sad history that permeated this place.

He followed me into a spacious, high-ceilinged opening, where a short few days ago I had looked up to a balcony where Dr. Mills hanged my sister and to the face I'd never forget: Eleanor's face, staring down at me from the third floor. I averted my eyes now from looking up, to concentrate instead on the solemn expression of John Weller.

"Why here?" he asked. "I'd think this would be the last place you'd want to see again."

I swallowed before speaking. "It's away from prying eyes, Mr. Weller."

He nodded, a half-smile on his face. "I think we can move on to John and Catherine, don't you?"

His smile was nice. I knew so little about him. He was a reporter. What else? Who were his friends? Did he ever laugh? What had been his life before being forced to come here? I would never know these things about him now, suddenly realizing I was sorry for it. What would a friendship with this brooding man have been like? I wondered. We had a connection, somehow. But friendship? Even now I found it difficult to look straight into his eyes when I said something to him. It was as if his eyes saw through me, to my heart racing.

"All right. John, it shall be." I answered.

He said dryly, "So, Catherine. How *is* that bump on your head? Jack told me you were as heavy as a sack of soggy crawfish getting you back to your quarters."

I took a step back and laughed. "What an image that is."

A few seconds of silence passed between us until he said, "Seriously, I'm glad he showed up when he did. Have you figured out who hit you?"

"I've an idea who it was. But no proof."

"David Mills?"

"More likely Eleanor. I think she saw me as a threat, as someone who knew what she'd done to Gretchen. Whatever she says to the contrary, I believe she knows she murdered my sister. Then when Sister Adelaide frightened her with questions about why she was hiding, it had to have set her on fire. Both Sister Adelaide and I were the enemy."

John's dark eyes delved into mine. "I'm glad Jack came along when he did."

His husky voice was unsettling, but I returned his gaze finally. After a few seconds, I said, "So am I. Clarice asked Jack to find her mother. He found me instead."

John Weller looked away, as though a passing thought had skimmed across his mind.

"What?" I asked.

He shook his head and looked away. "Nothing."

I asked, "Has anything turned up about Charles Bremmer being an imposter?"

"Not yet. Early days. I've some spies of my own looking into Herr Bremmer's past."

I nodded. "I thought you should know about the crates before I leave."

His attention returned. "Crates?"

"When I was under the chapel, I found some supplies. Food. Rope. I learned that Jack saw Polanie moving the Samoan's food away from their camp by canoe. It's being hidden under the church for some reason. There might be other things hidden under there as well. It was dark and I couldn't really see much. Someone has turned the crates the pews were shipped in into storage containers. And now I'm thinking maybe not all the pews were what they seemed on the barge, you know?" I paused, letting him comprehend. "I haven't said anything to the nuns."

"I see. But if Charles Bremmer is behind the pilfering or stealing of supplies for any reason, shouldn't you tell them?"

"Because you brought the marines to this place. Guarding the entrance now, aren't they?" I saw a glimmer of appreciation in his eyes.

"The fact one of Hitler's Nazi Party was living on the premises convinced the captain pretty quick his men needed to provide a twenty-four-hours-a-day presence here." He smiled. "And I told Yves just driving his fancy car gave me all kinds of credibility."

"I doubt that."

"I don't know. It's pretty snazzy."

I said, "It's going to get a bit hot for Charles Bremmer with them here."

"He's staying out of sight at the moment. I haven't seen him since yesterday."

"Maybe he's gone to Morley again."

"Where?"

"A deserted lumber town. Down in the swamp. Father O'Quinn said it's not had people there since the Morley Lumber Company left many years ago.

"When did he tell you that?"

"When I took the Ferry on Saturday, Charles was on board. He told me he was headed to White Castle, and he had one of those same crates in the back of a wagon. I didn't question it at the time, but now I do. I don't think he was going just to White Castle. I think his destination was Morley. In an old wagon owned by a colored man from Carville."

He shot a question at me like a reporter. "Who was the black man?"

"Old Jacques. He goes to Morley, according to Father O'Quinn, to harvest old cypress in the swamp." I paused then raced ahead, hoping my words didn't sound ridiculous. "I think there may have been things inside that crate Charles needed to get out of this place. Is that just too farfetched?

John Weller's eyes widened. A silent thought passed between us. He said, "A lumber company would have done more to the landscape than just build a village for the employees. They would have to create a channel in the swamp to get their lumber out."

"A deep channel," I said quietly. Then, "You decide when to tell Sister Paul about the crates under the chapel."

"If they haven't already been moved."

"Right," I agreed. "But it might have been hard to do

that with the sheriff and his men all around us." I paused. "Even harder with the marines."

He gave me a glance and another smile before answering. "I'll take a look."

I stuck out my hand to shake his. "Goodbye, John. I hope Adam Wolf finds a story."

He didn't take my hand but stared at me silently, searching my face as seconds ticked by. Then under his breath I heard, "You'll know if he does." He paused. A single finger touched my lips. "I've wanted to kiss you since I saw you looking down at your sister in the old cellar."

I trembled. Emotion I didn't know existed, a lightness in my body, a disengaged voice I didn't recognize was mine spoke. "You can, you know."

He stepped away, sadness in his eyes. His voice rough, barely above a whisper, said, "No, I can't." His eyes pulled at me. "But I wish things were different."

I stared at him, hardly seeing him standing there in front of me. His words lifted me out of myself. I knew I must say what I knew was true, yet I felt the flush of heat rising to my cheeks.

"What?" he asked, "What is it?"

"I'm not afraid of the disease, John."

He was surprised. "I can't believe you'd say that." He turned away, staring out the window but not seeing through it. Slowly, deliberately, he said, "I knew from the first time I saw you in that hallway how strong you were." Something had brightened in his eyes. "You're not afraid of much, are you?"

Now it was my turn to be surprised. "I've been terrified of everything all my life, John. Don't look at me like that! It's true. I've been boxed up inside my house for so many years I've lost count. I'm afraid of my own shadow."

"But you're not afraid of catching leprosy from me?"

I said quickly, "Not at all."

He said, "Then I think you're going to have to rewrite that story, aren't you?"

It took me several moments to digest his words. "I've changed, I know I have. But is that possible? In just these few days?"

"Sometimes, in the blink of an eye, you can see the light." He held my hands. In a quiet voice, he said, "I've changed too. I've decided maybe I want to live. To write again."

"To be Adam Wolf again?"

"Yes. And to beat this damn thing hanging around my neck." He raised my hand and lightly brushed his lips against my fingertips. "You're the reason."

When I tried to protest, he shook his head. "Yes. You." A hint of a smile made his eyes glisten. He took my hands in his. "I plan to be in touch when I can kiss you like I've wanted to."

Tears sprung to my eyes and I felt warmth rising on my cheeks.

"I love to see you blush." He reached up and touched my face with the smooth back of his hand. "Don't give up on me."

My voice was softer than I wanted. "I won't."

We walked out on the porch together. Gray clouds hung over us, promising rain. The river looked like a pewter ribbon, twisting and turning, an incessant, never-ending view of life flowing. And its uncertainty of which course it would take. Yves and Jack sat in the coupe, waiting for me at the ferry dock.

I watched Adam stride down the steps off the porch into the yard. He turned once and raised his hand in the air like a prizefighter after winning a fight.

I laughed, calling out, "Goodbye, Adam Wolf!" as he disappeared around the corner of the house.

Standing at the rail of the ferry, I saw the hospital, dull and faded inside the gray landscape around it. Even under a clear blue sky, sadness would cling to it. Sadness but also surprising happiness sometimes. I smiled, thinking of John Weller. But I wouldn't call him by that name again. He was Adam Wolf.

Standing there, I suddenly imagined myself afloat in an immense, airy space with wind and blue sky overhead. It was the strangest feeling because it occurred to me I was outside, in the open, with people standing nearby. Adam was right. It meant nothing. I wasn't afraid anymore. Not today. And maybe not tomorrow.

NEW ORLEANS PICAYUNE

AUGUST 5, 1941

GERMAN MISSIONARY CONVICTED OF ESPIONAGE

One man from island of German Samoa still sought for questioning

Charged with unlawfully obtaining information by photographs or through other means that affects the national defense, Charles Bremmer, a German national, who resided in St. Gabriel Parish, was convicted by jury in the fifth circuit federal court on Thursday.

Bremmer was arrested in December last year near the town of White Castle. Principal evidence obtained was the June 19, 1940, issue of a national magazine in which several pages were devoted to minute detail of the United States army, its personnel, mechanical equipment, and latest developments in large armament and small arms.

Also recovered was an expensive miniature camera, a small-bore target pistol, four albums of photographs, some of a chemical plant located along the Mississippi River, and several road maps of states located on the Gulf of Mexico.

The most telling evidence was a radio receiver buried at the site but recovered by Marines.

During the trial Bremmer maintained his innocence, claiming the one responsible for taking the photographs is a native from German Samoa, a patient at Marine Hospital No. 66, located near St. Gabriel. He stated he had been "watching suspicious actions" by the Samoan for some time. The man is still being sought for questioning.

Bremmer received the maximum prison sentence provided by statute of law, two years hard labor and a fine of $10,000.00.

Represented by Robert Weinstein, assistant United States attorney, bills of exception and an appeal on behalf of the defendant will be filed tomorrow.

Editor's note:
Adam Wolf's new book *Living with a Spy* warns Americans of the danger of Hitler's Third Reich. He was actively involved in the capture of Charles Bremmer. Published by Blue Water Press.

AFTERWORD

T HIS BOOK IS ENTIRELY A work of fiction, and characters are pure imagination. But the inspiration that led to its completion was the day I read *With Love in their Hearts*, compiled and edited by Julia Rivera Elwood, published in February 1996. Her booklet traces the story of the Daughters of Charity of St. Vincent de Paul and their dedication for one hundred years to the patients of a leprosarium created on 330 acres of an old plantation known as Indian Camp near Carville, Louisiana.

One nun in particular, Sister Hilary Ross, worked tirelessly at Carville from the years 1922 to 1960.

She was a pharmacist who fought against prejudice and hysteria by always treating patients with compassion and understanding. Her research into this incurable, infectious disease became a crusade for her, one that would eventually be won once sulfone drugs were introduced in 1941. In 1958 Sister Hilary received the President's Medal, an award given to a woman for the first time in eighty-eight years.

Through the years, the Daughters of Charity served in all capacities at the US Marine Hospital Number 66, now the Gillis W. Long Hansen's Disease Center. One can only imagine what sacrifices the nuns made and what trials they faced. But as Elwood writes, "They have managed to give not only committed, professional care to the patients, but they have added the human touch: hearts full of love!"

J. S.

CPSIA information can be obtained
at www.ICGtesting.com
Printed in the USA
FFOW03n0817121217
43958409-43071FF